MARGIN of ERROR

ALSO BY RACHEL LACEY

Learning Curves

Cover Story

Stars Collide

No Rings Attached

Read Between the Lines

MARGIN of ERROR

RACHEL LACEY

Montlake

This is a work of fiction. Names, characters, organizations, places, events, and incidents are either products of the author's imagination or are used fictitiously. Otherwise, any resemblance to actual persons, living or dead, is purely coincidental.

Published by Montlake, Seattle
www.apub.com

EU product safety contact:
Amazon Media EU S. à r.l.
38, avenue John F. Kennedy, L-1855 Luxembourg
amazonpublishing-gpsr@amazon.com

ISBN-13: 9781662529252 (paperback)
ISBN-13: 9781662529269 (digital)

Cover illustration and design by Elizabeth Turner Stokes

Printed in the United States of America

MARGIN of ERROR

PROLOGUE

Charlotte boarded the bus with a vague sense of urgency she couldn't explain. She'd left her apartment with more than enough time to make it to her first appointment of the day. Being a Realtor in New York City meant she was often in a rush, but she got to see so many unique and interesting spaces. Today, she would be showing one of her clients a showstopper of a condo near the financial district. But she couldn't shake the feeling she needed to hurry.

Eden Sands sang softly through Charlotte's earbuds as she made her way down the aisle. Since it was approaching midday, the bus was fairly crowded, filled mostly with commuters like Charlotte, riding into Manhattan from their homes in Queens. She spotted an empty seat next to a woman dressed in business attire.

Charlotte slid into the seat, then checked her phone to see that her daily horoscope had arrived. Most of her friends thought it was silly, but she'd always been a bit superstitious. She checked her horoscope almost every day, hoping it would give her some much-needed guidance. She tapped her screen, opening the app.

It's a good day to make a new connection, Taurus.

She smiled as she read the first line. Surely that was a good omen for her day. Charlotte loved striking up random conversations with people she met on her commute and while exploring the city, showing properties to her clients.

Change is the theme of the day, but what at first looks like a new beginning might actually be an ending.

"I love your scarf."

Charlotte glanced at the woman beside her, involuntarily touching the pink-and-green scarf at her throat. She had a weakness for colorful scarves, and this was one of her favorites, but the last time she'd worn it, her friend Liz told her it was too flashy, so to have it complimented by a stranger? Charlotte beamed. "Thank you."

The woman returned her smile before turning to look out the window. She wore a black pantsuit under a matching wool coat, and her brown hair was pulled back in a neat bun at the base of her neck. Maybe she was the connection Charlotte was supposed to make today. She'd always used her horoscope as an excuse to seek out new people and experiences.

Charlotte paused her music and removed her earbuds. "It's freakishly cold today for November, isn't it?" she asked, hoping to keep the conversation going. She still felt restless, and a conversation with her seatmate might help distract her from her weird mood.

"It is," the woman agreed. She tapped her phone to pause her own music, revealing that she'd been listening to "Turbulent," which coincidentally was the same song that had just been playing in Charlotte's earbuds. The Eden Sands / Anna Moss duet about female empowerment was one of her all-time favorites.

Charlotte held up her phone to show her seatmate their matching songs, and they shared a smile. "Hopefully tomorrow will be warmer."

"Actually, I don't mind snow, at least not when it's fresh." Her demeanor was friendly, but there was something indefinably sad about her expression.

Maybe Charlotte could help brighten her day. "I grew up in Vermont, so I'm certainly used to it, but it's different there. Snow in the mountains is beautiful, you know? Snow here in the city is just . . . dirty."

"You have a point." The woman laughed softly. "Vermont, hmm? I've always wanted to visit."

"Oh, you should," Charlotte said. "At least if you love scenery and maple syrup. I'm from Middleton, which is a college town, but there are so many nice areas to visit. If I was going as a tourist, I'd probably rent a cabin near Manchester. You've got the Green Mountains in your backyard for views and hiking, and a short drive to the shops and restaurants in town."

"Sounds perfect. I'm overdue for a vacation, actually." Something wistful passed across her face.

"I bet you'd love it, and it's only about a four-and-a-half-hour drive from here."

"Maybe someday." The woman's gaze flicked to Charlotte's phone, where today's horoscope was still illuminated, and her expression turned curious.

"Want to know yours?" Charlotte asked. "What's your sign?"

"I'm a Sagittarius, but . . ." She trailed off, and Charlotte realized what she'd initially thought was curiosity was actually skepticism. This woman probably didn't believe in astrology.

Nonetheless, Charlotte decided to see it through. She clicked on the appropriate link. "Let your true personality shine today, Sagittarius. There are greater forces at play, but if you're willing to open your mind, you might find just what you're looking for. Be open to new ideas and information, regardless of how unusual they may seem at first glance. The missing piece in your life may come from a place you least expect, but be confident that it *will* come."

The woman blinked at her, and Charlotte had no idea how to interpret her reaction to the horoscope. She looked almost gobsmacked, or maybe she couldn't believe Charlotte had actually read it to her. The bus had been stopped at a red light, but now it rumbled forward with a jolt. They were on FDR Drive, with the East River to their left.

"What did you think?" Charlotte asked.

She stared at Charlotte for a long moment, lips pursed. "I think . . . well, horoscopes seem like utter nonsense, but mine says to be open to new ideas and information, so explain it to me, then. You seem like a reasonable person. You put stock in what they say?"

"I do," Charlotte said, "but I think you need to approach astrology with the right mindset and expectations, or it *will* seem like nonsense. It's not a crystal ball. More of a guiding light, if you will."

"Interesting. I'm a statistician. I trust numbers and science, so I tend to avoid things that involve too much conjecture, but I've been looking for an excuse to broaden my horizons. At the risk of sounding like Agent Mulder, I want to believe."

Charlotte grinned. "You strike me as more of a Scully, and not just because you're a skeptic."

Something shifted in the brunette's expression. She seemed almost bashful. "I do have a soft spot for Dana Scully, and yes, we're both skeptics."

"Okay, Ms. Skeptic. Let's see if I can make a believer out of you."

The woman smiled, and it brightened her whole face. "I'm ready."

"So the first thing to keep in mind about astrology is that it's an ancient science. People were making predictions about personality based on the position of the planets when someone was born as far back as ancient Greece. Even further, I think."

The woman's eyebrows rose. "The ancient Greeks also believed that thunder was a result of angering the gods."

"Yes, but . . . think of it in terms of magnetism, like the way things turn toward the north and south poles and how the pull of the moon's gravity creates the ocean's tides. Is it so far-fetched to think there are greater forces in the universe that affect us, forces that shift and change based on the movement of the planets and other celestial bodies?"

There was something else in her eyes now, a spark of what might be interest. "Go on."

"There have been a lot of studies on the personality traits of people born to the different signs, and while it might not be based in the kind of science you're looking for, it does have some merit. And perhaps most importantly, it's just plain fun."

The woman's lips quirked. "Now *that* I can believe."

"I don't treat it as an exact science, but I look forward to my daily horoscope because often it helps me see meaning in what's happening in my life," Charlotte told her. "I use it as a motivational push, you know? Like today, my horoscope said it's a good day to make a new connection, and maybe that's why I struck up a conversation with you. If you use it as an excuse to push yourself out of your comfort zone, I can't see any downside."

"I suppose I could agree with that," her seatmate said, glancing out the window.

"So did I convince you?"

The woman turned her head, and their eyes locked. "I don't know yet, but I'm at least thinking about it, which is more than I ever thought I'd say about astrology."

Charlotte fist pumped the air. "Yes! And you're following your horoscope by keeping an open mind."

"That I am." She looked out the window again. They had entered the financial district, tall buildings on either side of the street, people in business attire hurrying down the sidewalks. "It feels almost . . ."

Charlotte waited a few seconds, curious what her seatmate had been about to say. "Almost what?"

"Well, I've been wanting to let my true personality shine—for lack of better words—so when you read that to me, it felt rather prophetic."

"Wow. Really?"

"Yeah." The woman looked down at her hands. "I don't believe in signs, but . . ."

"This certainly feels like one."

They smiled at each other, and that felt like a sign too. Of what, Charlotte wasn't sure. But . . . something. She was making the connection her horoscope called for, and this woman was taking a leap of faith. It was all so much deeper than Charlotte had expected when she boarded the bus thirty minutes ago.

In fact—

"Oh, this is me." Her seatmate stood, and Charlotte realized the bus had stopped. The doors slid open as a handful of people lined up to get off.

Charlotte stood automatically, moving into the aisle so the woman could exit.

"It was really nice to meet you," the woman said, and then she was stepping past Charlotte into the aisle. She joined the other people exiting the bus, gone almost before Charlotte registered that their conversation had ended.

She wished . . . well, she wished she had at least gotten the woman's name. Maybe they could have followed each other on Instagram or something. This was the problem she sometimes had when she started conversations with random people. She'd meet someone she'd like to keep in touch with, and while she did occasionally exchange names or social media handles with them, most times the connection ended just like this one.

Somehow, this moment, this connection had felt like . . . more.

Charlotte often felt adrift in her life, always making these fleeting connections. She sought new experiences, new dating apps, new coffee shops, sometimes even new cities in search of . . . well, she'd know when she found it, hopefully.

She slid into the seat the woman had just vacated and glanced out the window, watching her former seatmate cross the street. She was taller than Charlotte had realized, and there was an elegance to the way she moved. As Charlotte watched, the woman turned her head, looking back in Charlotte's direction.

The bus's horn sounded suddenly, long and loud. Charlotte jumped, glancing at the driver. What the hell? Someone screamed, and Charlotte looked back out the window just in time to see a black

SUV speed past the bus and slam into several pedestrians who had been crossing the street. *Oh god.*

The woman Charlotte had just shared a conversation with lay crumpled on the slushy pavement. Another woman was on her hands and knees beside her. It happened so fast that it hardly felt real. Charlotte's chest began to burn, and she realized she'd stopped breathing. A prickly feeling crawled over her skin, and for a moment, she thought she was going to be sick.

All around her, people gasped and cried out, their exclamations hammering home the reality of the situation. On the street, Charlotte's former seatmate hadn't moved. The other woman was sitting beside her now, cradling an arm against her chest. Charlotte heard a tinny voice nearby saying "911, what is your emergency?"

"Several people just got hit by a car!" a panicked man said.

Charlotte sucked in a much-needed lungful of air, and then she was moving. She lurched out of her seat and bolted down the aisle. On the street, there were more screams, more people on the phone—presumably with 911—but no one was *doing* anything. The SUV came to a stop about twenty feet down the road, and the driver got out and started shouting.

Charlotte couldn't make out the words over the roaring in her ears. She approached the women who'd been hit. One woman was clutching her arm, crying, while Charlotte's seatmate lay flat on her back at the edge of the street. Her eyes were closed, and her body was too still.

Fuck.

Was she dead? Charlotte's mind replayed how the vehicle had flung her, the brutal way she'd slammed into the pavement. Seeing something like that in person was so shocking, so *violent.* Blood stained the snow around the woman's head.

Stop the bleeding.

The thought popped into Charlotte's head, maybe from all the hours she'd spent watching one of her favorite TV shows, *9-1-1.* She dropped to her knees. Where was the blood coming from? Charlotte swept a quick gaze over the woman's body, and *oh god*, her right leg looked weird. Like, obviously broken. Charlotte's stomach lurched.

"Hey." She reached for one of the woman's hands. Her skin was cold and clammy against Charlotte's. "Can you hear me?"

The brunette's eyes fluttered and then opened, and Charlotte wanted to cry from relief because she was *alive*. Her fingers twitched, and her features twisted into an expression Charlotte knew she would never forget. To call it a grimace was too tame. The woman's face radiated a visceral kind of agony that was absolutely horrifying.

Her eyes met Charlotte's, glassy and desperate. "Help."

"I will." Charlotte darted another panicked glance down the woman's battered body. She seemed to have taken the impact of the SUV on her right side, which made sense from the direction she'd been walking. Her breath came in fast, shallow gasps, and her expression indicated a level of pain Charlotte couldn't even fathom.

By now, other passersby had gathered, surrounding them in a circle of concerned faces and anxious murmuring. Charlotte had no idea what to do. "Does anyone have medical training?" she called, her voice high pitched and shrill.

Heads shook all around her. Peripherally, she was aware that the other woman who'd been hit was sitting on the curb now while a passerby attended to her.

"Do you know where you're hurt?" Charlotte asked her seatmate as she debated her next move. She knew not to move the woman in case of a spinal injury. Trying to stop the bleeding still seemed like a good idea, though.

It felt like an eternity had passed since the accident, but it had probably been less than a minute. These moments felt so much more exaggerated in real life than they appeared on TV. In a TV show, you would see the accident, and then it would cut to the arrival of the ambulance. In reality, every second dragged.

There was *so much blood*. It had seeped into Charlotte's pants as she knelt in the street, but hopefully the snow was diluting it, making it look worse than it was. Maybe her seatmate wasn't as badly injured as it seemed. Charlotte would get her name and visit her in the hospital, bring her flowers and candy and read her another horoscope.

What at first looks like a new beginning might actually be an ending.

That ominous line from Charlotte's horoscope flitted through her mind, and she shuddered, rejecting what it might mean. But, as she watched, the woman's eyes closed. Her mouth hung slightly open. Her skin was ashen. Even her lips looked gray.

"I'm going to see if I can find where you're bleeding from, okay?" Charlotte spoke loudly and firmly, trying to sound more confident than she felt. The woman's eyes flickered open, a silent scream held in their depths, before closing again.

Charlotte felt another punch of adrenaline. With fingers almost numb from the cold, she ran a hand through the woman's hair, locating a gash in her scalp, which was hopefully the source of all the blood. Head wounds bled a lot. She remembered reading that somewhere.

In the distance, she heard sirens. *Thank god.* Her gut said this woman was in real trouble. The ashy tint to her skin was terrifying.

"The ambulance is almost here," Charlotte told her.

The woman's eyes opened sluggishly. "Help," she repeated.

"Can you tell me what hurts?" Charlotte asked somewhat desperately.

Her eyes rolled back for a moment, and then she blinked, looking up at Charlotte. "I can't feel . . . can't feel anything."

Charlotte's chest tightened. Did she have spinal cord damage? Charlotte had already noticed how shallow and rapid the woman's breathing was, but now she saw that the left side of her chest seemed to rise more than the right, as if the right side had . . . collapsed. A thin trickle of blood ran from the corner of her mouth. Her eyes were unfocused, the pupils blown wide.

Not sure what else to do, Charlotte took the woman's hand in hers the way she had before, trying not to notice how cold it was, how *limp*. "Stay with me," she said. "The sirens are getting louder. The ambulance must be almost here."

The woman's eyes focused on her for a moment, and Charlotte forced a smile. She gave her fingers another squeeze, then reached out with her free hand to brush a damp strand of dark hair from the woman's face, offering what comfort she could.

"I—" the woman gasped.

"What? You what?" Charlotte held tight to her icy fingers, willing the ambulance to hurry up. She felt something hard pressing into her palm and looked down. There was a gold band on the woman's ring finger. She was married. She had a family out there, people who loved her. She had to survive. Charlotte barely knew her, but she desperately wanted her to live.

"I don't think . . . I'm going . . . to make it," the woman whispered, her words broken by desperate gasps for air.

"Don't say that," Charlotte cried, but the woman's eyes had closed again. Her features went slack. She was so gray. *Lifeless.* "Hey! Just hang in there another minute."

Charlotte squeezed her hand, hard enough to hurt, in an attempt to revive her. The woman didn't respond.

A fire truck arrived on the street in a wail of sirens and a whirling mass of lights, followed rapidly by an ambulance. The crowd began to fall back as people made room for the first responders to come through. Soon two men in uniform had crouched beside Charlotte.

Someone took Charlotte's shoulders, guiding her backward to give them room to work. The crowd converged around her, people offering words of support and asking questions about the woman's status that she couldn't answer.

Charlotte wiped away a tear as the EMTs worked on the woman, their movements swift and efficient. They'd secured a plastic collar around her neck and were calling out medical jargon that sounded terrifyingly serious. She caught "vitals unstable" and "BP seventy-two over forty and falling."

One of them secured a brace to the woman's broken leg, and then they put her on a backboard. Through all this commotion, the woman remained unconscious.

"Sats are dropping," an EMT said. "We need to move now."

Then they were rushing toward the ambulance. Charlotte pushed forward, desperate to know what would happen next.

"She's crashing," someone called, just as an alarm began to scream.

Charlotte stared in horror. The blaring alarm made it abundantly clear that the woman's heart had stopped beating. The EMTs were still moving, working, trying to bring her back. As the ambulance's doors began to close, one of the EMTs shook her head, and the look on her face told Charlotte everything she needed to know.

The doors slammed shut, the sound reverberating in Charlotte's skull like a death knell.

They'd lost her.

CHAPTER ONE

Two Years Later

Watching someone die changed a person. Charlotte was not the same woman she'd been on that cold Manhattan morning. For starters, she no longer lived in Queens, or in New York, for that matter. As she sat facing her dad in a little café near the Northshire University campus in Middleton, Vermont, she tried to summon some enthusiasm for their conversation.

The truth was, sometimes she felt like a part of her had died that morning too. And yes, the woman from the bus had definitely died. Charlotte had found an article on a local news site that confirmed a pedestrian fatality in the financial district that morning.

Charlotte had always felt somewhat adrift in her life, moving from place to place, boyfriend to boyfriend, but after watching that woman die, she was more lost than ever. At the time, Charlotte had taken it as a sign to find purpose in her life, but she'd spent the last two years chasing one dead end after another. Now here she was, back in the town she'd grown up in, the town she'd sworn she would *never* return to after she left twenty-two years ago.

Famous last words. The truth was, Charlotte was getting desperate. When her most recent attempt at finding purpose ended in yet another failure, she'd found herself unexpectedly drawn to the place she'd spent most of her life running from. It was time to face her past. Thirty years ago, Charlotte's mother vanished without a trace, defining her childhood and shaping the adult she would become.

Yes, she had enough self-awareness to realize her wandering lifestyle was likely rooted in a search for answers she might never find, but she was going to try anyway, dammit. So here she was, back in Vermont and determined to finally find out what happened to her mom. And while she was at it, she also hoped to reconcile with her dad. Their relationship was a work in progress, but that was more than she could have said a few months ago.

". . . so I'd really appreciate it if you came." Her dad gave her an expectant look, drawing her back into the conversation.

"I'll think about it." But Charlotte knew she wouldn't be attending the faculty friends-and-family gathering he hosted every year at his home. The university was a bit of a sore spot for her, and they both knew it.

"I really hope you do." His smile was somewhat forced, as if he'd read the "no" in her expression.

"I'll let you know, but right now, I have to get going. I'm about to meet a new client to show her a house. She just moved to the area for a job at the university." Because everything in this town revolved around Northshire University.

"Oh yeah? What does she teach?"

Charlotte shrugged. "No idea. I'm just here to help her find a house."

"Okay. See you next week." Hope glimmered in his eyes. He wanted her back in his life too. Since her return, they'd met for lunch every Sunday after he got out of church, and slowly, things were starting to feel less awkward between them, but they still had a lot of lost time and hurt feelings to make up for.

"Yep. Bye, Dad." She walked outside, where a cold breeze whipped through her hair, tossing it in her face. Maybe it was time for a haircut.

She'd worn it long her whole adult life. Maybe she should get a bob. Or something even more drastic? Like a pixie cut.

It was January, after all. New year, new Charlotte? The problem was, she'd tried out a "new Charlotte" so many times, she almost didn't know who she was anymore. Had there really been no lesson to learn from that fateful day on the bus? Charlotte had thought that watching someone lose their life was a sign to find purpose in hers, except she'd tried everything she could think of, and nothing had panned out.

She'd gone after a big promotion at work, only to end up hating the new responsibilities she was given. So, she'd quit her job and left New York to chase a second chance with "the one that got away," her college boyfriend, Darren. Charlotte had tried out a new life in Washington, DC, with him, but they'd quickly fallen into old patterns, fighting constantly, so in the end, she'd left him . . . again.

Starting over in her hometown might be her last stab at figuring out what she was supposed to be doing with her life. Charlotte had moved back to Vermont four months ago, and it hadn't taken long for certain habits to reappear, like not putting on her coat if she was just running out to her car.

Luckily, the weather today was fairly mild, by Vermont standards. It was about thirty degrees and partly sunny. She slid behind the wheel, grateful for her gloves, since the steering wheel was absolutely freezing. As she drove, her thoughts meandered in an attempt to distract herself when the campus came into view.

There was a reason she hadn't attended Northshire University. It was a petty one, but it was hers. Both her parents had taught there. Her dad still did. Charlotte had spent countless hours as a child running around the campus, observing the college students as she dreamed of what her life would be like at that age, so mature and worldly.

But her mother's disappearance and her subsequently strained relationship with her dad had tainted all her memories of the campus. It lost its magic, feeling instead like a prison she'd been desperate to escape. When the time came, she'd chosen to leave Vermont, attending college in New Hampshire instead. She'd sworn she'd never come back, and yet, here she was.

Today's showing was at a small colonial just past the main campus. This was the perfect location for a professor, but Charlotte had concerns about the house itself. It seemed dated, and not in a charming way. It needed enough work that it might even be considered a fixer-upper, which wasn't what her new client was looking for.

The driveway was empty when Charlotte reached the small beige house. She parked at the curb and consulted the listing notes on her phone while she waited for her client, a woman named Marin Easterly. A few minutes later, a black Subaru Outback pulled up. This must be her.

Charlotte put on her coat, shut off her car, and stepped outside, flinching as the cold air gusted against her. A tall brunette was getting out of the Outback as Charlotte headed up the walkway to meet her at the front door.

"Hi, you must be Marin. I'm Charlotte. It's so nice to meet—" She froze with her hand extended in greeting as she got a good look at the woman in front of her. Everything seemed to stop as adrenaline punched through her system, making her heart race and her stomach tingle, because it was *her*.

The woman she'd watched die two years ago was standing right in front of her. Which wasn't possible, of course. Charlotte blinked, giving her head a slight shake. They said everyone had a doppelgänger . . .

"It's you." The woman's eyes widened as she stared at Charlotte with an expression of wonder. "It's really you."

This can't be happening.

"But . . ." Charlotte spluttered. "I watched you die."

For a moment, Marin could have sworn her heart stopped for the second time. But it was still beating. *Racing*, in fact. The woman who'd comforted her as she lay dying in the street, who'd shaken her out of the fog that had shrouded her for so much of her life, was standing in front of her.

That fateful day, Marin had felt such a strong connection to her that she hadn't paid enough attention to her surroundings as she crossed the street. She'd looked back over her shoulder, hoping for one last glimpse of the woman on the bus, a decision that had nearly cost Marin her life.

Now she knew that woman's name. Charlotte Danton. Her new Realtor. What were the chances? If this wasn't fate, she didn't know what was. Tears pricked behind Marin's eyes, and she felt the uncharacteristic urge to hug this woman she barely knew.

Charlotte's eyes looked suspiciously glossy, suggesting she was just as affected by their reunion. Her hair had gotten longer, blond curls falling halfway down her back. And her scarf . . . the pink-and-green scarf. She'd been wearing it on the bus. Marin had the inappropriate urge to touch that too. It had caught her eye that day, and it did again now. Those colors looked fantastic on Charlotte.

"I don't understand," Charlotte said. "How are you here? And in Vermont? I have so many questions."

"I'll answer them all, but let's go inside first, shall we? It's freezing out here." Her body had a lot of aches and pains these days, and the cold certainly didn't help. Perhaps she should have relocated to Florida instead of Vermont, but she'd had her reasons for coming here, reasons she never could have imagined would lead to this moment.

Charlotte reached for the lockbox on the front door and entered the code, then motioned Marin in ahead of her. She kept staring at Marin as if she'd seen a ghost, and she probably felt like she had, if she thought Marin had died that day. Obviously that accident had changed Marin's entire life, but she'd never really stopped to imagine its impact on Charlotte.

"Okay, Marin Easterly." Charlotte gave her an incredulous look. "You know, I always regretted not getting your name that day. It was hard to mourn you, not knowing. Now here you are, alive . . . and in my hometown, no less."

Marin's hands were shaking, and her heart pounded. "This feels like one of those 'small world' moments."

"For me, it feels like an impossibility because I watched your heart stop," Charlotte said. "And then I read a news article that said a woman died in that accident."

"My heart *did* stop, and a woman *did* die." Marin pressed a hand subconsciously against the organ in question. "I flatlined for almost two minutes. I had broken my right femur, fractured my pelvis, bruised my spleen, punctured a lung . . . the doctors said it was a miracle I survived. But there was another woman injured in that accident, Brenda Lewis. Initially, she only broke her wrist, but she had a massive heart attack on the way to the hospital. She didn't make it."

"My god." Charlotte's eyes were wide and watery. "That's . . ."

"It's terrible, a horrible tragedy, but I'm very much still alive."

"And here in Vermont." Charlotte reached out and touched Marin's arm, as if reassuring herself that she was real. "You have no idea how many times I've relived that morning, how I've gone back over our conversation. I see that SUV in my nightmares. I watch it slam into you, watch you *die*."

"I've thought about it a lot too. Your face is the last thing I remember when I was lying there in the street. I always wished I could thank you for that, for holding my hand and reassuring me. I thought I was dying, and it helped . . . knowing someone was there."

Charlotte swiped a tear from her cheek. "I wasn't sure if you knew I was holding your hand."

"I knew. I felt so disconnected from my body . . . it's hard to describe. But I knew you were there." She glanced around herself, suddenly aware that they were standing in the foyer of this house she'd wanted to see. "After we look at the house, do you want to maybe grab a coffee? I'd love to talk more, but I'm not sure this is the place."

Charlotte blinked as if she'd lost track of their surroundings too. "Yeah. This is my last appointment of the day, and I'd love to keep talking. You have totally blown my mind." She mimed her head exploding. "I don't even know what I'm doing right now."

Marin's lips twitched. "I feel the same way."

Charlotte blew out a dramatic breath. "Okay. Let's look at the house, and then coffee."

"Yes." Truthfully, Marin was already somewhat impatient to leave. She'd been so excited to start house hunting. She'd never owned a home by herself before, having gone straight from her parents' house into her marriage with Andrew. But while she was eager to find a house, she could already tell she didn't like this one. It had a musty smell she would never be able to live with. Meanwhile, she was dying—no pun intended—to sit down and talk more with Charlotte.

"So, I got the feeling from your initial email that you're looking for something move in ready," Charlotte said, shifting into what Marin suspected was her professional voice.

"Yes." Marin followed her toward the kitchen, looking around as she walked. "I'm renting now and can stay there as long as I need, but I'm eager to be in my own home."

"This house is technically move in ready," Charlotte said, "but it hasn't been well maintained. The current owner is an elderly widow who lives alone, and she's offering the house as is. It would mean a lot of updating and repairs for you to take on, so keep that in mind as you look around."

"I'm not very handy with that kind of thing," Marin admitted. Not only was she inexperienced with home repairs, but she also had physical limitations now that she hadn't had before the accident. On the flip side, the settlement she'd received from the driver who hit her was allowing her to build this new life for herself. "I have a feeling this house needs more work than I can put into it."

"I suspect you're right, but let's finish our walk-through anyway. If nothing else, it'll help you get a feel for what you do and don't like. Every home you look at will bring you closer to finding the right one."

"Okay," Marin agreed. Charlotte had pushed her out of her comfort zone on that bus two years ago, and maybe she could do the same today. Because the whole reason Marin was here in Vermont involved leaving her comfort zone. She was rebuilding her life, making it *hers*. She wanted to embrace her authentic self for the first time in her forty-seven years, and maybe part of that included figuring out what she truly wanted in a home. "What drew me to this one was mostly its proximity to the campus."

"That *is* a big plus," Charlotte agreed. "Were you a professor when I met you before?"

"No." Marin still couldn't believe she was really standing here with "the woman from the bus," as she'd called her in her head for the past two years. "I'm a statistician. I was working for an investment firm, and it was so unfulfilling. I lost that job while I was recuperating, and I'd always wanted to teach, so . . . here I am."

"We have a lot to talk about over coffee," Charlotte said, "but I love that for you."

Charlotte's reaction was validating. Marin was starting over here in more ways than one, and truthfully, it was intimidating. "Thanks. I'm just an adjunct, teaching two classes, but it's a start."

"A good start. Northshire University is a great place to teach, and now you've got your foot in the door."

"Do you know someone who teaches there?" Marin asked, undeniably curious to know more about Charlotte. She'd said she grew up here, but beyond that, Marin had no idea why she was back in Vermont.

"Both of my parents taught there," Charlotte said, turning to lead the way through the living room. "My dad still does."

"Interesting." Marin peeked out the window to see the small backyard. It had a storage shed in the corner and was bordered on both sides by other houses. The space was currently blanketed in snow, but Marin imagined how charming it might be in the summertime. "I'd like a nice yard, I think. I've never had my own outdoor space before."

"Had you always lived in the city?"

"My whole life," Marin confirmed. "I love the city, don't get me wrong, but I'm ready for something new. I wanted a change in my life . . . and here I am."

"Here we both are." Charlotte gave her a curious look. "Quite the coincidence."

"Not entirely. You mentioned Middleton that day on the bus," Marin reminded her. "You told me you'd grown up here, so when I saw a posting for an adjunct position teaching statistics at NU, it felt sort of fated for me to at least apply."

"You don't strike me as the superstitious type."

"I'm not, or . . . I wasn't before." Marin shrugged. "Maybe I am now."

"Color me intrigued," Charlotte said. "So, in the interest of going to get that coffee, what do you think of the house?"

"I like the yard and the proximity to campus, but the house itself feels a bit claustrophobic." Marin looked around herself at the dark paneled walls in the living room. She'd felt trapped most of her adult life, and now she was ready to free herself from those confines, including the proverbial closet. "And it needs a lot of work. I'm trying to be realistic about the sort of houses I'll find in my price range, but this one needs more than I'm able to give it."

"Totally fair. It's your house, Marin. You should have one you love."

She smiled. "Yes. I'm ready to fill my life with things I love."

CHAPTER TWO

Charlotte sipped her latte as Marin settled across from her. *Marin.* The name was unusual, much like the woman. Charlotte had imagined various names for her over the years, wanting to be able to memorialize her properly in her mind, but nothing had ever felt quite right. She'd never thought of Marin. It was a perfect fit for the tall brunette sitting across from her.

Marin looked a little bit older than she had when Charlotte last saw her. A little bit leaner, as if her recovery from the accident had toughened her up. Charlotte wanted to know everything she'd been through over the last two years. Since today's showing had been a bust, they'd see more houses together. Maybe this could turn into a friendship.

Charlotte could use a new friend, and more than that, she felt an indescribable desire to have Marin in her life for longer than it took to find her a house. She wasn't sure she believed in fate anymore, but surely there was a reason they'd found each other again. Sitting here now, Charlotte felt lighter than she had in months, maybe years.

"So," Marin said, then sipped her coffee. A bright smile lit her face. She'd smiled so much today. She seemed happier than the woman from Charlotte's memories, more vibrant in some indefinable way.

Whatever changes she'd made to her life recently, they seemed to suit her. In fact, Charlotte was a bit envious, given her recent downward spiral.

"Where do we start?" Charlotte asked, suddenly overwhelmed by all the things that had led them to this moment. *Tell me everything,* she wanted to beg. *I want to know absolutely everything about you.*

"Let's start with you, if you don't mind," Marin said, and there was something guarded in her expression now, as if she'd heard Charlotte's silent plea. "I feel like our interactions so far have revolved mostly around me."

Charlotte swallowed her disappointment. They had time. "Fair enough."

"What brought you back to Vermont?" Marin asked.

"I'm looking for answers." She sipped her coffee, debating how much of the story to share. Her mother's disappearance was common knowledge among everyone she'd known while she was growing up, but she'd lived outside that shadow for most of her adult life. It was one of the reasons she'd left this town in the first place.

Marin watched her, seemingly waiting for Charlotte to elaborate. She was a striking woman. Marin might not be considered conventionally beautiful, but she had such warm brown eyes. High cheekbones. And her chestnut hair was glossier than Charlotte remembered. Anyway.

Charlotte exhaled slowly. "My mom disappeared when I was ten, just . . . headed out for her monthly book club meeting, and no one ever saw her again."

"Shit." Those eyes Charlotte had just been admiring were wider now. "How awful. I'm so sorry."

"Thanks. It was pretty terrible. Suddenly everyone at school was whispering behind my back. There were so many rumors. You know how kids are. Some people said she'd run off with her secret lover. Some people figured my dad killed her and hid the body. There were a million theories, and they all hurt."

"Did the police have any theories?" Marin asked.

Charlotte lifted one shoulder, tracing a finger back and forth over her coffee cup. "They don't put in too much effort when an adult goes missing, if there's no evidence of foul play. I think they assumed she just left us. That's not a crime."

"No, but it's not an easy thing for a child to accept about her mother."

"Definitely not," Charlotte said. "My dad hired a couple PIs over the years, but neither of them was able to find her."

"What do you think happened?"

Charlotte sighed. "Honestly, I have no idea. I've gone around in circles about it most of my life. I just can't accept that she would voluntarily leave us to wonder if she's alive or dead, but there was never any evidence that something happened to her. Whatever I feel about my dad, there's not a violent bone in his body. I just can't imagine him hurting her."

Marin cocked her head slightly. "So you're here now trying to find out what happened?"

Charlotte nodded. "I know it's a long shot. I mean, it's been thirty years. The trail is cold, but I'm going to give it my best. My other reason for being here is to try to repair my relationship with my dad."

"Were you close before she disappeared?"

Charlotte rolled her lips inward. "Yes. My early childhood was magical, or at least that's how I remember it. My dad was the fun dad, you know? He'd take me on hikes and play with my toys, read me as many bedtime stories as I wanted. Then after she disappeared, he just . . . shut down. He left me with babysitters, never seemed to want anything to do with me. Looking back as an adult, I can see that he was grieving, but at the time, it felt like I'd lost both parents, and I hated him for abandoning me like that. I left Vermont after high school and never looked back."

"Do you have other family here in town or just your dad?" Marin asked.

"Just my dad. My parents had both moved to Vermont to work at the university, so my aunts, uncles, and cousins are scattered up and down the East Coast. I don't see them in person as often as I'd like."

"My family is somewhat scattered, too, so I get that."

"I pretty much cut ties with everyone in Vermont when I left, even my friends from high school." Charlotte sucked in a deep breath, meeting Marin's eyes. "After watching you die—or thinking I had watched you die—it felt like a wake-up call, a reminder of how short life can be. I've been running around ever since, trying to do all the things I would have regretted not doing if it had been me lying in that street."

Marin flinched. "I suppose I've been doing the same thing. Ironic that that moment somehow led us to this one."

"Feels kind of fated, doesn't it?"

"It does," Marin agreed. "And I say that as a person who—prior to almost dying—didn't believe in fate. I was the least superstitious person I knew. I didn't even believe in luck. I thought it was all nonsense. Give me numbers. Now those make sense."

"No wonder you looked so skeptical when I read your horoscope."

"Exactly." Marin pointed a finger at her. "You'll never know how close I came to telling you not to even bother. I was mostly humoring you to be polite, but then you read out the most eerily prophetic thing. It was like you'd peeked inside my brain and seen my most private thoughts and desires." There was that guarded look again.

Charlotte would have given anything to know what Marin wasn't saying. "Really? I honestly don't remember anything about the horoscope I read you."

"I do," Marin said quietly. "I remember every word."

Now Charlotte was desperate to remember what that horoscope had said.

"So," Marin said, one corner of her mouth quirking upward. "If you ever want to read my horoscope again sometime . . ."

"Would you believe I deleted my horoscope app a few months ago?"

Marin gaped at her. "What? Why?"

She sighed. "I got disillusioned with them. I spent two years after you died—*god*, I've got to stop saying that. I'm still trying to wrap my head around the fact that you're alive. But I spent two years trying to find purpose in what happened. I chased after all these things I thought I wanted, but none of them panned out. They were all mistakes."

Marin reached across the table, touching her fingers briefly to the back of Charlotte's hand. "This doesn't feel like a mistake."

Marin swiped a gloved hand over her car's windshield with a frown. A light snow had begun to fall while they were in the coffee shop, and now her car was dusted in white. Having lived her whole life in the city, she was unaccustomed to driving. She'd always had a driver's license, but she had mostly depended on public transportation.

She'd been intimidated by cars even before she'd been hit by one, but this year was all about conquering her fears, and that included becoming a more confident driver. So she brushed off her windshield and slid into the driver's seat, wincing at the fiery bolt of pain that shot down her right leg, making her toes tingle. Nerve pain, her new best friend.

Marin started the engine and connected her phone to the stereo. This was one thing she liked about driving, being able to blast her own music. Chappell Roan's "Good Luck, Babe!" started to play as Marin pulled out of the parking spot. Maybe she was too old to be listening to Chappell Roan, but she refused to apologize for indulging in whatever her heart desired this year. She liked catchy pop tunes, and it thrilled her that there were so many young artists these days who were out and proud.

If Chappell's music had been around when Marin was a teen . . .

But there was no sense lamenting things she couldn't change. She'd made it here in her own time. Well, she hadn't actually come out yet. She hadn't gotten past practicing the words in her head, but she would. Soon. She'd been stuck in her private fantasies, waiting for this moment for years. For *decades*.

Now that her divorce from Andrew was finalized, it was time. Vermont was her blank slate, the opportunity to introduce herself authentically. There would be no preconceived notions. She was finally free to be herself.

Her pulse raced just thinking about it.

Marin tightened her grip on the steering wheel, grateful that her apartment was only a few miles from the coffee shop. Tomorrow was the first day of classes, so she'd be spending more time on campus, but she should make time each day to just drive. She needed to get more comfortable behind the wheel, and she needed to get more familiar with her new hometown, so daily scenic drives seemed like a win-win.

Five minutes later, she pulled into an available parking spot near her new apartment. She was renting the first floor of a three-story building, an old house that had been divided into apartments. It was small and outdated, but it worked for now. It had been unexpectedly difficult to find a first floor unit, but stairs were sometimes hard for her on days when her nerve pain flared up. A first floor master bedroom was a must for her future house as well.

Marin grabbed her purse, locked the car, and made her way inside. The sun was low in the sky, casting her east-facing apartment in shadow, so she flipped on lights as she walked. She hung her coat in the closet and set her purse on the coffee table.

She'd had coffee with Charlotte today. *Charlotte.* Such a beautiful name for an equally beautiful woman. Marin pressed a hand to her heart, feeling it race. She'd been so shocked, so *thrilled* to see her and finally learn her name, she hadn't fully processed the ramifications of having Charlotte in her life now.

"You have my number already, as your Realtor," Charlotte had said before they left the café. "But feel free to reach out as a friend too. I'd really like to keep in touch."

Marin had promised she would. She needed friends here in Vermont, and she wanted to get to know Charlotte better. It was just . . . Marin had allowed her fantasies to run a bit wild over the last two years. She'd been immediately drawn to Charlotte that morning on the bus, had felt a little ping in her belly reminding her that, yes, she was a lesbian. A very, *very* repressed one.

As she'd rebuilt her life over the last two years, she'd spent a lot of time caught up in fantasies that often involved a certain nameless blond from the bus. So, seeing her today, learning her name, and laying the foundation for a friendship with her? That was confusing, to say the least. It had taken time for Marin to get past the shock of their run-in, but by the time they were having coffee together, that spark had rekindled.

Marin was attracted to her, no doubt about it, and the feeling only seemed to have intensified since the last time she saw her, probably because she'd spent so many hours thinking about her. She'd thought she was safe in her fantasies since she'd never see the woman from the bus again.

Fate had a funny sense of humor where Marin was concerned . . . if she believed in such a thing. Maybe, especially after today, she *did* believe in fate. At the very least, she was intrigued by the idea.

She walked to the fridge for a glass of water, idly wishing she had someone to talk to. She felt an unexpected tug of loneliness. Ordinarily, she'd call one of her siblings to chat, but she couldn't talk to them about this particular dilemma, at least, not until she'd come out to them.

A thump from upstairs indicated one of her neighbors was home. As far as she could tell, all the other occupants of this building were students at the university, which was yet another reason to find a house, and soon.

Marin was too old to be living with students, especially now that she was a professor. If any of them was in one of her classes, it might be awkward. She headed to her bedroom to change into more comfortable clothes. Yes, she knew it was only four thirty in the afternoon, but she was in for the day, and she'd fought hard for the freedom to make her own decisions.

Right now, she wanted to spend a few hours reading in comfort. Sapphic fiction—sapphic romance in particular—had gotten her through long years stuck in a loveless marriage. In those books, she saw women like herself living happily, loving each other . . . *thriving*.

It helped her to understand her sexuality, to accept herself for who she was, to know what she wanted in life. And the sex scenes? Suffice it to say, Marin had spent many an evening reading steamy books before indulging in some self-care with her vibrator, which was a million times hotter than anything she'd ever experienced with her husband.

Now, she could technically go out and find a woman to hook up with anytime she wanted, except Marin wasn't a hookup kind of woman. That wasn't how she wanted to experience the pleasure of a woman's body for the first time. Also, she couldn't even begin to contemplate dating before she'd said the words "I'm a lesbian" out loud for the first time.

She had to come out to the people in her life, including her family. She'd just seen them all at Christmas, but she hadn't been able to get the words out. It wasn't the right time, or maybe she just wasn't ready. Now she had a reprieve while she settled into her new life in Vermont. She wouldn't see her family in person for a few months, but she needed to make plans to tell them.

Soon. In the meantime, she'd start her new job. She'd find a house. She'd make some friends here in Vermont, find new hobbies, maybe even join a local pride organization. *Then* she could date. Hopefully that would all happen quickly, though, because after so many years of fantasies, Marin was fairly desperate to kiss and touch someone she felt a real attraction for.

She wanted a girlfriend, a life partner, a *wife*. Honestly, she could hardly wait. Dating was her top priority, just as soon as she'd taken the steps to get herself ready.

With a sigh, she settled on the sofa and reached for the throw blanket she'd left there earlier. Maybe she wasn't lonely so much as she missed having someone to talk to. Were those the same thing? She missed casual conversation, but she treasured these moments when she got to decide exactly what she wanted to do and when she wanted to do it.

She put on her glasses and scrolled Instagram on her phone for a few minutes to unwind before she started reading. She'd followed several accounts for house-decorating inspiration, and one of them had just posted a swoon-worthy photo of a home library. Okay, that was something she'd love to have.

Intrigued, she clicked on the post to see more photos. Built-in bookshelves. Were those expensive? She loved the look of them. Who cared if she mostly read on her Kindle these days? Maybe she could purchase print copies of her favorites to fill the bookshelves. A whole wall of sapphic books! Imagine?

She smiled. Oh yes, she could imagine it. She could see herself sitting in a cozy chair with her new girlfriend. As she swiped to the next photo, her gaze caught on an image of the influencer cozied up, reading with a dog nestled beside her. Hmm.

A dog? Yearning stirred in Marin's chest. Suddenly, she remembered how many times she'd begged for a puppy when she was a little girl. Her childhood best friend, Jenna, had dogs at home, and Marin had loved playing with them. She'd always wanted one of her own, but her parents had been staunchly anti-pet. Andrew had been the same.

"A dog," she murmured to herself. Yes, she should get one. As a bonus, she'd have someone to talk to at home without sacrificing any of her newfound freedom. Suddenly, she wanted a dog almost as much as she wanted a girlfriend, but one was certainly easier to obtain than the other.

She googled "getting a new puppy," and her feed flooded with articles advertising everything you needed to know about bringing home a new puppy . . . except where to get one. Then the website for the local animal shelter caught her eye. That was as good a place to start as any. Marin clicked on it, her gaze immediately drawn to a photo of puppies.

As it turned out, the shelter had a litter of five-week-old lab mixes that would be looking for homes soon. Marin tabbed through the photos, feeling a rising sense of excitement.

Getting a divorce, starting a new career, coming out . . . those were all changes made to reward her adult self. But a puppy? This would be a gift to her inner child, and little Marin was long overdue to have a puppy.

CHAPTER THREE

Anxiety twisted in Marin's stomach as she stood before her bathroom mirror, putting the final touches on her makeup. She hadn't expected to be this nervous about her first day at her new job. She was only an adjunct professor, teaching two classes. The stakes were relatively low, but regardless, she *really* wanted today to go well. It was a big deal, walking away from her former career and dipping her toes into something new.

She wanted to succeed, both at Northshire University and with the other ventures she was pursuing here in Vermont. It was time to make her mark. As she'd learned two years ago, tomorrow was never guaranteed. Blowing out a breath, she returned her makeup pouch to the drawer beside the sink and walked to the living room for her purse. As she picked up her phone, she saw a text from the new contact she'd saved yesterday.

Charlotte Danton: Good luck today!

Charlotte Danton: PS this is Charlotte in case you didn't save my # yet

She smiled as she also noticed a flurry of activity in her sibling group chat. Her brother Jed had been the first to wish her luck, but the rest of her siblings had chimed in soon after. Even a few of her nieces and nephews had texted, wishing her well. How sweet. She sent quick thank-yous to everyone, then tucked her phone into her purse and walked outside to her car.

Marin was grateful she lived close to the campus, especially since she didn't have an office there to use between classes. Technically, she and two other adjuncts had been assigned an office to share, but it meant each of them only really got to use it for office hours or meetings. Other than that, she would do all her prep work and grading at home.

She parked in the faculty lot, then picked up her briefcase to begin the walk to Ziegler Hall, where her classes would be held. Today, she'd be teaching Introduction to Statistics, which was held on Mondays and Thursdays. On Wednesdays, she had a three-hour-long course—Data Analysis Using Statistical Software.

Next semester, she hoped to pick up more classes to supplement her income, but two classes were enough to ease her back into the workforce for now. With her settlement from the accident, she would be able to buy her new home outright instead of having a mortgage, which meant her living expenses would be relatively small.

Still, she hoped to eventually be a full-time professor, if her injuries allowed her to push that hard. She had to stay in tune with her body and be mindful of her limitations. Thinking in terms of flare-ups and pain management was still a relatively new concept for her.

It was brutally cold outside this afternoon, and she felt it in every one of her healed fractures but particularly in her right thigh. The January breeze bit into her cheeks and whipped through her hair. Consequently, Marin arrived at Ziegler Hall feeling windswept and sore. She ducked into the ladies' room to touch up her appearance, then took the elevator to the third floor and walked to her classroom.

She blew out a cleansing breath as she made her way to the lectern at the front of the room. This was something she'd always wanted to do, and she couldn't wait to see the classroom filled with young faces. She wanted to show them that statistics weren't boring, that they could be exciting once you learned the power behind them.

The first student, a young woman in a pink puffy coat, entered the room and gave Marin a shy smile. She returned it with a friendly wave.

Ten minutes later, the classroom was filled with eager students. Well, "eager" might be overselling the level of enthusiasm Marin saw on their faces, but she was enthusiastic enough for all of them.

"Good afternoon, everyone," she began. "I'm Professor Easterly, and I presume you're all here for Introduction to Statistics?" She swept her gaze around the room, seeing a few students nod. No one got up and left. "Good. Now, I'm not sure if I should admit this to you or not, but this is my first semester teaching."

She raised her eyebrows for effect, hoping for a few smiles or even laughs in response, but the students mostly just stared, looking bored. *Yikes.* Tough crowd.

"I'm a statistician by trade, and I spent twenty years working at a financial firm in Manhattan, so not only am I here to teach you some interesting ways you can work with numbers, but I can also introduce you to potential career options. Please come see me during office hours if that interests you. I'd love to help."

Still nothing but bored expressions on their faces.

Marin did her best to shrug it off and move forward. "Now, let's take a look at the syllabus for this semester." She clicked a button on her laptop, relieved when the correct slide appeared on the screen behind her. She considered herself good with technology, but it was Murphy's Law that something would go wrong with the presentation on her first day at a new job with a room full of students currently forming their first impressions of her.

An hour and fifteen minutes later, Marin sent them on their way, feeling exhausted but hopeful. Sure, the students hadn't been as lively as she might have liked, but still, she'd enjoyed herself. Her corporate job had begun to bore her to tears. She'd dreaded going to work every morning. If today was any indication, she wouldn't have a boring day as a college professor. If only she could figure out how to get her students more engaged . . .

"Professor Easterly?"

She looked up at the sound of her name, glad she hadn't yet given in to the urge to rub at the ache in her right thigh. Standing around in heels—even low ones—had been a foolishly vain decision. She smiled at the young man in front of her. "Yes. Noah, right?"

"Yeah. Um, I wanted to talk to you about career options like you mentioned, but I looked at your office hours in the portal, and I'm not on campus on Tuesdays. I'm a commuter. I help my mom on our family farm when I'm not in class . . . um. You don't need to know that." He looked uncomfortable. "I was wondering if there's another time you're available?"

"Sure, Noah. We can definitely find a time that works." She pulled up the shared office-availability form on her phone. "Would you be able to meet me on Thursday before this class? Say one thirty?"

His face brightened. "Yeah, that would work. Thanks so much, Professor Easterly."

"You're very welcome. I'll see you then."

She watched until he'd left the classroom, feeling a hundred times better about the class now. For a minute there, she was afraid she'd bombed on her first day as a professor, but she'd made an impression on Noah, and that was a win.

Marin shifted her weight to her left leg. Flats. Maybe even orthopedic ones. She rolled her eyes at herself, but she'd decided on the day she finally went home from the hospital that she'd never again feel anything about her body other than gratitude. She could live with the aches, pains, and scars. Hell, she celebrated them because she was *alive*.

She tucked her laptop into her briefcase, then bundled up in her coat for the walk back to her car. She had just enough time to go home and change before her next appointment.

Because Marin was about to meet a litter of puppies, and she couldn't fucking wait.

"Leave your shoes at the door, please." A harried-looking woman about Marin's age stood before her in a long-sleeved shirt and leggings. She'd introduced herself as Susan, the puppies' foster mom. "They haven't had their vaccines yet, so they could be vulnerable to germs you track in."

"Of course." Obediently, Marin took off her sneakers and left them by the door. Already, she could hear puppy sounds, yips and squeals and the scuffling of paws.

"They're five weeks old right now," Susan told her. "So they won't be ready to go home for about three more weeks."

"That's fine. I'll need time to buy supplies and learn how to care for a puppy."

Susan gave Marin a guarded look. "You haven't had a puppy before?"

She shook her head. "I've never had a dog, but I've always wanted one. I'm recently divorced and looking for a new companion." She paused, feeling an uncharacteristic need to explain herself. "I'm a statistician, so I assure you I know how to conduct research, and I plan to learn everything I need to know about puppies."

"Good, because puppies are a *lot* of work, and I want to make sure they're all going to great homes," Susan said. "You'd be surprised how many people fall in love with them when they're tiny and cute and then return them to the shelter in a few months when they've turned into big out-of-control teenagers."

"That won't be me," Marin assured her. "I'm one hundred percent committed to having a dog, and I'm prepared for the rough spots. I take my responsibilities seriously."

Susan smiled. "Okay, come and meet them. Their mom is a black lab, but that's all we know about their pedigree. She was rescued from a house fire shortly before she gave birth, and her family couldn't afford her care, so they surrendered her. Anyway, we gave the puppies fire-themed names."

"That's adorable," Marin said, "but is their mom okay? Was she injured in the fire?"

"Only minor injuries, thank goodness. A few small burns and scorched foot pads. She's fully recovered and already has her forever home lined up, just as soon as they're weaned. She's in here." Susan led her into the living room, where a black dog waited, tail wagging. "This is mama Raven."

"Hi, Raven," Marin said, unsure how she was supposed to greet the dog. She really did have a lot to learn.

Susan kept walking, leaving Raven in the living room. They entered the kitchen, which had been blocked off with a baby gate. "And here are her puppies. There are six, and four of them are already spoken for. Do you want to know which ones are still available, or do you want to meet them first?"

"Um, I think I'd like to spend a minute getting to know them first."

Susan nodded. "Why don't you go on in? Just grab a toy and interact with them. Be gentle, though. Remember they're just babies."

"Of course." Marin fumbled with the baby gate before she figured out how to open the latch. As she stepped through the gate, she was immediately surrounded by puppies. Several of them bounced against her legs. They were mostly black, except for one honey-brown puppy, and several had white markings. "What are their names?"

"Spark, Blaze, Smokey, Ember, Ash, and Cinder."

"Those are adorable. I'll ask you who's who once I've gotten to know them a little bit."

"Take your time." Susan lingered in the doorway, watching as Marin lowered herself to the floor, maybe to answer questions, maybe to supervise Marin. Maybe both.

A black-and-white puppy launched itself into Marin's lap with a yip and grabbed a mouthful of her hair, then tugged. "Ouch," she laughed. "Here, let's chew on this instead." She offered the puppy a stuffed duck, which it immediately chomped down on.

"That's Ash," Susan said. "He's the biggest in the litter. The boldest too."

"Hi, Ash." Marin squeaked the duck for him, and the puppy snatched it from her hand, biting her fingers in the process. "You're a handful, aren't you?"

"He's also one of the puppies who's already spoken for," Susan said, voicing it as a warning when Marin wouldn't have chosen this puppy anyway. He was too brash for her taste. Ash liked to be the center of attention, and she'd had enough of those types in her life already.

Marin shifted her focus to the rest of the litter. A black-and-white puppy nipped at her sock, tail wagging, while several others lunged for her face, licking her cheeks and biting her hair. She laughed, a little bit caught off guard by how exuberant—and mouthy—they were. Was she cut out for a puppy?

Because now that she was paying attention, there were pee pads all over the floor to contain messes. At least Marin hadn't sat in a wet spot, and thank goodness she'd changed into jeans after class. But the longer she watched them play, the more she knew this was the right decision. She'd always wanted a puppy. She'd begged for one when she was a little girl, but her parents had said no.

As the youngest of five, Marin heard that word a lot while she was growing up. She'd been an afterthought, a later-in-life "oops," and so she'd been expected to go with the flow. With older siblings always being shuttled from one activity to another, no one had time to cater to Marin's whims. She'd worn her older sisters' hand-me-downs and lost herself in books while she sat through their lessons and games.

There had been perks to being the youngest, of course. Marin's parents had been less strict with her when it came to curfews or what TV shows she was allowed to watch. They simply hadn't had time to micromanage her the way they had with her older siblings. Still, she'd internalized from an early age that she should put her own wants and needs aside and go along with what everyone else wanted, but now . . . now it was finally her turn.

She picked up another toy and tossed it to a nearby puppy, laughing as several of them bowled each other over in their quest to get it. Her gaze caught on a small black puppy playing quietly in the back corner of the kitchen. "Hey, puppy," she called. Immediately, the puppies nearest to her barreled into her again. The black puppy lifted its head and looked at her.

"Hi there," Marin said, making eye contact. "Want to come over and say hello?"

"That's Ember," Susan told her, reminding Marin of her presence. "She's a little bit shyer than the other puppies."

"I see that. Hi, Ember." Marin waved at the puppy, feeling rather inept at how she was supposed to attract a shy puppy's attention.

"Try using a higher tone of voice, like 'Here, puppy, puppy, puppy!'" Susan called. Immediately, most of the puppies piled in her direction. The little black puppy trotted over, hanging behind her siblings.

"Here, puppy!" Marin said, making her voice high pitched and silly. "Puppy, puppy, puppy!" They bounded toward her, lunging across her lap in a whirl of tongues and paws and wagging tails. They were adorable. Little Ember still hung back, but she was close enough now that Marin could reach out to her. She scratched the puppy under her chin, feeling a burst of warmth in her chest when Ember's tail began to wag. "What a pretty name you have, Ember."

"She's the runt of the litter," Susan said. "We almost lost her that first week. She wasn't getting enough milk. The other puppies were pushing her out of the way, so I had to supplement her to get her back on track. I sat up with her one night, hand-feeding her until she was strong enough to rejoin the litter. I wasn't sure she would make it, but I saw a spark in her . . . an ember, I guess you could say, just waiting to burst into flame. She's still the smallest and quietest puppy, but I think she'll really blossom once she's away from her siblings."

"I bet she will." Marin had been taken with Ember from the moment she noticed her, and the feeling was stronger now. Marin knew a thing or two about being the smallest, about blossoming away from her siblings, about an ember smoldering until it had the strength to blaze. "You're a very pretty girl, Ember."

The puppy looked up at her and wagged again, and then she crawled into Marin's lap. Her little body was so warm, and her fur was so soft. Marin stroked her, laughing as the puppy rolled upside down and grabbed at Marin's hair with her mouth.

"Incidentally, Ember is one of the two puppies who's still available."

I'll take her. Marin bit back the words. She was a statistician, after all. She needed all the data before she made a decision. "Who is the other available puppy?"

"Blaze." Susan pointed to a black puppy with a white stripe down the middle of its forehead. "He seems to be a bit more rambunctious than Ember, but really, it's hard to say at this age how their personalities will develop."

"Hi, Blaze." Marin waved a toy in his direction, and the puppy bounded over. Meanwhile, Ember was still upside down in Marin's lap, mouthing at a stuffed pig Marin had given her. Her feet were disproportionately big for her body, and it was adorable.

Blaze came over to grab the toy she'd offered, and Marin spent a few minutes getting to know the two available puppies. They were both sweet, but her heart had already decided. Every time she looked at Ember, she felt a tug of affection telling her this was the puppy she wanted.

"I'd like to adopt Ember," she told Susan.

"Are you sure?" Susan asked. "We have adult dogs available too. You don't seem to have much experience with dogs, and puppies are a lot of work. She won't stay this small or this cute for long. None of them will."

"I know that, and I *am* inexperienced with dogs, but I've waited a long time to be in a position where I can bring an animal into my life. I promise you, I don't make commitments lightly. I'm prepared to give her everything she needs, no matter how challenging it is."

"Your application says you're a professor at the university. Young puppies can't stay home alone for very long. She'll need to go out every few hours."

"I'm only teaching two classes this semester, so that shouldn't be a problem. Plus, I live near the campus, so I'm sure I could hire a student to watch her while I'm working if she needs extra attention at first."

Susan nodded, seemingly pleased with that answer. "And how will you handle her exercise needs while you're living in an apartment?"

"I'm house hunting, hoping to buy something in the next few weeks, so by the time she's big enough to need it, I hope to have a nice yard for her to play in."

"I like the sound of that," Susan said. "And I like the way you've bonded with Ember."

Marin looked down, surprised to realize the puppy had fallen asleep in her lap. She cradled Ember in the crook of her arm like a baby, and the puppy let out a contented sigh. "She caught my eye the moment I noticed her hanging out in the back like that. I guess you could say we're both underdogs, both survivors."

"Sounds like a perfect match, then. I'll email you some literature and links to help you get started on your puppy research. She'll be ready to go home in about three weeks."

"Just enough time for me to get ready for her." Marin looked at the sleeping puppy in her arms. Ember would add so much joy and excitement to her life, not to mention love.

A half hour later, Marin was back in her car. Her phone was filled with puppy pictures, and she was *happy*. She'd only been in Vermont a little over a week, and already her life was so much richer.

Instead of going back to her apartment, Marin guided her car toward the winding mountain roads outside town. Time for her daily driving lesson. She would keep doing this until she got more comfortable behind the wheel. As a bonus, she was getting to know the area and experiencing the beauty of Vermont.

It was definitely beautiful here in January. Cold, but beautiful. As she pulled out of Susan's driveway, she was dismayed to see snowflakes in the air. The sky had turned heavy and gray while she was inside, something that seemed to happen often this time of year. Nonetheless, the forecast wasn't calling for any snow accumulation today, so she decided to forge on.

She turned onto a road that led away from downtown Middleton, driving carefully as it curved through a heavily wooded area. The ground beneath her tires was probably not paved. It was hard to tell for sure because of the snow, but she thought this was one of the many dirt roads in the area. It had been coated liberally with sand and gravel for traction.

She spent the next fifteen minutes taking random turns, meandering along various winding rural roads. Already, they felt slightly less intimidating than they had when she first arrived in Vermont. While she was driving, the skies cleared again, bright blue peeking through the clouds. The snow-covered field she was driving past began to glisten in the sunlight. Behind it, mountains appeared, a stunning vista that caused her breath to catch in her throat.

Her car's stereo dinged to let her know she had a text message from Charlotte, and Marin's stomach fluttered in anticipation of what her new friend had said. Since she was alone on this rural road, she pulled her car to the side and stopped. She sat there for a minute, gazing out over the field of sparkling snow. Here and there, small houses dotted the hillside. What a view they must have . . .

She could imagine herself sitting in the living room of her new house, gazing out at a view like that. It would be the perfect backdrop while she graded assignments and played with her new puppy. And entertained a new girlfriend . . .

With another deep breath, she checked her phone.

Charlotte Danton: How did it go?!
Me: Class was good, and I adopted a puppy afterward!
Charlotte Danton: A puppy? I need details!
Me: Saw an ad from the local shelter last night
Me: Who could resist this face?

She attached a photo of Ember. Charlotte responded with a series of heart eye emojis.

Charlotte Danton: No one surely! Awwwww
Charlotte Danton: So he or she is officially yours?
Me: Yes, although I can't bring her home for a few weeks. Motivation to find a house!
Charlotte Danton: Got it. On that note, I emailed you a few more houses to consider.
Me: Great. Do any of them have a view? Because I think I want a view.
Charlotte Danton: Not really. You wanted to be downtown, right? Near the campus?
Me: Suddenly thinking I'd be willing to commute a bit to have a view like this.

She snapped a picture of her current view and texted it to Charlotte.

Charlotte Danton: Solid goals! Ok I'll set up a few houses for us tmrw morning and then maybe lunch after?
Me: Sounds perfect

While she was parked, Marin sent a few pictures of Ember to her sibling group chat, and also to her niece Jen, who was a big dog lover. She was about to put her phone down and begin the drive back to her apartment when an email came in to her new university account. She didn't get many of those, or at least she hadn't yet, probably because she was a lowly adjunct. Curious, she clicked on the email, which was a newsletter from the department secretary, announcing several clubs and committees in search of faculty volunteers.

Marin was considered faculty, even though she wasn't full time, and she'd like the opportunity to get more involved on campus. Curious, she scanned the email. Her eyes snapped almost immediately to a posting for the campus Pride Coalition. They were looking for a faculty volunteer to oversee various activities.

She sucked in a deep breath. This could be the perfect opportunity for her. There was no requirement for faculty volunteers to be queer, but it could be a way for Marin to dip her toes into her new reality. She planned to debut herself here in Vermont as an out lesbian, as intimidating as that had turned out to be, and this could be the perfect first step.

Heart pounding, she clicked the link to submit her name.

CHAPTER FOUR

"Well, that was disappointing," Marin said as she followed Charlotte into her house, a cute little bungalow on the outskirts of town. They'd spent a fruitless morning house hunting, viewing four properties that had all ended up not working out for one reason or another. The last house they'd visited was only a few minutes from where Charlotte lived, so she'd invited Marin to her place for lunch.

"I'm sorry our morning was a bust, but I'm glad it led to us having lunch together." Charlotte was radiant today. Her curly blond hair was long and loose over her shoulders, slightly windblown from the mountain air. She had on just enough makeup to accentuate her features, and her blue eyes danced with energy and enthusiasm, accentuated by the royal blue scarf looped around her neck.

It seemed to Marin that Charlotte had only gotten more beautiful since they first met, or more likely, she looked the same, but after two years spent fantasizing about her, Marin had developed an unhealthy crush on her new friend. At least she'd had decades of practice hiding her feelings.

"Anyway," Charlotte said as she got a bowl of pasta salad out of her fridge. "Tell me more about how things are going. How was your first class? How are you liking Vermont? How did you end up adopting a puppy? I want to know everything."

So, they sat together at the kitchen table with fresh fruit and pasta salad, and Marin told her how much she'd enjoyed standing in front of a room full of students while she tried to engage them in the power of statistics. She told Charlotte about her appointment with Susan and the puppies and how little Ember had stolen her heart.

By the time they finished lunch, she was relaxed and happy, having forgotten all about the disappointing morning of house hunting. She and Charlotte relocated to the living room, where they settled together on an oversize blue sofa, leaving an empty cushion between them.

"The last time we talked," Charlotte said, "you mentioned that you're starting a new chapter here, that you're making some big changes in your life. What does that mean, exactly?" Her brow furrowed. "I just realized that might be too personal of a question. Sorry."

Marin felt a punch of adrenaline, because this was it. This was her moment to *finally* come out for the first time. She was equal parts bursting with anticipation and seized with a jittery fear. She'd been waiting such a long time to say these words, it was almost overwhelming. "It's personal, but it's something I think I'd like to share with you."

Charlotte shook her head. "Don't tell me unless you're sure. I wasn't trying to pry, honest."

"I'm sure." Marin sucked in a deep breath, steadying herself. "I . . . the thing is, I'm a lesbian."

"Oh." Charlotte's eyes widened for a moment, and then she grinned. "Is that all? I thought you were about to tell me something shocking, but that's cool. This is a very queer-friendly state. I don't know why I had it in my head that you were married to a man, though."

Marin exhaled with a burst of nervous laughter. After all this time, she'd finally said the words, but she'd forgotten to tell Charlotte a very important part of her truth. "I *was* married to a man. I mean, I've never actually . . . you're the first person I've told."

Charlotte's eyes went even wider this time. "Oh my god. You just came out to me? Like for the first time? Ever?"

Marin nodded. Hysteria bubbled up inside her, and she had the totally irrational urge to laugh again, but she swallowed it down. "Yes. That's exactly what I just did."

"Holy shit." Charlotte gaped at her. "I don't know what the protocol is here. No one's ever come out to me before . . . like, I mean, of course I know gay people, but I don't think I've been the first person someone's told. Oh my god, I'm blowing this. Congratulations! This is a big deal for you, and I'm so glad you felt like you could tell me. That's an honor. Really."

"Thanks." Marin wasn't quite sure what to do with herself. Her skin felt hot, and her heart was beating so fast, but she also felt lighter for having finally said the words out loud. Maybe she hadn't fully realized until that moment how much space they'd been taking up inside her.

"So is this a new realization for you, then, that you like women?" Charlotte paused. "And if I'm being nosy, please tell me to buzz off. I'm just curious by nature."

"It's not a new realization, actually. I've known for a while." Marin sucked in a lungful of air and blew it out slowly. "And you're not being nosy. I've been trying to find the courage to tell someone for a long time. I came to Vermont with the idea to just be . . . out, but now that I'm here, I realize it's not that simple. Telling my story for the first time is a big deal, even if people here don't have preconceived notions that I'm straight. It's been really intimidating."

"I'm sure it has. So would you like to, then?" Charlotte turned to face her, wrapping her arms around her knees. "Tell me your story, I mean? Because I'd love to hear it."

"I would," Marin said, suddenly bursting to share her truth. "And actually, I think I need to start all the way at the beginning, if you don't mind."

Charlotte nodded, eyes locked on Marin's.

"The first thing to know about me is that I'm the youngest of five. My parents never said so, but it's pretty obvious that I was a later-in-life 'oops.' My siblings are significantly older, and no one ever seemed to know quite what to do with me . . . like I was an afterthought. We weren't poor, but five kids definitely strained the budget."

"I can imagine."

"From an early age, I learned to go with the flow and do what was expected of me. I tried not to take up too much space, you know?"

"I guess I can see how that would happen," Charlotte said. "But it makes me sad to think of little Marin being afraid to take up space."

"Oh, don't feel sad. I had a happy childhood. There was plenty of love to go around, but I always felt somewhat disconnected from my siblings, being so much younger. They weren't my playmates so much as . . . babysitters, if that makes sense. By the time I was a teenager, they were grown. It was just me and my older and very conservative parents in the house. So when I went off to college, I was probably more naive than the average student. I had no idea who I was or what I wanted."

"I didn't really, either, when I started college," Charlotte said. "No clue at all."

Marin gave her a grateful smile. "There were . . . *signs* . . . in hindsight. Female friends I felt a little too close to, a female professor I definitely had a crush on." She rolled her eyes at herself. "But my parents had drilled into me from a young age that I was expected to get my degree and then get married . . . to a man. Again, I was naive. And eager to please. So when I met Andrew, I put all my energy into that relationship.

"He seemed perfect. He was charming. Funny. My parents loved him, and so did my friends. He was so romantic, always bringing me flowers and gifts, and I thought I was so lucky to have him. My friends started asking if I thought he was going to propose, and that felt kind of scary for some reason, but I wasn't sure why. I once confessed to a friend that our sex life wasn't that exciting for me, and she told me that's just how it is once you're in an established relationship, so when he *did* propose, I said yes."

Charlotte watched quietly, her eyes never leaving Marin.

"I was twenty-four when we got married, had just finished my master's and was planning to go for my PhD. I'd always wanted to teach, but Andrew convinced me I'd make more money, and sooner, going into finance instead. I'm not proud of the way I let myself be influenced back then, but . . . as they say, it sounded like a good idea at the time."

"Hey, I'm the last person to judge on past decisions," Charlotte said. "I've made more than my fair share of mistakes. Probably, most of us look back and wish we'd made different choices, but we were doing the best we could with the knowledge we had then."

"Yeah, so things were okay for a few years. Andrew and I were reasonably happy. Sex was kind of a chore for me, but it wasn't terrible. I . . ." Her cheeks felt uncomfortably hot. It was hard to share these intimate details about herself with someone, and while she felt close to Charlotte, they really hadn't known each other very long. "I was in denial for a long time, but on some level, I think I always knew. I fantasized about women . . . and *only* women.

"I've always been a huge book lover, but I think I subconsciously avoided reading queer stories because I was afraid of how they might make me feel. My book club chose *The Seven Husbands of Evelyn Hugo*, and my first thought was 'Ugh, seven men!' and then I found out it was a sapphic love story, and I balked. I actually considered skipping that month so I wouldn't have to read it. What can I say? The denial ran deep."

Again, Charlotte gave her an encouraging look.

"I read that book, and . . . let's just say, my eyes were opened." Marin exhaled. "I was forced to face reality. Not only did I not love my husband, I wasn't attracted to men at all. I started reading as many sapphic books as I could get my hands on, fantasizing that I could have what those women had . . . a passionate, loving relationship with another woman. Andrew and I still shared a bed, but I was dreaming about a different life."

"Is that when you decided to leave him?" Charlotte asked.

She let out a bitter laugh. "I wish, but no. He has a big personality, and by this time, we'd been married for a decade or so. I didn't want to rock the boat. Also, my parents were in their seventies then and having a lot of health problems. It was a difficult time. I lost my mom to cancer and my dad to a heart attack, both of them gone before I turned forty."

"I'm so sorry you went through that," Charlotte said, her tone sympathetic.

"A hazard of having older parents, I guess. Anyway, after they were gone, I started thinking again . . . I needed to divorce Andrew, but as much as I hated living in a loveless marriage, it was terrifying to think of blowing up my whole life by divorcing him, especially because he's not a bad guy. We had some good times together. So I kept putting it off, waiting for the right moment." She took a deep breath and stared straight at Charlotte. "Until you sat beside me on that bus and read me a horoscope about how it was time to be my authentic self. I was floored."

Charlotte pressed a hand to her mouth. "Wow, yeah. I could tell those words meant something to you, but I had no idea."

"I didn't believe in signs, but my god, how could I see that as anything but?"

Charlotte nodded, looking slightly breathless.

"I decided, okay, maybe it's really time." Her chest constricted, and she rubbed a hand against it. "I was feeling pretty determined when I got off the bus, and then, of course, that car hit me."

"Oh, Marin . . ."

"I could feel myself slipping away. I don't know how to describe it." She steeled herself against the shakiness that gripped her every time she relived her brush with death. "The pain was so overwhelming that I felt almost disconnected from my body. Not numb, but . . . separate.

It was a kind of terror I didn't know was possible, because I felt myself dying. I knew it was happening, and I was just . . . so scared. And so sad." A tear slipped over her cheek, and she swiped at it with a trembling hand.

"It was pretty damn terrifying for me just watching, so I can only imagine."

"People talk about your life flashing before your eyes, but it wasn't like that at all, at least not for me. I just kept thinking about all my regrets. I was devastated that I would die without ever having found the courage to *live*. It was a horrible feeling." She shuddered. Behind the fear and the crushing sadness, she'd been so cold. There'd been so much pain. It was disorienting and terrifying and so traumatic she could hardly bring herself to think about it at all.

"I'm so sorry." Charlotte touched her hand. Her fingers were so warm. It made Marin realize how cold hers had become by comparison, as if she were reliving the way it had felt to nearly die on a snow-covered street.

"I have no memory of the time my heart stopped. No white light. Nothing." She took another deep breath. "I was there on the street, and then I was in the hospital, hooked to machines and clinging to life. But I was alive, and I vowed right there in the hospital bed that if I made it home, if I got a second chance, I was going to start living my life the way I'd always wanted to. I wasn't holding anything back this time."

"Good for you. Goddammit, Marin, I'm so happy you're getting that chance."

"Yeah, me too." Another burst of anxious laughter escaped her. This didn't feel like the right moment to laugh, but she couldn't seem to stop herself. She laughed, and then she hiccupped, and suddenly she was crying. Her breath hitched as the tears started, and just like with her laughter, the tears seemed to pour out without permission. "I'm sorry. I just . . ."

"Don't you dare apologize." Charlotte scooted closer on the couch, resting a hand on Marin's shoulder. "That was a hell of a story you just told, and it sounds like you'd been holding it in a long time. I think these tears are a cleansing."

Marin pressed a hand over her eyes, embarrassed by her tears, because they just would *not* stop. But the ache in her chest lessened with each sob, like pressure had been building there for the last twenty years or so, maybe her entire forty-seven years, and now she'd finally found the release valve.

What must Charlotte think, first watching Marin nearly die and now watching her fall apart? Why couldn't Marin ever just act like a competent adult in front of her? "Sorry," she whispered, wiping furiously at her face.

"What did I just say? Please don't apologize. Here."

Marin looked up to see Charlotte holding out a packet of tissues, which she accepted gratefully. She wiped her eyes, removing most of her makeup in the process, but it was too late to worry about her appearance. Maybe this was one way to get her attraction to Charlotte under control, because even if Charlotte liked women—which was a big *if* since Charlotte had definitely responded to Marin's announcement like a straight ally—she certainly wouldn't be interested in someone as messy as Marin had been in her presence.

Friendship, though. Hopefully that was still on the table.

"Sometimes there's nothing better than a good cry," Charlotte said.

Marin managed a shaky smile, surprised to realize she *did* feel better. "Maybe. Still, I didn't mean to fall apart in front of you like that."

"Pfft." Charlotte made a dismissive gesture with her hand. "That's what friends are for, right? And seriously, I'm just so happy you're getting that second chance. You're going to have all the experiences you've been wanting. It's fantastic, and I'm gladder than ever that we've reconnected, because I can't wait to watch you *thrive*."

CHAPTER FIVE

"So what's next for you?" Charlotte asked Marin as they wandered down an aisle in the local pet store, looking at puppy supplies. "Any plans to start dating women?"

It'd been a week since Marin's unexpected and tearful confession, and Charlotte was still so honored that Marin had felt comfortable sharing something so important with her. She was grateful for this new friendship, hoping that maybe she'd finally found purpose in what they'd gone through together that day on the bus.

Surely this was it. Marin would be part of her life now, and maybe Charlotte would find the rest of what she was looking for here in Vermont, too, reconnecting with her dad and hopefully even figuring out what had happened to her mom.

"That's a terrifying question." Marin gave her a stiff smile, then rolled her eyes. "The easy answer is yes, god yes, I'm so ready to start dating. I've only been thinking about this for twenty years now, but that's also why it's *not* an easy answer, because it's intimidating as hell to think of putting myself out there. Most women my age will have . . ." She huffed, her cheeks going slightly pink. "They'll have *much* more experience dating women than I do."

"Okay, I get that." Charlotte picked up a purple stuffed dragon with shiny wings that crinkled when she touched them. "Is this not the cutest thing you've ever seen? I'm totally buying it for Ember."

"I love it," Marin agreed. Her shopping cart already contained a crate, a small dog bed, bowls, and several toys and treats.

Charlotte squeezed the dragon, producing a high-pitched squeak that made them both laugh. "As for dating, when you say you're worried about your lack of experience, you're talking about sex, right?"

Cheeks even pinker now, Marin nodded. "I'm forty-seven, and—"

Charlotte held up a hand. "Look, I know this is outside my wheelhouse as a straight woman, but first of all, I think you can't be the only forty-seven-year-old who's looking to date a different gender for the first time, and second, you can take dating at any pace you're comfortable with. I'm someone who needs to get to know a guy before I sleep with him, so when I use dating apps, I start with coffee, then maybe some other casual activity. There's a lot of 'getting to know you' before we make it to the bedroom, so even if that hasn't been your style in the past, maybe it's a good place to start now. Get coffee with a woman. Or go to a gay bar and see if someone buys you a drink. That's not so scary, right? Just ease your way into it."

"I like the sound of that, but does Middleton even have a gay bar?" Marin asked as she picked up a package of bright-red tennis balls.

"Good question. I honestly don't know the answer, because we don't have many bars in general. It's a college town, which means we have more inclusive spaces than some other parts of Vermont, but you don't necessarily want to look for women in places where students go."

Marin visibly shuddered. "God, no."

"So, online dating could be a good place to start. And we can look and see if there are any gay bars around. I'd be happy to go as your wing woman." Charlotte grinned at her, flapping the dragon's wings as she spoke.

Marin chuckled. "I appreciate that, and I could certainly use a wing woman. If nothing else, you can cheer me on while I set up my online-dating profile."

"Definitely. Just let me know when you're ready. We can open a bottle of wine and get you all set up to date."

Marin exhaled slowly. She did that a lot when she was trying to relax herself, Charlotte was starting to notice. "You've done this, then? Online dating?"

"Sure," Charlotte said, remembering that Marin said she had married Andrew when she was twenty-four. That probably meant she hadn't dated since her early twenties. It would be intimidating, getting back into the game after so long, no matter what gender you were dating. "I don't love it, but it's so hard to meet people any other way these days."

"I *want* to say it sounds exciting," Marin said. "But honestly, it sounds terrifying to click on someone's picture and invite them out for coffee. Chemistry is such an indefinable thing. How do you know who you'll hit it off with in person?"

"You don't. That's why you start with something simple like coffee. Then, if there are no sparks, you haven't wasted too much time and energy on that person. But online dating *does* open you up to a much wider dating pool than just hoping you'll randomly meet someone."

"True." They approached a long display of collars and leashes. Marin bypassed the camo and studs to pick up a small raspberry-pink collar with reflective strips on it. "What do you think of this one?"

"I think that color would really suit her. She's solid black, right?"

Marin nodded. "I don't wear much pink myself, but I think I like it for Ember. Okay." She placed the collar and a matching leash in her cart. "What else do I need?"

"Chew toys," Charlotte said.

"You seem to know a lot about puppies," Marin observed.

"An ex-boyfriend of mine was majorly dog obsessed. He raised several puppies while we were together, so yeah, I've spent a lot of time around puppies."

"One of my nieces is the same way," Marin said with a soft smile. "She's been texting me suggestions nonstop since I told her about Ember."

"I love that," Charlotte said. "How old is she?"

"Thirty-six," Marin said, then laughed at the surprise on Charlotte's face, because she'd been imagining an adorable little girl texting Marin about puppies. "Yes, my nieces and nephews are grown. I'm a great-aunt already. I'm the baby of the family, remember?"

"Right." They reached the aisle with chew toys, and Charlotte selected a package of puppy teethers, then tossed it into Marin's cart. "I'd be happy to come over when you bring her home and help you get her settled, if you like."

"That would be great, actually."

"Definitely, and before that, let's plan our wine night to get you set up for online dating."

"Maybe this weekend?" Marin suggested.

"Weekends are actually really busy for me with work. I can meet up, but it would be tricky."

"How about Thursday night? I don't teach on Fridays."

"Thursday should be perfect. Let's plan on it."

They went through the self-checkout, and then Charlotte helped Marin load her new purchases into the Outback before they went their separate ways. As Charlotte pulled into her driveway ten minutes later, she slowed automatically to check the mailbox, surprised to find a manila envelope wedged inside from the Middleton County Sheriff's Department. *Holy shit.* She'd been waiting on this for so long she'd decided it wasn't coming. It had been months since she'd requested a copy of the file from her mother's disappearance.

Charlotte's fingers tingled, and her stomach tightened. The sheriff's department had closed her mother's case within a few months of her disappearance, but what if Charlotte found something in here that gave her a new lead toward finding out what happened?

Since returning to Middleton, Charlotte had looked up as many of her mom's old friends as she could find, but none of them had anything useful to tell her. She was still trying to track down her mom's best friend, a woman named Beverly Sinclair. Charlotte remembered Bev being around a lot, almost like an aunt, and yet, they'd lost touch after her mom's disappearance. Charlotte hoped Bev might have something useful to tell her.

The problem was, Bev had left Vermont twenty years ago. She'd moved to Massachusetts with her husband, but they weren't there anymore, either, as far as Charlotte could tell. There were a *lot* of Beverly Sinclairs on the internet, and Charlotte had messaged as many of them as she could, but so far, the only responses she'd received were to say they weren't the Beverly she was looking for.

But now, Charlotte had the sheriff's report. She sat at her kitchen table and opened the envelope. The file looked alarmingly thin, all things considered. She'd known the sheriff's department hadn't spent much time investigating her mom's disappearance, but even so, this seemed light.

The private investigators her dad hired after the sheriff's department closed their investigation had done so much more legwork. She'd have to ask him if he still had any of their documentation, because she'd like to look through it too. She skimmed a report about her childhood home being searched but didn't learn anything useful.

She flipped to the next page, which contained an interview with a man named Allan Svenson. Who was that? The name tugged at something in Charlotte's memory, but she couldn't place him. Maybe he was another professor at the university? When she was little, it had felt like her parents' entire lives revolved around that university, and consequently, so had Charlotte's.

The interview had been transcribed from an audiotape by Deputy Lou Bouchard, noted as LB, Allan Svenson as AS.

LB: How do you know Mrs. Danton?

AS: We're colleagues.

LB: Phone records show you call her an awful lot for someone who's just a colleague.

AS: We teach in the same department.

LB: Is that all? Some of these calls are pretty late at night. You want to try again?

AS: We both like to talk about history. We enjoy each other's company. Is that a crime?

LB: It's a crime if you two were having an affair and she wanted to end things, so you did something to her before she could leave you.

AS: That's not what happened.

LB: I hope you're not lying to me, because if you are, you should know that I'm going to find out, and it'll be worse for you than if you just tell me the truth now.

AS: I didn't hurt Terri, and I don't know where she is. That's the truth.

The interview ended shortly after, but the report included his phone records and her mother's, showing they did indeed talk on the phone a lot, especially late at night. Charlotte got a sick feeling in the pit of her stomach.

Had her mother been having an affair? Had Svenson killed her? The room seemed to tilt as she processed what she'd just learned.

"Fuck." Of course, she'd known there would probably be things in the sheriff's report that she didn't want to hear. Difficult things. Maybe even shocking things. Over the years, she'd considered as many possibilities for what happened to her mom as she could think of, everything from her father killing her to her mom falling victim to a random crime to her disappearing on purpose to live a life somewhere else without the burden of her family.

Charlotte closed her eyes. She remembered sitting at the kitchen table with her parents on weekend mornings, reading together. Riding their bikes through downtown Middleton. Walking from one parent's office on the NU campus to the other between their classes.

They'd been an inseparable trio, or so Charlotte had thought. Yes, she'd considered that her mother might have had an affair. She'd done her best to consider *every* possibility, but apparently she hadn't taken this one seriously enough, because with the evidence in front of her now, Charlotte felt as if she'd been gut punched.

Maybe she'd never actually known her mother at all.

On Wednesday, Charlotte visited the one place she'd been avoiding since her return to Vermont: Northshire University. Even though she'd never been a student here, this campus held so many memories. As she passed the maple tree at the center of the quad, Charlotte saw herself as a little girl, climbing through its branches so she could sit and spy on the students as they walked below.

Today, salt crunched beneath her shoes, but the sidewalks were clear of last night's snowfall. According to his schedule, Allan Svenson was teaching until two. She planned to catch him as his class let out, having decided not to forewarn him that she was coming. She'd always thought you could learn a lot by watching people in those unscripted moments when they were caught off guard.

Charlotte drew in a steadying breath as Wallis Hall came into view. Her eyes were drawn to the last window on the second floor, her mom's old office. Her gaze dropped to the stretch of concrete beneath that window. A black bike rack stood there now, but in her mind's eye, she saw the makeshift memorial set up after her mom's disappearance, a cluster of flowers, stuffed animals, cards, and other offerings left by students and colleagues.

Just as clearly, she remembered the candlelight vigil held there in her mom's honor. So many people had attended, staring at Charlotte and asking if she was all right. She had *not* been all right, not then and certainly not now as she prepared to confront the man who might have been having an affair with her mom when she vanished.

Had he killed her?

After another fortifying breath, she entered Wallis Hall, lost for a moment as nostalgia crashed over her. She'd spent so many hours here as a child. She shook off the urge to gawk, instead making her way down the corridor to a large lecture hall at the end. Svenson was just finishing up a class about military history. Charlotte had a sinking feeling that she might have watched her mom teach in this very room. It was the *worst* kind of nostalgia.

Ugh.

She hated this, and she wasn't even sure why. Obviously, it sucked to confront Svenson, but her emotions felt bigger than that. Being back in this building had shaken her more than she'd anticipated. She almost expected to turn around and see her mother walking down the hall toward her.

Tears pricked behind her eyes, and she blinked, forcing them back.

Before she could spiral any further, the double doors in front of her swung open, and students began to spill into the hallway, backpacks slung over their shoulders. Many of them were in the process of putting on coats and hats in preparation for the winter weather outside.

Charlotte stood out of the way until the majority of students had exited the lecture hall. Then she stepped through the open door before she could overthink it. A tall, slim white man stood at the front of the room, talking with two students. He was probably in his mid-sixties, with gray hair that receded slightly in the front.

She walked down the aisle toward him, her stomach tight. No, she wasn't looking forward to this, but it had to be done. The students he'd been talking to turned to leave, and he looked right at Charlotte. Her lungs seized because she *knew* this man. His face was undeniably familiar to her, and based on the way his eyebrows rose, he recognized her too.

"I'm Charlotte Danton," she said, just in case she was reading too much into his expression. "I was hoping to talk to you for a few minutes."

"Terri's daughter." His posture seemed stiffer than it had been when she first walked into his classroom. Was he about to blow her off?

She nodded in answer to his question.

"You look so much like her." His eyes softened, and he reached for the briefcase on the lectern beside him. "Let's go to my office. We can talk there."

"Thank you." She fell into step behind him as he led the way out of the lecture hall, turning off the lights and then closing the door behind them. As they walked toward the stairs, she wondered if Marin was here today. She only taught a few days a week, but right now Charlotte couldn't remember which days. Her brain had turned into an anxious mess.

Svenson led her up two flights to the third floor. He unlocked the door to his office and motioned her in ahead of him. She stepped into a small room that smelled vaguely of old books. Unsurprisingly, the large bookshelf behind his desk was packed full of them.

"I didn't know you were back in Vermont," he said from behind her.

"I didn't know you knew anything about where I lived?" She turned to face him, wanting to hate this man and not even sure why. For all she knew, he'd brought some joy to her mother's life, not that she wanted to consider any aspect of her mom's love life.

He shrugged, gesturing for her to take one of the guest chairs in front of his desk. "Your mother was very popular in the department. A lot of us wanted to know how you were after her disappearance. People talk, that's all."

Charlotte resisted the urge to claw at her arms. Her skin was literally *crawling* with discomfort right now. "I left after high school. I just came back last fall."

He settled in the leather chair behind the desk. "I'm sure your dad's glad to have you back in town."

"I'm not sure you of all people should be talking about my dad." The words came out harsher than she'd intended, and Svenson flinched.

"Fair enough. I guess you've heard a few things about me too." He looked down at his hands, hiding his expression from her.

Charlotte sat, clenching her hands into fists in her lap. "You aren't even going to deny you were having an affair with her?" She hadn't actually prepared herself for this possibility. She'd been so sure he would deny everything. Hell, he hadn't even admitted to an affair in the police transcript she'd read.

"What would be the point?" He looked at her with sad, tired eyes. "It ended thirty years ago. I was married at the time. So was your mom. We were in love, but we were trying not to hurt our families . . . our kids in particular. But I'm divorced now. My kids are grown, and lying to you feels like it would hurt you more than telling the truth."

"You . . . I . . ." She was at a loss for words, angry tears gathering in her eyes.

"In anticipation of your next question, no, I don't know what happened to her." He looked down at his hands again. "We'd decided the affair would be enough, at least until our kids were grown. Neither of us wanted to break up our families. I was at a conference in Virginia the week she disappeared. The sheriff's department checked my alibi. I didn't hurt her. I would *never* have hurt her."

"I have no idea what to say to any of that."

He nodded. "I'm sorry I lied when it happened. I was scared, and I was trying to protect my family. I truly had no information about Terri's disappearance. If I had, I'd have spoken up immediately."

"What do you think happened to her?" Charlotte asked.

"I don't know." His expression seemed earnest, but Charlotte didn't know him well enough to know if he was a good liar. "And it's eaten me up inside all these years, not knowing. Maybe I shouldn't tell you this, but . . . Terri was the love of my life. I never fully got over her, never remarried after my divorce."

"Oh," Charlotte mumbled, more uncomfortable than ever.

The grief on his face seemed real and startlingly raw. "I can't imagine her leaving you behind, so . . . I've always assumed she's no longer with us. I'm sorry."

Charlotte inhaled sharply. Deep down, she'd always believed the same thing, but it *hurt* to hear it from this man. Most people she knew—including her dad—perpetuated the idea that her mom might still be alive. Perhaps that made it even more jarring to hear Svenson say he thought she was dead.

So few people had ever admitted that to Charlotte before.

How dare this man—her mother's lover, of all people—be the one who gave her brutal honesty, while her own father still tried to keep an unlikely fantasy alive?

Charlotte's vision blurred. Her throat ached. Suddenly, she was on the verge of tears. She swallowed hard, then pinched the skin between her thumb and index finger. It was a trick she'd learned after her mom disappeared, when she'd heard kids whispering about her and needed to fight back the tears. Thankfully it still worked.

"You must have a theory of what you think happened," Charlotte insisted.

"Honestly, I think it must have been something random. I assumed she met with some kind of random accident or crime, because I don't know what the alternative would be."

Charlotte stood on wobbly knees, suddenly desperate to get out of here. "Thank you for your time."

He nodded, reaching for something on his desk. He held out a business card. "If you ever have more questions, or . . . for any reason. Feel free to get in touch."

She grabbed it, muttered another thank-you, and bolted for the door. Out in the corridor, she leaned against the wall, gulping air. Why did he have to be so *nice*? Was this another dead end? Would she ever know what happened to her mom, or was she destined to spend her whole life chasing a woman she'd never find?

CHAPTER SIX

"That's a lot of wine for the two of us," Marin said with a laugh as Charlotte entered her apartment on Thursday evening, holding a tote that contained three bottles of wine. "Although I *do* have a pullout couch if you want to get drunk and crash here tonight."

Charlotte grinned. "Honestly, I brought a variety because I didn't know what you like. A client gave me this awesome sampler basket that I wanted to share, but I'm not opposed to crashing on your couch either. I don't have any appointments until after lunch tomorrow."

"And I have nothing on my calendar until late afternoon," Marin told her. "I'm volunteering at a Pride Coalition meeting on campus." Her cheeks warmed slightly as she remembered the things she'd confessed to Charlotte the last time they talked. She was out now, at least with one person, and it felt *amazing*. She was still in a little bit of disbelief that she had someone she could be completely herself with now. It was a heady feeling.

"That's awesome," Charlotte said, walking toward the kitchen with her wine tote. "Will this be your first LGBTQ event?"

"It will, although it's a student group. I'm just there as a faculty advisor. So, I'm also going to see if there are any adult groups in the area that I could get involved with."

"I hope you find one." Charlotte lined up the wine bottles and turned to face her. "What do you want to start with? I brought white, red, and sparkling."

"Which goes best with pizza?" Marin gestured to the box on the counter. "The students upstairs assured me this is the best place in town, and I splurged on cheesy breadsticks, too, because . . . why not?"

"Why not indeed?" Charlotte said, eyes sparkling. "And using that philosophy, I think . . . whichever you're in the mood for. Who cares if it goes with pizza?"

"Good, because I have a feeling red would be considered the proper pairing, but I prefer white. Maybe we could start with that, and then if I successfully get my online-dating profile set up, we can open the bubbly?"

"I *love* the way you think." Charlotte reached for the bottle of white. "Got a corkscrew?"

"I know there's one here somewhere." Marin rummaged through the junk drawer to the left of the sink until she found the corkscrew. She handed it to Charlotte, then turned to get two plates out of the cabinet.

Her stomach buzzed with a mixture of hunger and excitement. Tonight, she would take the first step toward dating a woman, and . . . she went weak at the knees just thinking about it. She might absolutely lose her mind when she finally kissed a woman. Sex? *Fuck.* It was going to rock her world, that was for sure.

She exhaled as Charlotte handed her a glass of wine. "Thanks. How's your week going?" She kept her tone light because Charlotte had texted her earlier in the week about learning her mom might have been having an affair. Marin wanted to see how she was feeling about things if Charlotte was in the mood to share.

Charlotte's expression flickered with something Marin couldn't identify. "I went to the university yesterday. I met Svenson . . . except it turns out, I already knew him."

"What? How?"

"I don't know exactly . . . his face is just familiar to me. I think my mom must have introduced us. I spent a lot of time on campus when I was a kid, and they taught in the same department. Anyway, he confirmed their affair, didn't even try to play coy with me. I wasn't expecting that." She paused to sip her wine. "But he says he was at a conference in Virginia the week she disappeared, and the sheriff's department confirmed his alibi."

"So where does that leave you?" Marin filled a plate with pizza and breadsticks and led the way to her living room. It was mind boggling how quickly their friendship had progressed. They'd reconnected less than two weeks ago, but it seemed that the incident on the bus had formed an instant bond between them, one that ran deep.

Hopefully that bond was at least partially responsible for the draw Marin felt toward Charlotte. She wasn't naive. She'd been attracted to Charlotte from the first moment she'd laid eyes on her, but she needed to move past it once she started dating other women, because Charlotte was straight, and Marin really, *really* wanted this friendship to last.

"I'm going to ask my dad about it when we have lunch on Sunday." Charlotte pressed her lips together. "I'm looking forward to that about as much as you'd expect."

Marin gave her a sympathetic look. "I bet."

"I'm still trying to track down my mom's best friend from back then. Other than that, I don't know. My mom disappeared before social media or smartphones or even doorbell cameras, so there's just not much information to track. The sheriff's report was disappointingly brief. There's no evidence anything happened to her, but something obviously did."

"In a way, not knowing almost seems harder than losing her."

"Exactly." Charlotte's eyes glistened with tears. "If she's dead, I'd at least like to be able to grieve, you know? Instead I'm left wondering if she decided to just leave me behind and start a new life somewhere."

"That seems unlikely." Marin sipped her wine, resisting the urge to hug her. It was hard to know where the bounds of friendship lay when her feelings were muddled by attraction. This had always been a problem for her, wondering if she wanted to hug a friend for platonic reasons or because she found her attractive. Consequently, she rarely initiated hugs with female friends.

"It does," Charlotte whispered, wiping away a tear. "Amnesia is pretty rare in real life, but the PIs my dad hired checked every Jane Doe—living and dead—in the country who even vaguely matched my mom's description, and none of them were her. So if she's out there, she never asked for help, which is why I feel like she's probably dead, but . . ."

"It's horrible not to know for sure. I'm so sorry."

"Thanks." Charlotte's voice wavered. She wiped away more tears, then let out a shaky laugh. "What is it with us? Always with the heavy conversations."

Marin offered a gentle smile. "I don't know, but I'm glad we can share difficult things with each other."

"I am too." Charlotte blew out a deep breath. "Anyway. Enough of that. Let's talk about setting up your online-dating profile . . . and this new puppy of yours."

"Both are simultaneously thrilling and stressful," Marin admitted with a nervous laugh. "The puppy will be lots of fun. I've always wanted a pet—a puppy specifically—so I hope she's really going to enrich my life. At the same time, she's also going to be a lot of work. I have a feeling I haven't even thought of half the ways she's going to trash this apartment yet."

Charlotte laughed. "I have a feeling you're right, but she's cute enough that you'll forgive her for the mayhem, and I do think she'll bring more joy than chaos to your life."

"I won't be bored, that's for sure." Marin grinned. "And one of the students upstairs has agreed to do some puppysitting for me, which will be a huge help. As for dating . . ."

Charlotte lifted an eyebrow. "Also fun with the potential for chaos?"

Marin laughed. "Yes."

She and Charlotte chatted through the rest of their dinner. Once they'd put away the leftover pizza and refilled their wineglasses, it was time to get to the main event. Marin chose a popular online-dating app and downloaded it.

"Here goes nothing." She clicked the button to sign up. As soon as she'd added some basic information to set up her profile, the app asked her to upload photos of herself, and Marin hit her first roadblock. "I don't have many recent photos. I've taken a few selfies since I got to Vermont. Will those work?"

"Show me what you've got." Charlotte made an encouraging gesture.

Marin opened her photo roll, then handed her phone to Charlotte. "Pick something for me?"

"Um, there's nothing in here I shouldn't see, right?" Charlotte flicked her gaze to the phone, then back to Marin.

She laughed. "I'm tragically boring. There's not much of anything in there at all, let alone anything embarrassing."

Charlotte clucked her tongue as she began to scroll through Marin's photos. "I'd never call you boring. I mean, your heart stopped for two minutes. How many people can say that? And here you are, exploring your sexuality for the first time at forty-seven. Starting a new career, getting your first puppy. You're doing so many new things, and they're all exciting. Not boring."

"Hmm." It did sound exciting when Charlotte laid it out like that . . . not that she recommended the whole "heart stopping" thing. But she *was* proud of herself for making so many changes in her life.

"Okay, I like this one of you in your winter hat. Do you mind if I edit it a little bit? Brighten the colors, maybe crop it?"

"Go for it," Marin said, desperately curious to see which photos Charlotte would pick.

Charlotte was quiet for a minute, clicking the screen as the tip of her tongue peeked out from between her lips. *Distracting.*

Marin looked down at her hands. Hopefully, she'd have someone new to daydream about soon. Someone she could do a lot more than fantasize about . . .

"Okay. I've got two photos here that you can use, but I'm not sure we've got the right cover photo. Would you be up for taking a few pictures with me?"

"Um." Marin touched her hair self-consciously. Suddenly, her cheeks were hot, and she wasn't even sure why.

"Just saying, I think we could really show off your assets."

"My assets?" Her cheeks were even hotter now.

Charlotte scoffed. "Please. You must know you're beautiful, and you've got a great figure too. Let's show you off a little bit. You're all bundled up in these photos." Charlotte held out the phone to show the two photos she'd chosen, one of Marin outside in her winter coat and hat with snowy mountains behind her, and another of her last year in Manhattan, a laughing selfie taken after a dinner with some of her coworkers.

Also, the woman she was currently attracted to had just called her beautiful and said she had great assets, so . . . "Why the hell not? Do you want to dress me up too?"

"I mean, if you've got something in your closet that shows a little cleavage, I think that would be the definition of 'showing off your assets,'" Charlotte said with a cheeky grin.

"Most of what's in my closet right now is casual stuff for home and business attire for work, but I must have a few nice tops in there too." Marin rose, realizing in a rush how tipsy she was. Maybe that was why she was going along with this, but then again, perhaps being slightly inebriated was helpful for taking photos and setting up an online-dating profile.

She went into her bedroom and rummaged through the closet, finally choosing a rose pink satiny blouse that dipped low in the front and an emerald green top that she remembered Andrew complimenting her on the last time she'd worn it, not that she wanted him in her mind tonight. She carried them both into the living room. "Thoughts?"

Charlotte looked carefully at both shirts and then at Marin. "Try the green one first. I think the color might really suit your complexion, and I like the neckline."

"Okay." Marin went back into her bedroom and shut the door behind her. She shed her long-sleeved tee and pulled on the green top, then walked to the mirror. The fabric folded at the neckline, giving it an understated look that nonetheless revealed a tasteful amount of cleavage.

What will Charlotte say when she sees me in it?

Marin's heart raced. Since she was already primping, she pulled out her makeup bag, then touched up her mascara and reapplied lipstick . . . a darker shade than she'd had on before. She added a diamond pendant that dangled just above her cleavage.

There. She looked nice.

Sucking in a deep breath, she went back into the living room. "So?"

Charlotte's gaze lingered on her face, then dipped to her chest before sweeping down over her fitted jeans. "I think this is perfect. You look *hot*."

The words produced a burst of warmth low in Marin's stomach. Had a woman ever called her hot before? She didn't think so, and now she felt hot in an entirely different way. Heat flushed her skin, and when she met Charlotte's gaze, she felt a throb of arousal in her core.

Well, this had gone off the rails alarmingly quickly. Marin cleared her throat, attempting to change the subject in her sex-starved brain. "So, where do you want to take these pictures?"

"Um." Charlotte swept her gaze around the living room.

It gave Marin a chance to watch her unobserved for a few seconds. She took in Charlotte's oversize gray sweatshirt and black jeans, letting her gaze linger on the way the denim clung to her hips and thighs, and yeah, the wine was definitely going to Marin's head . . . or maybe to certain other body parts. Thank god Charlotte was going to take these pictures and help her get a date, because she obviously needed one.

"What if we open the sliding door here—just for a minute because it's freezing outside—so I can use those lights strung across your yard as a backdrop?"

Marin followed her gaze. Someone had hung a string of large white lights that ran from tree to tree around the yard, which probably made it feel warm and inviting on summer evenings. "We can try that, but be quick or else I'll be showing more than my cleavage in this top." She pressed a hand self-consciously against her breasts.

Charlotte laughed. "Oh, I don't know, if you get cold enough, we might get you even more dates."

Marin opened her mouth to protest that those weren't the kind of dates she wanted before she saw the teasing twinkle in Charlotte's eyes. Marin laughed. *Okay, here goes nothing . . .*

Marin looked exceptionally beautiful tonight. The light illuminated reddish undertones in her brown hair, a depth to the color that Charlotte didn't remember seeing that morning on the bus. She wondered if Marin was dyeing it now, but it felt inappropriate to ask. Marin's eyes were what captivated her, though. They radiated such joy, such *life*, it was impossible to look away.

Charlotte held up her phone, angling it so the lights outside provided the perfect backdrop. She worked with a lot of photographers for her real estate listings, and while this wasn't the same kind of shoot, she'd still picked up a few tips over the years for how to frame attractive photos.

"Why don't you lean against the doorway?" she suggested.

Marin did as she'd asked, angling her body slightly and crossing her arms beneath her breasts. The lighting was softer now, away from the bright lamp in her living room. Charlotte snapped several photos and examined one, zooming in on Marin's face. It was nice, but there was a shadow across the right side of her face that ruined the effect.

"Angle yourself a little bit to the left?"

Again, Marin complied, turning slightly toward Charlotte. That top looked great on her. The color perfectly complemented her hair. Marin was tall and lean, maybe a little bit leaner than she'd been two years ago, the result of whatever grueling rehabilitation she'd gone through to get back on her feet.

Charlotte snapped a few more photos, but Marin's crossed arms were giving the wrong vibe, almost closed off. Too posed. "Hands in your front pockets, I think."

Marin pushed her hands into her pockets. A dog barked somewhere in the distance, and she glanced over her shoulder with a soft smile, maybe thinking about her puppy. Charlotte shot a burst of photos, capturing the unscripted moment, including the way Marin looked at her now, lips slightly curved, eyes burning with intensity.

Charlotte was pretty sure she'd gotten what she needed, but she snapped a few more photos anyway. Somehow, it felt impossible to break eye contact with Marin. The moment lingered, Marin staring at her with that indecipherable expression.

Eventually, Marin shivered, looking away as she rubbed her arms. "Okay, it's freezing outside. Can we close the door now?"

"Yep. Come on in, and let's see what we've got." Charlotte walked to the couch and sat, beginning to thumb through the photos. *Wow.* Those last ones, where Marin had her hands in her pockets, had come out fantastic. She looked soft, *warm*, both distant and not. She'd been lost in thought, but it added interest to the photos.

Marin looked like a woman with layers, someone you'd want to talk to, get to know . . . date. That was the whole point of this exercise, after all. It was obvious that these were casual photos taken on someone's phone, which was what you wanted on a dating profile anyway, but they also looked *good.*

Marin sat beside her, leaning over to peek at Charlotte's phone. "How are they?"

"They're fantastic." She held it up, displaying one of her early favorites.

Marin's eyes widened slightly. "Wow. That's nicer than I was expecting."

"I'll send them to you."

"Actually." Marin darted a glance in her direction. "Why don't you pick your favorite and edit it like you did with the others? I trust your judgment."

"Okay." Charlotte swiped through the photos, zooming in on a few until she found her favorite. Marin had just looked back at her after staring off into the yard, right at the end of their photo shoot. Her expression was intense, but sincere. Something about the way she stared into the camera was incredibly sexy without looking like she was *trying* to be sexy. Charlotte had always found that to be so much more appealing than someone who was trying too hard.

Not that she thought women were sexy.

She rubbed a hand over her face. The wine must be going to her head. Carefully, she cropped the photo and adjusted the color and lighting, then texted it to Marin. "This should be your profile photo on the dating site, the first thing people see."

"You think?" Marin's phone dinged, and she squinted at the screen.

"For sure. If I dated women, I'd click on that photo. You look hot but also approachable and real. It's perfect." She was suddenly aware that she'd called Marin hot twice tonight. She was, though. Even a straight woman could appreciate when another woman looked good.

"It *is* a nice picture. I would never have taken something like that for myself. It's a little out of my comfort zone, but I'm going with it." Marin was quiet for a few minutes, clicking away on her phone.

Charlotte sipped her wine and watched.

"Advice on what to put for my interests?" Marin asked.

"Be honest, but also try to make yourself sound interesting. Like, no need to mention that you'd rather be watching TV than out with friends, or whatever the case might be."

"Actually, I'd rather be out with friends. I haven't done nearly enough of that lately." Marin started typing again. "Do I . . . should I mention that I'm divorced?"

"I don't know. Maybe that's something you can mention once you start chatting with someone?"

"Okay. I like that idea."

They kept at it for another fifteen minutes or so as Marin completed her profile, and then with one final click, she sat back with a satisfied smile. "There. I'm live."

"Yes, you are." Charlotte held up a hand.

Marin slapped it with hers. "Live. Alivc. Living. All of the above."

"Get it, girl," Charlotte agreed. "Now, let's find you someone to date."

"Oh boy." Marin reached for her wineglass, which was nearly empty. They'd polished off the bottle of Riesling, and Charlotte was feeling pretty tipsy. She suspected Marin was, too, based on the frequency of her laughter and her increasingly relaxed posture. "All right, let's see who it suggests for me."

Charlotte scooted closer, so she could see Marin's search results. She pointed to a blond woman in a purple jacket. "She's pretty."

Marin exhaled audibly as she clicked on the woman's profile. "Damn. I think it just hit me that I'm really doing this."

"You really are."

"I don't think you realize . . ." She glanced at Charlotte. "Just how long I've waited for this moment. I've been thinking about it, wanting to date a woman for twenty years. This feels . . . I don't know. Momentous. But also, weirdly anticlimactic browsing profile pictures."

"I imagine anything's going to feel anticlimactic after you've built it up in your head for that long," Charlotte said. "But it'll be worth it when you kiss a woman for the first time."

Marin's breath hitched as if she'd just imagined it. "Yes. It will."

"So . . . can you imagine kissing Tammy?" Charlotte gestured to the woman displayed on Marin's phone.

Marin studied Tammy's profile for a minute in silence, then shrugged. "To be honest, I have no idea. I think online dating might be tricky for me. It feels so impersonal." She sighed. "But unfortunately, I searched the other night, and the nearest gay bar is in Albany."

"Damn."

"Right. That's what, an hour and a half from here?"

"About that, yeah," Charlotte confirmed.

"I'm not likely to meet anyone local there, so it's not a good option if I'm looking for a relationship, not a hookup, which means . . . online dating it is." Marin backed out of Tammy's profile and kept scrolling.

"No worries. We're going to find you the perfect woman."

Thirty minutes later, they'd narrowed it down to three women, all of whom seemed promising and lived within an hour of Middleton.

"Personally, I think you should message all three," Charlotte said.

Marin frowned. "Really? That feels like . . . cheating."

"Nah. You aren't dating yet. You're just exchanging messages to see if you *want* to date. Chances are, if you message all three, one won't respond, one will turn out to be looking for a hookup or say something really obnoxious in response to your message, but maybe, if you're lucky, one of them will interest you enough to keep chatting."

"That doesn't sound very encouraging." Marin pressed her lips together.

"It's the reality of online dating," Charlotte said with a shrug. "You'll probably strike out a lot before you meet anyone in person, so shoot all three of them a quick message, and take it from there. I like to start with something innocuous like 'How are you handling this cold weather?' or something like that."

"Are you using an online-dating site right now too?"

Charlotte shook her head. "No, but I have in the past. I just went through a pretty messy breakup, so I'm taking a breather from dating this year while I focus on family stuff."

"Gotcha."

"You know, there *is* an app I've been thinking of reinstalling, though." Charlotte darted a hesitant glance at Marin.

"Which one?"

"My horoscope app. I was feeling pretty disillusioned with the universe for a while, but maybe . . . I'm starting to have faith in the stars again."

Marin reached over and touched her hand. "I'm so glad."

Charlotte unlocked her phone and opened the app store. "Okay. I'm doing it. Now you message those women."

"Deal." Marin's thumbs flew over her screen. She typed for such a long time that Charlotte wondered if she'd done more than send a simple introductory question. Finally, she sat back, looking satisfied. "I messaged all three of them, said I was new to Vermont, and asked if they had any tips for handling the cold weather."

Charlotte laughed. "I'm waiting for someone to write back offering to keep you warm."

Marin cringed. "I walked right into that one, didn't I?"

"Yes, but it'll be a good way of weeding out the women who're only interested in sex."

"Let's hope. And hey, if you ever want to talk about that messy breakup, I'm here to listen. Anytime."

"I appreciate that, and I'll definitely take you up on it, but not tonight. I'm in too good of a mood." Charlotte looked at her newly reinstalled app, then put her phone down. The same thinking applied to horoscopes. She'd look at hers soon, but not tonight.

Marin's phone buzzed in her hand. "Oh my god. Someone already responded." She squinted at the screen. "And you called it. She says her favorite way to keep warm in the wintertime is by exercising in the bedroom. Delete." Marin tapped her screen.

"It's okay. Just laugh and move on."

"Even more anticlimactic now, but still . . . I'm glad we did this. It's a step. A big one."

"Damn straight." Charlotte giggled, embracing the tipsiness. "Or *not* straight. You know what I mean."

Marin rolled her eyes, but she was smiling too. "Thanks again for your help. You made this a lot more fun than it would have been if I'd done it by myself."

"I'm glad." Charlotte smiled. She and Marin both moved to put their empty wineglasses down on the coffee table in front of them, and the cushion shifted beneath them. Charlotte lost her balance and thrust a hand out to catch herself before she pitched face first onto the carpet. Her hand landed on Marin's thigh.

For some reason, Charlotte's heart was pounding as she righted herself. She never would have thought anything about having her hand on a straight friend's thigh, and she hated herself for feeling weird about it just because Marin was a lesbian. Charlotte had had gay friends before and never second-guessed herself, but right now, as she shuffled back to her previous spot, she was hyperaware of the warmth of Marin's skin through her jeans.

Marin wasn't even looking at her. She was laughing, completely unruffled by Charlotte's blunder. Charlotte was being weird about nothing. She got up and went into the kitchen for a glass of water. Maybe that would help clear her head.

From the living room, Marin's phone chimed again. "Oh wow. Someone just messaged me through the app . . . someone new. Not one of the women I contacted."

"Sound promising?" Charlotte asked as she filled her glass. She took several gulps of cold water.

"Actually . . . yes." Marin was staring at her phone with a giddy expression on her face. "She says she noticed I'm new to Vermont and that she is too. She wondered if I'd like to do some exploring together, and . . . she says she loves my smile."

"Okay, you're right. That's a good one." Charlotte rejoined her on the couch.

Marin didn't even look up from her phone. Her thumbs were flying as she responded to the message. Finally, she looked up. Her eyes were sparkling. Her whole demeanor seemed lighter. Energized. "I just wrote her back."

"Awesome. What's her name?"

"Laura." Marin was positively *beaming*.

Charlotte pulled out her phone and snapped a quick picture, then texted it to Marin. "I want you to remember exactly how you feel in this moment, because you're glowing, Marin. I'm so happy for you."

"Thanks." Marin looked down at her phone, then back at Charlotte. "This just got exciting. In fact, I feel like celebrating. Let's break out the champagne."

CHAPTER SEVEN

Marin woke slowly, tangled up in bits of dreams, fragments of future dates, conversations, *kisses*. She felt the ghost sensation of a woman's hands on her body, sending warmth through her system. Smiling, she kept her eyes closed, lingering in this half-awake place where her dreams felt so vivid, almost real.

She imagined feminine hands on her skin, soft lips pressed against hers. It felt *so* good, even though it was only a fantasy. A needy ache built between her thighs. She slipped a hand below the waistband of her sleep shorts, brushing her fingertips against her clit before dipping them lower, coating them in her arousal.

It wasn't unusual to start her morning this way . . . lost in sapphic fantasies. These days, she often felt insatiable, and with the added fuel of last night's online-dating adventure, she was needier than ever. Soon, she would actually have a woman's hands on her body, her lips on Marin's. A breathy moan escaped her at the thought.

Fingertips now wet, she brought them back to her aching clit. She rubbed gently at first, but fueled by her fantasies, her arousal quickly spiked. Her mind spun with hazy visions from her dream, blond curls and blue eyes . . .

Marin froze as she realized she was picturing Charlotte. Charlotte, who she'd laughed and drunk two bottles of wine with last night. Charlotte, who'd taken those ridiculously sexy photos of Marin for her dating profile.

Charlotte, who was asleep on the pullout couch in Marin's living room at this very moment.

Oh fuck.

Marin had completely forgotten that Charlotte was in her apartment. She yanked her hand from her sleep shorts as embarrassment burned through her system. She'd been lying here, dreaming about sex, touching herself, while Charlotte slept just on the other side of the door. Oh god. She'd moaned. How loud had that been?

Her core ached with unreleased tension, and her panties were wet. Holding in a sigh, she sat up in bed, and then she almost groaned for a completely different reason. Now that she was upright, her head ached from all the wine. Briefly, she wondered if she could get back to sleep so she didn't have to leave her room and face Charlotte, but she was fully awake now, and she had to pee.

Ignoring the discomfort, she reached for her phone. Anything to delay leaving her bedroom. It was only a few minutes past seven. Charlotte was probably still asleep, and Marin was being a thoughtful host by not disturbing her, not a coward for needing a few minutes to compose herself after her interrupted moment of self-pleasure. She still felt tense and restless. Frustrated.

Horny.

She was horny as hell, and there was nothing she could do about it. It didn't matter that she had extensive practice getting herself off silently, having spent years taking care of her own needs while sharing a bed with Andrew. It felt different to think about touching herself while Charlotte was here. For one thing, she'd never fantasized about

Andrew while she was getting herself off, but even if she had, he was her husband, so it wouldn't have been wrong.

Fantasizing about her friend—her *straight* friend—while she got herself off was wrong, especially while that friend was on her couch.

Marin squinted at her phone. In her distraction, she'd forgotten to grab her reading glasses, and these days she was helpless without them. Losing her perfect vision had been one of the more humbling aspects of entering her forties, at least until she'd gotten hit by a car. Now glasses seemed a small price to pay for the privilege of getting older.

Sliding them into place, she turned her attention to the notifications on her phone. There was some activity in her sibling group chat, but more interestingly, there were two new messages from the dating app. Laura had written her back, and so had Bridgette, one of the women Marin sent an introductory message to last night.

Marin gulped as a burst of excitement swept through her system. Maybe nothing would come of either of these connections—she was under no illusion that online dating was easy—but it was a start, and it was so freaking exciting. She was messaging with two queer women who were interested in dating her. This was, quite literally, a dream come true.

She responded to them both, not giving herself time to overthink her responses. She kept her messages short and sweet but with a flirty undertone . . . or at least she hoped that was how they would be read. The apartment outside her bedroom was still silent, but Marin's bladder was complaining pretty urgently now, and she needed ibuprofen for her head too. Like it or not, she had to leave her room.

She sat up, wincing as a bolt of pain shot down her right leg. The pelvic injury she'd sustained in the accident had damaged her sciatic nerve, leaving her with chronic nerve pain. She had a few tools and tricks to help manage it, but some days the pain was unbearable. Hopefully, today wouldn't be one of those days.

Then again, alcohol made inflammation worse, so perhaps she only had herself to blame for today's flare-up. But she so rarely indulged, she wasn't going to feel guilty about it now. She rubbed at the tingling sensation in her thigh, then stood and slipped her sleep shorts down her legs. She tossed them into the hamper and reached for a pair of flannel lounge pants. Then she pulled on a hoodie over her T-shirt.

Sufficiently covered to face company, she left her room. She glimpsed a tousle of blond hair in the blankets on the sofa bed, indicating Charlotte was indeed still asleep. Marin went into the bathroom, shutting the door quietly behind herself. She freshened up, then brushed her teeth and her hair. When she left the bathroom, Charlotte was sitting up on the sofa bed.

"Morning," Marin said. "I didn't wake you, did I?"

"Nope." Charlotte rubbed her eyes with a yawn. "I never seem to sleep well after I drink these days. Hazards of getting old."

Marin chuckled. "I'm fairly sure I'm older than you, but I know what you mean. My body doesn't let me get away with half the shit I did in my younger days, and that was the case even before I got run over by a car." She rolled her eyes to keep the mood light, but truthfully, her leg still hurt. Tingling pain had begun to radiate down the back of her thigh.

"I turned forty last year," Charlotte said, "and it seems like my body immediately started to rebel."

"I remember feeling the same way. Coffee?" She reached for the pot on the kitchen counter and began to fill the carafe with water.

"Definitely. Thanks. Do you want to grab breakfast before we go our separate ways? I need to go home by midmorning to shower and get ready for my first client appointment."

Marin would love the excuse to splurge on a nice breakfast—something she rarely did—but this morning, she needed to try to nip this nerve pain in the bud with some stretching exercises, an ice pack, and a muscle relaxant. "Rain check? I'd love to go out to breakfast sometime, but I need to stay in this morning."

"No problem. You okay?" She was looking at Marin like she could see her discomfort, which was unlikely because Marin was an expert at hiding pain, both physical and mental.

She'd been keeping it to herself for forty-seven years, which meant she was a master of disguise. But maybe she didn't need to hide from Charlotte. Friends shared this kind of thing, didn't they?

"Nerve pain," she said with a sigh. "Happens sometimes since the accident."

"I'm sorry." Charlotte's eyes were sympathetic. "Is it bad? Is there anything I can do to help?"

"Sometimes it is, but it's not too bad yet this morning." Marin reached into the cabinet where she kept her medication and took out the bottle. "I try to get ahead of it with meds and stretches, but that means I shouldn't go sit at a restaurant right now. Sorry."

"No need to apologize. I could pick something up for us if you like? Or if you'd rather that I get out of your hair so you can rest, just say the word."

"Um." Marin had assumed she would just leave, but her offer sounded tempting, actually. "You don't mind?"

"Of course not. That's what friends are for, right? What are you in the mood for?"

"This might be the hangover talking, but a greasy breakfast sandwich is calling my name." She pressed a hand against her stomach, which had growled obnoxiously at the thought. "Know a good place?"

"You bet I do. Bacon, egg, and cheese?"

"Is there any other way to eat a breakfast sandwich?" Marin was surprised by the teasing note in her voice. She liked who she was around Charlotte, a more fun version of herself.

Charlotte grinned. "Absolutely not. Okay, let me get dressed, and I'll go get us some greasy hangover cures."

At her words, Marin's eyes were drawn to Charlotte's bare legs. She wore a borrowed tee and sleep shorts that Marin barely remembered giving her last night when they decided they'd had too much to drink and Charlotte should stay. Just as quickly, she yanked her gaze back to Charlotte's face. "Sure. Help yourself to any toiletries you need."

"Thanks." Charlotte headed for the bathroom.

Half an hour later, Charlotte was back at Marin's apartment with two deliciously greasy breakfast sandwiches. She'd also bought a couple of donuts because they looked too delicious to pass up. She knocked at the door, wondering if it was her imagination that it took longer than usual for Marin to open it.

"Hi." Marin offered a smile that seemed slightly brittle. Her movements were stiff, and obviously this nerve pain was worse than she was letting on.

"The stretches didn't help, huh?" She stepped inside, shutting the door behind her.

"Sometimes they don't." Marin rubbed at her right thigh. "Breakfast smells delicious, though."

"It really does." Charlotte walked to the breakfast table. "What's more comfortable for you? Sitting? Standing? Breakfast in bed?"

Marin's surprise at the question was obvious, although she had probably tried to hide her reaction. She seemed somewhat hesitant to share her pain with Charlotte, and she hoped that was just Marin's nature and not a result of how her ex-husband had treated her. "Standing, probably. Then I may lie down after breakfast. Sorry."

"What in the world are you apologizing for? Pain happens. Just let me know if there's anything I can do to help."

"Breakfast definitely helps." Marin's expression softened. "Thank you."

"Anytime. So have you heard back from any of the women you messaged last night?" Charlotte pushed a breakfast sandwich and a donut in front of Marin and went to pour two mugs of coffee, eager to make herself useful.

"I had two messages waiting this morning, actually."

"Yeah?" Charlotte grinned as she placed a mug of coffee in front of Marin. "Good ones?"

"Yeah, they both sound nice. It's exciting. Thanks for helping me get started."

"You bet. I'm glad you're off to such a good start. You'll be on your first date with a woman before you know it."

"I sure hope so." Marin's face held a look of such raw, intense longing, it took Charlotte's breath away. She blinked, and it was gone, but Charlotte felt her whole perspective shift in that moment. She had no idea what it was like to be in Marin's shoes, to be forty-seven and never have dated someone she was physically attracted to. No wonder she seemed nearly overcome by the anticipation.

"This is a big deal for you," Charlotte murmured as she wrapped her hands around her coffee mug. "I think I just realized *how* big of a deal."

"The biggest. I'm overwhelmed just thinking about it." Her face transformed with a brilliant smile. "The best kind of overwhelmed."

"I can't wait to hear every detail." And yet, Charlotte felt a strange little ping of discomfort at the thought of Marin treating another woman to that beautiful smile.

"Every detail?" Marin's eyebrows rose, laughter sparkling in her eyes.

"I want to know everything about your journey," Charlotte clarified. "Anything you feel comfortable sharing . . . maybe not *every* detail when you finally have sex with a woman." She laughed, somewhat awkwardly.

"I'm not really one to share details about my sex life." Marin looked embarrassed now. "Not that I've ever had much excitement to share in that department."

"Soon you'll have all the excitement you can handle." Honestly, Charlotte couldn't even imagine what it would be like, having sex with someone she was attracted to for the first time at Marin's age.

"Hopefully." Marin took a big bite of her breakfast sandwich and moaned. "Okay, this is amazing. Just what I needed this morning."

"They're great, right? It's from Betty's Bakery in town."

Marin chewed and swallowed. "Noted."

Conversation became sparse as they ate. Charlotte was mostly enjoying her food, but she couldn't help noticing the pain tightening Marin's features. She was obviously trying to put on a brave face, but the pain seemed to be getting worse.

When they finished eating, Charlotte offered, "Why don't you let me clean up the kitchen while you lie down for a bit?"

"I should take a shower, but . . ." She winced, again rubbing at her right thigh. "Maybe I'll lie down first. You don't need to clean up, though."

"I got this. Go rest. Are you sure there's not anything else I can do to help?"

Marin shook her head. "I've already taken my medication. Sometimes there are bad days, and there's not a lot I can do about it. Such is life with chronic pain."

"I'm sorry." Charlotte pulled her in for an impulsive hug, loving the way Marin leaned into her and exhaled as if the hug had brought her some comfort. Charlotte never discounted the benefits of a good hug, or of comfort in general. Medicine wasn't the only way to help someone feel better. Care and compassion went a long way too.

"Thank you," Marin whispered before she pulled back. She opened the freezer and removed an ice pack, then headed toward her bedroom, walking slowly and with a limp.

It was another harsh reminder of what she'd been through. Yes, she'd survived, but there had obviously been a physical toll to pay. Not for the first time, Charlotte was so grateful that she'd lived.

And that fate had brought them back together.

She cleaned up the remnants of their breakfast, then spent a few minutes tidying Marin's kitchen. They'd left their pizza plates and wineglasses on the counter last night, both of them exhausted and more than a little bit drunk by the time they'd gone to bed. She took care of it now, then wiped down the counters.

Once she'd started the dishwasher, she went down the hall and peeked into Marin's room. She was lying on her left side, her right leg extended straight. The ice pack—one of those cloth-covered gel packs—was draped over her thigh. Her face was tight with pain, her fists clenched in the sheets. Charlotte's stomach dropped. It hurt to see her in such visible distress.

"Hey," she said softly.

Marin's face softened. "Hi. I really didn't mean for you to clean up my kitchen."

"I know you didn't, but I was glad to. What else can I do?"

Marin shook her head. "Nothing. I'm just going to lie here for a bit until it eases."

"Want company, or would you rather be alone?"

Marin lifted her head, staring at Charlotte in surprise. "You . . . you'd stay?"

"Of course," Charlotte said. "I've got another hour or so before I need to get ready for my first appointment of the day. I'd love to stay and distract you from the pain if you think that would be helpful. Now that I've reinstalled the app, I could even read your horoscope for you! But if you'd rather be alone and nap or whatever, just tell me to get lost."

"I'd really like some company, if you're sure you don't mind." Marin spoke softly, hesitantly, as if she wasn't accustomed to this kind of care. "And a horoscope sounds . . . fun."

"Awesome. Let's see what the stars have in store for you today."

On Sunday, Charlotte met her dad for lunch, as had become their routine. After decades of barely speaking, they'd taken the first tentative steps toward rebuilding their relationship since her return to

Vermont. Today, though, she was semidreading their meeting since she'd have to ask him about Allan Svenson. What if he didn't know and she ruined his memories of his wife by revealing her affair? By the time she reached the restaurant, she was a nervous mess.

Her dad was already seated at a table by the front window, and she made her way over to him. "Hi, Dad."

He inclined his head toward her. "Charlotte."

She shrugged out of her coat and hung it up before she sat. Her dad had on khaki pants and a blue blazer over a crisp white shirt and tie, as if he'd just come from the classroom, although he'd actually come from church. This was his forever uniform, though. She'd never seen him truly dressed down. In fact, she wasn't even sure he owned jeans.

"Been keeping busy?" he asked. "I can't imagine many people are looking for houses this time of year."

"You'd be surprised, actually. It's been busier than I was expecting." She'd been a Realtor for almost twenty years, but this was her first time working in Vermont. Also, she was stalling. She fidgeted with her menu, unsure how to even broach the subject.

Luckily or unluckily, the waiter chose that moment to approach their table. Her dad asked for a bottle of sparkling water for the table and ordered a chicken club. Flustered, Charlotte said she'd take the same.

"If you don't mind my saying so, you seem like you have something on your mind," her dad observed.

"I got a copy of the report from the sheriff's department about Mom's disappearance."

"Oh." He sipped from his water, then gave her a piercing look. "Any surprises?"

"Yes." She gulped from her own water, her throat gone dry. "Dad . . . do you know Allan Svenson? He teaches at the university."

Her dad flinched almost imperceptibly. "I know him."

"Do you know . . . ?"

"Yes." His voice held no inflection, and suddenly, she didn't know how to read his face either. "I know about his relationship with your mother."

"Did you know before she disappeared?" she asked quietly.

"Yes." He cleared his throat. "Our marriage wasn't perfect, Charlotte. We both had our . . . indiscretions, but we were committed to raising you together as a family."

What? Charlotte's face burned at the implications. "You both . . ." She coughed. Oh god, what was she supposed to say to that? What was she supposed to *think*?

"Maybe we should have made better choices, but we were doing the best we could. And the sheriff's department assured me that Allan had a rock-solid alibi for the day of her disappearance, so ultimately, I don't think he's relevant."

"But you? Who were *you* sleeping with?" This time, her voice came out sharp and biting.

"No one at the time of her disappearance. I'd been trying to convince Terri to give us another chance. I thought . . . well, it seemed like she was willing to try."

"I don't know what to think. You were both sleeping with other people? That's . . ." She mimed her head exploding.

He looked pained. "I know. I'm sorry."

"Is there anything else you haven't told me?"

He fiddled with his water glass, although she wasn't sure if he was thinking or stalling. "There was a duffel bag missing, a small bag your mother sometimes packed for weekend trips. I didn't notice right away that it was missing, and by the time I did, well, I was starting to second-guess myself." He shook his head. "I can't be sure when I last saw that bag. She might have lost it or thrown it away. It might have no relevance at all. I just don't know."

"A duffel bag." Charlotte didn't know what to say, what to *think*. But suddenly, it felt horrifyingly obvious what she'd be thinking if this was anyone but her dad. She'd be thinking the jilted husband killed his wife. It was *always* the husband. Everyone knew that. But she just . . . she couldn't believe it. Couldn't picture him ever being violent.

She also knew people made this mistake all the time. No one wanted to believe their family member was guilty of a crime. *He seemed like such a nice guy.* Wasn't that what people always said when they discovered that someone they knew had done something horrible?

She'd never imagined either of her parents capable of having an affair, and she'd been wrong about that. What if she was wrong about everything? What if neither of her parents had been who she thought they were? Was she about to lose her dad, too, like ripping off a mask and revealing someone she didn't want to know?

Charlotte had come to Vermont looking for answers, but if she discovered that her dad had murdered her mom . . . it might ruin her. Some of her thoughts must have shown on her face, because her dad's eyes flashed with pain.

"I didn't hurt her. She headed out to meet her friends for book club, and she never arrived. That's all I know." He looked devastated, and for the first time, she wondered what it had been like for him, living under a shadow of suspicion after his wife disappeared. If she'd heard the rumors that he killed her, surely he had too. That must have been terrible for him.

"I'm sorry," she said quietly. "You promise there's nothing else you're not telling me?"

He held her gaze, his expression earnest and unflinching. "I promise."

She exhaled. "Okay."

She believed him. She had to. What choice did she have? He was her father.

CHAPTER EIGHT

Marin attempted to project a confidence she didn't quite feel as she entered the classroom where Northshire University's Pride Coalition held its meetings. She was excited to get started in her new role as faculty advisor, but also . . . intimidated. She'd planned to walk into this meeting as an outwardly queer woman, to introduce herself that way from the start.

Now that it was time to actually *do* it, well, she was quaking in her boots. So far, she'd only come out to one person—Charlotte—and while the NU Pride Coalition was virtually guaranteed to be a safe place to share her truth, the words didn't come easily for her yet. She was nervous as hell as she lingered at the back of the room.

There were about ten students in attendance so far, a mixture of genders. They'd moved their seats into a semicircle and were deep in conversation, barely seeming to notice her arrival. Marin wasn't sure what was expected from the faculty in this situation. Should she join their conversation, or was she supposed to be more of an observer?

Before she could decide, another woman entered the room, a fellow professor if Marin had to guess. She looked to be in her early thirties, with light-brown hair and a warm smile. "Hi," she said to Marin before waving at the gathered group of students. "Are you Professor Easterly?"

"I am," Marin confirmed.

The woman's smile widened. "I'm Dr. Lind . . . Audrey. I'm an art history professor here."

"Please call me Marin. I teach statistics."

"Nice to meet you, Marin." Audrey extended her hand, and Marin shook it. "Are you new here this semester?"

She nodded. "New to teaching, actually."

"It's only my second year teaching too," Audrey said with enthusiasm. "Isn't it great? I hope you're loving it, and I'm glad you're here with the Pride Coalition. We've been short a faculty sponsor this year, and with the political climate being what it is, I was afraid the university might start trying to shut down the club."

"Really?" Marin frowned. "That would be terrible."

"You're telling me," Audrey agreed. "My fiancée kept it going while she was here, but she retired from teaching last year. We've been short a faculty sponsor ever since."

She. Marin's brain snagged on that word. Audrey's fiancée was a woman, and that made Marin irrationally pleased. "Well, I've only got two classes this semester, and I'd love to get more involved here, so just let me know how I can help."

"I'm really glad to hear that," Audrey said. "The students pretty much run things themselves, but the faculty sponsors help plan events and fundraisers. I also try to be available as a mentor, because while a lot of these kids are super comfortable with their identities, some aren't. Some of them really need an adult in their life they can trust."

Marin swallowed, humbled by the responsibility that entailed. "I wish I'd been comfortable with my sexuality at their age, but I hope I can help them have a better experience than I did." And she'd just come out for the second time, in a roundabout way. Her cheeks felt uncomfortably warm.

"Sounds like you're here for exactly the right reason, then," Audrey said approvingly. "Come on. I'll introduce you to the group."

Marin followed her to the front of the room.

"Hi, everyone," Audrey said. "Before we get started, I want to introduce you to our new faculty sponsor, Professor Easterly. She's new here, so let's help her feel welcome, okay?"

"New to Vermont too," Marin added. "And very glad to be here."

"Welcome, Professor Easterly," someone called out.

She exchanged greetings with the students before they got down to business, which today consisted of early planning for the Valentine's Day party. They were also organizing a fundraiser for a local LGBTQ center. Marin was pleased with how comfortable she felt in the group, and it only increased her yearning to further immerse herself in queer communities.

For now, though, it warmed her heart to see these kids having such a good time in a safe space. Well, most of them were having a good time. She noticed one student lingering at the rear of the group, listening and not contributing to the conversation. That was fine. Marin had been more of an observer than a participant in school herself, but this student's body language seemed anxious and uncomfortable.

"Before we go, I just wanted to remind you all that my office hours are posted in the portal, and my phone number is included there too," Audrey said. "You're welcome to contact me for any reason, even if you just want to chat. I'm always here for you, okay?"

"That goes for me too," Marin added. "I'm . . . I'm not only new to Vermont and to teaching, I'm also new to being out, so if any of you are going through that, too, I might be a good ear. Happy to try at least." She gave a nervous laugh, her stomach churning from coming out to a room of people.

She saw several appreciative smiles from the students. The meeting started to break up soon after, although a few people lingered, chatting with friends. Marin caught the eye of the quiet student in back and made her way over to say hello.

"Professor Easterly, right?" the student said, her expression hesitant. "I'm Brianna."

"It's nice to meet you, Brianna. Is this your first year at NU?"

She nodded. "Yeah. I'm a freshman. Um . . . I've got to run, but it was nice to meet you."

"See you here next week?" Marin asked in what she hoped was an encouraging tone.

Brianna nodded, then waved before she headed for the door.

As other students started to leave the room, a bubbly young woman with curly brown hair approached Marin. "Hi, Professor Easterly. I'm Gia, student president of the Pride Coalition. Just wanted to say welcome. We're glad to have you join us."

"Thanks, Gia. I'm very glad to be here." Marin felt warm all the way to her toes. The room emptied fairly quickly from there, and soon she and Audrey were exiting the classroom together. Audrey locked the door behind them.

"So where did you move from?" Audrey asked.

"Manhattan."

"Oh wow. Big change. Have you always lived in the city?"

"Yes," Marin said with a chuckle. "It was time—past time—for some big changes in my life."

"Good for you. I hope you're loving it. I went to college here, then left for a while and moved back last year, so I appreciate how different it is living somewhere rural when you didn't grow up here."

They stepped outside into the weak January sunshine. Marin pulled her coat more firmly around herself, but the cold at least was something she was used to. And in a minute, she'd be in her car, where she could blast herself with heat.

"Listen, I don't know if you know anyone in the area or not, but my fiancée and I would love to have you over for dinner sometime if you're interested. We're always looking to make more queer friends around here. The community is fairly small." She smiled at Marin, and Marin's stomach filled with a fizzy sensation at being so casually referred to as queer. It felt so *good*. So right. So validating.

"I'd love that," she said, trying not to sound overly eager. "I don't know many people in Vermont yet, and like I mentioned to the students back there, I'm very newly out as well, so I'd love to make some queer friends."

"Perfect," Audrey said. "I need to double-check with Michelle—my fiancée—but maybe this weekend?"

"Actually, I'm bringing home a new puppy on Friday, so my weekend is likely to be fairly hectic getting her settled," Marin told her regretfully.

Audrey's smile widened. "Aww, a puppy! How fun. Why don't I get your number? I'll check with Michelle and text you. Maybe we can squeeze in dinner before you bring home your puppy, since I imagine you'll be busy after."

"I imagine I will be, and that sounds great." She read off her number to Audrey; then they said their goodbyes, and Marin headed for her car. She was thrilled by the possibility of dinner with Audrey and her fiancée. She'd never hung out with a sapphic couple before, and she could hardly wait.

In the meantime, she was chatting with two women from the dating app, and her pulse kicked as she anticipated checking her messages once she got home. Laura was fun to talk to, although Marin still wasn't sure how to know if she had chemistry with someone before she'd met them in person. For now, they were sending a lot of messages, which made Marin happy.

Bridgette, the other woman she was messaging with, seemed a little forward for Marin's taste. She'd already sent several selfies of herself posing seductively. Marin had been putting off her requests to reciprocate. She wasn't a "sexy selfie" kind of woman, at least not until she knew someone well enough to have that level of comfort with them.

Sexy was the last thing she felt as she turned on the heated seat in her Outback to help loosen muscles that had tensed from nerve pain, but this heated seat might be what got her through the Vermont winter. It was seriously amazing, the best help she'd found for sore muscles since the Jacuzzi tub at the house she'd shared with Andrew. She would *love* to have one of those at her new house.

When she got home, she found another message from Bridgette waiting for her, as well as some new puppy pictures of Ember from her foster mom. She also had a text from Audrey asking if she could come over Thursday for dinner.

The selfie request from Bridgette was a no-go, but dinner with Audrey and Michelle? That earned a resounding yes.

Marin arrived for dinner with her new queer friends on Thursday feeling equal parts nervous and euphoric. Audrey greeted her at the front door, wearing burgundy corduroys and a black top.

Marin held out the bottle of wine she'd brought. "I hope you both enjoy red wine. I forgot to ask if you drink when we planned dinner."

"We do, and thanks so much." Audrey made a welcoming motion with her hand. "Come on in. Michelle's in the kitchen finishing up dinner."

Marin stepped inside and began unbuttoning her coat. "I'm obsessed with the location of your house. That view! I pulled into your driveway just in time to catch sunset over the mountains."

"Isn't it amazing? This was Michelle's house, and I loved it so much it was a no-brainer for me to move in here with her when the time came."

"Did I hear my name?" An elegant brunette entered the room, wearing fitted jeans and a pin-striped shirt. She offered Marin a polite smile. "Hello. I'm Michelle." She spoke with a crisp British accent.

"Marin," she responded. "It's so nice to meet you. I was just admiring your house. I'm house hunting myself right now, and this is definite goals."

"This house is the main reason I still live in Vermont," Michelle said. "I love it, and I love the location even more. You should see the views during the daytime."

"Excuse me," Audrey interjected, giving her fiancée a playful nudge. "The house is the only reason you still live in Vermont?" She gestured to herself.

"I said the *main* reason." Michelle gave her an affectionate look. "If you recall, you offered to move to London with me if it was what I wanted. So yes, I stayed for the house . . . mostly."

"I recall." Audrey kissed her cheek. "And I meant it too. London would have been a fun adventure, but I'm glad we stayed here."

Michelle gazed adoringly at her fiancée, and Marin felt a tug of yearning watching them together. This was what she wanted. She wanted a woman who looked at her the way Michelle looked at Audrey. It was the kind of sapphic love she'd spent so many years daydreaming about. Watching them made her want a girlfriend of her own more than ever.

"Anyway." Michelle turned toward her. "Welcome. Would you like something to drink? I've cooked a squash risotto for dinner."

"She's getting domestic now that she's quit teaching," Audrey said.

"And now that I have someone else to cook for."

"Cooking for one is a drag," Marin agreed. "Although I do end up with a lot of leftovers I can use for lunch the next day."

"No significant other, then?" Audrey asked. "I'm going to have a glass of wine with dinner, if that sounds good to you. Riesling, probably. Michelle usually goes for whisky."

"But I might have wine tonight too." Michelle led the way toward the kitchen.

"Wine sounds perfect," Marin said. "And no significant other. I'm recently divorced, actually. It's part of the reason I'm here in Vermont, starting over."

"Good for you," Michelle said. "I'm about three years postdivorce myself. I hope you find everything you're looking for."

"Thanks."

They fixed plates and poured wine and then sat together around a square table just off the kitchen. "So, Michelle, you used to teach at Northshire?" Marin asked.

Michelle nodded. "I taught art history for seventeen years."

"That's what you teach, too, right?" Marin asked Audrey.

"Yes. Michelle and I were colleagues last year. Actually . . ." Audrey glanced at her fiancée with a sly smile. "Do you mind if I tell her the rest?"

Michelle rolled her eyes. "Go ahead."

Audrey turned to Marin, eyes gleaming. "She was my professor when I was an undergrad. She inspired me to pursue a career in academia myself."

"Aww, I love that," Marin exclaimed.

"Well, don't leave out the best part," Michelle drawled, looking amused.

"Never letting you live down that you called this the best part," Audrey said smugly, then turned to Marin. "I had the *biggest* crush on her when I was a student, not that I ever would have acted on it then. When we reconnected last year, though . . ."

"Wow," Marin said ineloquently.

"Yep." Audrey grinned. "I like to think we're a perfect match. The universe was just waiting to bring us back together, right?"

"Right." Marin thought of herself and Charlotte and how the universe had brought them back together too. The romantic side of her wished they could have a similar outcome, but it wasn't meant to be. Charlotte was straight.

"Anyway, if you're at all interested in female artists, you've come to the right place. Michelle and I could talk your ears off for hours on the topic."

"I don't know much about female artists, unfortunately," Marin admitted. "In fact, I think I could only name a handful."

"That's true for most people," Michelle said. "Women in art rarely get their due."

"Well, now you've got me curious to learn more. Any suggestions?"

"So many," Audrey enthused before listing off a handful of books and articles Marin could check out, including a book called *The Story of Art Without Men*, which Marin was immediately intrigued by because, wow, what a title. She was in the mood to celebrate women in all facets of her life these days, it seemed.

"Marin, you mentioned that you're house hunting?" Michelle said.

"I am. Not having much luck yet, unfortunately. It's a slow time of year, I'm told."

"Well, if you were serious about a home with a view like ours, I happened to hear that a house a few miles down the road from this one is about to go on the market," Michelle said. "I could get the listing agent's information for you, if you're interested?"

Marin felt a ping of excitement because that sounded *perfect.* "I would love that."

On Friday afternoon, Marin picked up her new puppy. Ember and her siblings were gated in the kitchen like they had been last time, although several of them were gone now, having already been adopted, and Marin could hardly believe how much they'd grown. Yes, she'd seen pictures since her first visit, but photos didn't quite do justice to the fact that the stubby-legged pups she'd met three weeks ago looked like little dogs now. In fact, she even heard a bark or two as she walked into the kitchen.

"Hi, puppies," she said, already smiling. Ember stood at the back of the group, just like last time. As Marin approached, the puppy's tail wagged enthusiastically. If it was possible, Ember had gotten even cuter since Marin first met her. Marin felt a warm burst of happiness to know that this was *her* puppy now.

"I just need you to sign the contract," Susan said. "Then we'll go over the basics of her routine, vaccine schedule, and all that good stuff, but please feel free to email me with any questions once you get home."

"I appreciate that," Marin said. "As you know, she's my first puppy, so I'm bound to have questions, although I've done my research and I have a friend with puppy experience who's going to come over later today to help."

Susan nodded. "All right, let's get this signed so you can take your girl home."

They went through the paperwork together, and then . . . it was time. Marin clipped on the collar she'd brought with her, with Ember's name already inscribed on the name tag, and then she lifted the puppy into her arms. Ember whined, looking back at her siblings. This felt like a huge transition for her, going from living in a litter to being someone's pet, but every puppy did it, so hopefully she'd adjust quickly.

"Ready to go home?" Marin asked the puppy.

Ember stared at her out of big brown eyes, and there was that warm feeling again. This puppy was about to turn Marin's world upside down, no doubt about it, but she could already tell the reward was going to be worth the loss of sleep and chewed shoes.

After saying goodbye to Susan, they were off. Marin tucked Ember into a puppy carrier on the back seat before sitting up front. There was a whine from behind her. "Hang on, sweetie. We just have a short drive home."

She talked to Ember all the way to her apartment, and the puppy cried a few times but was mostly quiet. When they arrived, Marin tried walking her in front of the building, "tried" being the operative word. Ember yanked and rolled like a fish on a hook, clearly unfamiliar with being walked on leash.

And Marin had her first reality check about life with a new puppy. Ember was a baby. She had almost no training yet. Marin had her work cut out for her, maybe more so than she'd anticipated. It was intimidating to realize that this helpless little creature was entirely dependent on her now. It was a big responsibility. And more than ever, she needed a house.

This morning, Marin had driven past the house Michelle told her about, and it looked *really* promising. It was small, but it had so much charm, and honestly, small suited her right now. Best of all, it was situated in a wide-open field, surrounded by wooded hilltops, the perfect mountain hideaway. She and Ember would have all the space they needed for walks, hikes, and anything else they wanted to do together.

Marin couldn't do any vigorous hiking with her leg injury, but she hoped to at least do some exploring in the woods. Staying active was actually good for her recovery, as long as she didn't overdo it. There was a fine line that she was still adjusting to, but after months of rigorous PT, she was stronger than she'd ever been in many ways, despite the chronic pain.

She'd sent the link to Charlotte, although she wasn't sure how to coordinate seeing a house while also settling in a new puppy, because Ember obviously couldn't be left home alone so soon after adoption. Marin had to work on crate training with her this weekend. She had *so* much to do to get Ember acclimated before her class on Monday. It was daunting.

"Is this her?" a female voice called from overhead, and Marin recognized it as belonging to Ji-Yoon, the art history student who lived upstairs. Ji-Yoon would be puppysitting for Marin over the next few weeks, a fact she was extremely grateful for.

"Yes, this is Ember. Want to come meet her?"

"Try and stop me!" Ji-Yoon clambered down the steps from the upstairs landing and crouched in front of the puppy, who was currently eating snow. "Hi, puppy." Ji-Yoon knelt before Ember, arms outstretched. Ember's little tail wagged so hard it performed a full loop-de-loop. "Aren't you adorable?"

"She's very cute, and she seems to like you," Marin observed.

"I'm irresistible," Ji-Yoon said with a laugh as she leaned down so the puppy could kiss her face. "And animals generally love me. Just let me know when you need me to puppysit. I'm not seeing anyone right now, so I'm happy to hang out with this adorable girl while I study. Do you mind if I have a few friends over to play with her too?"

Marin smiled at the way the girl babbled on. She liked Ji-Yoon a lot, and it was handy that she lived upstairs. This was the positive trade-off of living in an apartment, something she'd lose when she moved into a house. "I think it would be great if you had friends over, actually. I'm told socialization is important at her age, and that'll be hard to accomplish in January since I can't take her around town very easily. So yes, please introduce her to your friends."

"Excellent. Ember, you and I are going to be besties," Ji-Yoon proclaimed before pressing a kiss between the puppy's ears. "See you around, Professor Easterly. You've got my number. Just text when you need me. Otherwise, I'll be here like we discussed to watch her during your class on Monday."

"Perfect, and it's Marin, remember? I'm not your professor. I'm your neighbor."

"Right, right. Feels weird, but okay, Marin." Ji-Yoon waved before heading back upstairs.

Ember whined, watching her go.

"You like her, huh? That's good. All right, Ember. Ready to see your new home?"

CHAPTER NINE

Charlotte arrived at Marin's apartment just past five, carrying a bag of burgers and fries for her and Marin, as well as a few goodies for Ember. She knocked quietly, not wanting to disturb the puppy if she was asleep. Sleeping puppies were like sleeping babies in Charlotte's opinion . . . never to be woken if it could be helped. A few seconds later, the door swung open to reveal Marin with a small black puppy cradled in her arms.

"Oh hi, puppy," Charlotte cooed.

"This is Ember." Marin looked a bit harried, locks of brown hair escaping her ponytail, slightly out of breath, and there was a wet spot on the thigh of her jeans.

Charlotte would guess that Marin had already gotten a crash course in how exhausting it was to keep up with a young puppy, but at the same time Marin's eyes sparkled with joy. She looked so happy, and maybe because Marin had been just a dim shadow of this woman when Charlotte first met her on that bus, she found she couldn't look away.

"I don't have to ask if you love having a puppy," Charlotte said.

"You don't?" Marin cocked an eyebrow. "Because I haven't sat down in three hours, I've lost count of how many accidents I've cleaned up, and I'm not even sure what's on my jeans, but I hope it's water."

Charlotte laughed, setting her bags on the table before she extended a hand to pet the puppy. "Yeah, but you're beaming, and I'm here now to help with the puppy wrangling. What do you say, Ember? Want to hang out with me and give your mom a breather?"

"You're a lifesaver." Marin passed the puppy into Charlotte's arms.

"Nah, I just love puppies. Go do whatever you need to do. We'll be fine." She turned toward the kitchen while Marin disappeared into the bedroom. The kitchen floor was strewn with toys and a cardboard box with puppy teeth marks all over the flaps. "Looks like you've been a busy girl this afternoon, hmm?"

Ember squirmed in her arms, but as Charlotte put her down, she saw the puppy start to circle and sniff on the linoleum.

"Uh-oh." She snatched Ember back into her arms and looked around for a leash. Luckily, she found it hanging from the same hook as Marin's keys, just inside the front door. Charlotte snapped the pink collar around Ember's neck and rushed outside to the snow-covered yard.

Ember took three steps across the snow before she squatted and peed.

"I knew you had to go! Good girl, Ember. Good puppy."

Ember wagged her tail at the praise, looking up at Charlotte with big brown eyes.

"You're a sweetheart, aren't you? No wonder Marin's smitten with you. I hope you two make each other very happy. She deserves all the happiness, you know?"

Ember pounced and grabbed a stick in her mouth, which she chomped on happily. Charlotte followed her around the yard for a few minutes, letting her sniff and scuff in the snow. Finally, she circled around and took a poop, which Charlotte collected using one of the bags attached to her leash while praising the puppy again for successfully doing her business outside.

As she walked back into the apartment, Marin was coming out of her bedroom in clean jeans, her hair neatly brushed. "Oh, did you take her out? Thank you."

"She peed *and* pooped," Charlotte said. "Where are you putting these?" She held up the bag in question before leaning down to set the puppy on the floor.

Marin gaped at her. "She did all that *outside*? Just now?"

"Yup." Charlotte unclipped Ember's collar, and the puppy raced toward Marin.

"Wow." Marin pushed a hand through her hair. "I haven't successfully gotten her to potty outside since I brought her home. As for the poop bag . . . uh, that's the first one, so I don't know where I'm putting them yet. Let me get a separate trash bag for them. I'll probably want to take them to the dumpster frequently so it doesn't get smelly in here."

"Good thinking." Charlotte waited until Marin had retrieved a trash bag and then dropped the one she held into it. "I've potty trained a few puppies so I'm happy to give tips."

"I need all the help I can get, clearly, so yes please."

"Definitely, but first, let's eat." She pointed toward the bag of burgers and fries she'd brought with her.

"Mm, yes, thank you." Marin gave her a grateful smile.

Charlotte washed her hands, and then they sat at the table together while Ember played behind the baby gate in the kitchen, energetically tossing a squeaky toy.

"She's really adorable," Charlotte commented.

"She is." Marin gazed affectionally at the puppy. "I love her to pieces already, but she might be just a *bit* more work than I had anticipated."

Charlotte laughed. "Puppies will keep you on your toes, that's for sure, especially if you're working on potty training and crate training and all that good stuff. You said one of the students upstairs is going to watch her while you're teaching?"

Marin nodded. "Yes, I introduced them today, actually. Ji-Yoon's going to be a big help, but I hope I haven't taken on too much at once, bringing home a puppy while I've got all this other stuff going on in my life."

"You'll be ridiculously busy for the next month or so, but you'll make it work. People do it all the time. You've got Ji-Yoon to help, and you've got me too. I love puppies, so I'm happy to hang out with her whenever you need a break."

"I appreciate that, but I don't want to take advantage of our friendship."

Charlotte scoffed. "You're the one who's going to be up half the night with her. Coming over to play for a little while is the fun part."

"I guess that's true, and I confess, I'm a little anxious about tonight. Do you think she'll cry all night in her crate?"

"Has she been in one before?" Charlotte asked.

"Her foster mom said she'd started some basic crate training with them, but not much. I've done my research, but if there's one thing I've learned from Ember so far, it's that putting these things into practice with a real, live puppy isn't nearly as straightforward or easy as the articles make it sound."

"Things rarely are." Charlotte looked at Ember, who had lain down on the kitchen floor and was chomping on the stuffed dragon Charlotte picked out for her that day in the pet store. "But one great thing about puppies is that they learn and grow so quickly. Anything that feels impossible today will be easier tomorrow, and if tonight is a nightmare, just remember that'll get better soon too."

"Okay, that *is* reassuring," Marin said. "It probably would have been easier to adopt an adult dog, but I've wanted a puppy since I was a little girl, and I'm pretty excited to finally live out this childhood dream."

"I love that for you. What's the point of getting a divorce and starting your life over if not to have the things you've always wanted, right?"

Marin's face brightened. "Exactly."

"Remember that when you're outside with her at three a.m., and you're exhausted and frustrated. It's all temporary, but the joy she brings into your life is something you'll cherish forever."

"Thank you," Marin said, her expression soft. "That was just the pep talk I needed."

"Anytime. Just tossing this out there, and feel free to say no, but I'd be happy to pack a few things and sleep on your pullout couch tonight if you think it would help. We had so much fun at our last slumber party." She gave Marin a playful smile.

"That was a fun night," Marin said, her expression fond. "And I'd love your help if you really mean that, but please don't feel obligated. I'll figure things out with her one way or the other. I mean . . ." She chuckled. "I can't imagine volunteering to help take a puppy out to potty in the middle of the night in Vermont in January."

"Well, I never said I'd be the one to take her outside in the middle of the night," Charlotte teased. "But honestly, I wouldn't mind. For one night, it's a fun adventure and a chance to help a friend. So . . . sleepover part two?"

Marin's expression was luminous. "Yes."

Marin sat cross-legged in her bed with a puppy lying belly up across her knees, gnawing happily on a piece of cardboard. It was almost ten, and Marin was about to try putting Ember to bed in her crate for the first time. Marin was already exhausted after fewer than twelve hours of puppy wrangling and feeling somewhat apprehensive about the night to come.

Charlotte sat in Marin's bed across from her, wearing flannel pajama pants and a blue hoodie. She was such a good friend. Marin had laughed so much tonight having Charlotte here, but there was nothing friendly about the way her pulse raced every time Charlotte's hand bumped hers. Charlotte just looked so *adorable* in her pajamas.

Marin's feelings for her were growing by the day. It was a good thing she'd had so many years of practice keeping her feelings to herself. Such a shame, though, that she was finally free to pursue a relationship with a woman, and she'd immediately gone and fallen for her straight friend. Fallen so hard that she was losing interest in the women she was messaging through the dating app. She and Laura were still chatting, but Marin didn't feel the same fluttery excitement with Laura that she did when she got a text from Charlotte.

"Are you going to be a good puppy tonight, cutie?" Charlotte reached out and rubbed Ember's tummy, and the little dog kicked her back feet happily. Marin tried not to notice how Charlotte's blond hair brushed her arm as she rubbed Ember, but goose bumps rose on her skin regardless.

Sitting together in Marin's bed this late at night felt unexpectedly intimate, and more than that, it hinted at the kind of domesticity Marin yearned for. How she wished she were sitting here with her girlfriend or wife, someone who'd share her bed forever . . .

"Oh," Charlotte said suddenly. "I meant to tell you, I called the Realtor who's listing that house your academic friends told you about. Showings don't officially start until Monday, but she said the owners might be willing to let you come out this weekend when I mentioned that you could make a cash offer. The current owners are moving due to an unexpected job transfer, and it sounds like they're looking for a quick, easy sale."

"That sounds promising. I'm not sure what I'd do with Ember, though."

"We'll figure it out if the showing comes through. I don't want you to miss out on the house because of logistics. I'll ask around and see if one of my coworkers might be willing to sit in the car with her while you walk through the house or something."

"I'll ask Ji-Yoon too. She seems eager to earn some pet-sitting cash . . . or maybe just to play with a puppy. Maybe both."

"Puppysitting would have been my dream job when I was a college student, so I can't say I blame her," Charlotte said.

The puppy in question wriggled out of Marin's arms and leaped into Charlotte's lap, then lunged up to lick Charlotte's face. Charlotte giggled, rolling backward so she lay on the bed with the puppy on top of her. Marin felt so *happy*. All those lonely years with Andrew, she never could have imagined the simple joy of this moment.

Charlotte lay on her back with a soft smile on her face, Ember sprawled across her stomach. "You look happy, Marin."

"Funny, I was just thinking the same thing. I spent so many years being *un*happy, and now I'm just so glad to be here, building new friendships and playing with my puppy. So far, divorced life is exceeding expectations, that's for sure."

"What was your ex-husband like?" Charlotte asked quietly. "I mean, if you don't mind talking about him. Is he supportive of your new life?"

"We've barely spoken since the divorce was finalized, so I doubt he knows much about my new life." She looked down at her hands, then back at Charlotte. "He's not the worst, by any means, but there's no love lost between us. Our marriage was on the rocks long before my accident. We'd grown apart. Maybe he felt frustrated that I didn't enjoy our sex life as much as he did, but eventually, he looked elsewhere. He slept with other women for years, and I turned a blind eye. Our divorce was long overdue."

A wrinkle appeared between Charlotte's eyes. "I'm sorry. How did he react to your accident?"

"Ironically, he was so caring and attentive during my recovery, and thank god for that because I needed his help whether I liked it or not. It's part of the reason I stayed married to him for another eighteen months."

"That's totally understandable, and honestly I'm glad you had someone to help you through your recuperation. No one should go through something like that alone. Did you have any close friends you could lean on?"

"Not really." Marin reached out to rub Ember, careful not to touch Charlotte in the process. "I think because I was hiding so much of myself, I found it hard to have close female friends. I felt like I was wearing a mask. I had a lot of casual friends, but no close friends."

"What about your siblings? You have four, right?"

"I do, and we're pretty close, although my relationship with them is a bit unconventional since they're so much older than I am. We've become more like peers now that we're all adults, but they've always considered me the baby of the family. I'm close with one of my nieces, too, Jen. In fact, I need to text her in the morning with puppy pictures because I know she's waiting. I got so busy tonight I forgot."

"And have you come out to them yet?"

"Not yet." Marin blew out a breath. "I've been putting it off, but it's on my to-do list for this year. I'll be visiting each of my siblings to come out to them."

"How do you think they'll take it?" Charlotte was still on her back in Marin's bed. Ember had fallen asleep with her head nestled between Charlotte's breasts, and the sight was enough to take Marin's breath away. How lucky she was to have a new friend and puppy in her life, even if she could never have Charlotte in the way she craved.

"I think most of them will be fine with it," she answered, her stomach tightening. "But my oldest sister, Nancy—Jen's mom—is fairly conservative. I'm worried she's going to react badly, but I'll tell her regardless. No more hiding. That's the promise I made myself when I left Andrew. I won't apologize for who I am, and I'm willing to lose family over it if that's what it comes to. It's that important to me."

Charlotte reached out and gripped her hand. "That's incredibly brave. You're a badass, Marin Easterly, and I hope your sister surprises you . . . the good kind of surprise."

Marin squeezed her fingers, reluctant to let go. "Me too."

A high-pitched whine yanked Marin from sleep, and she lurched upright in bed, momentarily disoriented. She felt a hazy sense of contentment from whatever she'd been dreaming about, but . . . there it was again. A whine.

The puppy.

She reached for her phone on the table beside the bed and squinted at the time. Just past one in the morning. Oh, this should be fun, taking a puppy outside in the middle of the night in January . . . in Vermont. "You chose this," she reminded herself, and despite her groan as she slid out of bed and reached for a hoodie, she had no regrets.

Already, she loved Ember with a sort of fierce protectiveness that was new for her. She was responsible for this tiny life in a way she'd never been responsible for anything or anyone before. She didn't take that responsibility lightly.

Marin knelt before Ember's crate. The puppy stared at her with big pleading eyes and let out another whine. "Gotta pee, huh?"

She opened the crate and tucked the puppy under her arm, then stumbled toward the living room, feeling a bit delirious after having only been asleep for about three hours. In the living room, she froze when she saw the pullout couch extended, containing a sleeping Charlotte. For a moment, she'd completely forgotten Charlotte was here.

Warmth spread through her belly. Marin hadn't had many sleepovers as a child, or as an adult for that matter, so seeing Charlotte in her living room, knowing she was here as a show of friendship and support, really meant a lot.

Marin clipped Ember's collar around her neck, fumbling awkwardly to avoid putting the puppy down, where she might pee on the floor, and then she opened the door. "Fuck," she hissed as the icy air hit her face.

She hurried down the steps to the walkway and set the puppy in the snowy area she'd designated as her unofficial potty spot. Ember circled in the snow and then squatted. "Good girl," Marin murmured. She watched until she was sure Ember was finished, then scooped her up and carried her back inside.

As she closed the door behind her, Marin shivered, having realized belatedly that she'd gone outside in her sleep shorts despite the single-digit weather. Her legs felt like ice. She could only hope it didn't cause her nerve pain to flare up.

"Potty call?"

She jumped at the sound of Charlotte's voice, shivering again for an entirely different reason. Charlotte was sitting up in the sofa bed, blinking at Marin out of sleepy eyes. Her hair was messy, curls sticking out in every direction, and god, she looked good.

"Yes," Marin answered. "Hopefully she starts sleeping through the night soon, because . . . brr."

Charlotte laughed quietly. "Maybe next time you should consider putting on pants." Her gaze lingered on Marin's bare legs in a way that sent another shivery jolt through her.

"Next time I'll definitely remember pants."

Charlotte laughed again, then lay back down. "Night, Marin."

"Night." She returned to her bedroom, tucked the puppy into her crate, and climbed into bed. As she drifted back to sleep, her last thought was of Charlotte on the sofa bed, staring at her legs.

She woke in a daze a few hours later to repeat the process. When Ember woke for the third time, it was nearly six. Marin decided to go ahead and get up, hoping Charlotte wouldn't mind the early morning. Decision made, she flipped on the light in her bedroom so she wouldn't have to get dressed in the dark.

Aware of the puppy waiting impatiently to go outside, she grabbed her flannel pants and had them halfway on before her gaze caught on the pink scar that ran up her right thigh. She'd had surgery to repair a broken femur, one of many surgeries she'd endured in the days after the accident. But her stomach dropped as she realized this was what Charlotte had been staring at last night.

In her sleepy haze, Marin had romanticized the middle of the night encounter, but *of course* her straight friend hadn't been staring at her bare legs for any nonplatonic reasons. She'd been looking at Marin's scar, probably remembering the way they'd met. Suitably chastised for her inappropriate thoughts, Marin knelt before the crate and lifted Ember into her arms.

The puppy whined again, squirming against her grip. Marin stood and rushed through the living room, grabbing Ember's leash on her way outside. When she returned to her apartment a few minutes later, Charlotte was waiting with arms outstretched.

"Let me take Ember for a minute. You've been running in and out with her all night. Go take a few minutes for yourself." Charlotte tucked the puppy against her chest and lay back with her. Ember immediately started kissing her face.

Marin *could* use a moment to freshen up. And warm up. "Thank you," she told Charlotte, then ducked inside the bathroom. While she was in there, she seized the opportunity for a quick, hot shower, then wrapped herself in a thick robe to cross the hall to her bedroom. Clean and refreshed, she reentered the living room to find Charlotte sitting on the floor with Ember while the puppy played with her stuffed dragon.

"Breakfast?" Charlotte asked hopefully. "I heard back from the listing agent for the house on Middleton Hill Road. She said we can come at two this afternoon and you can bring Ember as long as you keep her in a carrier so she doesn't make any messes in their house."

"Oh wow. That's soon." Marin walked to the kitchen to figure out what she had for breakfast. "Ember was really good in her carrier on the way home from her foster mom's house, so that should work."

"Awesome. I'll tell her we'll take it." Charlotte began to type on her phone, laughing as she held it out of Ember's reach.

Marin fixed two bowls of oatmeal and one bowl of puppy food. They ate breakfast together, and then Charlotte got dressed and headed out since she had several other showings before Marin's. Marin spent the rest of the morning with Ember, playing and practicing some basic leash training. Truly, she was exhausted. Her aches and pains were worse than usual today, and she yearned for a long soak in the tub and maybe a nap.

Ember had other plans. The tub in this apartment was small and cramped anyway. But maybe soon, she'd have something better . . .

Marin had a smile on her face as she arrived at the house on Middleton Hill Road that afternoon. She had a good feeling about this one, and that was saying something, coming from a skeptic like her. Marin had never been a "gut feeling" kind of person before she met Charlotte, but apparently she was now.

The house wasn't much to look at from the outside, with worn brown siding and no garage, but the location was exactly what Marin wanted. There was a small fenced area in back with a large deck, where she could take in the views. Already, she could picture herself and Ember out there this spring, enjoying wildflowers and butterflies. Hopefully the interior of the house was workable. Because the listing wasn't live yet, she hadn't seen any photos.

She parked along the narrow road and walked Ember until she pottied, before tucking her into her carrier to go inside. While she'd been walking Ember, Charlotte had arrived. She stood on the front porch, entering the code to unlock the door. "Hi," she called over her shoulder. "Come on in. They've asked us to leave our shoes by the door."

Marin joined her on the porch as Ember whined softly inside her carrier. Marin took off her boots on the welcome mat and followed Charlotte into the house.

"Let's see what we've got," Charlotte said. "I don't often view homes where I haven't seen any interior photos. I hope I'm not wasting both of our time."

"If you are, it would be my fault, not yours. I'm the one who got fixated on this house, and . . . I think I like it." Marin walked into the living room. It had light-colored hardwood floors and oversize windows on the far wall that looked out over the hills in back. The house was small. She'd known that going in, but so far at least, it felt cozy and inviting.

And because of all the windows, it didn't feel claustrophobic. Marin had spent too many years feeling closed in. She needed a home where she could breathe freely.

"I like it too," Charlotte said. "These windows are incredible, and there's a woodstove here in the living room. These things are so practical this time of year. You can heat most of the house with it, which saves you on propane and makes the living room super cozy."

"I love the sound of that."

"Let's see the kitchen," Charlotte suggested. "That's a room that can easily make or break a house for most people."

"Agreed. I'm not particularly fussy about the appliances, but my apartment doesn't have a pantry, and I'm constantly struggling to keep food off the counters. Like, seriously, where are you supposed to put stuff without a pantry?"

"Exactly. It's impractical. So let's see if this house has one."

Marin followed her to the kitchen, which was also small. The appliances were outdated, but there was a pantry and more windows overlooking the backyard, with stunning views. Marin could see herself sitting at the little breakfast nook, reading a book while she enjoyed her morning coffee with Ember lounging at her feet. "I'm still liking what I see."

"Yeah?" Charlotte turned to face her, eyes sparkling. "That's awesome. I like it too. It's cute, and it feels really livable."

"I can *see* myself here, and that's important."

"It is."

They walked through the rest of the house, revealing a guest bathroom, laundry in the partially finished basement, two small guest rooms upstairs, and finally the master bedroom. It, too, was small but indescribably cozy, and it was on the ground floor, which was a huge plus. Its windows shared the view, and the attached bathroom had one feature that Marin immediately focused on. "A soaking tub? A *jetted* soaking tub no less? Sold. I mean it."

Charlotte laughed. "Seriously?"

"Yes." Marin set down Ember's carrier so she could stretch her aching forearm. "Not solely because of the tub, but I think it just sealed the deal for me. I haven't had access to a soaking tub since my divorce, and while I've always loved a good bath, they're even more important for me now, for pain relief."

"Let's get you a soaking tub, then," Charlotte agreed. "Honestly, this house has a lot going for it. The price is a little high, but that's Vermont real estate for you, and it *is* within your budget. Getting in before the listing officially goes live means that if you want it, it's probably yours. So . . . you want it?"

"I do." Marin nodded briskly. "I wasn't an impulsive person before. I would have gone home and run numbers, calculated costs versus benefits, but the new me goes with my gut, and my gut says this is the one. I like it. It's cozy in a good way, the views are amazing, and that deck and fenced backyard will be perfect for me to hang out with Ember once the weather gets nicer."

"Did you map out your commute to the university? What's that like?"

"I did, and it's about a thirty-minute drive."

"That's reasonable, but also bear in mind that this is a dirt road, which means mud season will be an issue."

Marin gave her a questioning look. "Mud season?"

Charlotte laughed, a sound Marin loved. It was light and breezy, and it filled her with joy. "In the spring when the snow melts, the dirt roads turn to mud, and it's pretty awful. Honestly, Vermont has winter road maintenance down to a science. We're so well plowed and salted, it's fine. But the mud? It'll sink your car axle deep. It's the worst. You're driving an Outback, which will probably do well in the mud, but keep it in mind as you make your decision."

"I'll learn to manage mud season," Marin decided, because her gut was still saying *go for it*. "I leased the Outback because it would be practical on rural roads, so hopefully it'll do the job, and if it doesn't, I'll get something else."

Charlotte grinned. "That's the spirit. So this is it? You're ready to put in an offer?"

"I am. Let's do this."

Slowly but surely, she was completing her to-do list. Puppy—check. House—check. Now she needed a woman to hold. Looking at Charlotte, she felt that all-too-familiar jolt in the pit of her stomach. But no matter how badly Marin wished otherwise, Charlotte wasn't the one.

CHAPTER TEN

Charlotte stood in line at the deli counter at the Main Street Café, waiting to pick up sandwiches for her and Marin. It was Saturday, a full week since they'd looked at the house on Middleton Hill Road, and they were going to have lunch at Marin's apartment before Charlotte headed out for an afternoon of house showings.

Marin's offer on the house had been accepted almost immediately, with a closing set for the first weekend in March, which meant soon Charlotte would just be Marin's friend, not her Realtor.

"Charlotte?"

She glanced behind her, and everything seemed to freeze as her gaze settled on the woman standing there. It had been a long time—over twenty years, in fact—since Charlotte had last seen her, but the recognition was immediate and overwhelming. "Elena."

Elena Campos looked much the same as she had in high school, dark curls framing her face, light-brown skin that seemed sun kissed even in the middle of a Vermont winter. She was smiling at Charlotte, and . . . *that* was unexpected. "I heard you were back in town, but well . . . hi."

"Hi." Charlotte felt flushed and tongue tied, because how were you supposed to greet the woman who had been your best friend through high school, who you'd fallen out with just before graduation and hadn't spoken to since? "I . . . wow . . . it's really good to see you."

"You too." Elena was still smiling, but something hesitant had entered her eyes now, as if she was remembering the way they'd crashed and burned senior year, just like Charlotte was. "I'd love to catch up sometime."

"So would I." Charlotte's body was on high alert, a confusing cocktail of emotions sweeping through her veins as she realized that deep down, she'd been afraid of this, that Elena still lived in town and Charlotte might bump into her. Shame followed, because this woman had been her *best* friend, and their friendship-ending fight seemed petty and insignificant now. "I'm on my way to meet someone, but maybe we could grab lunch sometime?"

"I'd love that. Can I get your number?" Elena held out her phone.

Charlotte glimpsed a photo of Elena with two teen girls who were unmistakably her daughters on the lock screen, and it hit her like a punch in the gut just how much time had passed since they'd spoken. How had she let that happen?

Charlotte tapped her number into Elena's phone and said goodbye, but she was still reeling as she walked outside a few minutes later, holding a paper bag that contained her and Marin's lunch. Elena's family had moved to Vermont the summer before Charlotte and Elena started high school, and almost as soon as they'd met, they'd become inseparable.

Sometimes friendships were just like that, weren't they? One day, you didn't even know each other, and the next day you had connected on a soul-deep level. Charlotte had experienced it twice . . . first with Elena, and then with Marin. She and Elena had spent practically every free moment at each other's houses, talking about clothes and music and which boys they liked.

They'd both dated a lot, but senior year, they'd promised each other they would attend prom together. It was going to be their last hurrah before going off to college, and no boy would come between them. But midway through senior year, Elena had gotten serious with her boyfriend, Marcus. He'd asked her to the prom, and she'd said yes.

Charlotte, who'd been single at the time, had been so upset, so *hurt*. They had a huge fight, and in the end, Charlotte lost her best friend. It had felt like such a big deal at the time, and now . . . well, now it felt like she'd thrown away an important friendship over something trivial. But maybe she was about to get a chance to fix that mistake.

She got in her car and drove to Marin's apartment. Marin greeted her at the door, looking exhausted and a bit disheveled, but she was *radiant*. Having a puppy really agreed with her.

"Perfect timing." Marin spoke quietly, then put a finger to her lips. "Ember just fell asleep, so if we're quiet, we can eat lunch without puppy interference."

"Challenge accepted," Charlotte whispered.

"You okay?" Marin asked, giving her a questioning look. "You look kind of intense."

"I just bumped into my best friend from high school, and it really threw me." She spoke softly as they sat across from each other at the kitchen table. "We had a big falling-out senior year, and we haven't spoken since."

"That's a long time," Marin observed. "What did you fight about?"

"A guy." Charlotte rolled her eyes. "It seems so stupid now, and I guess . . . seeing her today made me realize that. Like, she has teenage daughters I've never met. I have no idea what's going on in her life. And we were *inseparable* all through high school."

"It happens, and you moving out of state certainly didn't help you two reconnect."

"No. If I'd gone to NU like so many kids from our high school—including Elena—we probably would have made up in college. If I'm honest, our fight was part of the reason I left Vermont after high school. Everything here felt so overwhelming and messed up, and I just needed a fresh start. Anyway, we exchanged numbers today, but I feel so weird about the whole thing. Our fight was my fault. At the time, I blamed her for choosing her boyfriend over me, but now I see that I was just being immature and stupid."

"It's what teenagers are best at, right?"

"I guess. I haven't spent much time around teens since I was one."

Marin chuckled. "I've spent enough time with nieces and nephews—and even great-nieces and nephews—to have experienced my fair share of teen drama."

"That must seem so weird, your siblings being grandparents already," Charlotte said. "I mean, I don't feel nearly old enough for that."

"Well, I'm a little older than you," Marin said, eyes sparkling playfully. "But no, it's not weird for me because of the age gap between me and my siblings. That's my normal. My mom was about my age now when she had me."

"Did you ever want kids?" Charlotte asked, then waved a hand in front of her face. "Sorry, that was insensitive of me to ask. A friend of mine went through years of infertility, and she told me how hurtful it was when people asked her why she didn't have kids."

"I don't mind you asking," Marin said. "I did want kids, but I never tried to have one. It never felt like the right time with Andrew, and he didn't particularly want them, so he never pushed me about it. In hindsight, I think I just didn't want to tie myself to him that way."

That was a more honest and in-depth answer than Charlotte had been expecting. "I get that. When I was younger, I wanted kids, too, but I never had the right partner, and I didn't want them badly enough to consider intentionally becoming a single mom. Now, I guess the urge has passed. I like my independence too much."

"The urge has passed for me too. There are a lot of things I want from my new life, but children aren't one of them."

"Except as their teacher?"

"College students aren't exactly children, but yes." Marin's face softened. "That I'm enjoying quite a lot."

"Good. So far, your new life here seems to be working out just as you'd hoped."

"Except for dating," Marin said. "That's going more slowly than I'd like, although Laura and I are actually hoping to meet soon."

"Exciting." But Charlotte felt something ugly twist in her chest at the thought of Marin going on a date with Laura. It was the same way she'd felt when Elena ditched her to go to the prom with Marcus. Maybe Charlotte was a terrible friend who wanted her friends to be single just because she was. She didn't like what that said about her.

"I'll just need to coordinate our date around Ji-Yoon's availability to watch Ember." She gestured toward the black puppy, who was still fast asleep in her dog bed.

"I can watch her if Ji-Yoon can't," Charlotte offered, determined not to repeat the mistakes of her past. She wouldn't lose Marin the way she'd lost Elena. "I'd be happy to."

"Oh, you've already done enough," Marin deflected.

"Nonsense. It would be fun to watch her for a few hours." This time, Charlotte would be a good and supportive friend. "Nothing's going to get in the way of your date with Laura."

Marin admired the framed photo of her and Ember on the shelf in her living room. Charlotte had taken the picture of them last week. In it, Ember sat on Marin's lap, gazing up at her with those big brown eyes while Marin smiled at the camera, and she almost didn't recognize herself, she looked so happy. She *felt* happy.

She'd been floored when Charlotte showed up at her apartment unexpectedly on February fourteenth, holding a pink-wrapped gift and a bouquet of flowers, telling Marin she didn't want her to go another year without receiving a gift from a woman on Valentine's Day. It had been such a sweet and thoughtful gesture, so *romantic* . . . in a strictly platonic sense. Not for the first time, Marin was grateful for their friendship.

Ember trotted into the room, and when she spotted Marin, her tail started doing full loop-de-loops of joy. Marin felt a burst of warmth in her chest. Oh, she loved this little dog. So much. "Want to go out?"

Marin fastened Ember's leash and led her outside, grateful for the relatively mild February day. Temperatures today had reached almost forty, and after a frigid few weeks, this felt positively balmy by comparison.

Charlotte would be here soon. She was going to puppysit while Marin went on her first date with Laura. Her body went haywire at the thought, heart racing, butterflies flapping frantically in her stomach. This date was the culmination of two decades of yearning, and two years of careful planning. It was thrilling and momentous, and now that it was nearly here? Marin was overwhelmed in the very best way.

She was going to do everything in her power not to let Charlotte enter her thoughts while she was with Laura. She had to stop pining for her straight friend. If she let her thoughts keep drifting in that direction, she was going to ruin her chances with Laura, who she genuinely liked. Things with Laura had the potential to be great as long as Marin didn't mess it up.

Today, she and Laura were going snowshoeing and then for coffee, and while Marin had eagerly agreed when Laura suggested it, now she was worried. Snowshoeing was likely to aggravate her bad leg, even though it also sounded fun. She should have been more realistic about her limitations, but there was always next time . . . assuming today was a success.

Marin needed to start getting ready as soon as she walked Ember. The puppy could walk all the way to the end of the block and back now. She was growing so fast! Currently, Ember was prancing adorably at the end of her leash, tail up and nose extended to sniff whatever scents carried on the breeze.

"Hi, Ember." Connor, one of Marin's upstairs neighbors, bent to pet her as he walked past. She wagged happily. She'd miss getting so much attention once they moved to their new house, but Marin hoped that having lots of open space to play would more than make up for it.

Back at the apartment, Marin shut the door behind them and unclipped Ember's leash. The puppy ran to her water bowl and took a big drink, then dashed to Marin and stood on her hind legs, begging for kisses with her face still dripping from the water bowl. Marin knelt and scooped Ember into her lap for sloppy kisses.

She was about to do her makeup, so she'd wash off the puppy slobber then. A burst of adrenaline filled her stomach as she thought of where she was going. A date. Her first date with a woman. Her breathing picked up speed. Oh god. This was such a big deal. *Huge.*

Ember grabbed a mouthful of Marin's hair and yanked, successfully distracting her from her rapidly spiraling thoughts.

"Ouch." Marin carefully extracted Ember from her hair. "Here, put this in your mouth instead." She gave Ember her toy dragon, and the puppy began to thrash her head back and forth so that the dragon's wings made a crinkly sound against the floor. "You're adorable."

Ember lunged at her face, and Marin gave her another gentle redirection to the toy. She'd been somewhat terrified when she brought Ember home three weeks ago, afraid she'd be terrible at puppy rearing, but she was getting the hang of it. In fact, she thought she and Ember were doing pretty damn well together.

Sure, she hadn't had an uninterrupted night's sleep in weeks, but that was to be expected. It was worth it to be tired when she felt so happy and fulfilled with this puppy in her life.

"I'm about to go on a date," she told Ember, who cocked her head to listen, purple dragon dangling from her mouth. "We're going snowshoeing, so I have no idea what to wear. I mean, I've got to stay warm, but I also want to look nice when we go for coffee afterward. Does that mean I need to wear jeans under my snow pants?"

Ember cocked her head in the other direction.

"Hopefully Charlotte has suggestions, because I'm clueless." Another benefit of having Ember around was that Marin could talk through her thoughts out loud under the guise of talking to the puppy. "Suddenly, I feel like I haven't thought through my date attire properly."

Ember shook her dragon, dragging it around the kitchen. It thrilled Marin that Ember's favorite toy was the one Charlotte had bought for her.

Right on cue, there was a knock at the door, and Marin rushed to answer it. "Help," she greeted Charlotte rather ineloquently. "What in the world do I wear on this date? A snowsuit won't be sexy at the coffee shop afterward, but I can't imagine snowshoeing in jeans. What if I fall and get soaked, and well, what if I look like a total idiot in front of Laura?"

"Whoa." Charlotte laughed, brushing a blond curl from her face as she stepped past Marin into the kitchen, where Ember was bouncing for her attention. "Hey, puppy." She bent to ruffle Ember's ears, then turned to face Marin. "Take a breath, Mare. I had a feeling you might be freaking out about your date, so I brought provisions."

For the first time, Marin registered the bag in Charlotte's hands. "What kind of provisions?"

"First, I brought my snowshoes in case you want to borrow them. They're way nicer than whatever the nature center will have available to rent."

"Oh, perfect. I really appreciate that."

"No problem." Charlotte reached into her bag and took out the snowshoes. "You and Laura are taking a beginners' lesson together, right? So you don't need to know how to use them yet?"

"Right." Marin held one of the shoes and examined it. She'd expected it to be webbed like a tennis racket, but this was made of plastic, almost like a short, wide ski that snapped onto a shoe. "These aren't what I expected."

"Modern snowshoes are pretty cool, right? Now, let's pick out your clothes. We want Laura to be absolutely bowled over when she sees you in person for the first time."

Marin scoffed. "That's not likely, no matter what I'm wearing."

"Are you kidding?" Charlotte waved a hand in Marin's direction. "You're *gorgeous*, and more than that, you have this irresistible energy that gets a little bit stronger and more magnetic every day of your new life here in Vermont. It's like I'm watching you evolve day by day, and it's mesmerizing. *You* are mesmerizing."

Charlotte reached out and cupped Marin's cheek. Her hand was so warm, so soft, and Marin couldn't breathe. Charlotte was staring at her with an intensity that made Marin's heart lose its rhythm and the fine hair on her neck and arms stand at attention. She'd been so focused on her date, on *Laura*, that she'd successfully tabled her feelings for Charlotte, but now . . .

Now she was looking at Charlotte, *really* looking, noticing the way her blue eyes sparkled and how they complemented the turquoise scarf at her neck. The way Charlotte's fingers brushed gently against Marin's cheek like a lover's caress. Marin turned her face toward the touch, inhaling the scent of Charlotte's skin as arousal flared inside her.

Good god. What was *happening* right now?

Ember barked, and Charlotte jumped, yanking her hand from Marin's face.

For a moment, they just stared at each other. Marin swallowed with an audible click. Her mind reeled with confusion. Arousal still swamped her senses. Then some instinct made her look down just as the puppy squatted on the linoleum. *Fuck.*

"Ember, no!" She scrambled for the leash and scooped the puppy from the floor before she could pee, feeling slightly dazed, almost dizzy, because what in the world had just happened between her and Charlotte?

She rushed out the door without her coat and set Ember in the trampled-down patch of snow designated as her potty area. The puppy immediately squatted. That had been a close call, especially since Marin had just walked her. Puppies were unpredictable that way, though.

Whatever had happened between her and Charlotte was a close call, too, because what if Marin had let her feelings show? Ordinarily, she had an uncrackable poker face, honed by decades of hiding herself from everyone around her, but she'd almost slipped for a moment there with Charlotte.

It couldn't happen again.

Already, Charlotte was too perceptive where Marin was concerned. Usually, she loved how easily Charlotte read her, but in this case . . . it could prove disastrous.

Marin led Ember back into the apartment, almost afraid to look at Charlotte, afraid of what she might see on her face. Certainly that touch had been platonic on Charlotte's part. What if Marin had made her uncomfortable with her reaction?

But Charlotte gave Marin an easy smile as if nothing out of the ordinary had happened. "So, I also brought my favorite snow pants. They're lightweight and kind of cute. I think they'd look good on you."

"Oh. Okay." Marin stared at the black pants Charlotte held. They looked almost like regular pants, not bulky like the ones Marin had bought. She liked the pants, and maybe . . . maybe things with Charlotte were still fine. She exhaled, releasing some of her tension. "Thank you."

"You're welcome." Charlotte held the pants out to her. "Go get dressed, and I'll help you finish getting ready for your date."

An hour later, Marin stepped out of her car in the parking lot of the nature center where she was meeting Laura. She was so nervous her whole body practically vibrated, and she felt 1,000 percent off balance by that weird moment with Charlotte. She'd done so well psyching herself up for her date with Laura, and now all she could think about was the warmth of Charlotte's fingers on her cheek.

She was so fucked.

Here she stood, wearing Charlotte's pants, holding Charlotte's snowshoes, trying ever so desperately not to think about Charlotte. Trying and failing. She pulled on her coat, hat, and gloves, watching idly as other vehicles pulled into the parking lot, people here for the lesson and random people out to enjoy the sunny February day.

"Marin?"

She spun to find herself facing a tall brunette, so tall that she almost made Marin feel short by comparison, and she was five foot seven. Marin's stomach filled with a tingly burst of adrenaline as she recognized Laura from the photos on her profile. Oh. Oh wow. Her date.

She was almost surprised to realize she was grinning, her heart pounding. "Hi, Laura. It's so great to meet you in person."

"You too." Laura walked over, wearing black snow pants and a hot-pink puffy jacket. Her hat was a mixture of vibrant colors, and it seemed to suit her. Some people just looked great in bright colors, like Char—*nope*, not thinking about her right now. "I've been so nervous . . . and so excited."

"Same." Marin laughed, as some of the tension left her body. "So much of both."

"That's a good sign, I think, right?" Laura's voice was different from what she'd expected, slightly husky. She had laugh lines around her eyes, and Marin had always found those so attractive on a woman. Now that she was paying attention, she was thrilled to realize that she *did* find Laura appealing, and not in a platonic way, but as someone she might want to kiss.

She exhaled in relief. "This might've been the hardest part, right? Actually meeting each other for the first time. Now we've gotten through it." She mimed wiping her brow.

"Definitely," Laura said. "This is my least favorite part of online dating, honestly, but it's so hard to meet people organically these days, especially as a lesbian in a small town."

"I'm sure it is. As you know, I'm new to all this." She gestured around herself, relieved that she'd already given Laura some of her backstory. Not all of it, but Laura knew this was Marin's first time dating a woman and that she'd just moved to Vermont. Laura was new to Vermont, too, but she'd moved here from rural New Hampshire, so she wasn't new to small-town New England life.

"I do know, and I'm so excited for you." Laura rested a hand briefly on Marin's shoulder as they began walking toward the welcome center together. "How are you feeling about things so far? Was this something you'd wanted for a while? Dating women, I mean?"

"It was," Marin confirmed, feeling a lump in her throat at just *how* long she'd wanted it. "I've been waiting a long time."

"That makes me extra glad to be here with you. I've been out since I was a teenager, but I know people who've come out at our age or even later, and I can't imagine how freeing that must feel . . . but also how overwhelming."

"So far, more freeing than overwhelming, but there are just . . . a lot of emotions." And just like that, Marin was on the verge of tears. Her eyes stung, and her throat ached. She gulped, pulling herself together.

Laura walked ahead, oblivious, chatting happily about snowshoeing. "I watched a few videos on YouTube, and it looks really fun, but I'm a woman who once got stuck halfway down the ski slope when one of my skis came off and went down without me, so no guarantees, right?"

Marin laughed, and it was a much-needed release for the emotions building inside her. "Look, I lived in the city for forty-seven years. I've never even been on skis. If anyone's going to fall and make a fool of herself today, it'll probably be me."

"If you go down, I'm going with you . . . for emotional support if nothing else," Laura offered with a silly smile, and Marin was laughing again.

And . . . the date she'd been so anxious about was off to a promising start. They joined their group and received a brief but informative demonstration on snowshoeing before they strapped into their awkward-looking footgear and tromped into the woods behind the welcome center.

It was more difficult than Marin had anticipated. The snowshoes used muscles she'd apparently never used before, and within minutes, her calves and feet were on fire, although she kept the discomfort to herself. She and Laura were both in their forties, but still, it seemed like bad form to complain about aches and pains on a first date.

Laura kept the conversation going while they walked. She seemed to be naturally chatty, with a gift for putting Marin at ease. They separated from the group, walking through an undisturbed part of the forest, and while her legs complained at every movement, Marin was mesmerized by the beauty of her surroundings.

The snow made a satisfying crunch beneath her shoes, while overhead, the wind whistled through the bare tree branches. The sun made everything sparkle, which was so damn pretty. Marin hadn't spent a lot of time in nature before, but she hoped that would change now that she lived in Vermont.

Laura's cheeks and nose were pink from the cold, and it made her look even prettier. Marin was thrilled to feel a visceral hit of attraction when she looked at her. When they returned to the parking lot an hour later, Marin was sweaty beneath her winter clothes, her legs hurt like crazy, and she was *happy*.

So. Incredibly. Happy.

"So," Laura said after she'd unclipped from her snowshoes. "Still up for that coffee?"

"Yes," Marin agreed quickly. "Definitely yes."

"I really like that 'definitely.' The Pleasant Rock Café is just down the street, if that sounds good to you?"

"It sounds perfect."

"Great." Laura leaned in, and Marin's whole body tingled as adrenaline flooded her system, because *oh god*, was she about to have her first kiss with a woman? Was she ready for this? God *yes*, but also, god *no*, and *Charlotte* . . .

Laura's lips brushed her cheek, warm and soft. Marin's skin flushed. Her heart raced. Her lips curved in an involuntary smile, even as they ached to be kissed, just maybe not by Laura.

What? Stop!

Laura's kiss had been perfect. It had been just what Marin wanted and needed. She'd had her first kiss with a woman, and for a moment there, she hadn't even thought of Charlotte . . .

CHAPTER ELEVEN

It was almost four, and Charlotte was restless. Marin and Laura had been out together for hours now. Were things going well? Had they gone for coffee after snowshoeing the way Marin had mentioned? Given the time, it seemed like they must have.

As Charlotte sat alone in Marin's apartment, her thoughts kept roaming to that moment in the kitchen right before Marin left, when Charlotte had touched Marin's cheek while she told her how beautiful she was. Marin had turned her face into the touch, or at least, that was how it happened in Charlotte's memories, but she felt so confused about the whole damn thing, she wasn't sure she could trust her mental replay.

Had Marin leaned into the touch, or had she just been flattered by Charlotte's praise? Charlotte's stomach squirmed. She hadn't been able to settle since it happened. Why had she touched Marin's cheek?

Why couldn't she stop obsessing about what was happening on Marin's date? Charlotte wanted Marin to find happiness with a woman. No one deserved it more than Marin. So what if Marin might have less time to spend with Charlotte once she started dating someone?

Charlotte should *not* be thinking about that. She really was the worst friend. This was exactly how she'd ruined her friendship with Elena.

Charlotte placed a hand on the sleeping puppy beside her. Ember loved to cuddle, and Charlotte loved that about her. Ember rolled belly up against her thigh, and Charlotte obediently began to rub her tummy as her tail swished happily against the upholstery.

"I hope your mom's having fun on her date."

Ember's tail wagged harder.

"You're a really good puppy, aren't you?"

The sound of the door opening had both Charlotte and Ember lifting their heads. Charlotte experienced a strange burst of excitement in anticipation of seeing Marin, while Ember slid down Charlotte's legs and bounded to the door, wagging so hard her whole body swayed from side to side.

Marin stepped into the apartment. She still wore Charlotte's snow pants, paired with a navy blue top that looked great on her. Marin's hair was a bit tousled from her outdoor adventures, her cheeks flushed a healthy pink. That sense of excitement increased to full-fledged tingles in Charlotte's belly.

"How was it?" she asked, surprised to realize she sounded vaguely out of breath.

Marin's smile was dazzling. "It was great. Really great."

Charlotte's stomach swooped with disappointment, and she immediately hated herself for it. Why was she such a terrible friend? Regardless, she feigned excitement. "I'm so glad! Tell me everything."

"Well." Marin scooped Ember into her arms and sat beside Charlotte on the couch. A faintly sweet scent lingered on her, maybe from the coffee shop. "She kissed me."

Charlotte let out an embarrassing squeak, feeling like she'd been punched in the gut. Everything inside her rejected the idea of Marin kissing Laura, to the point that she felt physically sick just thinking about it. "Oh my god," she managed.

"Yeah." Marin had a dreamy smile on her face. "Just on the cheek, but still . . . it was really nice." She turned her head, staring at Charlotte.

Charlotte felt some relief to learn that no one's lips had been on Marin's today. Although there was no reason why Marin shouldn't have kissed Laura on the mouth. None at all. So why was Charlotte having a weird, totally inappropriate freak-out just thinking about it?

"Are you okay?" Marin was still looking at her, those rich brown eyes locked on Charlotte's, and Charlotte's heart was about to burst out of her chest. Her body felt overheated, and her pulse was racing.

What was happening to her right now? This wasn't right. This wasn't . . .

This wasn't the reaction of a straight woman learning that her friend had been kissed by someone else. What . . . ?

She gulped, and another strange sound escaped her lips, something akin to a gasp. Not straight. Was she not straight? But . . .

"Charlotte?" Marin's head was tilted now, her expression one of concern.

Charlotte was ruining her moment. She sucked in a deep breath and pushed her emotions down deep. Marin had called her first date with Laura *great*. This was a big deal for her. The biggest! And Charlotte would *not* mess it up for her. She gave her head a quick shake. "I'm fine. I think I dozed off here with Ember on the couch, and now I feel a little delayed."

Marin's smile widened. "I know that feeling. Total disorientation. Even worse when someone's talking to you, and you're not quite awake yet."

"Exactly," Charlotte said, relieved her body had returned to normal. "I should probably run Ember outside since she hasn't been in a bit, and then I want to hear absolutely everything about your date."

"I'll take her." Marin started to stand, but Charlotte caught the wince she tried to hide. Had snowshoeing caused her nerve pain to flare up?

Charlotte scooped the puppy into her arms and stood. "I've got her. You should go change out of those snow pants, put on something more comfortable."

"Okay," Marin acquiesced, wincing again as she stood. "Thank you. I appreciate it."

"Not a problem. I love hanging out with Ember as long as I'm not the one who has to get up with her at three a.m."

Marin huffed. "Isn't that the truth? Those middle of the night calls are rough, especially this time of year. It's *cold* out there."

Unbidden, Charlotte remembered that first night when Marin had come stumbling through the living room in her tiny sleep shorts. Charlotte had caught herself staring at Marin's long, pale legs for reasons she hadn't understood at the time. *Oh.*

Feeling flushed all over again, Charlotte hurried toward the door. She clipped on Ember's leash and stepped outside, then set the puppy down in the snow. Ember whined, probably disappointed to have been whisked outside right after her mom got home. Charlotte might have lied about falling asleep on the couch, but she hadn't lied about Ember needing to go out.

Sure enough, the puppy ran to her usual spot to take care of business. Meanwhile, Charlotte turned her face toward the late-afternoon sun, grateful for the cold breeze that slapped some sense into her, cooling off her malfunctioning hormones.

Not. Straight.

Was that possible? She was forty years old. She'd had queer friends her whole life. She'd even gone to gay bars with them. She'd been hit on by women, and she'd never felt *anything*. She'd only ever been attracted to men. So this was . . . surely it wasn't what it felt like.

Because this wasn't what Charlotte had come to Vermont for. Marin was the one who'd come here looking to explore her sexuality. Charlotte just wanted to reconnect with her dad and to find out once and for all what happened to her mom. She wasn't looking for a relationship right now, not with a man or anyone else, not after making such a mess of things with Darren.

Ember turned and ran back to the apartment door, eager to see Marin. *Relatable.* Charlotte checked her attitude, making sure she reentered the apartment ready to show the appropriate amount of enthusiasm as Marin told her about her date.

Pain radiated down Marin's right leg, and her foot tingled with pins and needles. She grimaced as she shuffled toward her bedroom after taking Ember out for her bedtime potty trip. She'd had the *best* time on her date with Laura. It had gone better than she'd even dared to hope. They'd had fun. They'd had *chemistry*. The kiss—even though it was only on the cheek—still made Marin's heart race every time she thought about it.

But now her right thigh was on fire. She bit back a whimper as a particularly vicious jolt shot down her leg. She'd heard nerve pain described as feeling like an electric shock, and right now? Yeah, that felt accurate. Briefly, she remembered the way Charlotte had cared for her the last time this happened. She'd almost mentioned her discomfort tonight but hadn't wanted Charlotte to feel obligated to care for her again, especially since things had felt strange between them a few times tonight.

Marin wasn't sure if she was reading too much into it. Certainly her emotions had been all over the place before and after her date. Maybe she'd given off some weird energy that Charlotte was responding to, because Marin couldn't figure out a logical explanation for why things had gotten weird. Maybe she'd only imagined that it had been awkward. With all her internal drama, it was hard to be sure.

Ember looked up at her and whined.

"You're so intuitive, aren't you?" Marin eased herself onto the edge of the bed. "I'm okay. The pain will pass. I'll be fine in the morning."

Ember whined again, then climbed onto the stool Marin had left by the bed for this exact purpose. From the stool, she hopped into bed with Marin. She pressed herself against Marin's thigh, right where it hurt, in an unmistakable gesture of support.

Marin's eyes filled with tears. How many nights had she lain awake beside Andrew, in agonizing pain but trying not to make noise so she didn't disturb his sleep, wishing she had someone to hold her when she was hurting?

She could care for herself. She was doing it right now, after all. But to receive support from Charlotte and now Ember? It filled a void inside her she hadn't realized existed. It felt so *good* to receive comfort from someone who genuinely cared about her.

"I love you," she whispered to the puppy as tears slid over her cheeks. "I don't know how you know I'm hurting, but you're really helping me right now."

Carefully, Marin slid all the way into bed and stretched out. She needed to put Ember in her crate for the night, but right now, she couldn't bring herself to move again or to break this connection with the puppy. Ember stretched out beside her, keeping her body pressed against Marin's right side, and not only was it comforting on an emotional level, but Ember's body heat soothed her pain too.

Just a few more minutes. Usually she'd start with an ice pack to reduce inflammation before moving on to heat to relax her stiff muscles, but she'd forgotten to get a gel pack out of the freezer before she lay down. Anyway, Ember's presence was more soothing than an ice pack at the moment.

Marin reached over and shut off the light. She touched her cheek, remembering the way it had felt when Laura kissed her there. Not that there had been any doubt in Marin's mind that she was a lesbian, but that kiss surely validated all her private fantasies. It felt *right* in a way nothing else in her life ever had.

Charlotte's face flitted through her mind, and Marin's pulse jumped. Yes, she was still powerfully attracted to her friend. It didn't help that Charlotte was so fucking beautiful. So sweet and thoughtful and supportive. She was everything Marin wanted in a life partner, except for being straight.

Marin exhaled, and she heard Ember do the same in the darkness beside her. Maybe they could just lie here together until the next time Ember needed to go out. Marin rested a hand against Ember's soft fur. Darkness had sometimes felt so suffocating in the past.

She'd lain beside Andrew, feeling like the night was about to swallow her whole. She'd felt so devastatingly alone despite the man sleeping a few feet away. Sometimes, it had been hard to breathe. And now . . . now she was gulping air, filling her lungs with it.

Now, she was free.

She inhaled, and as she breathed back out, a sob escaped. Hot tears spilled over her cheeks and onto the sheets as she let the emotions surface, as she acknowledged how many nights, how many *years*, she'd suffered alone.

Today, she'd gone on her first date with a woman. Laura had kissed her. Somehow it had been overshadowed by Charlotte's hand on her cheek and the way she'd looked at Marin when she got home. Marin had no idea what any of it meant. She only knew that it was confusing and overwhelming at a time when her emotions were already out of control.

She sobbed, lying flat on her back since it hurt too much to move, until the pressure in her chest had eased. Her eyes slid shut, one hand still pressed into Ember's fur. When she woke, early-morning sunlight filtered through the window. She was still on her back with Ember snuggled against her, and without warning, her eyes filled with tears all over again. Her puppy was so intuitive, it boggled her mind.

Ember had known what Marin needed last night and had given it to her instinctively. She'd slept in the bed instead of her crate, slept through the night even though she usually got up for a four a.m. potty trip, providing emotional and physical comfort to Marin all through the night.

Marin sat up, relieved to realize her nerve pain was gone. As she moved her legs, she could tell she had some sore muscles from yesterday's snowshoeing adventures, but that was to be expected. Ember must be bursting to go outside. Marin sat up, reaching for the sweatpants and hoodie she kept beside the bed for quick overnight potty trips.

She stood, slipping them on over her sleep shorts and tank top, as Ember let out an urgent whine and trotted toward the door. Marin followed, wincing because Ember wasn't the only one whose bladder was bursting. She stepped into her boots and took the puppy outside, grateful when Ember did her business quickly.

Back inside, Marin unclipped Ember's leash and hustled to the bathroom. Once she'd freshened up, she fixed breakfast for herself and her puppy, then put Ember in her crate while she took a quick shower. The hot water felt like heaven on her sore muscles. Marin smiled as she reminisced about her date with Laura. It really couldn't have gone any better.

Speaking of Laura . . .

Marin shut off the shower, wrapped herself in a towel, and sat on the bed with her reading glasses to check her phone. Sure enough, she had a text from Laura saying how much fun she'd had and asking Marin if she'd like to meet for dinner one night this week.

Marin responded with an enthusiastic yes but with the caveat that she'd have to coordinate with her puppysitter. With her suddenly busy social life, she looked forward to Ember getting bigger so Marin could regain more of her independence, but at the same time she couldn't imagine wanting to rush her puppyhood.

Already, Ember was so much bigger and more mature than she had been when Marin brought her home three weeks ago. Would it be too forward if she invited Laura to have dinner here at her apartment to accommodate Ember? If only the weather were warmer so they could eat somewhere with an outdoor patio.

Laura texted right back, mentioning a casual restaurant nearby that was dog friendly. How perfect! Marin agreed to a dinner date there on Thursday as excited butterflies flapped around in her belly. She shifted her hips. Maybe it was more than excitement . . .

Marin was still sitting on her bed, wearing only a towel. She hadn't managed much time for herself since Ember came into her life, and now, with all these thoughts of kissing and dates and hopefully much more happening soon . . . well, she was feeling a little frustrated. She needed a release, preferably soon.

She glanced at Ember's crate, relieved to see that the puppy had fallen asleep while she was in the shower. It was Sunday. Marin had no plans. Well, now she had plans for a little self-care before the puppy woke. She closed her eyes, focusing inward. A faint hum of arousal already buzzed through her system. Oh, she needed this so much . . .

Marin slipped a hand inside her towel, exhaling as she touched her breasts. She cupped them, enjoying the warmth of her own skin and the ache that built between her thighs as she teased her nipples. Unable to wait, she slid her fingers down her stomach to the part of her that was begging to be touched.

She ghosted her fingers over her neatly trimmed curls, imagining another woman's hand on her body instead. She always imagined someone else touching her. Marin had an entire mental playlist of the hottest sex scenes from her favorite sapphic romance novels that she used to get herself in the mood.

But this morning, she found herself remembering the way Laura's lips felt on her cheek. Her lips had been so much softer than any man's Marin had ever kissed. Everything about sapphic sex would feel soft, she imagined, soft in the very best way.

Soft fingers, soft lips, soft, smooth skin . . .

Marin opened her eyes and darted another glance at the crate. Ember was fast asleep. Thank god, because she'd hate to stop now. Marin lay back in bed and removed the towel, but then she felt too exposed . . . like if Ember woke up she might see Marin touching herself, which was ridiculous because the puppy would be clueless.

Silly or not, Marin slid beneath the sheet for privacy. She closed her eyes, circling her clit with her index finger. She inhaled sharply. Already, her core ached for release, and as she brought her fingers down to her entrance, she found that she was wet.

Soon, she would be having sex with a woman instead of lying alone in her bed, fantasizing about it. Just the thought made her throb, and she started to stroke herself. She imagined a lover straddling her, hips pressed against Marin's, whispering naughty suggestions into her ear. There was only so much Marin could do with her own hand, but her lover could surprise her, try out moves she'd never thought of.

Her lover could put her *mouth* on her.

Marin gasped, rubbing almost frantically. She couldn't wait for that. Oh, how she wanted to experience the pleasure of a woman's mouth. She'd had oral sex before, of course, but Andrew wasn't very good at it, and she'd never liked the scratchy feel of his facial hair against her inner thighs. It left her feeling chafed afterward.

Soon. She'd have all the pleasure she could handle, whether it was with Laura or someone else. Marin was finished compromising. She wanted love, and affection, and companionship, and *passion*. She wanted it all.

Her body tensed, and her breath hitched. Just like that, she was about to come. *Wait.* She stilled her fingers. She knew from experience that if she rushed herself to a quick orgasm after not masturbating for a while, it would be underwhelming. But if she took her time and really worked herself up, the payoff would be *so* worth it.

So she ignored the relentless ache in her core, skimming her fingers lightly over herself until the urge to come had passed, until her breathing had slowed and she'd regained control. Ignoring her clit, which was *begging* for her attention, she slipped two fingers inside herself. Again, she summoned an imaginary lover.

In her mind's eye, Marin saw blond curls, so soft beneath her fingers, curls that smelled vaguely of wildflowers. She saw pink lips curved into a vibrant smile and bright-blue eyes that sparkled with laughter. Though she tried to deny it, she had been fantasizing about the same woman for two years now, long before she'd known her name, long before she'd shared that heated moment in her kitchen when Charlotte touched her cheek.

Marin felt the warmth of Charlotte's fingers as though they were still there. She ached to feel those fingers elsewhere on her body, and she knew she shouldn't fantasize about Charlotte now, but no matter how hard she tried to replace the images in her mind, to picture Laura or perhaps a hot actress instead, it was no use.

Maybe she needed to indulge in the fantasy to help herself get over it, to get Charlotte out of her system once and for all. *Been there, done that,* at least in her mind. She was getting close again. Her clit ached fiercely. Her hips pushed against her hand. Her brain chanted an internal chorus of *please please please* . . .

She replayed the moment when Charlotte had cupped her cheek, but in her fantasy, Charlotte used that hand to draw her in and kiss her. Marin imagined Charlotte's mouth ravaging hers as her hand slid down to the front of Marin's pants, then pushed inside. Charlotte's fingers against her clit, stroking as she took Marin right there in the kitchen.

Marin swallowed a moan as she rolled to her side, grinding her hips against her hand, vaguely aware that her skin was covered in a fine sheen of sweat and she was breathing heavily. Her eyes were closed, lips pressed together to keep herself quiet so as not to wake the puppy. She lingered in that in-between place, so close to coming she was practically there, body tense and shaking, frantic and loving every moment.

She gasped, hips bucking as everything inside her clenched. Almost . . . so close . . . so fucking close. Marin rolled to her stomach, grinding herself against her fingers. Panting. *Desperate.* The tension inside her reached its breaking point, and *oh* this was going to be a good one. She felt the beginnings of a massive orgasm building in her core, hot and tingly. A low groan escaped her throat.

Banging. Something was banging.

Marin froze. From the crate, Ember rustled and whined.

"Marin?" Charlotte's voice called from the direction of the door.

Fuck. Marin was face down in bed, one hand between her legs, sweaty and breathless and moments from coming. And Charlotte was at the door . . .

"Marin?"

Charlotte's voice was an echo of Marin's fantasy, and it shot straight to her core. Her hand jerked almost involuntarily, pressing hard against her clit, and for a moment, she was in ecstasy. A blinding flash of pleasure. Of release. Of pure bliss. *Charlotte . . .*

It was over before she could process it because she'd lurched to her feet, heart pounding for an entirely different reason. *Charlotte was at the door.*

"Just a minute," she called, hoping she sounded normal and not like she'd just been interrupted while she came. Her core tingled with the aftershocks of that tiny but mighty orgasm. *God.*

She blew out a shaky breath as she reached for the towel she'd discarded earlier, using it to clean herself up. Then she dashed to the bathroom to wash her hands before sliding them through her hair, which was standing out in all directions. Her cheeks were flushed, her eyes bright. She looked like she'd just been . . .

No time to think about it. She scrambled into the sweatpants and hoodie she'd worn to take Ember out, then rushed to the door. She yanked it open, realizing as she locked eyes with Charlotte that Marin wasn't wearing a bra or underwear. Charlotte's tongue darted out to wet her lips, and Marin's clit throbbed as fiercely as if she hadn't come at all.

"Hi," Charlotte said. "I just came from a showing near here, and I decided to grab coffees and stop by to see how you were feeling after yesterday's adventures, but . . ." A slight furrow appeared between her brows.

Marin concentrated on steadying her breathing. "I love the way you think. Sorry it took me a minute to get the door. I was just getting out of the shower when you knocked."

Charlotte's wide eyes suggested Marin was a terrible liar.

CHAPTER TWELVE

Charlotte stepped into Marin's apartment and looked around. "Where's Ember?"

"In her crate. Let me get her." Marin turned and walked into her bedroom, leaving Charlotte standing inside the front door, heart racing. She wasn't sure why she was here. Yes, she'd wanted to make sure Marin was okay. Marin had been in obvious physical pain when Charlotte left last night, so it was only reasonable to check in.

But that didn't explain why Charlotte had gone home last night and spent the rest of the evening thinking about Marin, about the way she'd looked when she got home from her date, about the light in her eyes when she'd told Charlotte that Laura kissed her. It didn't explain why Charlotte had woken up feeling like she'd dreamed about Marin, or why Charlotte's heart had nearly burst out of her chest when Marin opened the door just now.

The look on Marin's face . . .

Charlotte didn't know how to define it, only that it had caused her body to react instantly and uncontrollably, stomach sparking, cheeks blazing with heat. She was so confused about what she was feeling, which meant she should probably keep her distance, and yet she craved Marin's presence every time they were apart.

So, here she was. She walked to the kitchen table and set down the coffee cups and brown paper bag she'd brought with her, just as a black puppy burst into the kitchen, tail wagging in a happy swirl. "Hi, Ember."

"Can you watch her for a minute while I get dressed?" Marin asked, sounding vaguely embarrassed. She gestured to the hoodie and sweatpants she wore. "I tossed on the first thing I could find when you knocked, but . . ."

Suddenly, Charlotte was aware that she could see the hard points of Marin's nipples beneath the fabric. Marin wasn't wearing a bra. Charlotte swallowed as her cheeks grew even warmer. "Sure. I've got her. Does she need to go out?"

"She might, but she can wait for me. I'll be right back." The bedroom door closed with a click.

Charlotte stared at that door for a moment, alarmed to realize she was thinking about Marin getting dressed on the other side of it, picturing Marin as she lifted that sweatshirt over her head, baring her breasts, and . . . *stop it.* Charlotte blinked the image away, then spun to look for Ember. Marin had said the puppy could wait, but taking her out now would give Charlotte something to do and hopefully help clear her head. Plus, she still had her coat on.

"Come on, puppy." She clipped the little pink collar around Ember's neck and guided her out the door. Ember wandered around the yard, then led Charlotte toward the sidewalk that ran along the street. Charlotte followed her down the block until she'd taken care of business, and then they walked back to the apartment together.

Marin was standing in the kitchen when they returned, wearing dark-gray jeans and a rose-colored top, her hair neatly brushed but still damp around her face. She looked calmer now. There'd been something about her when Charlotte first showed up, an energy that made Charlotte blush. She *still* felt flustered just thinking about it.

"Thank you for walking her . . . and for bringing goodies." Marin smiled at her. She had the *best* smile. It brightened her whole face and made her eyes sparkle, filling Charlotte with joy every time she was on the receiving end of it.

"I could tell you were in pain last night," Charlotte said. "I wanted to make sure you were okay. Plus, I just wanted to see you."

"Thank you. Yeah, last night was a rough one, pain-wise, but this girl . . ." Marin gestured toward Ember, who ran over to press her head into Marin's hand. "She lay beside me in bed all night. It was such a comfort. I don't know how she knew, but . . ."

"Animals can be really intuitive about things like that. What a sweet girl you are, Ember."

The puppy wagged her tail, then bounded across the kitchen to grab her stuffed dragon.

"I'm lucky to have her." Marin gave the puppy an adoring look, then turned her gaze to the kitchen table. "And you. I had oatmeal earlier, but this looks way better."

"Betty's Bakery has the best lattes in town, I swear." Charlotte sat at the table. "And the coffee cake muffins looked irresistible, so I got two of those too."

"Yum." Marin sat across from her, and for a moment, they just stared at each other.

It seemed to Charlotte that these moments kept happening, these little pauses when their eyes caught or their hands bumped, and Charlotte's heart would race. She'd get flustered and not know what to do with her body. She knew this feeling with a man, but with a woman?

It was foreign and confusing, and Marin was her *friend*. Marin was dating Laura now anyway. Yesterday, Laura had kissed her, for crying out loud. On the cheek, but still. This wasn't the time for Charlotte to question her sexuality, and Marin was absolutely not the woman she should be having these kinds of feelings for.

Charlotte wouldn't let anything ruin their friendship. Marin thought Charlotte was straight, and that was for the best. For all she knew, she *was* straight. She and Marin had been through an incredibly intense situation together the morning they met. She'd held Marin's hand and watched her heart stop. She'd thought she watched Marin *die*. Maybe Charlotte was confusing that connection for something more than it was.

Deep down, she knew that was a flimsy excuse, but whatever. Marin was dating someone, which meant Charlotte couldn't act on her feelings anyway. So, Charlotte's sexuality was irrelevant right now. And anyway, she didn't want to date *anyone*, not a man, woman, or anyone else, until she'd accomplished the things she'd come to Vermont to do.

"Awfully quiet," Marin observed as she reached into the bag and pulled out the two muffins, then placed one in front of Charlotte.

"Sorry. Got lost in my thoughts for a minute." Charlotte reached for her latte and took a big sip, grateful it had cooled enough that she didn't burn her tongue.

Marin picked up her own latte. "That's a measure of getting to know someone, isn't it? When you feel comfortable zoning out in front of them."

"Yes," Charlotte agreed. "That is nice. So are you feeling better today?"

"The nerve pain is gone. I still have some sore muscles, but those are from snowshoeing, which was fun, so they're totally worth it."

"Good."

"Laura and I are having dinner together on Thursday." Marin was beaming now.

Charlotte forced herself not to flinch. "Really? Wow. That's a big step."

"It is." Marin broke off a piece of muffin and popped it in her mouth, making the sexiest little moan as she chewed. "God, that's good. We're going to this place called Erin's that's apparently very casual and dog friendly, so I can bring Ember with me."

"Erin's isn't the most romantic place, but bringing Ember along is a plus." Charlotte tried to inject some enthusiasm into her tone. "You know I'm always happy to watch her for you too."

"I know, and I appreciate it." Marin's expression had gotten . . . "Dreamy" was the best word Charlotte could think of to describe it, and now she felt sick. "Laura suggested Erin's, and it was so thoughtful of her to accommodate my puppy. I really like her."

"That's amazing." Charlotte picked at her muffin. "I'm so happy for you. I can't wait to hear all about your second date."

"Second date. I like the sound of that." Marin grinned as she took another bite of her muffin. "Things are starting to feel real now. Next weekend, I'm driving out to visit my brother Jed." Her expression dimmed, worry wrinkling her brow. "I decided I'll come out to him first."

"Yeah? That's a huge step. How are you feeling about it?"

"Honestly? Terrified," Marin admitted, "but there's a reason I'm starting with Jed. He's pretty laid back. I think he'll be supportive."

"Good. Where does he live?"

"Saratoga Springs. It's about an hour and a half from here, so it'll be a day trip for me."

"Is Ember going with you?"

"I think so," Marin said. "I'll double-check with Jed first, but I don't think he'll mind. If he does, I'll see if Ji-Yoon can watch her. I know you're busy on Saturdays."

"I am," Charlotte admitted ruefully. "Working nights and weekends is the biggest downside of my job."

"Well, I'm awfully grateful for your job, or else we might never have reconnected." Marin reached out and gripped Charlotte's hand, and the look they exchanged was so intense, surely it was imprinted on Charlotte's soul.

It was also too much, with her newly realized feelings. Charlotte pulled away somewhat awkwardly. "I'm glad for that too." She searched desperately for a subject change to lighten the mood. "Um, I haven't checked my horoscope yet today. Want me to read yours too?"

Marin's lips quirked. "I thought you weren't reading those as often these days?"

"I wasn't, but lately I've started keeping up with them again." Charlotte shrugged. "I'm starting to feel curious about what the universe has in store for me . . . thanks to you."

"So you're married?" Charlotte gestured awkwardly toward Elena's left hand, where a gold band rested. They'd met for lunch at a little café near the university, and Charlotte was unreasonably anxious about attempting to reconnect with her former best friend. "Tell me about him. Anyone I know?"

Elena shook her head. "We met through a dating app, of all things. His name's Carlos, and you can just imagine how thrilled my mom is that I did indeed find a nice Puerto Rican man to marry, even living all the way up here in Vermont."

"Oh, I can imagine," Charlotte said with a laugh. She'd spent countless hours at Elena's house in high school, enough that Elena's parents felt like an extension of her own family. She'd learned to make mofongo and pasteles in their kitchen, and yes, she'd heard Elena's mom carry on about wanting her to marry a Puerto Rican, despite living in a state without a large Hispanic population.

Elena rolled her eyes playfully. "Right, so she *adores* him, but obviously, I do too. We have two daughters, Emily and Sophia." She held up her phone to show Charlotte the lock screen photo she'd glimpsed last time.

"Wow, they look so much like you. That's great. I'm really happy for you." It was the truth, but she also felt a heavy sense of regret for all the time they'd lost.

"Thanks," Elena said. "What about you? Husband? Kids?"

She shook her head. "None of the above, surprisingly enough. I definitely thought I'd be married by now, but it just never quite worked out for me."

"Yet." Elena raised her eyebrows for emphasis. "We're still young. You might find the man of your dreams any day now."

Marin's face flitted through her mind, and Charlotte wondered if she was looking for a man at all. "Maybe."

"Forgive me if I'm bringing up a painful subject, but did you ever find out what happened to your mom?" Elena asked.

Charlotte reached for her soda and took a long drink. "No, but that's part of the reason I'm here. I'm determined to get answers."

"Good for you," Elena said. "I hope you do. I figured if there was ever a break in her case, I'd have heard about it, but I always wondered if she reached out after you and I lost touch, you know, if she'd just started over somewhere."

Charlotte's stomach clenched. "No, she never got in touch. It's hard to think she could be out there, living her life without me."

"Amnesia?" Elena suggested. "I know that doesn't happen as often in real life as it does in the movies, but it *does* happen. She could have had an accident, a brain injury . . . who knows."

These were the scenarios that kept Charlotte up at night. She'd never truly have peace until she had answers. "If she got hurt, she never sought help. My dad hired two PIs who spent years looking through all the Jane Does out there, living and dead. She wasn't one of them." Charlotte paused. "You don't happen to know Bev Sinclair, do you? She and my mom were close, but I can't track her down. I feel like if anyone knew what happened, it would be her."

"I don't, but I know a lot of people in town, and my mami knows even more. I'll ask around for you. Surely someone knows Bev."

"I would really appreciate that," Charlotte told her, surprised to feel tears pressing at her eyes. "I'll owe you one if you can track her down for me. And on that note, I owe you an apology for how I acted senior year. I was a terrible friend, and sitting here with you now, hearing about your husband and kids, it's really hitting me that I lost twenty years of knowing you. I don't think I can ever truly tell you how sorry I am."

"Listen." Elena put down her sandwich, her expression serious. "I certainly cursed you out plenty back then. I hated you with the fiery passion of a teenager scorned, but in hindsight, we were both so freaking immature about the whole thing. Honestly, did we really throw our entire friendship away because I got a date to the prom after promising to go with you?"

"It sounds so stupid now, but it felt like the end of the world then." Charlotte sighed. "I was so hurt, which is just silly. I mean, that much angst over the prom?"

"And it was so bad! I didn't even have fun," Elena exclaimed. "Marcus was a tool. I ended up wishing I'd blown him off and gone with you like we'd planned. Of course, by then we weren't speaking, so I couldn't tell you that."

"Teenagers are clueless," Charlotte said. "I hate that I never tried to look you up later on, once I'd grown up enough to realize how stupid I'd been."

"Same, girl. *Same.* We're both just as guilty on that front."

"So are you a teacher?" Charlotte asked. For as long as they'd known each other, Elena had wanted to teach elementary school. She'd had her career path all mapped out, while Charlotte hadn't had a clue what she wanted to do. She'd stumbled into realty, and it stuck.

Elena grinned. "Nope. I took an introductory psych class freshman year of college and realized I'd found my actual calling. I'm a child psychologist now, and I absolutely love it."

Charlotte blinked. "Wow. That's . . . different."

"Does anyone really know who they are in high school?" Elena shrugged. "What about you? What are you doing these days?"

"I'm a Realtor," Charlotte told her.

Elena snapped her fingers. "I can totally see it. You've always been great with people, and you have impeccable taste."

"Thanks." Charlotte studied the woman sitting across from her. Elena was as vivacious as ever, but she'd matured from the teenager Charlotte used to know. Now Elena oozed competence with an undercurrent of compassion, and yeah, Charlotte could see her as a child psychologist. In fact, she wished she'd had someone like Elena when she lost her mom. Her dad had never mentioned therapy, so Charlotte was left to deal with her feelings alone.

When Charlotte left the café two hours later—with plans to see Elena again next week—she felt light on her feet. She was *so* grateful to have reconnected with Elena. Maybe they'd become good friends again. Charlotte hoped so.

It was just past one on Monday afternoon, and she was right down the street from the campus. Maybe it was the sense of nostalgia brought on by her lunch with Elena, but she felt suddenly drawn toward the place she'd spent so much of her life avoiding. Other than her visit with Allan Svenson last month, Charlotte hadn't set foot on the Northshire University campus since shortly after her mother's disappearance, and now that felt like an oversight.

Charlotte needed to visit her mom's old building to see if anyone there still remembered her. Maybe someone at NU could help her uncover a new avenue to pursue, because Charlotte was dangerously close to running out of leads.

Decision made, she unlocked her car and got in. She put on her favorite upbeat playlist and turned the music up loud as she drove to the university. To refamiliarize herself with its layout, she turned onto the road that ran around the campus perimeter.

As she drove, she took in the stately brick buildings she remembered. There were also quite a few new, modern-looking additions, some of which seemed to be academic halls, some dorms. The university had evolved, just like Elena had. After looping the campus, Charlotte parked in the visitor's lot and started walking.

She'd visit Wallis Hall first, where her mom had taught. When she was here last month, Charlotte had been completely focused on

Allan Svenson. This time, she would go inside with her mom in mind. Hopefully something or someone there would give her a new lead.

Two young women passed her, walking in the other direction, laughing as they looked at their phones, and something about the closeness between them reminded Charlotte of her and Elena at that age. How different might Charlotte's life have been if she'd attended NU with Elena the way they'd always planned?

"Charlotte?"

Her stomach pinged with that all-too-familiar fizzing sensation before her brain even recognized Marin's voice. Charlotte spun to face her with an almost embarrassing amount of enthusiasm. "Marin, hi!"

Marin's brow wrinkled. "Are you looking for me? What are you doing on campus?"

"I . . ." Charlotte gave her head a quick shake, trying to clear her muddled thoughts. "I had lunch with Elena near here, and then I decided to stop by the campus, maybe wander around my mom's old building and see if anything new shakes loose. It sounds silly, I know, but . . ."

Marin's expression softened. "That's not silly. It's a good idea to talk to people who knew your mom, and there are certainly people in her department who've worked here that long."

"That's exactly what I'm hoping." But now she was distracted by looking at Marin.

A slate-gray pencil skirt peeked out from below Marin's maroon wool peacoat. Her hair was pulled back, emphasizing her cheekbones and the graceful slope of her neck, and goddamn she looked good in her professional attire. Like, ridiculously hot.

"I'm off to my introductory statistics class," Marin was saying as Charlotte spiraled about how hot she was. *Get a grip, Charlotte. Seriously.* "Feel free to stop by and observe after you're finished poking around campus, if you like." A smile flitted across Marin's gorgeous face. "You can let me know if I'm a boring teacher or a fun one."

"I'm sure your students find you fascinating." Charlotte certainly did. "I won't be interrupting if I come in halfway through your class?"

"Not at all. I'd love for you to come. Ziegler Hall, room 311."

"Okay then." Charlotte hoped she didn't look as smitten as she felt. "I'll stop by in half an hour or so."

"See you then." With a wave, Marin walked away.

Charlotte glanced over her shoulder, hoping for a glimpse of Marin's ass in that skirt, but it was hidden by the peacoat. Not straight, indeed. Charlotte's body was sending some pretty serious signals on that subject. She shook herself out of her Marin-induced stupor and kept walking toward Wallis Hall.

It looked the same as it did in her memories, a stately but somewhat dated brick building. Charlotte entered the hall, breathing in its musty scent, like old books and dust. God, it even smelled the same. A directory on the wall nearby caught her attention, and she crossed to it, hoping she would recognize a few names, people her mom might have introduced her to.

But none of the names looked familiar. Not a single one . . . aside from Allan Svenson, of course. The department chair was a woman named Karen Canterbury. Maybe she'd been here awhile? Charlotte took a photo of the faculty directory so she could do some internet sleuthing later and see who had been teaching here thirty years or more. There probably weren't many. She'd gather a list and contact them all to see if anyone remembered her mom.

It was a long shot, but if she took enough of those, hopefully one of them would yield answers. After all, she'd already uncovered her mother's affair and learned about the missing duffel bag. Who knew what else she would learn? Even if it took the rest of her life, she wouldn't stop searching until she'd found out what happened. She couldn't keep living in the shadow of her mom's disappearance.

Charlotte was sick and tired of feeling adrift, of *searching*. One way or another, she had to know the truth. Maybe then she could finally find where she belonged and settle down. She wandered through

Wallis Hall, feeling a slight pinch as she passed what had been her mother's office. It belonged to a professor named Kristina Liang now.

"Can I help you?"

Charlotte was startled to realize she'd been lingering in the doorway to this woman's office, and now Professor Liang was watching her. "I, um, this used to be my mom's office. She . . . we lost her about thirty years ago."

The professor's expression turned sympathetic, although Charlotte couldn't tell whether she knew who Charlotte's mom was. Certainly, she was too young to have been teaching here then. "Would you like to come in and have a look?"

Charlotte's feet made the decision for her, carrying her over the threshold. "Thank you."

"Of course. I've only been here a few years, but I've heard about Dr. Danton's legacy. I assume she was your mom?"

"She was." Charlotte swallowed over the lump in her throat. She hated talking about her mom in the past tense, even if present didn't feel quite right either. Being stuck in limbo like this was hellish. And being in her mom's old office was . . . hard. The weathered desk looked to be the same one that had been here then.

Curious, Charlotte stepped forward, checking the corner by the wall, and *god*, there was her name scratched into the finish. She'd done that one afternoon when she was bored, then spent months waiting for her mom to notice and fuss at her for it, but she never had.

Charlotte was surprised to realize she was smiling. Maybe not all her memories of this place were bad ones. "Thank you," she told Professor Liang before she went back into the hall.

She walked through the rest of the building and spoke to a few more people, but no one here this afternoon had known her mom. Once her curiosity was satisfied, she left Wallis and crossed the quad, looking for Ziegler Hall. Charlotte didn't think she'd ever been inside the mathematics building before. She asked a student for directions, and soon she was walking up the wide front steps of one of the newer buildings on campus.

Inside, she went upstairs and found room 311. There was a small window in the door, through which she could see Marin at the front of the room, looking professional as hell as she taught her students. Charlotte slipped through the door and took an empty seat in the back row. It was a small classroom, though, and Marin looked right at her, flashing a warm smile that set Charlotte's heart racing all over again.

"As we dig deeper into the relationship between causation and correlation, let's look at a real-world example. A recent study found a correlation between the number of hours a student spends on social media and their academic grades." She clicked a button on her laptop, and a graph appeared on the screen beside her.

"But does spending more time online distract students from their studies, resulting in lower grades, or do students who are already struggling academically turn to social media as a form of escape? This is where causation comes into play, and it's crucial when analyzing data not to jump to conclusions." Marin looked so confident up there, so natural and in command. Her entire demeanor was different from that of the casual woman Charlotte had known. She sounded smart, competent. Who knew statistics could be sexy?

"Confirmation bias can cause you to interpret the results in a way that reinforces your existing beliefs. In my previous example, it would be all too easy for parents to see those results and conclude that they need to limit their child's time on social media to improve their grades rather than looking deeper at the underlying reasons that the student is struggling.

"Now consider a different scenario." She stared right at Charlotte, then winked. "How many of you read your horoscope at least once a week?"

Charlotte raised her hand. Probably a third of the class also had a hand in the air.

"Who wants to tell me how confirmation bias could affect how you interpret the contents of your horoscope?" Marin swept her gaze around the room, nodding at a young woman in the front row.

"We're more likely to notice the parts of the horoscope that apply to us and disregard the rest," she said.

"Exactly." Marin gave her an approving look. Meanwhile, Charlotte's stomach had tightened because she wasn't sure where Marin was going with this. Was she taking a dig at the way they'd met?

"Aww, come on, Professor E. Don't hate on horoscopes," another student called out, voicing Charlotte's concern.

Marin chuckled. "I'm not hating on them. In fact, if I've learned anything over the last few years, it's this: Not everything can be explained by statistical models, even when you account for the margin of error. Sometimes, you have to trust your instincts and believe in the unbelievable."

CHAPTER THIRTEEN

Marin came to the campus on Tuesday afternoons for office hours. Her schedule this semester was sporadic and poorly spaced, but she hoped to plan things better next year, and in the meantime, it did allow her to be home more often with Ember.

Footsteps approached Marin's office, and she looked up in anticipation, but the student kept walking right past her door. So far, not many students had come to see her during office hours, which was disappointing. It gave her mind too much time to wander, and her thoughts were a dangerous place these days. If she wasn't obsessing about Charlotte, she was spiraling about her upcoming date with Laura.

She spent a half hour responding to emails before a hesitant knock made her look up from her laptop. Brianna from the Pride Coalition stood in the doorway, which was a surprise, but Marin made sure that didn't show on her face. While office hours were primarily for students from her classes, she'd extended an open invitation to the members of the Pride Coalition.

Since that first meeting, Marin had been making an extra effort with Brianna, often saying hi after meetings. The girl never said much, but Marin kept trying. Her gut said Brianna needed someone to talk to, and now it seemed her gut had been correct.

"Brianna," she said with a smile. "It's nice to see you."

Brianna shifted uncomfortably in the doorway. "Hi, Professor Easterly. I hope it's okay that I'm here?"

"Of course. Come on in and have a seat. Close the door if you'd like, totally up to you." Usually Marin preferred to keep it open, but it seemed prudent to offer Brianna the option of privacy if she'd come to discuss something personal.

Brianna closed the door, then stood there, twisting her hands in front of herself. She looked like she might bolt at the slightest provocation.

"Can you believe we're expecting more snow tomorrow?" Marin said, hoping to help put her at ease with a neutral topic. "I don't know about you, but I'm ready for spring."

"Yeah. I, um, I like skiing, but I'm ready for warm weather. Vermont winters can get really long." Brianna came forward hesitantly and sat in one of the guest chairs.

"Did you grow up here?"

"No, I'm from Connecticut. We get snow there, too, but not as much as Vermont."

"I'm from Manhattan," Marin said. "It's the same there . . . plenty of snow, but not nearly as much as we get here."

Brianna looked down at her lap. She was shaking, Marin noticed, and her stomach tightened in anticipation of whatever the girl was here to tell her.

"Take your time," Marin told her gently. "Whatever's on your mind, I promise to be a judgment-free listener, and I'll do my best to help."

"You mentioned that you'd come out recently?" Brianna looked up at her with wide, fearful eyes. "I was wondering if you have any advice? Because I . . . I need to do that. I need to tell my parents I'm gay, and I'm so scared."

Marin inhaled. Oh wow. This was a big deal. She hadn't anticipated providing this kind of guidance quite so soon. "It's a big step. To be honest, I'm still in the process of coming out to my family." Marin wasn't sure how much to share with a student, but Brianna still seemed skittish. More than that, she looked *terrified*, so maybe a little honesty from Marin would help. "I'm planning to come out to my brother this weekend, and I'm scared too."

Brianna leaned forward in her seat. "Really?"

"I imagine coming out is always scary," Marin said. "Do you have any idea how your parents will react?"

"I think they'll be upset." Brianna's voice lowered almost to a whisper, and her shoulders slumped as she seemed to fold inward.

"I'm sorry." Marin's heart went out to this vulnerable young woman who might be about to lose the love and support of her parents.

Brianna made a quiet sound of distress. "I'm really dreading it."

"That's very understandable, but remember, there's no rush. You should do this on your own terms and in your own time."

Brianna's hands clenched into fists in her lap. "It seems like everyone else at the Pride Coalition is already out. They're all so . . . authentic, you know? So sure of who they are. They aren't afraid."

"Oh goodness." Marin shook her head. "I guarantee you some of them are just as scared as you are. The Pride Coalition is a safe place, right? Just because you see people feeling comfortable with themselves in those meetings doesn't mean that's how they act all the time."

Brianna's brow furrowed. "But . . ."

"Is someone pressuring you to come out before you're ready?"

"No." She frowned. "Well, I did hear someone at a meeting say that you're living fraudulently until you're out as your authentic self."

Marin straightened in her chair. "That's just not true. No one can decide when the right time is except you, and it's important to keep your mental and physical well-being in mind as you make that decision. Would coming out now endanger you when you return to your parents' house this summer? Might your parents stop paying your college tuition? On the flip side, do you feel like it's having a negative effect on your mental health *not* coming out to them?"

Brianna stared into space for a few seconds. "I don't think I'd be unsafe, but they'll probably be upset. They might try to convince me to leave this school, if they think it's putting radical ideas in my head, but they aren't paying my tuition. I've got loans, so they can't make me leave. I'm eighteen. They can't *make* me do anything." Her jaw clenched.

Marin drew in a quiet breath. She desperately hoped she was giving good advice. Being so newly out herself, she felt a bit out of her depth here, but she wanted to help Brianna so badly. If nothing else, she understood Brianna's fear on a soul-deep level. She also knew better than most how beneficial it could be to wait.

"I guess my next question is," Marin said, "Do you see a benefit to telling your parents now versus waiting until after you've graduated and are living on your own? That way, you'd be less dependent on them in case it doesn't go well. And remember, I'm not judging either way. I'm just trying to help you consider your options."

"I don't know. Telling them might make me feel better at first, but it might end up being worse if they react badly. I just . . ." Tears ran down her cheeks, and her bottom lip shook. "I *do* feel like a fraud sometimes. I go to the Pride Coalition meetings, but otherwise, I hide in the closet. I'm not out to *anyone*, except you, I guess. I play it safe. I'm straight passing, you know? I'm not as brave as those students who walk around campus being visibly queer."

"I'm honored you felt comfortable coming out to me, but I have to disagree with you about one thing, Brianna. You *are* brave. Choosing to make the right decision for yourself is honestly the bravest thing you can do. It's better than letting someone you barely know convince you that you need to come out before you're ready."

Brianna shook her head, more tears falling. "It doesn't feel brave."

"Trust me, it is," Marin said firmly. "I recently came out to a friend for the first time, and it was a big deal. A *huge* deal."

"Was she supportive?" Brianna asked hesitantly.

"Yes, she was, and it made me so glad I'd waited for the right time and the right person."

"I . . . I think my best friend would be supportive too."

"Maybe that's a good first step for you," Marin suggested. "Maybe start by telling your friend, if you think they would be supportive and if that feels right to you."

Brianna sat up straighter, hope blooming on her face for the first time since she'd entered Marin's office. "Yeah, I think she would be. Maybe . . . maybe I'll tell her first."

"That sounds like a good option," Marin told her with an encouraging smile. "But remember, not telling anyone is perfectly valid too. I waited a very long time before I came out to anyone. That was the right decision for me, and I don't regret it. The only one who can make your decision is *you*. Got it?"

"Yeah." Brianna wiped the tears from her face, looking calmer now. "Thanks. I wasn't sure whether to come or not. I know you said we could stop by your office for advice, but . . ."

"I meant it, and I'm really glad you stopped by."

"I'm glad too," Brianna said quietly. "This really helped. I had convinced myself that if I didn't come out to my parents right now, I was being inauthentic and a coward, but what you said makes a lot of sense."

"I'm glad. Come back and see me again, okay? My door is always open. You might also consider visiting the campus counseling center. Regular counseling can be a big help with working through something like this."

"I'll think about it. Thanks." Brianna stood, gave Marin a shy wave, and left her office, looking more confident than she had when she entered it.

Marin watched her go, feeling cautiously proud of herself. This was one of the reasons she'd wanted to become a professor. She wanted to help guide young people, and while she'd envisioned helping them with statistics, in the long run, guidance on coming out might be even more important.

As the baby of her family and then someone who'd been in the closet for so long, Marin hadn't had many opportunities in her life to give advice or be a mentor. It felt good. *Really* good. Hopefully, she'd have more opportunities like this here at NU.

Marin was a big believer in doing things at your own pace, and while she couldn't regret the long and winding journey that had led her to Vermont, right now, it felt like an *eternity* to wait two more days until her date with Charlotte.

Marin's mind stuttered. *Laura.* Two more days until her date with Laura.

"I have a question for you." Laura regarded Marin over her nearly empty beer mug, brown eyes sparkling. "A really important one, so answer wisely."

"Okay." Marin felt a flutter inside her rib cage, anticipation or dread, she wasn't sure, because while she liked Laura as a friend, the more time she spent with her, the more Marin couldn't help feeling like the romantic element was lacking. And . . . okay, she was definitely dreading Laura's question.

"Do you want dessert?" Laura asked dramatically. "And more specifically, do you want to split the brownie sundae with me? Because it's *amazing* here, but it's way too big for one person."

Marin laughed as the knot of anxiety in her belly loosened. "Yes, I'd like that."

"Awesome. I think they do a pup cup too." Laura leaned down to rub Ember where she lay beneath the table, chewing on the Kong toy Marin had brought for her.

"She's been a very good girl tonight," Marin agreed. "She deserves a pup cup."

"Yes, she does. I'll be right back." Laura stood, grabbing her purse.

"Oh, but you got dinner too . . ."

Laura held up a hand. "You can pay next time."

"Okay," Marin acquiesced. Next time. That should make her happy. Thrilled, even. Laura was fun to spend time with and patient with the puppy. Marin had enjoyed dinner. But when it came to kissing . . .

Marin could only think about kissing Charlotte, which was ridiculous. Anger rose inside her because she was *furious* with herself for ruining this. She had this wonderful woman here with her. Laura was everything she wanted in a partner, except . . . she wasn't Charlotte.

Ugh.

Marin had already waited forty-seven years. She couldn't waste any more time, sitting home and pining after her straight friend. She had to find a way forward that would let her keep Charlotte as a friend but also have the passion she craved with someone else. Maybe that meant pushing ahead with Laura. She'd enjoyed the kiss on the cheek last weekend, after all.

So Marin smiled eagerly as Laura returned with a large brownie sundae for them to share and the pup cup for Ember. She joked and flirted as she ate. The ice cream was delicious, and Marin's mood had rebounded by the time they walked outside. Ember whined, tugging Marin toward a nearby snowbank.

"I think she needs to potty. Be right back," Marin said apologetically before hustling the puppy to the edge of the parking lot to take care of business.

When she returned, she found Laura leaning against the side of Marin's Outback, a relaxed smile on her face. "I had fun tonight."

"I did too," Marin told her.

"Dinner again soon? Or maybe more adventuring? Maybe both? I don't know about you, but I'm having a really good time." Laura stepped forward, taking Marin's hand in hers.

Marin's body went warm, and her stomach tingled. See? She could feel something for Laura as long as she was careful to keep Charlotte out of her head. She shivered involuntarily as images of Charlotte swamped her mind, making Marin's heart pound for all the wrong reasons.

For fuck's sake.

She was hopeless. But also . . . hopeful. She'd lived on hope for so long, and now it was time to act. She took a small step toward Laura, who gave her an encouraging smile. Laura rested her hand on Marin's waist, and that felt so nice, so different from how Andrew's hand had felt there. Marin leaned forward so their bodies were right up against each other.

This is it.

She was about to have her first kiss with a woman. Her heart was beating out of control, her pulse thudding frantically in her ears. She didn't realize she'd closed her eyes until she felt the gentle press of Laura's lips on hers. Marin's eyes popped open as she took a step back, stumbling over Ember's leash. *Wait . . .*

Her body flooded with a combination of adrenaline and embarrassment, because she'd stepped backward before Laura could do more than brush her lips against Marin's. Technically, they'd kissed, and it hadn't been bad.

Hadn't been bad?

That was the best thing Marin could say about her first sapphic kiss? She'd been fighting so damn hard to keep Charlotte's face out of her mind, she'd barely registered anything about Laura's kiss at all. *Fuck.*

"That was nice," Laura said, but she looked vaguely confused, as if she'd realized Marin hadn't enjoyed it as much as she should have.

"It was." Marin forced a smile. "I'll text you?" She scooped Ember into her arms, vaguely aware she was using the puppy as a barrier between them.

"Definitely do. Good night, Marin . . . and Ember." Laura ruffled the puppy's head, then leaned in to press another quick kiss to Marin's cheek before getting into her car.

Marin's head was swimming, and her emotions were in chaos. She unlocked her own car and tucked Ember into her crate on the back seat. As she started the drive home, tears gathered in her eyes because the more she thought about it, the more she wondered if she was leading Laura on. Laura seemed genuinely interested in her, while Marin was so hung up on Charlotte, she couldn't even think straight.

Back at her apartment, Marin changed into her hoodie and flannel pants, still fighting tears. What was she going to do? How long would it take to get over Charlotte? Marin was finally dating, and she couldn't even enjoy it because she'd fallen for the wrong woman.

A tear broke free as she sat on the couch. Ember leaped onto her lap and licked it from her face. "I'm so glad I have you," she whispered to the puppy. Sometimes lately, it felt like Ember was the only thing in her life that made any sense.

Her phone pinged with an incoming text, and Marin tensed, unsure if she wanted it to be from Laura or Charlotte. She probably shouldn't talk to either of them right now, not while she was this upset. She reached for her phone with a sigh.

Charlotte Danton: How was your date? Hope it was GREAT & need all the details!!

Marin had no idea how to respond. The date itself had gone well. The kiss? Well, the more Marin thought about it, the more that kiss slammed home the reality that she didn't have chemistry with Laura. She felt more attraction for Charlotte than she did for the woman she was dating. Which meant . . . what?

More tears fell as she stared at Charlotte's text. Charlotte was such a good friend. She'd consistently been so supportive of Marin's dating endeavors, and it really meant the world. Marin dug deep for the right words to reply with, because she needed to sound enthusiastic enough to keep Charlotte from asking questions Marin had no answers for.

Me: Really nice! Even Ember had fun.

Charlotte Danton: Squeeeeeeee!!!

Charlotte Danton: Was there more kissing?!?!

Me: Yes

Charlotte Danton: OMG

Charlotte Danton: I want to know everything!

Me: Yes but not tonight. I'm exhausted.

Charlotte Danton: Hang out soon?

Charlotte Danton: I've got showings all day tmrw & most of Sat too unfortunately

Me: I'm driving out to see Jed on Sat anyway

Charlotte Danton: Oh right! Maybe Sat evening after you get back?

Me: That should work

Charlotte Danton: Ok putting it on my calendar

Charlotte Danton: I'll bring wine, make it a girls' night

Me: Sounds perfect

That was the truth, unfortunately. She enjoyed every moment spent with Charlotte so much more than she enjoyed her time with Laura or anyone else. Marin would wait to officially make the decision when her emotions weren't so raw, but deep down she knew the truth.

She would have to end things with Laura.

CHAPTER FOURTEEN

"We need to do this more often." Jed smiled as he settled in the chair across from Marin. They were seated in his kitchen with cups of coffee while Ember napped on a dog bed at Marin's feet, wearing her leash so she didn't get into trouble in Marin's brother's house.

"We really do. Now that I'm in Vermont, it's only an hour and a half drive."

"Let me know once you're settled in your new house and ready for visitors. I'd love to come see it, and you." Jed was the youngest of Marin's siblings at fifty-seven. For that reason, she'd always been closest with him out of all her brothers and sisters. That, and he was one of the most laid-back people in her family.

His dark hair had faded to salt and pepper, and his hairline receded slightly at the temples. Jed had married young, and his two kids were grown now. He and his wife had divorced about ten years ago, which had earned the disapproval of his and Marin's father, who was still alive at the time. Now it felt like something else she and Jed had in common.

"I'd love for you to visit," Marin said. "Maybe this spring, once the weather warms up. I think the views from my new house will be amazing." She showed him a photo of the house on her phone.

"Wow," he said. "That's great scenery."

"Vermont is a beautiful state."

"Glad you're settling in." He gave her what he probably thought was a casual look. "How's it going otherwise? That leg giving you much trouble?"

Of all her siblings, he'd been the most involved after her accident, and she appreciated it immensely. "The nerve pain comes and goes, but I'm doing really well, thanks."

He nodded. "Glad to hear it. Hey, Fran said she saw Andrew in the city last weekend. Did she tell you?"

Marin frowned. "No. Guess she didn't put it in the group chat." Fran was the middle child of the five Easterly kids. She was an investment broker in Manhattan, completely focused on her career. Even when Marin had lived in the city, she'd rarely spent time with Fran.

"She mentioned it when I talked to her a few days ago. Anyway, seems he's engaged to that secretary he started dating after your divorce." Jed gave her a sympathetic look.

"Good for him, I guess." Marin sipped her coffee, surprised to realize she didn't feel much of anything in response to the news.

Jed chuckled. "He didn't waste any time. Meanwhile, you and I are taking it slow, am I right?"

"Well . . ." Her stomach tightened, and she felt acid from the coffee climbing back up her esophagus. This was what she'd come here to tell him, and now the moment had arrived.

"Wait a minute. Are you seeing someone?" He looked pleased at the thought.

"Not exactly, but . . . I'm getting back out there. I set myself up on a dating site, because I do want to find someone new."

"Good for you." Jed reached for his coffee. "I've dated a little bit here and there, but I'm not sure I'll get serious with anyone again. I guess I like having my own space now."

Marin looked down as her stomach twisted and a million excuses flitted through her mind. Then she exhaled, steeling herself. She'd come here to tell him the truth. Jed was a reasonable guy. He'd understand. She needed to just say it.

He was regarding her with interest. "You look like you've got something on your mind, sis. Something more serious than a dating app."

"I do." She exhaled, breathing through the tightness in her chest. "It's important to me to start dating again because I want to date women."

"Well, holy shit." Jed's eyebrows went up. "You're a lesbian?"

She nodded. "I've known for a while, but it took time to find the courage to end things with Andrew."

"I guess it would." He rubbed a hand over his jaw. "You know, I want to say I'm shocked, because I certainly never suspected you were into women, but I don't really feel shocked at all."

"No?" Her shoulders unclenched as the tension left her body. Her gut instinct had been right, and maybe his had, too, since it seemed that somewhere deep down, he'd already known.

"Nah, you never looked happy with Andrew. Maybe this is why. Hope you have better luck with women than I have." He offered a self-deprecating smile.

Marin let out an unexpected laugh. "I hope so too."

It was nearly seven that evening by the time Marin made it back to her apartment. She was exhausted, stiff, and sore from the drive, but happy. Before she left, she'd asked Jed to keep her news to himself until she'd had the chance to tell the rest of her siblings in person. Some things weren't meant for the group chat.

Now she was home. Ember was passed out on the couch, and Marin was . . . restless. When they'd texted on Thursday, Charlotte mentioned stopping by tonight with wine, but Marin hadn't really talked to her since then. She'd ended things with Laura, and she had no idea how to explain the whole thing to Charlotte.

Charlotte had sent several texts over the last few days, but Marin had kept her responses short and avoided making plans, hoping a little space might help her figure out what to do. It wasn't like her to stall, though. She picked up her phone and opened her text thread with Charlotte. Should she ask if Charlotte still wanted to come over tonight?

Marin had plenty of practice hiding her feelings, but she'd never had a close friendship with someone she was so over-the-top attracted to before. It was really testing her self-control. She'd hoped a few days of space would give her clarity, but it hadn't.

She stared at the text box, at a complete loss for what to say. "Hi, I missed you today?" Definitely not. "I came out to my brother, and it went pretty well?" Technically true, but it felt trite to make such an announcement after practically ignoring Charlotte for two days. "Still want to come over?" That felt too forward, and honestly, having Charlotte over tonight might be too much for her to handle. Maybe Marin needed a quiet evening to herself.

Decision made, she stood and walked to the refrigerator to see what she might be able to rustle up for dinner. Ember had already eaten. Puppy food was easy that way. As for Marin? Well, she had bread, and . . . that was about it. Eggs and toast for dinner? It wasn't exciting, but it might have to do.

A knock at the door had her turning in surprise. She wasn't expecting anyone tonight, unless . . .

Her stomach fizzed. Marin rushed to the door, and sure enough, Charlotte's smiling face was on the other side. Marin's skin flushed hot, and her heart lurched. She opened the door.

Charlotte held up a bottle of white wine and a reusable shopping bag. "I wasn't sure if you were still up for drinks tonight, so I grabbed a few things that will keep if needed. Your apartment was on the way home from my last showing, so I figured if your light was on, I'd knock, and if you're not up for company, just say the word and I'm gone."

Charlotte's smile was both hopeful and hesitant. Her hair was down, and it tumbled somewhat messily over her shoulders, and . . . Marin's body made the decision for her, stepping back to invite Charlotte inside.

"You sure?" Charlotte asked. "I could drop off the wine and food and go if you'd rather be alone?" Her eyes were questioning. She must wonder why Marin had been so quiet the last few days, and Marin had no good answer to give her.

"I'm sure," Marin told her as Ember joined them at the door, wagging enthusiastically to see Charlotte there. "You're one of her favorite people, you know."

"Well, her mom is one of *my* favorite people, so . . ." Charlotte passed the shopping bag and bottle of wine to Marin, then knelt to pick up the excited puppy. "Who's a good puppy? That's right, Ember, you are. You're the *best* puppy." She cooed over her while Ember writhed happily in her arms, tail thrashing and tongue trying to reach any part of Charlotte she could kiss.

"Now that she's up, I better—"

"I've already got shoes and a coat on. I'll take her." Charlotte reached for Ember's leash and fastened it before setting her down. "Right, baby girl? Let's go outside real quick, and then we'll have some snacks and hear all about your mom's hot date and visit with her brother." She turned and led Ember down the walkway.

Now that Charlotte was here, Marin felt foolish for even considering keeping her distance while she tried to get this attraction under control. It just wasn't an option. Charlotte was too important to her. So Marin did the only reasonable thing. She set the shopping bag on the counter and got out a corkscrew to open the wine.

Charlotte reentered Marin's apartment determined to get their friendship back on track. She wasn't sure what had happened this week, why Marin seemed to pull away, but she was going to do everything in her power to repair things. Maybe Marin had been distant for reasons that had nothing to do with Charlotte. Maybe she'd had more nerve pain than usual.

Or maybe she'd noticed that Charlotte was being weird around her, and this was her reaction. Whatever the case, Charlotte was here, determined *not* to be weird, determined to make things right between them. "I brought a charcuterie plate and some cookies along with the wine, in case you haven't eaten. I haven't had dinner yet, at any rate. I just finished work for the day."

Marin gave her a grateful smile as she got out plates and wineglasses. "I haven't eaten, either, so let's dig in. Thank you for saving me from my empty pantry, and . . ." She hesitated, and something unreadable passed across her expression. "Sorry for disappearing on you this week. I was trying to work through some stuff in my head, and not very successfully, it seems."

"It's okay," Charlotte said, wondering what that meant. She couldn't separate her feelings about Marin kissing Laura from her feelings about Marin avoiding her, and it all left her head such a mess that she figured it was better to just move on. "Did you get things sorted, at least?"

"Not really." Marin's lips twisted to the side as she poured two glasses of wine. "I just . . . I didn't feel the sparks I was hoping to feel with Laura, and it really threw me for a loop. I was having so much fun with her, and I didn't want it to end, but I realized I had to." She sighed. "End it, that is."

Charlotte snapped her mouth shut so she didn't gape at Marin's news. "I thought you were really into Laura."

"I thought so too." Marin busied herself opening the charcuterie tray. "I guess I wanted to be into her more than I actually was. When she kissed me, I didn't feel anything." She looked up at Charlotte, and the expression on her face was heartbreaking. "I've already wasted too many years kissing someone I feel nothing for. I know better than anyone that sparks are unlikely to develop later on. If they're missing from the start, well . . . that told me everything I needed to know, but it sent me into a bit of a tailspin."

"I'm so sorry." Charlotte placed a hand on Marin's shoulder. She knew how much Marin had been anticipating her first kiss with a woman, how eager she was for every part of this journey. It must have been devastating to have a disappointing first kiss.

But Charlotte had spent the last two days torturing herself as she pictured Marin and Laura passionately locking lips outside the restaurant, and now she felt a completely inappropriate surge of relief to know she'd been imagining it wrong. She internally berated herself for being such a terrible friend.

Charlotte and Marin were quiet as they fixed their plates and sat at the kitchen table. Marin sipped her wine. Once half the glass was gone, she sighed. "It wasn't much of a kiss, to be honest. Her lips touched mine, but that was about it."

"Well, we've got to make sure your next kiss really knocks your socks off, then." Charlotte picked up her wineglass, but she wasn't sure how to read the look on Marin's face right now. She looked intense but also sad.

"Here's hoping," she said finally. She made a little sandwich out of a cracker, prosciutto, and cheese, and popped it in her mouth, then chased it with more wine.

Charlotte was still staring at her mouth. "Have you told Laura?"

"Yes." Marin stared into her wineglass. "I gave her the dreaded 'It's not you, it's me.'" She rubbed a hand over her face. "Ugh. I hate that it came to this."

"I do, too, but good for you for ending things before you got any more invested. I always found it harder to break up with someone when we'd been dating longer, even if I felt no chemistry. It seemed like such a waste to have invested that much time and energy on someone only to have it not work out."

"I guess." But Marin looked even sadder now.

"When you think about it, the chances of finding love with the first woman you went on a date with were slim."

That brought a slight smile to Marin's face. "Statistically improbable."

"Totally. So, um, any other contenders? Or do we need to browse some new dating profiles tonight?"

Marin's smile wilted. "I think . . . maybe I'll wait until tomorrow to think about that."

"Okay." Charlotte tried not to let her relief show. "Tonight's just for fun and friendship. Hey, how did it go with Jed, or is that another conversation for tomorrow?"

Marin's expression softened. "It went really well. He was very laid back about the whole thing. I got so nervous in the moment, but he was fine."

"I'm so glad." Charlotte reached out and touched her hand, aware it was the second time she'd touched Marin tonight, and that Marin hadn't pulled away either time. On the contrary, Marin stared down at their hands with unmistakable fondness. "I can only imagine how nerve racking that would be, even if you're hoping for the best."

"It was." Marin exhaled. "I got really scared for a minute, and then I was like . . . fuck this. I came all the way here. I mentally prepared myself to lose relationships with my siblings if they won't accept me as I am, so I just blurted it out, and you know what he said?"

"What?" Charlotte asked, while her mind reeled around Marin's reality, that she was prepared to lose family members if they didn't accept her. Marin had mentioned that before, but that was before Charlotte started questioning her own sexuality, before she'd had reason to imagine herself in a similar situation, and the reality was . . . horrifying. To think of losing a family member over who you are? Charlotte wasn't prepared for that.

"Jed said that in hindsight, he wasn't all that surprised I'm a lesbian, that I'd never seemed happy with Andrew and maybe this explained it."

Charlotte laughed. "I mean, he's not wrong."

Marin's lips twitched. "No, he's not. And now I get to do it all again in a few weeks."

"Who's next?" Charlotte asked.

"Fran and Tom both still live in Manhattan, so I'm driving down to have lunch with them together."

"That's convenient."

"Yes. Then there's just Nancy, and I saved her for last for a reason." Marin drained her glass and stood to retrieve the wine bottle. She brought it back to the table with her.

"I hope she pleasantly surprises you," Charlotte said.

"I hope so too." Marin refilled both their glasses. "You know, I used to think coming out was an event, like . . . once I was divorced, I could finally come out, but now I realize it's an ongoing thing. It's a million little moments. I'll never stop coming out. There will always be someone else to tell."

"Yeah, I guess you're right. I never thought of that."

"It feels exhausting." Marin ate more of her charcuterie, looking almost as sad and defeated as she had when Charlotte first met her. She hated seeing that look on Marin's face now.

They didn't talk much as they ate, both of them polishing off several cookies after they'd finished their charcuterie. The first bottle of wine was gone, and Marin went to the kitchen and pulled out a second.

"More?" she asked, holding it up.

Charlotte nodded. She wanted Marin to smile again, and if more wine helped with that, she was on board.

"Sure you don't want to look at online-dating profiles?" she asked, hoping to cheer Marin up.

"Positive." Marin settled on the couch with Ember beside her. "Tomorrow I'll get back on the wagon with dating."

"Fair enough." Charlotte sat at the other end of the couch, watching as Marin sipped her wine. Marin's flushed cheeks were the only indication of how much she'd had to drink, but if she was anywhere near as tipsy as Charlotte was right now . . .

"I just . . ." Marin rubbed a finger back and forth over her wineglass, staring at it intently. "I want to feel passion with someone. I've waited *so long*, and when Laura kissed me . . . I thought that would be it, you know? I'd finally get to feel the sparks that everyone talks about."

Charlotte sat with Marin's words for a minute, digesting them, because maybe she hadn't fully understood Marin's reality before, that she'd never felt passion with a partner. That was so . . . sad. Charlotte was terrible for letting her conflicted feelings get in the way of wishing Marin the best on her date. No one deserved passion more than Marin.

"In the early years of my marriage, I tried *so hard* to find that passion," Marin said. "I bought lingerie, I asked Andrew to try new positions, and nothing ever did it for me. Deep down, I already knew I was gay, but I was in such denial. I thought if I just tried hard enough . . ."

"You never . . ." Charlotte stumbled to a halt, unsure how much was appropriate to ask about Marin's sex life.

"Never what?" Marin looked right at her, and those brown eyes were brimming with so many things, they made Charlotte's heart race.

"You never enjoyed sex with Andrew?" She settled on a slightly less direct way of asking her question, when what she really wanted to know was if Marin had ever had an orgasm with a partner.

Marin swirled her wine. "It wasn't all terrible, but it certainly wasn't great. I faked so many orgasms, and I'm not proud of that, but I didn't want Andrew asking too many questions about why he couldn't get me off. I just . . ." She shrugged, then drank more wine.

Charlotte's head was swimming. She was so drunk, and she suspected Marin would never tell her these things if she weren't drunk, too, but Charlotte's own blurred inhibitions only made her want to know more. "I think you did what you had to do to get through that part of your life."

"I guess so," Marin agreed. "Eventually, we pretty much quit having sex entirely. He went elsewhere, and I couldn't even really blame him."

"I could blame him," Charlotte said bitterly.

Marin gave her an amused look. "I mean, I don't excuse his cheating, but our marriage was doomed from the start with me being a lesbian, so he shouldn't shoulder *all* the blame."

"I guess."

"Anyway, I discovered sapphic romance books, and let me tell you, that was life changing." Marin was talking faster now. She seemed looser. *Drunk.* She was drunk, and Charlotte should stop her from sharing too much, but she was drunk, too, and she desperately wanted to know everything Marin was telling her. "I read every chance I got, and those books . . . they made me feel things my husband never could."

Charlotte exhaled in a shocked laugh. "Oh my god."

"Right?" Marin's lips quirked. "There I was, ignoring my husband, spending every free moment with my Kindle and my vibrator."

"Marin!" Her hand was on Marin's arm now, and she didn't remember putting it there. Marin's skin was so warm beneath hers, and she couldn't quite bring herself to move, especially not when Marin was looking at her through slightly hooded eyes. Maybe she was thinking about those books right now. Charlotte certainly was.

"It was so validating, though." Marin's voice was a little bit quieter now, a little bit deeper, and it seemed to rub over Charlotte's nerve endings, making her want, making her *ache*. "Once I started reading those books, everything made sense. I related to stories of two women falling in love in a way I'd never related to a straight romance book. I swooned for them. I *yearned* for them. And when there were steamy scenes . . ." She bit her bottom lip.

Charlotte felt an answering clench somewhere deep inside herself. "Yeah?"

"Those scenes made me *feel* things," Marin whispered.

"That's really hot." Charlotte's voice was a whisper now too.

"Books were enough excitement while I was married, but now . . ." Marin looked down at Charlotte's hand, which was still on her arm. "I want to feel a woman's hand on my skin."

"Like this?" Charlotte trailed her fingertips up the inside of Marin's arm. She had no idea what she was doing, or why she was doing it, but her heart was pounding so hard, and a delicious ache built between her thighs as her fingers slid over Marin's skin.

Marin's breath hitched, and her eyes fell shut. "Yes," she whispered.

"Do you . . . do you like that?" Charlotte's head was spinning with a combination of wine and arousal until she had no idea what she was doing or saying, except that she wanted to give Marin all the pleasure she'd waited so long to experience. Charlotte wanted to keep touching her. She wanted to kiss her. God, she wanted to kiss her so badly.

Goose bumps had risen on Marin's arm where Charlotte touched her, and Charlotte didn't want to read too much into this, but . . . Marin opened her eyes, and *god*, she looked aroused. She looked like she craved Charlotte's touch every bit as much as Charlotte craved touching her.

Charlotte almost felt as if she'd stepped outside her body as she watched herself take Marin's hand and lift it to her mouth. She pressed a kiss to the tender skin on Marin's wrist, and Marin's lips parted as she sucked in air. Emboldened, Charlotte kissed her wrist again, and Marin's features tightened with what looked unmistakably like pleasure.

Her eyes shut, and her mouth hung open in a silent moan. She looked like . . .

Charlotte's clit throbbed because Marin looked like she was in the throes of passion. Marin's chest heaved for breath, and her nipples were hard beneath her shirt. She'd just told Charlotte that she'd never experienced passion with a partner before, and now . . .

"Marin, look at me."

Marin did. Her eyes opened, pinning Charlotte in her gaze. She licked her lips, and her gaze dropped to Charlotte's mouth. Charlotte watched in real time as Marin's pupils dilated, and there was no other way to interpret what was happening. Surely there wasn't.

Yes, Charlotte was drunk, but she didn't think she was imagining this. Warning bells clanged in the back of her mind that the alcohol was affecting her judgment. Likely, it was affecting both their judgment . . . or maybe it had loosened their inhibitions? Maybe the wine had freed them to do what they wanted, and *oh* how Charlotte wanted.

Her body flushed hot, and she just . . . she had to kiss her. Charlotte leaned in. She didn't pause, didn't give herself a chance to change her mind. Marin wanted passion. She wanted the pleasure of a woman's kiss, and now so did Charlotte. More than anything. She wanted the pleasure of Marin's kiss.

She pressed her lips to Marin's, and several things immediately became clear. One, Charlotte was definitely not straight. She was attracted to women, or at least, to *one* woman . . .

And two, Marin was finally experiencing passion. A guttural sound of pleasure escaped her throat as her lips moved against Charlotte's. Her eyes slammed shut, and her free hand slid onto Charlotte's thigh, gripping her over her jeans. She looked absolutely overcome, and honestly? Same.

Charlotte slid closer, pressing Marin into the couch as she kissed her the way she'd been wanting to kiss her all week. And nothing, *nothing*, had ever felt so right.

CHAPTER FIFTEEN

Marin felt like she was dreaming. One minute, she'd been spilling her most embarrassing secrets to Charlotte—the wine had *definitely* loosened her tongue—and the next thing she knew, Charlotte was touching her arm, kissing her wrist, kissing her *lips*, and Marin's body was on fire in a way she'd never felt before.

She had sparks. An inferno of them. And they were worth every moment she'd waited to experience them. Oh *fuck* . . .

Charlotte's tongue teased the seam of Marin's lips, and she opened to her, inviting her in, *welcoming* her, because good god this was the best thing she'd ever felt. Marin thought she'd known what she was missing, but she'd underestimated just how amazing it felt to kiss the person you wanted. She needed Charlotte's mouth on hers like she needed air to breathe.

Marin pressed forward, an embarrassingly needy sound escaping her throat as Charlotte's tongue swept into her mouth. They were facing each other on the couch now, one of Marin's hands on Charlotte's thigh while one of Charlotte's hands drifted up Marin's arm toward her shoulder.

Her fingers left a trail of sparks in their wake. Marin was exquisitely aware of every millimeter of skin Charlotte had touched. She thought she'd feel those places forever, a permanent imprint of Charlotte. She could hear herself breathing, hear *both* of them breathing, quick gulps of air between kisses, breathy gasps, and murmurs of pleasure.

Marin closed her eyes and soaked it in, the warmth of Charlotte's fingers on her skin, the pressure of her mouth against Marin's. Laura's kiss had left her cold, but this one . . .

This kiss made Marin feel *alive*. Her body thrummed with pleasure from her scalp to her toes, centered in the needy ache between her thighs. She felt the gust of Charlotte's breath over her cheeks, the softness of her lips. They were as soft as Marin had imagined. Charlotte's hair tickled her neck, and it was soft too. It was *wonderful*.

A distant part of her brain wondered if this should be happening, *why* this was happening, if she wasn't careening wildly toward wine-induced regret when it ended, but here and now, she was too enraptured by Charlotte's kiss to question it. Marin wanted to drown herself in this kiss and never surface.

She must have opened her eyes, though, because now she saw the hazy shape of Charlotte before her. Charlotte's face was too close to hers for her eyes to focus. Marin just saw blond hair and Charlotte's upper body twisted toward hers, reminding her that they still sat side by side on the sofa. Without pausing to think, Marin gripped Charlotte's hand and tugged.

She wanted Charlotte in her lap, and that was exactly what happened. Charlotte's knees slid down to settle on either side of Marin's hips. Her warmth covered Marin's thighs a moment before her weight settled there, and Marin couldn't have kept herself quiet if she'd tried. She let out a whimper that bordered on a sob. It was lust and desire and desperation, and Marin was all those things.

The ache between her thighs was so intense, she thought she might combust. Her entire body felt overheated. Her panties were soaked. She couldn't seem to draw enough air into her lungs. With shaking hands, she cupped Charlotte's cheeks, kissing her deeply and thoroughly.

Passion. Marin had thought she knew what that meant, but she hadn't known it would be this intense, that she could crave quite this much, that her body could sizzle with a need this powerful. This kiss was everything she'd been waiting for and more. She hadn't known it could be this much *more.*

"Charlotte . . ." Her voice was little more than a needy rasp. It was the first word spoken between them since they'd started kissing, and it hung in the air like a warning bell now.

"Marin." Charlotte blinked at her as if she'd just awoken from a trance. Then she scrambled backward out of Marin's lap, landing awkwardly on the floor.

Marin stared at her for several long seconds as her senses cleared . . . at least as much as they could. She was drunk, both from wine and from arousal. Her thoughts were muddled by both, spinning out of control because *she'd kissed Charlotte*. Well, technically, Charlotte had made the first move, which she never in a million years would have imagined happening.

Why had Charlotte kissed her? Was Charlotte queer? Or was she just trying to give Marin what she'd been missing? Marin's intoxicated brain couldn't make sense of anything except how much she had loved every moment, how ridiculously turned on she was, and how desperately she wanted to be kissing Charlotte again.

Except Charlotte was sitting on the floor with her arms wrapped around herself, looking like she'd made a terrible mistake, and that was the metaphorical bucket of ice water dumped over Marin's head. *Fuck.*

"Charlotte . . ." She reached for her, but Charlotte scrambled to her feet.

"I shouldn't have . . . we shouldn't have . . ."

Marin snatched her hand back. She felt sick. *Oh god.* Had she ruined their friendship? "I'm so sorry."

"It's not your fault. I . . ." Charlotte gave her head a quick shake. "I just, I should go."

"No, please. We should talk about this."

"I can't." Charlotte was still shaking her head. She grabbed her coat and purse and backed toward the door. "Not right now."

"You're too drunk to drive."

"I'll call a cab."

"Please wait . . ." Marin's whispered plea sounded desperate and dejected, but Charlotte was already out the door. It closed behind her with a solid thump, and then Marin was alone. It had all happened so fast, the kiss and its aftermath, and her head was spinning.

She pressed her hands over her face, and a miserable moan tore from her chest as she processed Charlotte's abrupt departure and what it likely meant. Tears burned her eyes, and a painful lump rose in her throat. *Oh god. Oh no . . .*

A high-pitched whine yanked her from her downward spiral.

Marin opened her eyes to find Ember crouched on the floor in front of her, eyes wide and worried. "I'm okay," Marin told the puppy instinctively, but she wasn't.

She was very much *not* okay. Tears blurred her vision, and her stomach churned with a sickening combination of disappointment and fear. Marin had spent decades making sure she kept her desires locked down so tight that nothing like this could ever happen. She hadn't even allowed herself to initiate hugs with her female friends. She'd toed such a hard line to keep from ever crossing one . . .

And now she'd crossed it in the most devastating way, because it had happened with Charlotte. She needed Charlotte in her life. Charlotte's friendship meant the world to her. Marin wrapped her arms around herself, suddenly cold all over. She squeezed her eyes shut, trying desperately not to cry.

Something nudged her leg, and she looked down to see Ember standing there. The puppy whined again, visibly distressed by Marin's anguish. She'd ruined her friendship with Charlotte, ruined her first time making out with a woman, and now she was upsetting her puppy because she couldn't get control of her emotions.

Marin pressed a hand over her eyes, trying to calm down when all she really wanted to do was curl in a ball and sob. She'd gone from such intense pleasure to misery in such a short time, it left her head spinning even more than it already had been from the wine. The emotional whiplash felt strong enough to rip her apart.

She sucked in several deep, desperate breaths until she was able to give the puppy a fake smile and lift Ember into her lap. "Sorry about that. Do you need to go outside, sweetie?"

Ember squirmed in her arms. Not sure if that was a yes or just general puppy restlessness, Marin stood and fastened Ember's leash, then led her outside. She'd forgotten her coat, and the cold air was a shock to her system, but it did help sober her up. Charlotte's car was still here, a visual reminder of what they'd done and how it had ended.

When Marin got back inside, she picked up her phone and sent a difficult but necessary text.

Me: I'm so sorry. I never meant to overstep my bounds with you.

The text was almost immediately read, but no dots bounced to let Marin know that Charlotte was responding. Charlotte sent nothing back, and that made Marin feel even worse. She was half delirious now from the aftereffects of the wine and her emotional upheaval. Her body felt sweaty and wrung out, and she desperately needed a shower and a good long cry.

Ember had other ideas. The puppy was bouncing off the walls, demanding Marin's attention, so she did her best to fake a cheer she definitely didn't feel as she sat on the floor to play with her.

Marin could fake a smile with the best of them, but inside . . . she felt irreparably broken.

Charlotte was the worst friend in the history of friends. Last night had been 100 percent her fault. Marin had shared deeply personal things with her, and Charlotte had responded by kissing her. It had been one of the hottest kisses—if not *the* hottest kiss—of Charlotte's life, and that had completely thrown her world off its axis. Then she'd panicked and bolted, thinking only of herself and how she felt in that moment.

But how had it felt for Marin? After telling Charlotte how long she'd craved a woman's touch, how she'd waited to feel passion with a partner, Charlotte had kissed her, touched her, straddled her lap until Marin looked like she was completely overcome with pleasure, and then Charlotte had just . . . left her there.

Now Marin had sent multiple apologetic texts—as if any of this were her fault—and to make matters worse, Charlotte hadn't responded. She just couldn't. Every time she even thought about what happened last night, she started to panic. *Why* had she kissed Marin?

Charlotte had spent so much of her life searching. She'd chased men, chased jobs, chased the possibilities offered in her daily horoscopes. None of it had helped her find what she was looking for, probably because she didn't know *what* she was looking for, other than answers about her mom.

Which was why she was in Vermont, attempting to find those answers. Charlotte didn't have the time or energy to question her sexuality right now. A relationship—with someone of any gender—wasn't something she had the bandwidth for this year. Bottom line, Charlotte was a mess, and Marin deserved better.

It made her physically ill to think of how Marin must be feeling about the whole thing. Charlotte had ruined an important milestone for her—her first passionate kiss with a woman—and she would have to live with that knowledge. More than anything, Charlotte wanted to hide from what she'd done, but first, she had to respond to Marin's texts. It was the decent thing to do, even if their friendship didn't survive this.

Me: You have nothing to apologize for. This was 100% my fault.
Me: I need some time but I'll talk to you soon. Promise.
Marin Easterly: Take all the time you need. I'll be here.

Damn her. Why did she always have to be so *nice*? Charlotte didn't deserve her kindness, not today at least. She deserved to be told she was a shitty friend if not worse. Her phone vibrated again, and she tensed in anticipation of what else Marin would say, but the text was from Elena instead.

Elena Campos: I asked around and found Bev Sinclair. She's in Burlington now. Here's her #
Elena Campos: also found these pix of us from high school when I was going through old photo albums with the girls. How cute were we?!?!

Elena had attached several pictures of her and Charlotte from high school. Charlotte clicked on the first one to enlarge it. Elena and Charlotte had their arms around each other, hamming for the camera. In the next one, Elena was striking a silly pose while Charlotte gazed at her with unabashed adoration. The look of yearning on Charlotte's face in that photo . . .

Oh.

Fuck.

Her chest seized and her heart knocked into her ribs because those photos stirred feelings and emotions she'd long forgotten. They made Charlotte remember how it had felt to hold Elena in her arms, the obsessive need to be around her all the damn time. It was the same way she felt now with Marin.

But that meant . . .

Was it possible that Charlotte's feelings for Elena had run deeper than friendship? That she'd fallen for her best friend in high school, and that was why she'd been so irrationally upset when Elena went to the prom with Marcus instead of Charlotte?

Oh god.

If that were true, it explained why Charlotte had gotten so emotional about the whole thing, why she'd let it ruin her friendship with Elena. It also suggested Marin wasn't the first woman Charlotte had been attracted to, that Charlotte in fact had a history of falling for her female friends.

And that . . . well, she just couldn't deal with this right now. Charlotte was here in Middleton to find her mom and reconnect with her dad. She wasn't here to question her sexuality.

Tears stung her eyes, and she clenched her hands into fists until she got her emotions back under control. The photos from Elena had sent her into such a spiral, she'd almost missed the fact that Elena had also given her a lead: Bev's phone number.

Thank god. She'd been trying to track Bev down for months! Grateful for the distraction, Charlotte dialed the number and waited. She doubted Bev would pick up. No one answered their phone for an unknown number anymore, but after two rings, she heard a voice straight out of her childhood memories.

"Hello?"

"Hi, Bev Sinclair?"

"Yes. Who's this?" Bev asked.

"This is Charlotte Danton. I'm . . . I'm Terri's daughter."

There was a sharp intake of breath. "Oh my goodness. Charlotte. What a surprise! How did you get my number?"

"Elena Campos tracked it down for me," Charlotte stammered, suddenly realizing she didn't know Elena's married name. "I hope you don't mind."

"Of course not," Bev exclaimed. "I'm glad to hear from you. I think of Terri often, but I . . ." She faltered. "Oh goodness, is there news?"

"No, but that's why I wanted to talk to you. I'd like to ask you about my mom. I'm trying to find out what happened to her, and I'm talking to everyone I can who knew her. Do you think we could meet? Would you be willing to talk to me about her? I'll drive up to Burlington. I don't mind."

"I'd love to sit down with you and talk, but my husband's immunocompromised, and it's been a tough cold and flu season, so we're limiting visitors. How do you feel about saving yourself a drive and we can chat on Zoom?"

"Zoom would be great," Charlotte agreed. "When would work for you?"

"Well, like I said, my husband's had a rough go of it recently. He's recovering from pneumonia, so I've got my hands full right now. Can I call you in a week or so to set something up?"

Charlotte felt tears pricking at her eyes all over again because she wanted answers *now*, but obviously Bev's husband's health came first. Charlotte was just an emotional mess today. "Of course, and I really hope your husband is on the mend."

"I do, too, honey. Thank you."

"I'll talk to you soon, Bev, and thanks again. I really appreciate this."

"Nonsense, it's my pleasure. If there's anything I can do to help track Terri down, I'm happy to do it, but try not to get your hopes up. I told the police everything I knew thirty years ago, so I doubt I have any new information for you."

"I understand," Charlotte said.

A tear broke free as she ended the call. What would she do if Bev turned out to be another dead end? Because Charlotte had already tracked down and talked to everyone at the university who'd known her mom. She was out of leads.

Bev might be her last hope.

Marin arrived at the lawyer's office for her house closing five minutes early and with her heart in her throat. As her Realtor, Charlotte would be here while Marin signed all the paperwork and received the keys to her new house, but this wasn't how Marin had imagined seeing her for the first time since their kiss. They hadn't spoken since those awkward texts last Sunday, nearly a full week ago.

They wouldn't exactly be able to hash things out here at the lawyer's office, but Marin hoped she could convince Charlotte to stop by the house afterward, because they desperately needed to talk. She'd wondered at first if Charlotte was attracted to her, too, if maybe she wasn't straight after all, but after six days of avoidance, Marin was forced to admit it seemed unlikely that Charlotte wanted to pursue anything with her romantically.

So Marin would try to repair their friendship. Whatever it took. She needed Charlotte in her life. Marin had made peace with the knowledge that they couldn't be more than friends a long time ago. Of course, it would be harder now that she knew what it felt like to kiss Charlotte . . .

Her stomach tingled. She couldn't even *think* about that kiss without getting hot, but she would move past it. She had to. As Marin got out of her car, she spotted a familiar SUV parked farther down the street. Charlotte was already here.

Marin gulped, wiping her clammy palms against her jeans. Then she straightened her jacket and walked calmly up to the door, or at least she was reasonably sure she *looked* calm. Internally, she was in chaos, but this was the benefit of so many years of masking. She was a master at hiding her feelings. She entered the lawyer's office and greeted the receptionist, who guided Marin to a small conference room in back.

Charlotte stood at the window with her back to the door. She turned, and their eyes met. Marin gave her a friendly smile and a little wave.

See? Everything's fine. We can still be friends.

That was what she attempted to tell Charlotte with her eyes. Charlotte's smile, in return, looked stilted. Brittle. And that cut like a knife to Marin's sternum, all the way to her heart.

"Hi," Charlotte said after a slightly awkward pause. "Excited?"

Marin exhaled as she nodded. "Thrilled. I can't wait to walk into my house in a little while."

"I bet. Word of warning: The paperwork is a *lot*."

Marin chuckled. "I'm ready."

A middle-aged white man walked into the room, his graying hair neatly combed back, perhaps to cover a bald spot. "Good morning, ladies. I'm Peter Harkness."

Marin recognized his name from the paperwork. This was the attorney who would be handling today's closing. "Nice to meet you, Mr. Harkness."

"Please call me Peter. You must be Ms. Easterly?"

"Marin." She held out a hand, and he shook it.

The sellers had already left town, so they had completed their part of the paperwork electronically. It would only be Peter, Marin, and Charlotte signing documents in person today. Marin sat at the conference table and spent the next hour completing what felt like hundreds of documents. She signed until her hand cramped, but with Charlotte and Peter's guidance, she eventually got through it.

And then, he handed her a set of shiny keys.

Marin couldn't have stopped grinning if she'd tried as she walked out of the office, and she definitely wasn't trying. She was *ecstatic* to be a homeowner.

Charlotte followed her outside. "Headed over to your house right now?"

"I need to swing by the apartment and get Ember first. She and I will check it out together." Marin paused. "Would you stop by for a few minutes? So we can talk?"

Charlotte's gaze dropped to the sidewalk. "I have a showing to get to now, but maybe I could stop by in an hour or so? I'd like to see the house, now that it's yours."

"Okay. Please do." Marin gave her what she hoped was an encouraging smile. They needed to clear the air between them. Right now, that kiss hung like a neon sign over their heads, a reminder of the line they'd crossed.

As she watched Charlotte walk away, Marin hoped desperately that they could redraw that line. Her attraction was stronger than ever now that she knew how it felt to actually kiss Charlotte, but she also knew this was more than chemistry. She had real feelings for Charlotte. If things were different, she could fall for her.

If things were different, Charlotte could be *the one*.

Because not only was Marin ridiculously attracted to her, she loved being around her. She enjoyed sharing meals with her and watching Charlotte play with Ember. She loved every moment they spent together, and if she closed her eyes, she could see a future where she spent *all* her moments with Charlotte.

Well, fuck. This was a bigger problem than she'd realized, a problem she wasn't sure how to remedy. Had she already fallen? Was it too late to rein herself in to preserve their friendship? Maybe it would be less painful to walk away rather than continue to pine over a woman she couldn't have. No. She would find a way to fix this. They certainly weren't the first friends to share an ill-advised kiss. They could move past it.

Besides, the universe clearly wanted them to be part of each other's lives. There was no other explanation for how they'd both ended up in Vermont two years after the accident.

So, Marin drove to her apartment to pick up Ember. Last week, she'd gone on a bit of a shopping spree, buying furniture for her new bedroom and living room, kitchen essentials, and other things she needed to furnish her new house. When those items were delivered, she could officially move in. She hoped she and Ember would be sleeping in their new digs within a week.

The drive to the house took almost thirty minutes. A light snow had started to fall, which almost made her turn around and head back to the apartment. She'd gotten more comfortable behind the wheel over the last few months, but driving in snow still made her nervous. Fresh snow was so pretty, though. It sparkled where it had drifted along the side of the road.

Marin's muscles were clenched tight by the time she pulled into the driveway. It was long, with a slow curve leading to the house, and today, it was covered in about an inch of fresh powder. She needed to hire someone to plow for her.

Living outside the town limits meant she'd have a lot of things to consider now that she hadn't before, but she was up for the challenge. This house and the twenty acres of unspoiled nature it sat on would be more than worth it.

"What do you think, Ember?" she asked as she parked in front of the house.

The puppy stared out of her crate on the back seat, expression curious. Marin came around to get her and set Ember on the ground beside the car. There was a fenced-in yard in back, but the front yard should be safe enough, as long as Marin kept an eye on her. Her driveway was pretty long, and she lived on a dirt road with little traffic even if Ember wandered that far.

The puppy trotted across the driveway and climbed a snowbank, tail wagging as she realized the snow was firm enough to support her small body. Marin snapped a quick picture of her up there, which she texted to her niece Jen. Then she took a selfie of herself with the house visible behind her, which she sent to her sibling group chat.

Immediately, excited responses started rolling in. Even Nancy commented with congratulations on the new house. Jen sent a string of excited emojis and promised to visit as soon as tax day was over. As an accountant, she was extremely busy this time of year.

Smiling, Marin called Ember to follow her to the front door. "Let's go inside and check out our new house, okay? We've got so much land here, Ember. I think you're going to love it. I can't wait to watch you grow up in these hills."

Already, Marin felt calmed by her surroundings. There was no sound but the rush of wind through the trees. She'd never lived anywhere this remote. The prospect of privacy and space was intoxicating. She used her new key to unlock the door, immediately grateful that the previous owners had left behind a mat inside the door where she could dry Ember's feet before she tracked wet paw prints all over the hardwood floors.

"I'm never getting over these views," she told the puppy as she walked to the windows along the back of the house, looking out at the mountains in the distance. Ember stood at the window beside her, tail wagging.

Marin turned to survey her new home. The living room felt bigger without furniture, a blank slate for her to decorate exactly how she wanted. Despite the house being relatively small in square footage, the oversize windows and sprawling fields outside helped to make it feel open. Marin had spent so much of her life feeling confined, trapped in the metaphorical closet. Here, she was free in the most literal sense.

Marin lost all track of time as she wandered through the house, taking pictures and measurements, planning out where her furniture would go and what she had left to buy. The next thing she knew, there was a knock at the front door.

Charlotte was here.

CHAPTER SIXTEEN

Charlotte tried to act as if she weren't coming apart at the seams as Marin invited her into the house. But she was, and being in the same room with Marin only made it worse because now Charlotte's hormones had entered the equation. Her body kept reminding her how it felt to kiss Marin, while her head was reminding her that she didn't need a relationship right now.

"How does it feel to be a homeowner?" she asked, trying to sound casual.

"It's great. A little daunting because I'm realizing how many things I still need to buy and how much there is to do now that the house is mine, but still . . . great."

Charlotte crouched to greet the puppy bouncing excitedly against her legs. "And how do you like the new house, Ember?"

"Safe to say she's a fan," Marin answered.

"Has she checked out the fenced-in yard yet?"

"No, but now's as good a time as any. We've been here longer than I realized, and she probably needs to go out. Want to go outside,

Ember?" Marin led the way to a sliding door that opened into the backyard.

Ember cocked her head, staring at the door in confusion.

Marin opened it, gesturing toward the snow-covered yard beyond, and the puppy just stared harder. "You're allowed to go out by yourself now. Did you know that?" When the puppy made no move, Marin sighed and went to get her shoes, then led the way out the back door with Ember at her heels.

Charlotte waited inside, using the opportunity to observe Marin as she interacted with her puppy in the backyard. Somehow Marin got more beautiful every time Charlotte saw her. She was thriving in her new job and with her puppy and the house and her tentative steps into the dating scene. Maybe her newfound confidence caused the radiance that seemed to surround her like an aura every time Charlotte looked at her.

Or maybe the difference was Charlotte. Maybe she'd started out thinking of Marin as a friend and as Charlotte's feelings became more complicated, more *romantic*, she'd started to see Marin in a new light. Now, Charlotte was looking at the woman she wanted to touch and kiss, and yes, Charlotte found her captivatingly beautiful.

Currently, Charlotte was fixated on the raspberry-hued lipstick on Marin's lips and the way snowflakes glittered in her dark hair as she tromped through the yard with Ember. Marin laughed as the puppy dove into a snowdrift, and the sound was so beautiful. It made Charlotte ache with yearning. How was she supposed to get them back in the friend zone when she wanted Marin this badly?

When had she gone from being a straight woman with a female friend to . . . *this*? Charlotte rubbed a hand over her eyes, trying to get control of herself. Marin had asked her to stop by so they could talk, and suddenly, she had no idea what to say.

What *could* she say?

"She likes the yard."

Charlotte blinked. While she'd been spiraling, Marin and Ember had come back into the house. "I thought she would."

"We're making a mess." Marin looked down at her shoes, which were making puddles of melted snow on the hardwood floor. "But I didn't bring any towels with me, and well . . . I have cleaners coming tomorrow, so I guess it doesn't matter. Charlotte . . ."

Her tone changed on that last word. Marin was staring at her in a way that said she was ready for that talk. Charlotte swallowed thickly.

"I wish I could at least get us some water," Marin said. "I didn't plan this very well."

"You're on a well here, so your tap water is probably the best water you've ever tasted. If there's a cup or anything already in the kitchen . . ."

"Let's see." Marin took off her shoes and padded to the kitchen in her socks. She poked through cabinets, eventually saying "Aha! I found a package of plastic cups. Okay, let's test out my well water." She filled two red Solo cups and handed one to Charlotte, then sipped from her own. Her eyes widened. "That *is* good water. Now I understand why the refrigerator here doesn't produce filtered water."

"No need. Mother Nature's already given you the best, right from your backyard." Charlotte stared into her cup. "Marin, I'm sorry."

"For?"

"For kissing you." Charlotte looked up, gripping her cup so tightly it crinkled beneath her fingers. "You were drunk, and I took advantage. I have no idea what I was thinking."

"I'd love to know what you were thinking," Marin said softly, "and why you'd say you were taking advantage. To me, it felt like two people enjoying a kiss." Her gaze dropped to the counter, something vulnerable flitting across her face.

"That's how it felt to me too," Charlotte rushed on, still trying not to crumple her cup as her nerves sought an escape. "But I . . . I was drunk."

"You kissed me because you were drunk?" Marin looked at her, and there was no mistaking the hurt in her eyes, or in her voice.

Charlotte was messing this up, but she couldn't admit this confusing attraction . . . could she? Certainly she couldn't admit it to Marin before she was ready to fully acknowledge it to herself. "I don't know."

"Did you feel something for me in that moment?" Marin pressed. "Or was it a pity thing because you knew how badly I wanted to kiss a woman?" Her eyes filled with anguish.

"No!" Charlotte exclaimed. "It wasn't pity. I was thinking about how much you deserve passion with a woman, and I . . . I . . ."

"You what?" Marin was still staring at her, and all that newfound confidence Charlotte had just been admiring seemed to evaporate, leaving behind a woman who was unsure and vulnerable, a woman Charlotte had hurt.

She hated this. "In that moment, I wanted it to be me," she whispered. "*I* wanted to be the one to give you that passion."

"Because . . . what? You were doing me a favor or something?" Marin sounded even more hurt now, and to Charlotte's horror, her eyes shone with tears. "How is that not pity?"

"Because that's not what I was feeling. It wasn't like that at all."

"But you told me you're straight," Marin's voice wavered, "which means presumably you didn't enjoy kissing me, and now you've told me you were trying to give me what I wanted, which was to kiss a woman, but I wanted to kiss a woman who wanted to kiss *me*, not someone who was doing me a favor. Don't you see the difference?"

"I do." Charlotte nodded frantically. "And I did, Marin. Maybe it was the wine, but I *did* want to kiss you."

"Why?" Marin asked in a heartbreakingly brittle voice.

"Because . . ." Oh god, how could she answer without admitting to everything she'd been agonizing over for the last few weeks? But Marin had made herself vulnerable to Charlotte enough times, and Charlotte couldn't bear for her to think that kiss had been some pathetic attempt by a straight woman to let Marin experience a sapphic kiss. "I truly wanted to kiss you, and I *did* enjoy kissing you . . . a lot. I wanted that kiss so much, for myself as much as for you."

Marin's eyes were pleading. "Please tell me what that means."

"It means . . ." Charlotte gulped. "I have some soul-searching to do, but I need you to understand that this is about me, not you. Right now, I'm not ready to face what this means about *me*." She exhaled shakily. "Is that okay?"

Marin blinked. "Of course."

So many emotions flickered across Marin's features in that moment, Charlotte couldn't read them all. But she'd just realized something. Marin had kissed her back enthusiastically. She'd moaned. She'd pulled Charlotte into her lap. She'd looked *aroused*, so aroused that Charlotte still felt flustered every time she remembered it. Marin had told her she felt nothing when Laura kissed her, so her reaction shouldn't have been due solely to Charlotte being a woman.

So did that mean . . . did she dare hope . . . Marin was attracted to Charlotte too?

"Hey, have you moved into your new house yet?"

Marin turned at the sound of Audrey's voice. They'd just wrapped up another meeting with the Pride Coalition. Marin was really enjoying her involvement with the group and her new friendship with Audrey. "I'm actually planning to stay there tonight for the first time."

"How exciting," Audrey said. "Michelle told me she noticed that the for sale sign was down, so she thought the sale must have gone through. I don't usually go out that way."

"Yeah, I closed on Saturday." It was Wednesday now, and Marin couldn't wait to make things official. Her bedroom furniture had been delivered yesterday, so while the house would still be pretty bare, it was ready for a sleepover.

She talked to Audrey for a few more minutes. As she was leaving the building, she saw Brianna coming out of the bathroom. Marin had been hoping for a chance to check in with her and see how she was feeling about things. "Hi, Brianna," she called.

"Hi." Brianna gave her a stiff smile, but she waited outside the bathroom and fell into step beside Marin as she walked past.

"How are things?" Marin asked.

Brianna shrugged. There were several other students nearby, and maybe that was why she didn't say much, because she stayed close to Marin as they walked outside. The afternoon had turned frigid as the sun settled low in the sky. Marin couldn't wait for spring to officially arrive. Today was March tenth, but here in Vermont, it still mostly felt like winter.

Brianna kicked at the fresh dusting of snow that covered the walkway, then looked at Marin. "I'm a coward, that's how I'm doing."

Marin frowned. "Why do you say that?"

"Because I haven't told anyone. I'm still walking around campus—around my whole life—letting everyone assume I'm straight, and I *hate* myself for it." There was such vitriol in her words, it drew Marin up short.

"Oh, Brianna, no. Taking the time you need to come to terms with your sexuality, waiting until you're ready to come out . . . that is *not* cowardly, no matter how long it takes, even if you never come out. If you're not ready, for literally any reason, then you need to cut yourself some slack. You're being your own worst enemy here, you know?"

Brianna looked down at her hands, scowling.

"It took me twenty years to come out. Do you think I'm a coward?"

"Well, no, but times were different twenty years ago, and—"

"Ah, see?" Marin interrupted. "You're willing to make excuses for me but not for yourself. Why?"

Brianna opened her mouth, then closed it. She looked away, her expression heartbreakingly vulnerable.

"Be kind to yourself," Marin told her gently. "Coming out is something you do for *you*, right? Not for anyone else."

"Do you ever wish you'd been braver?" Brianna asked quietly. "That you'd found the courage to come out sooner?"

Marin exhaled. Brianna's question landed like a gut punch, but she knew it had been asked in innocence. "Of course I sometimes wonder how different my life might be if I'd come out sooner, but mostly, I try to take my own advice and cut myself some slack. I was doing the best I could at the time, and . . ." She looked up at the gray, cloudy sky, then back at Brianna. "I try to live my life without regrets. It's an exercise in frustration to spend too much time on what-ifs. They keep you mired in the past instead of looking ahead to the future."

Brianna was quiet for several long seconds, lips pursed.

"Don't rush this, okay?" Marin pressed. "You've got your whole life ahead of you. There is absolutely no reason that you need to come out in college. The fact that you're having such a hard time with it tells me that it's probably not the right time for you yet. So just . . . give yourself a break. It's okay to take your time."

"I guess." Brianna shrugged, but she looked calmer now. "Thanks for the pep talk."

"Anytime," Marin told her. "I mean that. Also, I really do think it could help to talk to one of the counselors here. It's free and confidential."

"It's free? Like, totally free?"

"Yes, and your parents don't need to know you're going. Think about it."

"Okay." Brianna gave her a small smile and started walking in the direction of the dorms. Marin watched her for a few seconds, then turned in the opposite direction. She was headed to her apartment to pick up the last few boxes and Ember, and then they were going to spend the evening together at the house.

Yet another fresh start in a year that had already been full of them. Marin had spent most of the week distracted by her feelings for Charlotte and the mess that had become of their friendship. She hadn't heard a word from Charlotte all week, and it was killing her.

Her advice to Brianna was ringing in her ears as she walked to her car. No regrets. Right? She wouldn't take back her kiss with Charlotte, the intensity of the passion, the need, the *yearning* she'd felt in those moments. But as much as that kiss had rocked her world, if it ruined her friendship with Charlotte . . .

Okay, Marin might have *some* regrets.

More than anything, she wanted to know what Charlotte was thinking. She'd mentioned soul-searching and figuring out what this meant for her. Was she questioning her sexuality? Did she feel pressured to come out before she was ready, much like Brianna? Had Marin inadvertently made her feel that way? She understood why Charlotte wouldn't want to discuss it with her, after their kiss, but she hoped Charlotte had *someone* she could talk to.

With a sigh, Marin slid into her car. Ten minutes later, she let herself into her apartment. Immediately, she heard Ember bouncing excitedly in her crate. Ember was old enough now to stay by herself for a few hours while Marin taught.

"Hey, puppy!" She walked into the bedroom, eyeing the boxes stacked against the wall. She'd arranged for the college guys upstairs to come down shortly and load them into her car, a fact she was intensely grateful for now, because her whole body ached.

Maybe it was the weather or the extra stress she'd been under. Some days, her body just felt the trauma of what it had endured two years ago. She had an appreciation for the pain, though, because it was a reminder that she'd survived. Not many people could say their heart had stopped. Marin was a member of the near-death experience club, and she didn't take that lightly.

Rubbing absently at her hip, she opened the crate and greeted the excited puppy who bounded into her arms. "Hey, you. Let's go outside, okay? Then it's time to load up and head over to our new house. I don't know about you, but I'm excited."

Ember's whirling tail indicated she was excited too. Marin took her outside, then tossed a few last odds and ends into a box and began moving what she could to the car. A few minutes later, the students from the top floor arrived to load the rest of the boxes for her. She paid them, and then . . . it was time.

She put Ember in her crate on the back seat. "Ready, puppy? We're going home."

CHAPTER SEVENTEEN

Marin lost track of time as she unpacked boxes and got everything set up for her first night in the new house. She hadn't brought much with her to Vermont, mostly clothes for her new job. She'd let Andrew keep the house they'd lived in when they were married, accepting payment for her half of the property as part of the divorce settlement.

Consequently, the new house was looking pretty bare at the moment. She'd purchased a few essentials over the last few weeks, including bedroom furniture and a sofa for the living room, but the walls needed art and shelves and all sorts of things that she absolutely couldn't wait to find. She was going to have so much fun making this house *hers*.

"Ember, where are you?" she called, realizing she hadn't seen the puppy for a few minutes. Ember was having a blast exploring every nook and cranny of her new home, but while there wasn't much here yet that she could get into trouble with, Marin also didn't like to let her out of her sight for too long. A quiet puppy generally meant trouble, in her experience.

Marin walked toward the bedroom, trying not to limp. Her leg was so stiff, but favoring it usually made it worse, so she did her best to walk normally. She'd do extra stretching exercises this evening to compensate. She found Ember in the bedroom, ears back and looking chagrined. A puddle of pee was nearby on the floor.

"Uh-oh," Marin said. "We lost our potty routine in the new house, didn't we? You didn't know how to ask. Okay. Let's clean that up and go outside."

Luckily, she knew where the box containing her cleaning supplies was, so she dropped a few paper towels over the puddle, then took Ember out back, in case she still needed to go. Sure enough, she squatted again now that she was outside.

It took Marin longer to find the bottle of enzymatic cleaner she used on puppy accidents. She was getting frustrated by the time she finally found it, not in the box of cleaning supplies, but with the toiletries in the master bathroom. "For fuck's sake," she muttered as she crouched awkwardly to clean up the mess. Her leg was *really* angry with her today.

There was a knock at the front door, and Marin tensed. Already frazzled and in pain, she wasn't in the mood for company, and who could it be? She didn't have any nearby neighbors who might want to stop by and introduce themselves. In fact, she couldn't see a single house from here. The privacy was one of the things she loved most about her new home.

She failed to hold in her groan as she stood, sending a bolt of pain all the way to her toes. Aware she had cleaner and probably pee on her hands, she rushed into the bathroom to wash up, then hurried to the door. Where was the puppy now?

But Ember was sitting at the front door, staring through the pane of glass beside it at whoever waited outside. Her tail was wagging, and hopefully that was a good sign that Marin would be happy to see whoever it was too.

Charlotte? Her heart gave a hopeful leap, and she hurried the last few steps to the door. But it wasn't Charlotte. Marin absorbed a moment of disappointment before her smile rebounded because Audrey and Michelle were on her front porch, and she was actually thrilled to see them.

She opened the door, running a hand through her hair. "Hi! Sorry it took me a minute. I was in the middle of cleaning up puppy pee when you knocked."

Audrey burst out laughing while Michelle's nose wrinkled. Both of them looked down at the puppy, who'd dashed out the door to circle their feet, bouncing and wagging enthusiastically.

"You must be Ember," Audrey said, sounding amused. "Did you make a mess in your new house?"

"She did. I've disrupted her routine, I guess, but . . . anyway." She waved a hand to invite them inside. "Come in, and yes, this is Ember. She's about three and a half months old now."

"Hi, Ember," Audrey cooed, crouching to greet the puppy. "Aren't you adorable?"

"We wanted to welcome you to the neighborhood, so to speak," Michelle said in her crisp British accent. "We're only, what, three miles down the road?" Her lips quirked.

"Around here, that practically makes us next-door neighbors, and I'm really glad about that, by the way. I'd love to have you both for dinner now that I've got room to host."

"We'd love that." Audrey stood, holding out a blue-and-green-painted vase filled with white flowers, peonies, Marin thought. "A housewarming gift for you."

"We also brought champagne for a toast and a lasagna you can put in the oven later in case you haven't shopped yet," Michelle added, holding up a bottle and a covered dish.

"Oh wow." Marin pressed a hand to her chest. "That's really nice of you. Thank you so much."

"Our pleasure." Audrey beamed, still holding out the vase.

Marin took it from her and held it up to admire it, realizing it was likely handmade, since Audrey was a potter. "Did you make this?"

"I did," Audrey confirmed. "It's my standard gift when I visit someone's home. I love giving out ceramics. If there's a certain color scheme you're going for in your new house, I'd be happy to make you something to match."

"Oh goodness." Marin examined the vase more closely. It was gorgeous, with a delicate design carved into the clay that added texture and style. "This is such a unique and thoughtful gift. I love it, and the colors are perfect."

"Keep hanging out with her, and you'll probably receive more," Michelle said, gazing around the entranceway with interest. "She does love to give out ceramics."

"Well, I have a whole house to decorate, so I won't complain. Thank you, Audrey. This is wonderful, and the champagne and dinner are much appreciated too. I haven't shopped yet, so I wasn't sure what I was going to have tonight."

"I suspected as much when I talked to you this afternoon at the Pride Coalition meeting," Audrey said.

"Come in and have a look around," Marin invited, turning to lead the way toward the kitchen. "If I can find glasses, I'd love to share a toast while you're here. I'm really glad you two live nearby."

"We're glad too," Michelle said. "And if you need help decorating these walls, you've got two art historians here who'd love to make recommendations."

"God, yes," Marin said. "I could use some help. I haven't picked out much artwork on my own. What do you think?" She gestured around herself at the mostly empty house.

"I think we bought our houses for the same reason," Michelle said with an approving nod toward the back windows. "The views and the solitude. That porch and fenced-in yard will be wonderful once the weather warms up."

"I can't wait to sit out there with Ember," Marin agreed. "The views and the space definitely sold me. The house itself is small, but well, I'm only one person."

"No progress on the dating front?" Audrey asked, and Marin must have been losing her touch when it came to hiding her feelings, because Audrey gave her a knowing smile. "Looks like you might have something to share after all."

"It's complicated."

Michelle snorted. "Isn't it always?"

"I guess." Marin shrugged helplessly. "I don't have much experience dating. I met Andrew in college, what feels like a million years ago, and we only divorced last year."

"I can relate," Michelle said. "I met my first wife at uni as well."

"Oh?" Marin started rooting through boxes as they talked, looking for flutes so they could share a champagne toast.

"Yes, we were together for over twenty years, so I know a little bit about how it feels to get back into the dating game after so long."

"I guess you do. Yeah, Andrew and I were together about twenty-five years." She pulled three small wineglasses out of a box. "Think these will do?"

"Absolutely." Audrey lifted the bottle of champagne and wrapped a dish towel around the cork, then twisted it off with a satisfying pop. She poured three glasses and handed one to each of them. "To Marin's new house."

They clinked glasses, and then Marin took a sip. The champagne was light and sweet, fizzing against her tongue. She rarely drank it, because she hadn't felt as if she had many things in her life to celebrate, but she loved champagne. She ought to drink it more often. She *would*.

"Now let's hear about whatever woman drama you've got going on. Someone you met on the dating site?" Audrey asked. She, Marin, and Michelle settled on barstools at the kitchen island with a view of the backyard. Ember was on the floor nearby, chewing on a Nylabone.

"I did go on a few dates with someone I met on the app." Marin took another sip of champagne, deciding how much she could share. If Charlotte was questioning her sexuality, then she needed to remain anonymous in Marin's story, at the very least.

"And?" Audrey pressed.

"And she should have been perfect for me. We had a lot in common, but there was just no chemistry."

Audrey frowned. "Bummer, but yeah, you can't force it if there's no spark."

"But there's someone else you're interested in?" Michelle asked.

"I've become a lesbian cliché and fallen for a friend." Marin was suddenly glad to have friends to talk this through with, because it had been eating her up inside, and maybe they could help her sort it out.

"Sounds like us last year," Michelle said, giving Audrey a fond look.

"We tried so hard to fight it." Audrey laughed. "Then I invited her over for a lesson on the pottery wheel, and one thing led to another . . ."

Michelle looked suspiciously flustered.

Marin found herself laughing. "I can see how that might happen. I mean, we've all seen *Ghost*, right?" She pretended to fan herself.

"Right." Audrey grinned. "I'd always wanted to recreate that scene with someone, and well . . . it was even hotter in real life, but that's a story for another day. Right now, we want to hear about this friend you've fallen for. Any chance she feels the same way?"

"That's the question." Marin stared into her champagne, watching as bubbles climbed the glass. "She had told me she's straight, so I assumed I was the only one catching feelings. I was trying so damn hard not to let it interfere with our friendship. Being closeted for so long, married to a man while knowing I preferred women, I know a thing or two about keeping my feelings to myself."

"That sounds miserable," Audrey said.

"It was, and that's how I started to feel when I was around her. I didn't know how to move past it so I could focus on the women I met on the app. And then, about a week and a half ago, we were hanging out at my apartment, and we had a bit too much wine. I was telling her . . ." Marin paused, cheeks heating. "I was disappointed because it hadn't worked out with the woman I went on a date with. I'd been anticipating kissing a woman so much, and it was a bust. I was devastated about it, and the next thing I knew, Ch—my supposedly straight friend kissed me."

Audrey straightened on her stool. "Oh shit! Maybe not so straight after all. Was it hot? The kiss?"

Marin's cheeks were burning now. She felt as flustered as Michelle had looked a few minutes ago.

Michelle smirked. "I think it's safe to assume the answer is yes."

Marin nodded, then coughed awkwardly. "It was . . . hotter than I knew a kiss could be."

"Good for you," Audrey said. "Sounds like you were overdue for that kind of passion. How are things with you and your friend now?"

"Terrible." Marin sighed. "We've barely spoken since. I think it really freaked her out."

"But *she* kissed *you*, not the other way around?" Audrey asked.

Marin nodded. "I was drunk, but I'd never lose control like that. I won't even initiate a hug with a female friend for fear of overstepping boundaries. She initiated the kiss."

"Sounds like it was pretty intense for you both." Audrey looked thoughtful. "My guess is that your friend might have just realized she's not straight, which you've probably realized, too, since you're protecting her identity. She's probably really freaked out right now."

Marin's vision blurred as tears filled her eyes. "Yes, I think so, and it's killing me because, as her friend, I want to help her through this, but as the woman she kissed, I understand why she doesn't want to be around me right now. It's an awful situation."

"Especially unfortunate for your first kiss with a woman," Michelle said, her tone sympathetic.

"You said you don't initiate hugs with female friends, but you look like you need one." Audrey stood and wrapped her arms around Marin, and she was right. Marin *did* need this.

"Thank you," she murmured, hugging Audrey back. "I feel so much better after talking about this with you."

"I'm glad." Audrey patted her back and then released her. "That's what friends are for, especially queer friends. We get the nuances of this situation, right?"

"Right," Marin agreed.

"So how have you left it with her?" Michelle asked.

"She said she needed time, so I'm giving it to her." Marin stared at her empty glass. "And then, if she decides it was a mistake, I'll get back to my dating app, because if there's one thing I've realized since kissing her, it's that I want a relationship with a woman even more than I thought."

"You've waited long enough," Michelle agreed. "And . . . if you do give things a try with this friend, it would be both of your first times with a woman, I assume? That could be complicated."

"Or like *really* hot," Audrey cut in with a cheeky grin. "Both of you experiencing sapphic sex for the first time together? That could be off-the-charts sexy, just saying."

Marin's cheeks were on fire, and she wished she had more champagne. As if she'd read her mind, Michelle reached for the bottle and refilled Marin's glass. "Or it might be awkward," Marin said. "Neither of us knowing what to do . . ."

"It's so intuitive, though," Audrey said. "And you've known you're a lesbian for so long, I bet you've done your research, maybe read some sexy books, at least?"

"Feel free to ignore her if she's too much." Michelle rolled her eyes at her fiancée. "She's much more open when it comes to talking about sex than I am."

Marin drank more champagne. She'd had enough now to be tipsy, and yes, she was embarrassed by Audrey's question, but she was also loving the chance to talk about these things with queer friends. She'd never done this before. "I've done my research, yes."

Audrey cackled. "I knew it. See? You'll be fine. I hope your friend decides to go for it. I really do."

So did Marin.

An hour later, she was alone in her kitchen waiting for the lasagna to heat up, having been unsuccessful at convincing Audrey and Michelle to stay for dinner. She'd fed Ember and taken some ibuprofen for her pain. In a few minutes, she'd sit down to a home-cooked meal by herself. That was okay, though.

She was too excited about being in her new house tonight to feel lonely. She was here with her puppy. She'd enjoyed champagne with her queer friends, and the vase! She couldn't forget the vase. It was beautiful, and she couldn't wait to put up some shelves to display it on. Her love life might be a mess, but she had so many other things to be thankful for.

The oven beeped, letting her know the lasagna was ready. She peeked inside to check on it. The lasagna bubbled on top, and it smelled delicious. She'd be eating it for a week with no one to share it with, but she'd always been a fan of leftovers.

She'd better leave the lasagna out to cool for a few minutes before she tried to eat it, though. Ember probably needed another trip to the backyard. Marin didn't want any more puddles on her new floors. She'd just turned to look for the puppy when she heard a knock at the front door. Who in the world could it be this time?

Confused, Marin walked to the door. She flipped on the porch light belatedly, because it was pitch dark outside, but she hadn't been expecting visitors. The porch flooded with light, revealing a tousle of blond hair that made Marin's heart jump into her throat.

Charlotte blinked at her through the glass, startled by the sudden light.

Marin opened the door. "Charlotte? This is a surprise."

Charlotte gave her a tentative smile. "I wasn't sure if you'd moved in yet. How are things going so far?"

"This is my first night here." Marin's confusion must have shown on her face, because Charlotte dropped her gaze to her hands, then looked up again, her expression determined this time.

"I . . . I can't stop thinking about you, and . . . can I come in?"

CHAPTER EIGHTEEN

Marin was flushed and flustered as she invited Charlotte into her house. The champagne was long gone from her system, but she felt drunk as she faced Charlotte. Her heart pounded, and her head spun. "I don't have much furniture or anything else to offer yet, but I do have a lasagna I was about to eat if you'd like to join me?"

"You don't have furniture, but you baked a lasagna?" Charlotte followed her toward the kitchen, taking off her coat as she walked. Then she froze, her gaze locked on the wineglasses on the counter. "Do you have company?"

"Audrey and Michelle stopped by earlier to welcome me to the neighborhood, so to speak," Marin said. "They brought the lasagna—and the champagne—although they couldn't stay for dinner, so I was faced with eating the whole thing myself."

Charlotte stared at the lasagna, then at Marin. "Oh."

So this was what had become of them . . . constant awkwardness. Marin hated it. As much as she had enjoyed the kiss in the moment, she could see now that they would have been better off if it hadn't happened. Marin would have eventually found chemistry with someone from the dating app, and she and Charlotte would still have their friendship.

Instead, Marin had to try to pretend she hadn't experienced the most intense passion of her life with Charlotte, like that kiss hadn't absolutely rocked her world. Charlotte clearly regretted it, and Marin was stuck in this awful purgatory with the woman who had been her best friend.

Ember dashed into the kitchen, cutting the tension between them. She had her favorite purple dragon in her mouth, and she dropped it at Charlotte's feet, then bounced adorably, inviting her to play. Charlotte crouched to pet her, then squealed as Ember promptly launched at her face.

"Watch out," Marin warned. "She's been mouthy lately."

"Ember, what's up, girl? Why are you trying to bite my face?" Charlotte laughed as she scooped the puppy into her arms and stood. Ember took this opportunity to give toothy kisses all over Charlotte's cheeks until Charlotte realized her error and put her down.

"It's a phase," Marin said. "Or at least I hope it is. We start puppy class in a few weeks, thank goodness, because I obviously need some help with her manners."

"I think you're doing great with her," Charlotte said. "All puppies like to bite, especially while they're teething." She paused, looking down at her hands. "Marin . . ."

"Yes?" Just like that, the tension in the room rose again. Marin's chest grew so tight she could hardly breathe.

"I need to know . . ." Charlotte took a hesitant step forward, and Marin's pulse started to rush frantically through her veins.

"Yes?"

"I need to know how you felt about that kiss," Charlotte said quietly.

Marin inhaled roughly, crossing her arms over her chest. "No. That's not a fair thing to ask of me. You know better than anyone how long I'd been anticipating that moment, not with you, but with someone. I *never* expected it to be you."

"But did you *want* to kiss me?" Charlotte persisted, her eyes locked on Marin's.

This felt like a trap. Marin had no idea how to answer, and suddenly her discomfort morphed into anger because how dare Charlotte put her on the spot like this? "You're still not playing fair. You initiated that kiss, then refused to talk about it. Now everything's weird between us, and I think . . . whatever happens next, it has to come from you."

"I started it, yes." Charlotte nodded, tears welling in her eyes. "I just wondered if you wanted to kiss me, too, but I get what you're saying. I just . . ." She inhaled roughly, and then she flung her arms around Marin. "I need to fix things with you, and I don't know how."

"Just be honest with me." Marin's hands were on Charlotte's hips, and everything about this moment felt too intimate. Their faces were only inches apart, and Marin was about to hyperventilate. She needed to either return some space between them, or—

"Honest?" Charlotte's gaze dropped to Marin's lips. "The honest truth is that . . ." She searched Marin's face, her blue eyes intense.

Marin had no idea what Charlotte was looking for, and although she tried to keep her expression neutral, Charlotte had to feel Marin's pulse racing. She couldn't seem to catch her breath, and there was no hiding that.

Charlotte licked her lips. "I want to kiss you again."

Marin didn't even recognize the sound that came from her throat. Her lips were parted, but she didn't remember opening them. Her grip had tightened on Charlotte's jeans-clad hips, and her breathing was even more out of control now. "Then kiss me," she managed, her voice low and rough. "For the love of god, *please* kiss me."

Charlotte pressed her lips to Marin's, and it wasn't a gentle kiss. It wasn't tender or hesitant. This kiss was hunger and passion and desperation. Charlotte's lips crushed against hers. Her body pressed into Marin's until her back met the kitchen counter. Marin clutched

Charlotte against her as she savored the heat of her lips. She traced the shape of them with her tongue, and Charlotte moaned.

Then Charlotte's tongue was in her mouth, and it was Marin's turn to moan. She'd closed her eyes at some point, and while she wanted to see the look on Charlotte's face, she couldn't seem to focus long enough to open them. Charlotte's tongue thrust against hers, and Marin felt something clench deep inside her body.

For now, she just needed to *feel.* The warmth of Charlotte's body, the softness of Charlotte's fingers where they cupped Marin's cheeks, the firm press of Charlotte's breasts against hers. Where their hips met, she felt only the gentle slope of Charlotte's stomach. No hard bulge like she'd become accustomed to in her marriage. This was what Marin had longed for, and it felt so right.

Tears filled her eyes. She was nearly overwhelmed with relief to feel a woman's body pressed against hers, to finally have the validation that this was exactly what she'd been wanting all these years. And it was better . . . so much better than she'd anticipated.

Charlotte's fingers traced Marin's jaw, then swept down to cup Marin's breasts over her shirt. She arched her back, pressing her breasts more firmly into Charlotte's hands as a guttural sound of pleasure tore from her throat.

Marin had been gripping Charlotte's hips, but her hands had drifted upward without her knowledge, and now they rested against the bare skin above the waistband of Charlotte's jeans. Marin traced the dip of her waist and the swell of her hips, enraptured by her feminine shape. It was perfect. *Charlotte* was perfect.

Charlotte's lips were on hers again, kissing her like she couldn't get enough. Neither could Marin. Charlotte nipped at her bottom lip, and Marin felt it in her clit. Her hips surged forward, pressing into Charlotte's. She pulled Charlotte closer, instinctively seeking pressure where she ached for it, but their hips lined up too perfectly for her to get any friction.

Then Charlotte was sucking at the delicate skin below Marin's ear, and her brain promptly short-circuited. Charlotte nipped and kissed that tender spot, and Marin's awareness distilled to the sting of Charlotte's teeth and the hot, wet trail of her tongue as it explored Marin's skin.

Marin had read about this kind of pleasure. She'd read about it and thought *yes, that's what I want.* She'd spent so long anticipating it, and yet she'd still underestimated just how aroused she would be once she finally experienced it, because this kiss was *everything*.

Marin's knees shook. Her core ached, and she could feel that her panties were soaked. Her pulse roared in her ears, and she felt so breathtakingly alive. If she could feel this much from a kiss, imagine how incredible it would be if they ever had sex?

Charlotte pinned Marin against the kitchen counter, clutching at every part of her she could reach. As she pressed closer, one of Marin's thighs slid between her own, and she let out a surprised gasp when it pressed into her right where she ached.

Marin's hands were on Charlotte's ribs, tracing up and down in a way that lit Charlotte's body on fire. She leaned forward, bringing their mouths back together. Their thighs were interlaced now. They were touching almost everywhere, and it was sensory overload. She loved kissing Marin, and who cared that she was a woman?

Charlotte certainly hadn't come here intending to kiss Marin, but here they were, and . . . she just couldn't seem to stop. She didn't *want* to stop. Charlotte sank her hands into the silky depths of Marin's hair. She'd known plenty of passion in her life, but this was different. Everything felt softer in the most literal sense, but also, this was *Marin*. This woman meant the world to her, and that made kissing her even hotter.

Marin had confessed to Charlotte how she'd yearned for this kind of passion, how many years she'd spent holding herself back. Now her hands were on Charlotte's body, and Marin was making the sexiest sounds, gasps and whimpers, as if she was so turned on she was about to lose her mind.

Charlotte wanted to give her even more pleasure. She had no idea what she was doing, but kissing was kissing, right? And a woman's body, well . . . Charlotte knew what *she* liked. So she palmed one of Marin's small breasts as she licked her tongue into Marin's mouth, leaning her body into Marin's. Marin's eyes fluttered shut, her head falling back to expose the pale skin at her throat. That skin already sported a few blotches where Charlotte's mouth had been, and she intended to leave even more before they were finished.

As she moved, Charlotte's thigh bumped the juncture of Marin's, and Marin groaned, grasping at Charlotte's hips to bring her back there. Charlotte shifted her weight, this time intentionally pressing her thigh into Marin, giving her pressure where she needed it.

"Oh," Marin whispered in awe, pressing her hips more firmly against Charlotte's thigh. Her eyes were bright, her cheeks flushed, and as Charlotte watched, she rocked her hips just the tiniest bit. "Oh, that's . . ."

"Good?" Charlotte had had no idea how arousing it would be to watch Marin. The ache in her core was almost unbearable. Truly, she'd had no idea she could be this aroused from a little bit of making out. They'd barely even touched each other yet.

"'Good' isn't a strong enough word." Marin was panting for breath. She hooked her fingers through the belt loops of Charlotte's jeans and dragged Charlotte even closer.

They fumbled against each other, both of them groping and grasping, frantically moving their hips in a clumsy attempt to find friction. Marin's nose bumped Charlotte's chin, drawing a startled laugh from them both.

"Remember that Sarah McLachlan album *Fumbling Towards Ecstasy*?" Marin's eyes sparkled as she brought a hand against the bare skin on Charlotte's lower back.

"Feels pretty accurate right now," Charlotte agreed.

"Yes." Marin spread her knees, inviting Charlotte to step between them.

Charlotte moved in, and Marin closed her thighs around Charlotte's hips. Then they were kissing again, Marin's hand on Charlotte's back, holding her close while Charlotte slipped her fingertips into the back pockets of Marin's jeans.

Nothing about this felt familiar, but everything about it felt *good.* Great, even. Everywhere their bodies touched reminded Charlotte that she was kissing a woman. Even Marin's lips felt different from a man's. Her cheeks were so smooth, and while there was a tiny part of Charlotte's brain that wanted to overthink this, wanted to freak out about what it meant, she was doing her best to live in the moment.

So what if she wasn't straight? So what if she was falling for her best friend? How could that be anything but wonderful? Charlotte would think through the ramifications later. Right now, she just wanted to enjoy every moment of this incredible kiss.

She savored the feel of Marin's tongue as it touched hers, Marin's fingers on her skin, Marin's heat where her hips met Charlotte's. Charlotte pressed closer, and Marin rocked into her, making a little whimper that might have been the sexiest thing Charlotte had ever heard. Her clit throbbed as Marin's movements pressed the seam of her jeans against it.

Charlotte couldn't get any real traction in this position, but it was enough to get her pretty damn worked up. They moved against each other with increasing desperation.

Emboldened, Charlotte brought a hand between their bodies. She slid her fingers over the front of Marin's jeans, cupping her over the denim, and *fuck* she could feel the dampness of Marin's arousal through her clothes. Marin's hips jerked, and her breath hitched. She looked at Charlotte out of lust-glazed eyes, her pupils completely blown.

Charlotte had no idea what she was doing except that she loved every moment. "Mare?"

Marin slow-blinked. Her lips were swollen and glistening from Charlotte's kisses. "Mm?"

"I love kissing you. I don't know anything else about, well, *anything*, but I know that."

"Same." Marin's voice was deep and raspy. One corner of her lips quirked in a smile. "Safe to say this means you're not straight?"

"Yes," she confirmed, but insecurity had begun to seep through the haze of arousal now that they were talking. "Although I don't . . . I don't know what it means for me, label-wise."

"That's fine. No rush." Marin cupped Charlotte's cheek. "I'm just . . . really happy."

"Is that all you are?" Charlotte teased, even as her heart clenched at the adoring look on Marin's face.

Marin let out a breathless chuckle. "No. I'm so fucking turned on, I'm about to lose my mind, but also . . . really damn happy."

"Did you want to kiss me?" Charlotte asked hesitantly. This was what she'd wanted to know when she knocked on Marin's door, what she'd been dying to know since that first kiss. "Had you thought about it before I kissed you? Were you attracted to me?"

Marin looked away, drawing a deep breath. They were still pressed against each other, bodies melded together from chest to thigh, so Charlotte felt the tension seep into Marin now. "Yes," Marin admitted quietly. "I was attracted to you. It's probably why things didn't work out with Laura, because how could I even look at her when I was absolutely obsessed with *you*?"

Charlotte gulped. "Oh."

"And you? Had you thought about it before you kissed me?" Marin's gaze was steady and intense, leaving Charlotte nowhere to hide.

"Yeah." Charlotte swallowed again, her throat dry. "I knew I was attracted to you, but I only realized it for sure a week or so before I kissed you. Before that, I was in denial, even though I was absolutely *obsessed* with you, because I had never considered that I might not be straight, you know? I've been in love with a man. You told me how long you'd waited to feel passion, and that's not how it is for me. I've felt passion . . . with men."

Marin cocked an eyebrow. "There's a word for that, you know?"

"Bisexual, I know." She exhaled. "Or maybe pan. Maybe I'm attracted to the person, not their gender. I just . . ."

"You aren't ready, and that's fine," Marin told her. "But it does mean we should probably stop for now. We need to slow down and make sure we're on the same page."

Charlotte huffed. "I feel like a tease. I don't want to make you wait any longer."

Marin pressed a gentle kiss to Charlotte's cheek and then slid sideways away from the press of Charlotte's body. Charlotte missed the contact immediately. "I can wait, and honestly, we have a lot to talk about before we go any further . . . *if* we go any further."

"I want to. I do, but you're right." Charlotte looked down at her hands. "I'm not ready. I haven't thought any of this through. I don't know what I'm doing."

"That's fine. No pressure, but . . . *shit.*" Marin's tone changed on that last word, rising in pitch.

Charlotte stiffened. "What?"

"Ember." Marin ran a hand through her hair. "I totally . . . I wasn't paying attention."

Charlotte spun, spotting the puddle by the back door and the shamefaced puppy sitting beside it. "Oh, Ember. We totally ignored you, didn't we? I'm sorry. Here, let me take you out—then we'll clean up your accident."

She hurried to the door, grateful for the distraction but also eager to help because she was fond of the puppy as well as her human. Charlotte opened the door and ushered Ember into the darkened backyard. Since she didn't have on shoes or a coat, Charlotte watched from the doorway as the puppy scampered across the snow. Ember took care of business, then ran back toward Charlotte.

Charlotte let her inside and closed the door. Marin had just finished cleaning the floor. She stood, not quite managing to hide her grimace as she straightened.

"Nerve pain?" Charlotte asked. "Here, let me help."

She rushed forward, but Marin waved her off. "It's mostly just general soreness from moving today. My body feels like I'm eighty sometimes." She rolled her eyes playfully, but there was something vulnerable in her expression.

"I imagine your body aches like it survived a near-fatal ordeal two years ago," Charlotte said. "I was there. I saw . . ." But she didn't want to remember how Marin had looked, crumpled and broken in the street, right now. "Anyway, I'm sorry you're in pain. I wish I'd been here to help you move."

"The college kids upstairs loaded boxes for me," Marin said.

"I'm glad you had help." Charlotte took the dirty paper towels from her and brought them to the kitchen, where she found a trash can. She was washing her hands when Marin joined her at the sink to do the same. Charlotte blanched as a new thought occurred to her. "I didn't hurt you just now, did I?"

"No, you didn't." Marin pressed a firm kiss to Charlotte's lips. "I wasn't feeling any pain while we were kissing, trust me."

Charlotte grinned against her lips. "Good."

"Very good." Marin kissed her again. "While we were ignoring my puppy, we also forgot about the lasagna. Want to stay for dinner, maybe talk some more? I'd love to know more about how you're feeling. I've been where you are, figuring out your sexuality, you know?"

"I'd like that. And maybe after dinner, I can help relieve your pain."

Marin lifted a brow. "I thought we were slowing things down?"

"We are." Charlotte rested a hand on Marin's thigh, then winked. "For the record, I was talking about a massage."

CHAPTER NINETEEN

The lasagna was delicious, although Marin could hardly focus on eating it, she was so distracted by Charlotte sitting on the stool beside her. Charlotte, on the other hand, seemed extremely focused on her lasagna, and Marin suspected she was using it as a distraction while she processed what had happened between them.

Marin was content to give her all the time she needed, as long as Charlotte didn't shut her out like she'd done after their first kiss. Marin could handle anything but that. "It was lucky that Audrey and Michelle dropped this lasagna off, or I might have been eating oatmeal for dinner. I'm not sure I have much else in the pantry at this point."

"I'm glad you've made friends here," Charlotte said, darting a glance at her.

"It's been wonderful getting to know a sapphic couple. I've always wanted more queer friends." Marin meant every word, but she was also trying to get some conversation going.

"And fellow academics," Charlotte said.

"Yes, definitely. Maybe I can introduce you sometime."

"Maybe." Charlotte gave her a tentative smile, then looked at her plate, brow furrowed. "I worry, Marin. You've been on this path for so long. You've worked *so* hard to get here. You've really embraced your identity as a lesbian, and you're ready for a real relationship with a woman, and I'm just . . . none of those things."

"None of what things?" Marin asked, trying to keep her anxiety at bay. This was the conversation they needed to have, after all.

"I'm not out. I'm not comfortable in my identity. I don't even know what my identity *is* at this point." She sighed. "And I'm generally terrible at relationships. I told you before that I'd just been through a bad breakup, but I didn't tell you how messy it was."

"No, I guess you didn't." Marin reached out and touched her hand. Sitting side by side on stools in her kitchen made this easier than if they'd been seated across from each other at a table.

Charlotte flipped her hand to grip Marin's fingers. "Darren was my college boyfriend. He had wanted me to follow him to DC for his new job after we graduated, but I wasn't ready for that kind of commitment yet, so I broke up with him, but I always wondered 'What if?' You know? I thought he was the one that got away, so one of my misguided attempts to find purpose after I thought I'd watched you die was to track him down and give things another chance."

Marin kept her hand in Charlotte's, not wanting to interrupt her story.

"It was great at first. We fell right back into each other's arms like no time had passed. I left the real estate firm I was working for in Manhattan and took a position in DC. Darren is a congressional aide, and he's doing some interesting work, really trying to make change. I thought, this is it. This is what I've been looking for. Darren might be the one."

Charlotte's eyes were glossy now. Marin scooted her stool closer so she could press her shoulder against Charlotte's, offering support. It thrilled her that she could touch Charlotte more freely now, that she didn't have to worry about these touches being misinterpreted.

"We were madly in love for a little while, but there were warning signs from the start," Charlotte continued. "He put his job before me, before *everything*. Aside from our chemistry, we had very little in common. It didn't take long before we were fighting again, just like we did in college. We sniped at each other constantly. It was just . . . a train wreck."

"I'm sorry," Marin murmured.

Charlotte sighed, her eyes downcast. "I uprooted my whole life for him, gave up my job and my apartment in New York. I'd been so obsessed with finding meaning in my life, and instead I got myself into this relationship where I was miserable all the time, and I realized I'd gone after the wrong thing *again*. It was so demoralizing."

"How did you end things?"

"He went out of town on business, and I just packed my stuff and moved out. I left him a note, which is so pathetic of me, I know. I just cleared out of his apartment. I had no idea where I was going, but I'd been thinking about my mom a lot, and my dad had been asking me to visit, so I drove straight from DC to Vermont, and here I am."

Marin wasn't sure what to think of that. Moving out of someone's apartment without saying a proper goodbye seemed kind of harsh, even if the relationship hadn't been great. But she'd already noticed Charlotte had a tendency to run from difficult conversations. Hopefully, it was something they could work on together.

"How long ago was this?" Marin asked.

"September."

"And I arrived in January."

"And turned my life upside down in an entirely different way." Charlotte gave her a shaky but sweet smile. "After I left Darren, I decided to take a break from dating. I put my focus on figuring out what happened to my mom and trying to reconnect with my dad, no distractions."

"I respect that," Marin said, and she did, although it hurt to think her relationship with Charlotte might be over before it had begun.

Charlotte blew out a breath. "I'm not saying I don't want to be with you."

"No?" Marin tried not to let her insecurity show.

"I didn't want to date, and like I said, I have a terrible track record with relationships, but I can't seem to ignore my feelings for you. I'm not ready to come out. I'm not even sure if I'm ready to take things beyond kissing yet. Would . . . would it be enough for you if we take it slow? Just let me try to sort myself out before we put a label on anything?"

"I can go as slow as you need," Marin told her. "There's no rush, as long as you see yourself dating me publicly at some point. Eventually, I do want a partner who shares every facet of my life."

"No rush, hmm?" Charlotte gave her a playful smile that faded abruptly. "I was going to tease you about how desperate you were earlier, but Marin, I'm not sure any of this is fair to you. I know how long you've waited, how serious you are about dating and finding a life partner. I totally understand if you want to look for someone who can offer you that *now*, because I just don't know how long it will take me to catch up to you. I'm sorry, but I don't."

Marin looked down at her half-eaten lasagna as she gathered her thoughts. "It's easy for the logical side of my brain to agree with you. Statistically, I have a higher chance of success if I keep using the dating app, but if there's one thing I've learned since I met you, it's that statistics don't apply where we're concerned. My heart wants what it wants, and that, my dear, is *you*."

Charlotte's bottom lip quivered. "Your . . . your heart?"

"Yes." Marin felt vulnerable for the admission, but she wouldn't apologize for it. "It's not a declaration of love, at least not yet, but you can consider it a declaration of intent. I like you a lot. I'm ridiculously attracted to you and have been since the moment I first laid eyes on you on that bus."

Charlotte's eyes went wide.

"Yes, from the moment we met," Marin told her. "I was so distracted by you . . . and the horoscope you read me. When I was crossing the street, I looked back at the bus, hoping for one last glance."

"I saw you look back. I was watching you too. *God.*" Charlotte's eyes filled with tears.

"I spent two years thinking about you," Marin admitted quietly. "When we reconnected here in Vermont, I thought you were straight, and I was thrilled for the chance at friendship. I thought I could move past my attraction, and I probably would have. I'm very good at keeping my feelings to myself." She shrugged. "But then you kissed me . . ."

Charlotte grinned, and then she was doing it again . . . kissing Marin. They leaned toward each other on their kitchen stools. Their lips met with just as much urgency as before, and Marin's body awakened all over again, aching and yearning, a reminder that *this* was what she craved and that it was worth waiting for because this kind of magic . . . who knew if she'd ever find it again?

"Statistically, our chemistry is off the charts," she murmured against Charlotte's lips, "and I can't guarantee I'll find this anywhere else."

"I can't disagree with that," Charlotte responded breathlessly.

"So yes, I'm willing to go as slow as you need," Marin told her. "If you just want to kiss and fool around until you've figured things out, I'll wait for you."

Charlotte rested a hand on Marin's waist. "I don't think I deserve you, but if you're willing to wait for me, I promise I'll work as hard as I can to figure my shit out sooner than later so we can be together for real."

Marin nodded. She was certain Charlotte would be worth the risk . . . and the wait. "Then it sounds like we have a plan."

"God, that's good," Marin practically moaned, and *phew* that sound did things to Charlotte. Marin was on the couch in a T-shirt and leggings while Charlotte gave her that massage she'd promised earlier, and the whole thing was sexier than Charlotte had anticipated.

She kneaded Marin's right thigh through her leggings, trying not to become distracted by how close she was to other parts of Marin's anatomy. It was awkward giving her a massage over her clothes, but they'd both thought undressing—even for a massage—was too much too soon.

"When did you first suspect?" Marin asked, making a little sound of pleasure as Charlotte's fingers worked the tension from her muscles.

Charlotte looked up to find Marin watching her with surprising intensity. "That I'm not straight?"

"Yes. I want to know everything about your journey, or everything you feel comfortable sharing, at least."

"After your snowshoeing date with Laura." Charlotte shifted her focus to Marin's calves, smiling as she felt the puppy curl up on her own lower legs. "You came home and told me she kissed you, and it felt like a gut punch."

"Wow," Marin murmured. "That's so recent. You must still be reeling, trying to figure it all out."

"I am," Charlotte admitted. "I'm so confused and unsure, and . . . nothing makes sense, except it does because I love every moment I'm with you, and there's no denying how much I love kissing you. I still don't know if that's enough, but . . ."

"It's enough." Marin reached down and squeezed her hand. "We have time. You need to get comfortable with your sexuality before we move forward."

Charlotte sighed, sliding her hands over Marin's calves, which were surprisingly well defined. "Your legs are sexy as fuck, by the way. You're way more toned than I am."

Marin chuckled. "That's a nice bonus from all the PT."

"Very nice indeed." Charlotte scooted forward, disturbing the puppy in the process, so she could kiss Marin's lips. "Remember how you told me once that you could look back and see early signs that you liked women, things you missed at the time?"

"Yes. I think a lot of people find that to be the case. You too?"

Charlotte nodded, suddenly desperate to get this off her chest, to share it with the one person she knew would understand. "I realized . . . I mean, I'm pretty sure I had feelings for Elena back in high school. I had no idea at the time, but now . . ."

Marin looked thoughtful. "You know, that makes total sense, actually. It's probably why you got so upset when she took her boyfriend to the prom instead of you."

"I think so, yeah." Charlotte was nodding almost desperately, but it felt so good to finally discuss this with Marin. Not being able to share it with her before had been one of the hardest parts about questioning her sexuality.

"I bet you'll find more early signs now that you know what you're looking for," Marin said. "A celebrity crush? A teacher?"

Charlotte laughed somewhat awkwardly. Had there been others? She hadn't prepared herself for that. "You mean Eden Sands might be more than just my favorite singer?"

Marin's eyebrows rose, and her lips quirked. "I don't know, is she?"

"I'm a pretty big fan, and I *do* think she's beautiful." Charlotte's cheeks flushed hot. "I had her poster on the wall of my dorm room in college. Shit. I *did* get really invested when she came out a few years ago. I read every article about it because I was just so happy for her and Anna . . ."

"Sounds like a crush to me," Marin said with a coy smile. "Welcome to your sapphic side."

Charlotte spent the next few days texting Marin every chance she got. They met for dinner on Friday—which led to more kissing—and generally acted like any other newly dating couple. Charlotte was completely smitten, thinking about her when they were apart, cherishing every moment together . . . just like she had with her previous boyfriends.

So, she definitely wasn't straight. She'd given it a lot of thought and even researched different sexualities on the internet, and so far, she thought pansexual was going to be the label that fit her best. She was attracted to a person, not their gender. While she'd been attracted to more men than women in her life, there was no denying she liked women too. And nonbinary people. She could be attracted to anyone, but right now, she only had eyes for Marin.

Now that Marin had brought her attention to it, Charlotte could look back over her life and recognize so many other female crushes—TV characters, celebrities, and of course Elena. It seemed so obvious now, and yet she'd totally missed it for what it was at the time. It gave her a new perspective on herself, though, to know her pansexuality was nothing new. She'd *always* been attracted to women.

Wild.

Marin drove to Manhattan on Saturday to have lunch with—and come out to—two more of her siblings. While she was out of town, Charlotte had dinner with Elena and her family. It was wonderful to meet Elena's daughters and husband, but Charlotte understood what Marin meant when she said she'd felt like she was wearing a mask around her friends while she was in the closet. Charlotte felt like she couldn't fully be herself around Elena while she was keeping this secret, but she just wasn't ready to share it with her.

Yet.

On Monday, Charlotte had her Zoom chat with Bev. This was her last lead. Where would she look next if Bev didn't have new information for her? Because Charlotte didn't know how to move forward with her life without getting closure about her mom.

She got dressed for the day since she had several showings that afternoon, and then she sat at her laptop and opened Zoom. She'd joined the session a few minutes early, so Bev wasn't online yet, and

Charlotte had to sit there, trying not to stare at herself on the video feed, wondering if she looked as nervous as she felt.

And suddenly, Bev was smiling at her from her computer screen. She looked older than Charlotte remembered, of course. Her brown hair was mostly white now, short and spiky, and her smile was as infectious as ever. Charlotte's heart gave a funny little squeeze because the sight of Bev brought back so many fun memories from her childhood. She remembered the way her mom would laugh when Bev was around, and how Bev seemed to genuinely enjoy letting Charlotte join their conversations, even though she was just a child.

"Charlotte," Bev exclaimed, and her wistful expression made Charlotte think Bev might be reliving some of the same memories. "Look at you, all grown up." Her eyes grew misty, and she pressed her knuckles to her mouth. "My god, you look like Terri did at your age. Wow."

Charlotte's smile felt brittle on her face. She knew she looked like her mother, or at least, she knew she looked like photos of her mother, but Charlotte's memories of her were so hazy. She'd been only ten when her mom disappeared. She wasn't sure how much she really remembered and how much she knew from looking at photos and hearing stories about her. "Bev, it's so good to see you. How is your husband doing?"

"Oh, he's much better, almost fully recovered from the pneumonia. Thanks so much for asking."

"I'm really glad to hear that," Charlotte said.

"Me too." She sighed. "Now that we're talking, I regret not doing a better job of keeping in touch. I looked you up on Facebook about ten years ago, but I wasn't sure you'd want to hear from me. Now I know I should have gone ahead and sent you a friend request."

"It's okay. I could have looked for you sooner too." Charlotte took a deep breath. "But we're here now."

"And you want to know what became of your mom." Bev rested a hand beneath her chin. She was in what looked to be her kitchen, with white cabinets visible behind her.

"I do. When I moved back to Vermont last fall, I decided I was going to find out what happened to her once and for all, but I'm already running out of leads."

"It's hard when people go missing," Bev said. "So many questions left unanswered. But let me see if I can answer some of yours. Since the last time we spoke, I've racked my brain for information about your mom, and I've come up with a few tidbits you might be interested in. First of all, your parents' marriage had hit a bit of a rough patch. I'm sorry if that's hard to hear."

"I know about the affair. I've spoken to Allan Svenson already."

Bev's face showed no surprise, which confirmed Charlotte's suspicion that her mom had kept few secrets from her best friend. "Good. I'm glad you know. That was something I didn't want to have to tell you myself. I'm not sure if it's relevant to her disappearance or not, but . . . your call got me thinking about things."

"And?" Charlotte pressed, stomach tight.

"When I think back to that time, actually the last few years before Terri disappeared, I think . . . well, she might have been depressed. I didn't know much about mental health back then. I didn't recognize it for what it was at the time, so I didn't mention it during the investigation, but she'd lost interest in a lot of things she used to enjoy. She stopped wanting to play tennis with me. I'm not sure she even enjoyed teaching anymore. The affair was, I think, an attempt to bring some excitement back into her life, and maybe it did. She did seem happier those last few months before she disappeared."

"Depressed," Charlotte repeated, reeling. She hadn't realized her mom was unhappy, but she didn't remember her as particularly happy either. "Do you think . . ." She couldn't even say the words, but when depressed people disappeared, it generally meant they'd taken matters into their own hands.

"I don't think she killed herself," Bev rushed to add. "Although at this point, I guess we can't rule it out, but I never thought she was suicidal. She just seemed . . . sad."

"Then what do you think happened?" Charlotte asked, her voice hoarse with emotion.

"At the time, I tried not to speculate. It was just too painful. But like I said, I've done a lot of thinking since you called, and I've come up with a theory. It's not a very *likely* theory, mind you, but it's the best I've got. The thing is, Terri had been talking about taking a vacation. She wanted to just get away from it all, you know? Go someplace tropical with turquoise water and sandy beaches. She mentioned it to me several times, and I didn't get the feeling she was talking about a family vacation. She wanted time alone. I didn't put two and two together at the time, but again . . . hindsight and all that."

Bev stared at Charlotte from the screen, suddenly serious. "I remember Terri telling me that if she made it down there, if she put her toes in the sand and had a tropical drink in her hand . . . she might not want to come back."

CHAPTER TWENTY

On the following Saturday, Charlotte stopped by Marin's house with coffee and breakfast before Marin set out to visit her sister Nancy. Her visit with Fran and Tom last weekend had gone pretty well, but Charlotte knew Marin had been dreading this one. Nancy was likely to disappoint her, and Charlotte wanted to offer as much support as she could beforehand.

Internally, she was spiraling over her conversation with Bev. She hadn't realized until Bev suggested that Charlotte's mom might be living a new life on a tropical island just how firmly her subconscious had believed her mom was dead. Deep down, she'd assumed she was looking for her mom's body. And if, by some miracle, her mom was still alive, Charlotte had assumed something happened to keep her from coming home.

So to think her mom might be out there, living and loving life without her? That was absolutely devastating. Nonetheless, Charlotte was putting on a brave face today because Marin was about to face her conservative and likely homophobic sister.

Nancy lived outside Rochester, New York, which was about a five-hour drive from Middleton, so Marin would be spending the night there. Charlotte was disappointed that Marin would be gone most of the weekend, even though Charlotte would be working for the majority of it.

She'd done a lot of soul-searching since she and Marin agreed to take things slow, and while she wasn't ready to come out to anyone else in her life yet, she got more comfortable with her sexuality every day. Marin had become so important to her in such a short time, and it just felt . . . right. Charlotte knocked on Marin's door, surprised to hear a tiny bark from inside the house.

A few seconds later, Marin opened the door, looking somewhat frazzled. "Oh, Charlotte. Hi." She stepped forward to give Charlotte a quick kiss as Ember barreled past her to bounce against Charlotte's legs.

Charlotte smiled against Marin's lips. "I brought coffee and breakfast to share with you before you leave. When did she start barking when someone knocks on the door?"

"It's new." Marin rolled her eyes. "Either a developmental phase or a response to the new house, like she feels like it's hers and needs to be protected."

"That might be adorable?" Charlotte asked, bending to pet the puppy.

"It's adorable now but maybe not when she's older. I'm going to do some research on how to discourage the barking."

"Good idea." Charlotte stepped into the entrance hall and slipped off her shoes, then wrapped an arm around Marin's waist and drew her in for another kiss. She could hardly believe how natural this already felt, how much she enjoyed it, how much she craved more . . .

"I'm glad you stopped by." Marin swayed into her touch, resting her forehead against Charlotte's. "I was hoping to see you before I left."

"My first showing isn't for an hour, so I'm all yours until then." Charlotte slid a hand down to Marin's hip, caressing her over her pants.

"I like the sound of that," Marin murmured. She shifted on her feet, and because Charlotte was still holding her, she felt the tension that seized Marin's body.

"You okay?" she asked.

"Just some nerve pain," Marin said. "I'll be fine."

"You have a five-hour drive this afternoon. Won't that make it worse?"

"It might," Marin admitted. "But I'll get through it. Now that I've told the rest of my siblings, I'm afraid Nancy's going to hear my news through the grapevine if I don't hurry up and tell her myself . . . and I really want to be the one to tell her."

"I get that." Charlotte pulled back, eyeing her critically. Now that she was paying attention, she could see the strain on Marin's face and the stiffness in her posture. "Come enjoy your latte while it's hot. I brought muffins, too, cranberry this time."

"Sounds perfect." Marin led the way to the kitchen, which was now furnished with a small round table and chairs. She'd done a lot of work this week, filling her house with furniture and accents that helped it feel more like a home.

Marin eased herself into one of the chairs, obviously trying to minimize her pain, but Charlotte wasn't fooled. She sat across from Marin, wondering what she could do to help. She was worried about her making that five-hour drive alone.

Well, she'd have Ember along for company, but the puppy actually made the journey more complicated, as she'd need frequent potty stops that would require Marin to lift her in and out of the vehicle. Plus, the pain was in Marin's right leg, so she couldn't exactly stretch it while she was driving.

"What if I tag along to do the driving?" Charlotte suggested, speaking her idea out loud almost before it had formed in her mind. "I'll stay at the hotel while you meet with Nancy, but I'd love to help with driving and puppy wrangling."

"I'll be fine," Marin insisted, sipping her latte. "You've got showings scheduled all weekend. We already discussed this when I made my travel plans."

"Yes, we did, but you're in pain, and I want to help. Surely you'd be more comfortable in the passenger seat so you can recline with an ice pack. I can cancel today's showings or try to get another agent to cover for me. It's not that big of a deal. Let me help. Please?"

"I . . . really?" Marin's expression had softened now. "You'd do that for me?"

"Of course I would. Even if we were only friends, I would, but I especially want to help now that we're more than friends. You mean so much to me, and I hate seeing you in pain. If I stay home, I'll worry the entire time, wondering if you're okay."

"I'll be fine on my own," Marin said. "But it *would* be more comfortable if I could recline in the passenger seat, and if I had someone to help with Ember."

"Then it's settled. I'm coming." Charlotte nodded decisively. "You're planning to leave around noon, right?"

Marin nodded. "I'm staying overnight near Rochester. Is that okay?"

"Yes." Charlotte would have to rearrange most of her showings this weekend, but Marin was her priority right now. Health and happiness came before work, which was something she hadn't always realized in the past. "Okay, I'll call around to see if a coworker can cover some of my showings. I'll cancel the rest, then go to my ten o'clock, pack an overnight bag, and meet you back here around noon."

"We can leave a little later if that's better for you. I was originally planning to have dinner with Nancy, but she rescheduled on me. I'm not meeting with her until breakfast tomorrow, so as long as we make it to Rochester tonight, we're fine."

"Okay, it would actually be amazing if I could keep my ten *and* my eleven this morning. Those are the most important showings I have scheduled this weekend. So I'll be back to your house around one?"

Marin reached out and gripped her hand. "Take your time. I really appreciate this."

"I know you do, and I'm happy to do it. We'll have a fun road trip adventure."

Marin smiled, looking excited for the first time since Charlotte had arrived at her front door. "Yes, we will."

Marin still felt a little bit guilty that Charlotte had rescheduled her weekend appointments for her, but she couldn't deny she was glad to have her along for the trip. Charlotte drove, chatting energetically and singing along with the radio while Marin reclined in the passenger seat with a gel pack wrapped around her thigh.

"Your turn," Charlotte announced. They'd been playing car games to pass the time, and right now they were playing a modified version of truth or dare that basically just involved sharing truths.

"Your first kiss," Marin said, looking over at her.

"Dylan Cranston in tenth grade. It was gross." Charlotte scrunched her nose. "He stuck his tongue in my mouth, and there was way too much spit involved. I didn't kiss anyone again for like a year after that."

Marin laughed. "'Gross' pretty much sums up all my high school kissing experiences."

"Well, you were kissing the wrong gender."

"I didn't know that yet, though," Marin said.

"When *did* you know?" Charlotte asked.

"College, probably. I had a few crushes that I tried really hard to convince myself were women I admired, but deep down, I think I knew. I just didn't want to admit it, not even to myself. I knew my parents would be disappointed, that they might even disown me if I was gay. I felt as if I'd be making life so much harder for myself if I 'chose that lifestyle,' which was of course bullshit because it's not a choice. My denial led to me being stuck for way too long in a marriage I never truly wanted."

"I'm sorry," Charlotte said. "I hate that society puts so much pressure on us to fit in and conform to other people's ideas of who we should be. And I hate that homophobia is still so prevalent, but here you are, being all loud and proud in spite of it. I think you're incredibly badass, Marin Easterly."

Marin chuckled. "So badass I'm basically flat on my back while you drive me to my sister's house."

"For the hundredth time, you are *extremely badass* for surviving what you did, and I have nothing but respect for how you've rebuilt your life and all the risks you're taking. Driving to Rochester to come out to your conservative older sister who's probably not going to take it well? Brave as fuck."

"Thank you." Marin swallowed over the lump in her throat. "Okay, your turn."

"Let's see." Charlotte glanced at her with a smile. She had on sunglasses, her blond hair was loose over her shoulders, and she was so gorgeous, she took Marin's breath away. "Dream vacation?"

"Goodness, I don't know." Marin turned to look out the window. "I was so focused on getting divorced and starting my new life, I haven't given much thought to vacations."

"I hear you. I haven't taken many fancy vacations, either, mostly just ski trips or weekends at a local beach, but it's fun to think about, right? Like, if money and time off and all those other logistics weren't an issue, where would you want to go?"

"Hmm." Marin wasn't playing coy. She honestly had no idea. "I suppose a tropical beach sounds nice. That clear blue water? I'd love to see it, and sit in one of those fancy chairs with an umbrella so I don't burn. Maybe I'd like to go snorkeling and see the fish up close." Now that she was picturing it, the ideas kept coming. "Or scuba diving? Do you think that's too hard? I want to see a coral reef and pretty fish, maybe even a shark, if it's not the man-eating kind."

"A shark, hmm?" Charlotte smiled, but it seemed somewhat fragile.

"You look upset. Was it something I said?"

Charlotte huffed, then shook her head. "No, I was just thinking about what Bev said about my mom wanting to go to a tropical island and how she might not come back."

"Shit, that was insensitive of me. I'm sorry."

"Don't be sorry. It just shook me up. It made me realize that deep down, I assumed my mom was gone." Charlotte drew in a sharp breath. "I feel terrible admitting this, but somehow imagining her on a tropical island somewhere, happily living her life without me? That feels . . . worse." Her voice faded out on that last word.

"I can see how it would." Marin reached over and gripped her hand where it rested on the steering wheel. "But if that's what she did, hopefully she had a reason for it."

"The worst part is that I'll probably never know." Charlotte sighed, and it carried a sadness that made Marin's breath catch. "I'm talking to a PI who specializes in finding people who've disappeared on purpose, but he's really expensive, and I don't know how likely it is that he could track her down after all this time . . . if that's really what she did."

"I truly hope you find the answers you need."

"I do, too, but I'm trying to make peace with the possibility that I won't. And I hope you get to take that tropical vacation someday . . . hopefully with me."

"I like the sound of that." Marin's attention caught on a sign for an upcoming rest area, and she pointed. "Do you mind?"

"Course not. Need to stretch your legs?"

Marin nodded. Actually, she didn't have any pain at the moment. Reclining the seat had done her a world of good, but she'd stayed in the car at both their previous stops while Charlotte walked Ember, and now her bladder was complaining. "So what's your pick for a dream vacation?"

Charlotte looked thoughtful. "I think for me it's more about who I'm with than where I am. I don't care all that much about seeing specific places, I guess. I care more about having fun experiences with my favorite people."

"That's a great way of looking at it."

A few minutes later, they stopped at the rest area, and Marin was relieved to find that she had no nerve pain when she stood. "Resting while you drove really did the trick. I'm feeling completely better."

"Yay." Charlotte leaned in and gave her a quick kiss.

Since they were hours from home and anyone who might know them, Marin grabbed Charlotte's hips and pulled her in for another deeper kiss. "I love kissing you."

"Same."

And then, because she really did have to pee, she let Charlotte go. "Do you mind watching Ember while I go inside?"

"Nope. Take your time."

Marin and Charlotte took turns going into the rest area, and then they got back on the road. The last two hours of the trip passed uneventfully, with Ember napping in back while Charlotte and Marin played more silly car games.

It wasn't until they were pulling into the lodge that Marin thought through the logistics for the night ahead. "Um, I picked this place because it had individual cottages instead of a central hotel building, for Ember's sake, but I don't remember what the bed situation is." She hadn't paid the least bit of attention, assuming she would be alone in the room. She'd been more focused on finding pet-friendly accommodations for the night.

"No worries," Charlotte said. "We'll figure it out."

"Okay," Marin agreed, but she had a sneaking suspicion they might have a single-bed situation on their hands, and she had no idea how Charlotte would feel about that.

They stopped at the office, and she walked inside to check in. "Can you remind me what the sleeping arrangement is in the cabin I booked?" she asked the clerk.

"The bedroom has a king-size bed, and there's a pullout sofa in the living room," he told her.

"Oh, good." A pullout sofa was better than nothing. "Are there any other cabins available, just in case my friend doesn't want to sleep on the sofa?"

"I'm sorry, ma'am, but we're fully booked tonight." His tone was polite but firm. "It's one of the last big ski weekends around here."

"I understand. Thanks for your help." She took her key card and went back out to the car. "Good news and bad news," she told Charlotte. "There's a pullout sofa and a king bed."

"I'll take the sofa, no problem," Charlotte agreed easily.

"Okay." Marin shouldn't feel disappointed that Charlotte didn't want to share her bed, and yet . . . maybe she did. Even if they didn't have sex, she'd love to sleep beside Charlotte.

They drove to cabin twelve and took the parking space in front, then spent the next few minutes carrying their bags inside and getting Ember's crate set up. The cottage was cozy, with a little living room and kitchenette and a separate bedroom.

The windows probably had pretty views during the daytime. The pictures on the website looked nice, anyway, but it was approaching seven now, and the sun had set. They were both starving, and Ember probably was too. Marin fed and walked the puppy while Charlotte went over to the diner next door, returning with sandwiches and milkshakes.

Then they watched TV together for a little while, cuddling on the sofa with Ember nestled cozily between them. It felt like a scene from a future Marin desperately wanted, the three of them making a happy little family unit. Honestly, she couldn't think of anything more perfect. As she rested her head on Charlotte's shoulder, breathing in the fruity scent of her shampoo, she thought this must be love.

Both her heart and her body craved Charlotte every moment of every day. She felt happy in Charlotte's presence, content, safe.

Of course that was love. Maybe she'd been a little bit in love with Charlotte since they reconnected back in January.

She remembered what Charlotte had said in the car about her dream vacation being more about the person than the place, and Marin felt the truth of that here on this slightly stiff sofa in a little cabin outside Rochester with a potentially unpleasant meeting with Nancy looming in the morning. The circumstances were far from ideal, but Marin felt warm, relaxed, and happy simply because she was with Charlotte.

"What are you thinking?" Charlotte asked. "Looks intense."

"Just thinking how glad I am that you're here." Marin brought their lips together. "And that you don't need to sleep on the sofa tonight if you don't want to."

Charlotte's eyes widened.

"We don't have to do anything but sleep, but it's a big bed, Charlotte. Share it with me."

Charlotte looked down at her lap. "Funny you should mention that, because I actually checked out the sofa bed earlier, and it's broken. Totally unusable."

"So you're telling me there's only one bed?" Marin couldn't help laughing.

"Yes?" Charlotte gave her a questioning look. "What am I missing?"

"Sorry, it's a romance-novel thing. 'Only one bed' is a *very* popular trope."

"Oh," Charlotte said. "I mean, I was just going to sleep on the couch itself."

"That sounds so uncomfortable. Please share the bed with me. We can just sleep."

Her bottom lip trembled. "I want to do more than sleep. I hope you know that. It's just . . . I'm scared. I don't know anything about sex between two women. I've been meaning to research it, but I got caught up in everything with my mom. Meanwhile, you've been waiting such a long time, and I feel like you deserve more than I can give you."

"Impossible," Marin assured her, one of her hands stroking the skin above Charlotte's jeans, and even that simple touch had her pulse racing. Once they made it to the bedroom—whenever that happened—she was going to absolutely lose her mind. She got wet just thinking about it. "I'm so attracted to you, anything we do will be amazing. We're both going to be feeling our way, so to speak, but I think that could make it even more special. We'll have to check in a lot, right? Ask each other what we like and what feels good. Trial and error sounds really fucking sexy, if you ask me."

"Yeah." Charlotte's breath hitched as Marin scratched her nails lightly over her skin. "I like *that*, by the way." Charlotte slipped a hand beneath Marin's shirt, then slid it up to cup her over her bra, and Marin ached to feel that hand on her bare skin. She *throbbed.* All this foreplay with Charlotte was the sweetest kind of torture.

"See?" Marin's voice was raspy with need. "Feeling our way. We're already good at it. I'm one hundred percent confident we'll figure the rest out . . . when the time comes."

Charlotte blinked at her out of lust-drunk eyes. "One hundred percent?"

Marin nodded. "And as a statistician, I don't say that unless I mean it."

"Mare," Charlotte whispered, and something in her tone only increased the ache between Marin's thighs. "I'd like to share the bed with you."

"What are you saying?" Marin asked, because she had to be sure. She couldn't stand much more teasing, not if Charlotte was going to share her bed platonically tonight.

"I'm saying, I want to do more than sleep in that bed."

"Are you sure you're ready? I know you wanted to focus on family before relationships this year . . ."

Charlotte's gaze never wavered. "I'm sure. I thought a relationship might distract me from my goal of finding my mom, because my previous relationships *were* distracting, but it's different with you. You're my best friend *and* my partner, and you encourage me in everything I do. If I get a new lead, you'll help me chase it, whether we're sleeping together or not."

"Oh, Charlotte . . ." Marin blinked the tears from her eyes.

"So yeah, I'm ready. Let's live out your 'only one bed' trope. What do you say?"

"Yes. I say yes."

CHAPTER TWENTY-ONE

Charlotte trembled with anticipation as she stood in the doorway to the bedroom, watching Marin tuck Ember into her crate. Anticipation . . . and maybe a little bit of fear. Not fear of having sex with Marin, but what if Charlotte didn't know what to do? What if she failed to live up to whatever fantasies Marin had in her head from the romance novels she loved so much?

With Ember put away, Marin shut off the overhead light, then crossed the room to stand in front of Charlotte. They'd left the light on in the kitchen, and it cast a warm glow over Marin's features. "I'm not trying to hide from you, Charlotte. I just didn't think Ember would settle for the night with the light on."

"Why would you hide from me?" Charlotte asked. After all, of the two of them, Marin had been the most eager to move things to the bedroom.

"I have scars." Marin held her gaze, not flinching away, but even in the low light, Charlotte saw the insecurity in her features. "I know you know that, but I haven't been with anyone since before the accident, and . . . I've *never* been with anyone I was attracted to. This is a pretty big deal for me."

Somehow, it was a relief for Charlotte to realize they both had some insecurities about tonight. "It's a big deal for both of us. Your scars are a testament to what you survived, Mare. I understand why you might feel self-conscious, but I've always found wrinkles and scars to be a beautiful and intriguing part of someone's body. They're marks of a life lived, right?"

Marin smiled, eyes glossy with unshed tears. "That's a lovely way of looking at it. I'm not ashamed of my wrinkles or my scars, but I'm *aware* of them . . . and that I didn't have them the last time I undressed for someone new."

"It's safe to say I find everything about you beautiful." Charlotte rested her hands on Marin's hips and drew her closer. "I always have. I didn't know *why* I found you so captivating at first, or why I always wanted to find excuses to touch you . . ."

"I never dared to hope you felt the same way," Marin said softly. "I thought I was doomed to the purgatory of lusting after my straight friend."

"Have you thought about me?" Charlotte asked, toying with the waistband of Marin's pants. She had on gray pants that looked like jeans but felt soft and stretchy beneath Charlotte's fingers, probably in deference to the long car ride. Charlotte traced a finger over the front of them, loving the way the fabric hugged Marin's curves. "When you touch yourself?"

She felt Marin inhale, a soft sound catching in her throat, and it made Charlotte ache with desire. It felt like a yes. It *sounded* like a yes. And it was unbelievably hot to picture Marin in bed, touching herself while she thought of Charlotte.

"Yes," Marin whispered. "I have . . . even before we reconnected. I've thought about you a *lot* since we met on that bus."

"Oh." Charlotte gulped. Marin had mentioned that before, but maybe it hadn't fully sunk in then. It had now. *Fuck.* She surged forward, capturing Marin's mouth. This kiss was different from the ones they'd shared before. This kiss felt like a lit fuse, like they'd ignited something that was barreling toward combustion. There was no stopping them now, and beneath the heated onslaught of Marin's mouth, Charlotte relinquished her insecurities about being able to satisfy a woman.

They both wanted this. They'd figure it out. And it was going to be amazing. How could it not be?

Charlotte fumbled with the button on Marin's pants, loving the needy sound Marin made as it opened. As Charlotte pushed down the zipper, her fingers brushed against the front of Marin's underwear. The fabric was delicate and undeniably feminine, and for a moment, her brain screeched to a halt at this tangible reminder that she was about to have sex with a woman. *Record scratch.*

Then Marin moaned, her hips pressing into Charlotte's touch, and the sound provoked an answering ache in Charlotte's core. She wanted this. So much. And as much as she couldn't wait for her own orgasm, she was going to take even more pleasure from fulfilling Marin's needs.

Charlotte thought of how many nights, how many *years* Marin had lain in bed beside her husband, dreaming about the day she could finally be with a woman, how she'd lain awake alone in bed after the divorce, still waiting. She'd anticipated this moment for so long, and now it was finally here.

And Charlotte was going to do her damn best to blow Marin's mind.

"Lie on the bed."

Marin heard the words through a haze of arousal, and it took a moment for them to register. Then she felt herself nodding, stepping backward, pulling Charlotte with her as Marin's brain went into overload because she was getting into bed with Charlotte. This was really happening.

She sat on the edge of the bed, inhaling sharply as her pants pressed against her where she ached. Oh, this was the most delicious form of anticipation. To be this aroused just from a little kissing and touching . . .

"Can I undress you?" she asked Charlotte. "Please?"

Charlotte stood before her, cheeks flushed, hair messy, nodding eagerly. "God, yes."

Without hesitating, Marin gripped the hem of Charlotte's shirt. Charlotte lifted her arms, and Marin tugged the shirt over her head, revealing a flesh-toned bra. It was simple, an everyday bra, smooth and seamless so as not to show beneath her top, but to Marin, it was the most beautiful thing she'd ever seen because it was on Charlotte.

Charlotte was watching her again, lips slightly parted as she lowered her arms back to her sides. Her chest rose and fell with rapid breaths.

Running on instinct, Marin slid her hands greedily over Charlotte's bra-covered breasts, then reached for the clasp between them, feeling a bit clumsy as she unfastened it. It fell away, baring Charlotte's breasts, and it took a moment for Marin to realize the gasp she heard was her own. Charlotte's breasts were so beautiful, large and firm, her pink nipples already tightened into hard buds. Marin wanted to take her time touching them, but first . . .

She unbuttoned Charlotte's jeans, then lowered the zipper, baring the front of pink cotton panties. Marin's core clenched at the sight. She pushed at Charlotte's jeans, and Charlotte helped, shoving them down her legs and stepping out of them. Her panties had a delicate lace trim that Marin was entranced by.

She traced it with her fingertips, rewarded as Charlotte's breathing picked up speed. Marin touched her over the cotton, feeling how damp it was, and she knew her own underwear was just as wet, if not more so. She was already throbbing just from touching Charlotte.

Marin felt as if she'd gone into a trance. All she could think about was exploring Charlotte's body. She'd waited so long to touch a woman, and for two years now, she'd dreamed of touching *this* woman. Marin felt eager and greedy as she slid her hands over Charlotte's skin. Every touch aroused her as much as it seemed to arouse Charlotte.

Charlotte stepped forward, pushing Marin flat on her back on the bed. In the next moment, Charlotte was straddling her, and Marin nearly lost her mind. Charlotte's warm weight pressed into her right where she ached. Their bodies touched in the most intimate way, although separated by far too much clothing.

Marin gripped Charlotte's ass, moving her against her, whimpering as Charlotte's hips rocked against her clit. It was too much and not enough, and Marin was so overwhelmed—she had no idea what she wanted to do next when everything felt so goddamn wonderful.

"Can I touch you?" she managed, her voice low and rough.

"You're still dressed," Charlotte responded, reaching for the waistband of Marin's pants.

"I know, but I . . . I need . . ." She gulped. "I need to know how you feel. Please."

Charlotte let out the sexiest little whimper, nodding almost frantically. "Yes. Touch me."

She rolled to the side, scrambling out of her panties, and Marin took a moment to appreciate the sight of her naked body, the golden curls between her thighs, glistening with her arousal. Marin had imagined this moment so many times. She'd looked at sexy images online, but she'd never actually seen a naked woman in person . . . other than herself, of course.

Now Charlotte was laid out before her, looking so goddamn beautiful. She was a feast, and Marin couldn't wait to devour her. Marin slid a hand almost reverently over the dip of Charlotte's waist to her hip. Her skin was so smooth, so warm, so *soft*. Goose bumps rose beneath Marin's touch, and seeing them thrilled her, because it meant Charlotte was affected by this too.

Marin reminded herself to breathe, sucking in air as she trailed her fingers over Charlotte's stomach, and then her fingers slid through Charlotte's curls to the hot, wet folds beneath. *Oh wow.* Charlotte's breathing became labored as Marin explored her, slowly moving her fingers over Charlotte's delicate flesh, familiarizing herself with Charlotte's body.

"You feel so good," Marin whispered. Her core ached more fiercely than ever, but it was a good ache. The *best.* She fought the urge to grind herself against Charlotte's thigh, instead savoring the anticipation, because tonight she was going to experience the pleasure she'd been craving. Tonight, it was all within her reach.

But first, she wanted to lose herself in the pleasure of Charlotte's body, because Marin had looked forward to this just as much. She'd wanted to touch a woman, to please her, to feel her come apart beneath Marin's fingers. Later, beneath her tongue. *Oh*, she couldn't wait for that either.

Marin was surprised to realize she was trembling in anticipation. She found Charlotte's opening and dipped her fingers into the wetness waiting for her there. "Is this okay?"

Charlotte nodded frantically, pressing one of her hands over Marin's, pushing her more firmly against her. "Please."

The sight of Charlotte's desperation sent a sharp surge of arousal between Marin's thighs, and she pressed them together, feeling rather desperate herself. Thank goodness she was still fully dressed, because if her bare skin touched Charlotte's? She might come before she was ready. Already, her hips moved almost without her knowledge, rocking to mimic the movement of her fingers as she stroked Charlotte.

Carefully, Marin pushed two fingers inside her, and then she groaned at the velvety soft feel of Charlotte surrounding her. God that felt good. Her hips moved more insistently now, and so did Charlotte's. They bumped against each other with Marin's hand trapped in between, and it was hot, so fucking hot.

Marin pumped in and out of Charlotte's body, then retreated, sliding her fingers up. This was the one part she'd been unsure about, finding Charlotte's clit. She knew how to find her own, of course, but how would it feel on another woman's body? Her fingertips were wet with Charlotte's arousal, sliding easily over her flesh.

She searched, feeling . . . feeling . . . Oh god, what if she couldn't find it? That would be so embarrassing, but before she could panic, Charlotte gasped, her back bowing, and her reaction alerted Marin that she'd reached her destination. Sure enough, as she focused her touch, she felt the little bud beneath her fingertips.

Marin gasped, her clit throbbing as she touched Charlotte's. "Right here?"

"Yes," Charlotte said, then moaned. "You're a natural. Don't think a man's ever found it that quickly."

Marin let out a hoarse laugh, grateful for the validation that she wasn't bumbling around like she had no idea what she was doing, even if that was occasionally how she felt. She circled Charlotte's clit and then tapped her fingertips gently against it, drawing a wheeze from Charlotte's lips. "Tell me what you like."

"I . . . I don't know." Charlotte sounded almost confused by the admission. "With guys, it's usually a race to the finish line, getting the condom on so he can get inside me, but with you . . . I don't know what comes next, except that I like everything you're doing."

"Do you want my fingers inside you?" Marin asked.

Charlotte nodded. "I think I do, yeah."

Marin brought a hand between Charlotte's thighs, testing her with her fingertips before she pushed inside. Charlotte's back bowed again, her stomach pressing into Marin's as she gasped with pleasure.

"You're so . . . so thoughtful with how you touch me," Charlotte said, panting. "You keep checking to make sure I'm ready for you, and I . . . that's really sexy."

"I'm glad." Marin thrust with those fingers as she used her other hand to touch Charlotte's clit, rubbing and circling it, watching

Charlotte's reactions to see what she liked best. Yes, she was very intentional in how she touched her. She wanted to give Charlotte as much pleasure as possible.

Emboldened by Charlotte's reactions, Marin hooked her fingertips forward, searching for her G-spot. She'd found hers before, although it was hard to reach on her own body. In theory, it would be easier to find on someone else. She fumbled around for a few seconds like an amateur, before she felt the soft, spongy area beneath her fingertips.

Charlotte went rigid against her. "I'm coming," Charlotte whispered before letting out a wild cry. Her inner walls pulsed around Marin's fingers, and she felt an answering clench inside herself. She clutched Charlotte against her, still stroking her with her fingers, wanting to feel every moment of her pleasure as she rode out her orgasm.

As for her own pleasure? This was already the most intense experience of Marin's life, and she hadn't even taken off her clothes yet.

Marin closed her eyes as Charlotte lifted Marin's shirt over her head. Her fingers brushed against Marin's bare skin, and *oh* it felt amazing. Then Charlotte began to push her pants down her legs. Marin did what she could to help, but snug, stretchy pants were a pain to get out of. There was simply no sexy way to get them off, except . . .

Charlotte scooted lower, kissing each inch of Marin's skin as she exposed it, and Marin was wrong. This was incredibly sexy. Her pants slid lower, and Marin heard herself wheeze as Charlotte kissed her upper thigh. Charlotte's tongue swirled against her delicate skin, and Marin arched off the bed.

"I love seeing you so worked up," Charlotte whispered against her thigh.

Marin sank her hands into the sheets, desperate for something to hold on to. She tried to respond to Charlotte, but the only thing that came out of her mouth was a shaky gasp.

"You like this?" Charlotte asked.

Marin could only nod, panting and clutching at the sheets. Charlotte tossed Marin's pants to the floor and then gently kissed her way down Marin's legs to her calves. Now Marin wore only her bra and panties. Charlotte kissed her way back up Marin's legs, drawing ever closer to the place where she ached so fiercely for her.

In all her many, *many* fantasies about her first time with a woman, she'd never imagined it quite like this. She hadn't thought to fantasize about Charlotte's lips on her inner thigh, and holy fuck that was amazing. Maybe somewhere in the back of her mind, Marin had worried that after so many years of anticipation, there was no way this experience could live up to her wildly inflated expectations, but in reality, it was *better* than she'd imagined.

Better because everything Charlotte did was unexpected. Not knowing where she'd kiss next, where she'd put her hands? It was blowing Marin's mind. And because she already felt so comfortable with Charlotte, so safe, she knew every touch was going to be wonderful.

Charlotte kissed her way over Marin's stomach, up her chest, to her mouth. Her naked body covered Marin's, soft skin sliding over hers, creating a delicious friction. Their mouths met, and Marin kissed her with mounting desperation, her hands clutching Charlotte's hips. Charlotte hovered over her somewhat awkwardly, not giving her any pressure where she needed it, heightening her anticipation.

They kissed for several long, delicious minutes. Marin's skin was sweat damp where it met Charlotte's, her heart racing out of control. Marin could feel that her panties were soaked. The ache in her core was almost unbearable, and yet, she was loving every moment. She was doing her very best to savor the wait, but if she didn't get some friction against her clit soon . . .

Then one of Charlotte's hands was beneath Marin's back, working the clasp of her bra until it released. She stripped the garment from Marin's body before scooting down to take one of Marin's breasts in her mouth. Her tongue laved at Marin's nipple, and it shot a bolt of fire straight to her core that hat her hips surging upward. Oh *fuck*. That felt amazing.

"You like that, hmm?" Charlotte asked before swirling her tongue around Marin's nipple again, and she could only nod frantically. "What else do you like?"

Too aroused to form words, Marin gripped one of Charlotte's hands and placed it over the band of her underwear, then pushed. Taking the hint, Charlotte stripped Marin's panties down her legs and dropped them on the floor. Now Marin was naked, cool air greeting her overheated skin.

Charlotte slid her hands up and down Marin's sides, fingertips skimming over her skin. One of her hands swept across Marin's lower stomach, lingering briefly over her scars, and Marin felt the briefest flash of insecurity before Charlotte was kissing her again. This time, Charlotte swirled her tongue over the tender skin below Marin's jaw, and she sank right back into the blissful haze of arousal.

Charlotte's hand slid down the front of her thigh, and Marin arched beneath her in a fruitless search for friction.

"Please . . ." she begged, too desperate to care how needy she sounded.

"Marin, I have no idea what I'm doing," Charlotte admitted quietly. "I know this is your first time with a woman, too, but I would have never known that from the way you touched me. What if I can't give you as much pleasure as you gave me?"

Marin exhaled, attempting to compose herself as she realized Charlotte hadn't been teasing. She'd been too intimidated to touch Marin. Now that she was paying attention, she saw the insecurity on Charlotte's face. "You'll be fine. Really. I'm . . . I'm so close it won't take much."

"Sorry." Charlotte gave her head a quick shake. "You've been so patient with me, and I'm just sitting here, making you wait. Okay, here goes." She slid her hand to the juncture of Marin's thighs, and they gasped in unison. Marin's hips bucked as Charlotte's fingers finally touched her pussy. Her touch was soft, tentative, and even so, Marin wanted to cry because it felt *so good.*

"It's your turn to tell me what you like," Charlotte said as she began to stroke Marin.

"Just . . . keep doing what you're doing, but . . . harder."

Charlotte's brow furrowed in concentration. She sucked her bottom lip between her teeth, which turned Marin on even more . . . if that was possible at this point. She was so aroused she could hardly think straight. Already, she felt the tingly heat of her impending release building low in her belly. She'd been so close just from getting Charlotte off. Marin canted her hips, increasing the pressure of Charlotte's fingers, and just like that, she was coming.

The orgasm rushed through her fierce and fast, a blinding wave of pleasure that left her shuddering and limp with relief. She gasped and grinned as she clutched Charlotte tighter against her. "Fuck. Oh god, that was amazing."

"I'm glad you think so, because I feel like I hardly did anything." Charlotte smiled back at her. "In fact, I don't think I'm finished with you yet. Watching you come was so hot, I want to see it again . . . and again."

"Oh." Marin stretched against the sheets, blissed out and relaxed, but already she felt the stirring of arousal again as a result of Charlotte's words. "I mean, I wouldn't say no to that. I wouldn't say no to anything with you." A lump rose in her throat at the admission, emotions surging to the surface because she just loved Charlotte so much. She loved lying here with her, holding her, touching her, literally everything.

"I thought it would be weird, being with a woman," Charlotte said as her fingertips traced circles on Marin's stomach. "I mean, not 'weird,' that's a terrible word to use when I'm talking about having sex with you, but I was a little unsure what constitutes sex between two women. I guess I grew up thinking that anything you do with your hands is foreplay and sex is when a man penetrates you, so . . ." She shrugged. "I didn't know what to expect. Maybe part of me worried

I wouldn't enjoy sapphic sex as much, but actually . . . this feels more intimate somehow."

Her hand dipped lower, cupping Marin intimately.

She throbbed at the touch. "Men need so much time to recharge, but women . . . we can go again and again. It's one of the things I've been most looking forward to."

"Does that mean you're ready to go again?" Charlotte asked, pressing down with her hand.

Marin gasped. "I'm always ready where you're concerned."

"That's hot." Charlotte grinned, looking much bolder now than she had a few minutes ago. "Then you won't mind if I do a little exploring?"

"Please do." Marin's breath hitched as Charlotte's fingers found her clit, circling it lightly.

"Right here?" Charlotte asked breathlessly.

Marin nodded somewhat desperately. "That's the spot."

"Noted." Charlotte toyed with Marin's clit, seeming to familiarize herself with it, and then she slid her fingers lower, pressing her fingertips to Marin's entrance. "And here? Do you want my fingers inside you?"

Marin considered that for a moment, but ultimately the fact that she was coherent enough to think about it told her everything she needed to know. "I don't hate it, but I don't think I particularly care for it either."

"Got it." Charlotte captured her lips as her fingers continued to explore. She slid them over every intimate inch of Marin's body, seeming to catalogue the places that made Marin gasp and moan. It was incredibly erotic, as was the knowledge that Charlotte wanted to please her, that Marin's pleasure was the most important thing.

In the past, sex had been something she tolerated. She would close her eyes and hope Andrew hurried up so she could go to sleep. She'd experienced pleasure only by herself, with her own hand or her vibrator . . . or by losing herself in a book, submersing herself in a world where women's pleasure was valued and celebrated and even prioritized.

Now she had a woman in her bed worshipping her body, prioritizing her pleasure, and it was . . . there weren't words. She kissed Charlotte with increasing desperation.

"Whoa. Are you okay? Did I hurt you?" Charlotte touched Marin's cheek, drawing her attention to the fact that she was crying.

"I'm fine. I'm so much better than fine. It's just . . . emotional for me, being here with you, *good* emotions, I promise. Sex used to be something I dreaded, but I fantasized about a future where I would enjoy it. Now you've made that fantasy a reality, and I . . . I'm emotional."

"Well, now you're making me emotional." Charlotte blinked, her own eyes glossy. "I think I love you, Marin Easterly." She slapped a hand over her mouth. "Oh my god, I didn't mean to just . . . blurt that out."

"I'm glad you did, because I love you too." Marin was crying in earnest now, and she certainly hadn't imagined saying those words for the first time while Charlotte's hand was between her thighs, while she was breathless and aroused and crying from how good everything felt, but now . . . she wouldn't have it any other way.

"Oh, Marin." Charlotte's bottom lip trembled, and the way she was looking at Marin right now . . . it was love, all right. It was the kind of love Marin had always wanted to see on a woman's face, and she knew her face reflected the same emotion. She was overflowing with it, and it was the most wonderful feeling in the world.

"It's true." Her voice was soft and tremulous as she cupped Charlotte's cheek. "I love you."

"I never saw this coming." Charlotte blinked, looking surprised and so fucking happy. "I just . . . wow. I had no idea how this would play out when I met you that day on the bus, but I knew *something*. You caught my eye from the first moment I saw you. I didn't know why, but I knew you were important. Then I thought I watched you die, and then I found you again, and now you've turned my world upside down in the very best way."

"The very best," Marin echoed, then gasped when Charlotte's fingers started moving again, slipping over her sensitive flesh.

"I love you." Charlotte kissed her fiercely, hungrily, and then she dipped her head to kiss Marin's neck. She kept going, placing hot, wet kisses over Marin's chest, teasing each of her nipples until Marin was whining and writhing against the bed. She had never known her breasts were this sensitive. It hadn't done anything for her when Andrew kissed them, but Charlotte . . .

Oh, Charlotte . . .

Marin moaned as Charlotte ventured lower, licking around her navel before traveling the expanse of her stomach, drawing ever closer to where Marin ached for her, where Marin *throbbed* for her. If it was possible, she was even more turned on now than she had been the first time. Her core clenched in anticipation, and her breath came in rapid pants.

"I want to taste you."

Marin let out the most outrageous moan. "Oh please. *Please.*"

She felt Charlotte's warm breath first, gusting against her hypersensitive skin, and even that felt fantastic. Marin again clenched her hands in the sheets to have something to hold on to.

"Look at me," Charlotte whispered.

Marin opened her eyes and looked down, and *oh god*, the image of Charlotte lying between her parted thighs was almost enough to make her come. Charlotte's blond hair was wild, tumbling over her shoulders. Strands of it fell across Marin's thighs, and she could think of nothing better than this, soft hair and soft skin, Charlotte's plump pink lips smiling up at her.

"You're so gorgeous when you're this turned on," Charlotte murmured, and then, while Marin watched, she leaned in, pressing her tongue firmly against Marin's clit.

"Oh fuck." Marin's hips bucked, and her eyes slammed shut almost without her knowledge. Her entire consciousness narrowed to the hot, wet pleasure of Charlotte's mouth.

Charlotte flicked her tongue back and forth, pausing from time to time as if to judge Marin's responses to each of her movements. She licked and kissed, occasionally moving from Marin's clit to lavish attention on the rest of her, but she always returned to the spot that made Marin squirm and moan, that had stars bursting behind her eyelids.

She wanted this to last forever, but Charlotte's mouth had other ideas. She swirled her tongue around Marin's clit again, and the tension inside her crested. This was it, and it was going to be a big one. *Oh fuck.* Marin ground her hips against that talented tongue.

"Please," she begged. "Please don't stop."

Charlotte didn't stop. She kept licking, lavishing Marin with pleasure as she tipped over the edge. This orgasm was exponentially stronger than the first one. It radiated out from her core in blissful waves that just kept coming. A hot, tingly sensation swept through her body, the best feeling in the world, the best orgasm she'd ever had, the best *everything*.

Marin moaned and writhed until she was a limp, shuddering heap against the sheets, weakly pushing at Charlotte's shoulders when her pleasure ebbed and she became too sensitive.

Charlotte looked up at her, wiping her chin with one hand. "Wow, that was . . . wow. This time I felt like I earned it. Watching you come is so fucking hot." She gasped, and Marin realized that Charlotte had a hand between her own thighs, rubbing frantically.

"Wait," Marin said, surprising even herself with how quickly she moved, considering she'd been boneless with pleasure a few moments ago. She rolled them so that she landed between Charlotte's thighs, pushing Charlotte's hand aside to replace it with her face.

Marin had anticipated giving almost as much as receiving, and she groaned as her tongue met Charlotte's intimate flesh, savoring her unique flavor. Marin licked and sucked eagerly, because she sensed

Charlotte was close, and also, because she had been looking forward to this so much. Within minutes, Charlotte arched and bucked against her, shouting her release.

"Get up here," Charlotte said hoarsely. "Because I need to kiss you."

Marin obeyed wordlessly because she needed the same thing. Here in Charlotte's arms, Marin felt a soul-deep contentment she hadn't even known was possible. Yes, this was love, all right.

Tomorrow might be difficult. It probably *would* be difficult, but right here, right now, Marin was happy. At peace. In love.

She felt like the luckiest woman in the world.

CHAPTER TWENTY-TWO

Charlotte woke with a smile on her face, because last night? Well, it might have been the best night of her life. She hadn't known how wonderful sex between two women could be. Hell, until last month, she hadn't even known she was attracted to women.

And now here she was, in love with a woman, wrapped up in her arms with a pleasant soreness between her thighs from a night well spent. But then she heard it again, the high-pitched whine that had awakened her.

"I'm coming, Ember," Marin mumbled sleepily from behind her.

"That's what she said . . ." Charlotte teased.

Marin's arm, which rested on Charlotte's stomach, tightened. "Damn right, it is."

"I'll take her out. You stay right here, looking beautiful." Charlotte sat up, leaning over to give Marin a quick kiss before she slid out of bed.

Ember whined again, and it sounded fairly urgent. Charlotte rushed around to find her clothes, which were discarded all over the floor. That showed how distracted she'd been last night, because she never let her clothes touch a hotel room floor. Yuck. She'd toss these in the dirty pile as soon as she took the puppy out.

She yanked on her shirt, buttoned her jeans, and slipped her feet into sneakers, then opened the crate. The black puppy barreled into her arms, licking her face as she squirmed to get free. Charlotte stood with her and hurried toward the door, looking around for Ember's collar and leash as she went. She found them on the table by the door with both their purses.

Two purses. Because Charlotte was dating a woman. Charlotte was *in love with* a woman. She grinned as she fastened Ember's collar and opened the door. She hadn't even known before last night, but it was true. She was in love, *so much* in love.

The cold air outside was a rude interruption to her warm, happy introspection, but luckily Ember didn't mess around. She took care of business and scampered right back to the door. Charlotte followed her in, shutting the door behind them.

Marin was just coming out of the bathroom, wearing nothing but an oversize blue T-shirt. Charlotte opened her mouth to say something but promptly forgot whatever it was as she got lost staring at Marin's bare legs. She didn't even notice the scar running down Marin's right thigh until Marin's hand shifted to cover it.

"You know that's not what I was staring at, right?" Charlotte asked.

"I . . . wasn't sure."

Charlotte stepped closer, sliding a hand beneath the T-shirt to cup Marin's bare ass. "I was admiring your legs because they're sexy as hell, and seeing you nearly naked is really turning me on."

"Oh," Marin said somewhat bashfully.

"I'll tell you as many times as it takes. Your scars are part of you, and since I think all of you is beautiful, that means I find your scars beautiful too."

"I really love you." Marin leaned in for another kiss. Her mouth was minty from toothpaste, while Charlotte still had morning breath.

"Love you, too, but let me go freshen up, okay?"

"Mm-hmm. I'll take this one." Marin reached for the leash Charlotte had completely forgotten she was holding.

Charlotte went into the bathroom. When she reemerged a few minutes later, she was wearing only her T-shirt, having left the rest of her dirty clothes behind. She found Marin in bed with Ember curled up against her chest. "Mind if I join this snugglefest?"

Marin held the sheet up, inviting her in. "We insist that you do."

Charlotte slid into bed, giggling as the puppy started energetically licking her face. "Love you too, Ember, but I was actually hoping to kiss your mom instead."

Marin laughed softly. "She's kind of a mood killer, but this is our morning routine after she goes out for the first time."

"It seems like an awfully nice way to start the day." Charlotte leaned around Ember to place a quick kiss on Marin's lips. "I didn't expect any of this, but I'm so glad I tagged along on your trip."

"I'm glad too." Marin kissed her again, one hand coming to rest on Charlotte's hip.

"We did pretty well last night, considering it was both of our first times with a woman," Charlotte said.

"I'd say we did better than 'pretty well.'" Marin winked, her expression heating.

"Yeah, we did." Charlotte found her hand beneath the covers and squeezed. "I was kind of fumbling my way through it, but you seemed to actually know what you were doing, which means when we get back to Vermont, I need you to introduce me to sapphic romance novels because they sound hot and seem to give some very good pointers for the newbies like me."

"I would be *thrilled* to do that."

They dozed in bed together with Ember cuddled between them until it was time for Marin to get ready for breakfast with her sister. Charlotte felt the mood shift as they got out of bed. It was as if a weight had settled over Marin's shoulders, and Charlotte wasn't sure how to ease it for her.

First, they stepped into a shower together, where Charlotte got her first real look at Marin's naked body in the light. There were a *lot* of scars, but Charlotte appreciated them all. Standing here now, kissing Marin under a cascade of hot water, hands between each other's thighs as they indulged in some quick shower sex, Charlotte couldn't believe how close she'd come to losing her, that she'd spent two years thinking she *had* lost her.

It made this moment even more meaningful. Charlotte came first, gasping beneath the spray as Marin's fingers took her over the edge, but Marin followed moments later, hips bucking into Charlotte's hand as she found her own release.

"Love this." Charlotte stroked a hand through Marin's wet hair as she caught her breath.

Marin smiled, water droplets glistening in her eyelashes. "Love how much we've both been using that word. Can't wait to go home and use it even more."

"So much more. In the meantime, I'll be here with Ember, waiting for you. Whatever happens with Nancy, you'll have us here to hug and kiss you afterward."

Marin drew her in so that Charlotte's forehead rested against hers. "I appreciate that more than you could know."

"I know why you're here." Nancy settled across from Marin at the table. Her husband, Rick, sat beside her, sipping his coffee and looking like he'd rather be anywhere else.

That made two of them. Marin's stomach sank. "You do?"

"Yes." Nancy gave her a disapproving look. At sixty-five, eighteen years Marin's senior, Nancy had little in common with her. Marin didn't even have any memories of them growing up together since Nancy had already been away at college when she was born. Nancy brushed back a strand of short silver hair. "Fran called last week. I don't know why you asked her to keep secrets from me, but it was shortsighted of you since she and I are close."

The way she said it emphasized the fact that she and Marin were *not* close. "I didn't ask her to keep secrets. I just asked her to give me the chance to tell you myself." Marin fiddled with her coffee cup. Nancy had invited her for breakfast, but so far, coffee was the only thing she'd served, and without food as a buffer, it was making Marin's stomach sour.

"Well, you could have saved yourself a trip because I've already heard your news, and it wouldn't have been worth a visit even if I hadn't. I don't need you to rub your lifestyle in my face." Nancy's expression was pinched. "Some things are better kept quiet."

"I just wanted to be honest with you about who I am, who I've always been."

"You don't *look* like a lesbian." Nancy sniffed, giving Marin a pointed once-over. "I suppose this is why you divorced Andrew?"

"Yes, it is." Marin had prepared for this reaction, and yet, it hurt more than she'd expected. She'd come out a handful of times now, and until this moment, she'd received only support in response. This was the first time someone had rejected her to her face, and it felt like being kicked in the gut.

Nancy tsked. "What a way to repay that poor man after he dropped everything to care for you after your accident."

"It had nothing to do with that. We weren't in love. Getting divorced was for the best, for both of us." Marin hated the defensiveness in her tone.

"What happened to your vows, hmm? For better or for worse? Marriages take *work*." Nancy took Rick's hand as if to emphasize her point. Rick remained fascinated with his coffee.

"We did work at it," Marin said, "but sometimes it's better to part ways. I'm happier now, *so* much happier. I thought that might matter to you."

"I would have preferred if you kept your private business private."

Marin stood, leaving behind her half-finished coffee. "I'm sorry for wasting your time. If you ever want to talk, you know where to find me."

Nancy picked up her coffee and sipped, her expression as sour as Marin's stomach.

"I'll walk you out." Rick got to his feet, speaking for the first time.

"Thank you."

"Sorry about that," he said once they'd left the kitchen. "I think her feelings were hurt that you told Fran first."

"I think she'd have reacted badly either way, but thank you." Marin had always liked Rick. Too bad he didn't have more influence over his wife.

"You might be right. I'm still sorry, and I'll do what I can to help bring her around. For what it's worth, I hope you find the happiness you're looking for." He rested a hand on her shoulder.

Marin forced a smile. Nancy's words had cut deeply, but his kindness was appreciated. Marin left the house feeling deflated, tired, and sad. Fifteen minutes later, she pulled up in front of the cottage to find Charlotte on the front porch, tossing a ball with Ember.

Charlotte stood, watching as Marin parked and got out of the car. "How did it go?" she asked, but her pinched brow suggested she'd already read the answer on Marin's face.

"About like I expected. No, actually it was worse." Marin sighed. Even though she'd known Nancy's rejection was a real possibility, she felt absolutely sick now that it had happened. "I didn't anticipate that Fran would have already told Nancy my news. She was upset before I even arrived."

"I'm sorry." Charlotte walked straight to her, wrapping her arms around Marin. "I'm so sorry."

"Thank you. I'll be okay." Marin blew out a breath. "It's her loss."

Charlotte could still see the hurt on Marin's face a week later. Sure, she'd tried to shrug it off, but Charlotte could tell just how deeply

Nancy's rejection had cut her. It was a harsh reminder, as she headed to her weekly Sunday lunch with her dad, that people still could and did lose family members by coming out to them.

How would her dad react when and if Charlotte told him she was in love with a woman? She honestly didn't know, and that was terrifying. For the first time since her mom's disappearance, she and her dad were back on solid ground with each other. Was she willing to risk losing him if she told him the truth?

It was a question for another time, though, because today she had a different difficult topic to discuss with him. "I got in touch with Bev," she told him as they waited for their entrées to arrive.

He smiled. "Oh yeah? How's she doing?"

"Really good. She's living up near Burlington these days."

"Ah." He gave Charlotte a curious look. "Did she have any insight for you? I know you were hoping she'd be able to shed some light on your mom's disappearance."

"Yes and no." She fidgeted with her water glass. "She said she thought Mom seemed depressed before she disappeared, that she'd lost interest in some of the activities she used to enjoy. Did you notice that too?"

He was quiet for a long time, staring out the window beside them. "I'm not sure," he answered finally. "Certainly, she was distant in those final months, but I assumed it was because of the affair. I thought she was just unhappy with *me*."

"Did she mention wanting to go on vacation, maybe somewhere tropical?"

He shook his head, his expression wistful. "We never really talked about vacations. Maybe we should have. I'm sorry, Charlotte. Why do you ask?"

"Bev mentioned that Mom wanted to get away, somewhere tropical. Probably doesn't mean anything." Charlotte swallowed her disappointment. How could she accept that she might never know what had happened?

More than that, how could she accept that there was a possibility—perhaps even a strong one—that her mom had simply left her behind to start a new life somewhere? Charlotte didn't know how to make peace with that.

And hadn't she more or less done the same thing, leaving town after high school and cutting ties with everyone in Middleton? What if her constant need to wander and start over in new places was actually a trait she'd gotten from her mom? Tears burned her eyes.

"You know." Her dad interrupted her introspective spiral, tapping a hand against the table. "I *do* remember her mentioning a tropical vacation. It was something she threw in my face during an argument. She said something about how she'd always wanted to visit a tropical island, and I'd never taken her." He looked chagrined.

That backed up what Bev had said, but did it mean anything?

"If you're thinking she moved to a tropical island without telling us . . . I don't buy it." He shook his head. "You were just a child. She wouldn't have left you."

"People do unpredictable things when they're depressed."

"Anything's possible, I suppose, but the woman I knew and loved would never have abandoned her daughter." He placed a hand on hers.

"Well, she's not here, so whatever happened, she *did* abandon me." Charlotte swallowed, hard. "And Bev's tropical-island theory aligns with you saying that one of her bags was missing."

"Yes." He looked thoughtful. "But it was a small bag, so if that's what she did, she didn't take much with her."

"I found a PI who specializes in finding people who've run away. He says it's a long shot that he'd be able to find her after all this time, but . . . I think I'm going to let him try."

He nodded. "I support that. I'll even help pay if you need it. As you know, the PIs I hired never found anything, but I never asked them to treat her as someone who'd voluntarily run off."

The waiter arrived with their lunch, and her dad shifted the conversation to the spring semester, talking about classes and students, a topic that was always one of his favorites and one Charlotte tended to dislike. Now that she was dating Marin, though, she found that her attitude toward the university had changed. She loved hearing about Marin's students and classes. Maybe it was time to let go of childhood resentments.

So she asked a few tentative questions, trying to sound interested in the answers, and in the process, she discovered that she *was* interested. He told her about a young woman he'd been mentoring who was the first woman in her family to attend college.

"That's wonderful, Dad."

"I'm really proud of her." He looked across the table at Charlotte. "I'm proud of you, too, you know? I respect how you've chased your dreams wherever they take you, and everything you're doing in your search for your mom. I know she'd be proud of you too."

Charlotte blinked rapidly against the tears in her eyes. "Thank you."

"What else is new with you? Are you seeing anyone?"

She thought of Marin, and a smile immediately bloomed. "Yeah, I am, actually."

Her dad smiled. "That's wonderful. I can tell by the look on your face that things are going well. Maybe I'll get to meet him sometime?"

"Oh . . ." *Him.* Her dad assumed she was dating a man. She remembered the haunted look in Marin's eyes after she'd left Nancy's house. Charlotte wasn't prepared to lose her dad, not yet, not so soon after mending their relationship. "Um, maybe. Things are still pretty new."

Shame rose in her chest, and just like that, her eyes welled with tears all over again. She was a coward for not using this opportunity to tell him about Marin. After everything she'd put herself through to reach this point in her life, Marin deserved so much better.

CHAPTER TWENTY-THREE

Over the next few weeks, Marin and Charlotte settled into their new relationship. They spent plenty of time together at home, but they also went snow tubing and took a pottery class at the community center, taught by Audrey. They did all the couply things Marin had been yearning for, although they couldn't acknowledge that they were a couple when they were in public since Charlotte wasn't out yet.

And that was fine. Marin would give her all the time she needed. She was happy, *truly* happy, maybe for the first time in her life. Sure, she'd been reasonably content since the divorce as she made strides in her new life, but there'd always been a missing piece, a yearning she'd known wouldn't be satisfied until she found a life partner.

She'd never dared hope that person would be Charlotte. Nor had she imagined herself as the more "experienced" person in her first sapphic relationship, but actually, she loved helping to guide Charlotte through her sexual awakening. Marin hadn't had many opportunities in her life to provide guidance or nurturing. Now she found herself in that role not only with Charlotte but also in raising Ember and mentoring students on campus. It was incredibly gratifying.

As March became April, the snow finally melted, and the trees began to bud. Spring had officially arrived, although spring in Vermont also meant mud. Ember got into endless messy situations outside. Marin had to wipe her down multiple times a day, but she didn't really mind, because she loved her puppy *so* much.

Not that Ember looked much like a puppy these days. Gone was the tiny runt of the litter Marin had brought home back in January. Ember was big now, full of energy but also settling nicely into adolescence.

There was still one thing weighing Marin down, though, and that was Nancy's rejection. The sibling group chat had proceeded as usual, but Marin couldn't help noticing how superficial it had gotten, as if Jed, Fran, and Tom were all waiting for Nancy and Marin to patch things up. If only Marin knew how . . .

She strolled through the campus quad, enjoying the daffodils and crocuses as they bloomed along the sidewalks. It was the second week in April, and her weather app was calling for heavy rain later this evening, but right now, it was a perfect spring afternoon.

She and Charlotte were going on a double date tonight with Audrey and Michelle, and Marin could hardly wait. She walked faster, impatient to get home, even though she had plenty of time before she needed to start getting ready.

"Professor Easterly!"

She turned to find Brianna on the sidewalk behind her. "Hi, Brianna. How are you?"

"I'm good." There was a bounce to Brianna's step that hadn't been there when Marin first talked to her over the winter, and she was so glad to see it. "I was actually planning to stop by your office soon to tell you, but I did come out to my best friend, and she's been great about it."

"That's wonderful," Marin exclaimed.

"Yeah. So far I'm only out to her, but that feels okay for now. I can swoon over the cute girls in the TV shows that we watch together, and she points out girls on campus that she thinks I might like." Brianna grinned. "I feel like *me* when I'm around her."

"I'm so glad." Marin was so proud of Brianna, and happy for her. "I've been thinking about you and hoping you were doing okay."

"Yeah. Sorry for being so dramatic before." Brianna rolled her eyes, and Marin chuckled. "I was in such a rush to come out to my parents, but you were right . . . I've got time."

"You do," Marin said. "You've got plenty of time, but I'm really glad you have someone you can be yourself with now. That's a great feeling, isn't it?"

"Yeah, it is." Brianna's smile was luminous. "Anyway, I just wanted to say thanks. See you at the next Pride Coalition meeting?"

"Yes," Marin said. "See you there."

Marin walked to her car with a newfound bounce in her step. At home, she fed and walked Ember, then changed from her work clothes into date-night attire. She decided on fitted black slacks and a royal blue top. By the time she'd finished getting ready, it was almost time for Charlotte to pick her up. They were meeting Audrey and Michelle at a new restaurant in town, and everything about the evening promised to be wonderful.

Her phone rang, and Marin rushed to find it, hoping nothing had come up with dinner, but it was her niece Jen's name on the screen. Marin's chest tightened. She hadn't talked to Jen since her falling-out with Nancy, unsure what to say or how Jen felt about the whole thing, which was probably cowardly of her in hindsight. "Jen, hi."

"So I just came from Mom and Dad's house," Jen said, sounding pissed, and Marin sat abruptly on her bed. "Dad finally clued me in about what's been going on between you two, and first of all, I gave Mom a huge piece of my mind over how homophobic she's being, but secondly, why didn't you tell me, Aunt Marin?"

The hurt in her voice was unmistakable, and Marin's stomach plummeted. "I'm sorry. I should have. I guess . . . coming out to my siblings felt like all I could handle, and I figured I'd let them tell the rest of the family."

"But you and I are close," Jen protested. "We've chatted so much since you adopted Ember. You didn't think I'm a homophobic asshole, too, did you?"

"No." Although the truth was, she hadn't been sure. Maybe she'd been afraid to find out, afraid of losing Jen too.

"Well, I'm a little pissed at you for not telling me, but also really proud of you for living your truth. Are you seeing anyone?"

"I am," Marin admitted with a smile. "Things are going really well. I'm . . . happy."

"That's awesome. You deserve all the happiness, and now that tax season is finally almost over, maybe I can drive up and see your new house and meet Ember . . . and your girlfriend."

"I'd like that."

"Great. Oh, and leave Mom to me. I'll get through to her," Jen said. "She's not hopeless, at least I don't think she is. She's just set in her ways, which is a lame excuse, I know, but she loves you. I'll make her realize how ridiculous she's being."

Marin sighed. "I appreciate that, but please . . . I don't want to come between you and your mom."

"You aren't. This is all on her, but I'm going to fix it."

Marin heard the sound of Charlotte's SUV pulling into the driveway. "Thank you. I really appreciate that, and I wish I could talk longer, but my girlfriend just got here. We're going out to dinner with another couple tonight."

"Ooh, a lesbian double date," Jen said with a laugh. "Sounds awesome. Okay, enjoy dinner, and email me with some dates that work for me to visit. My schedule's about to be wide open, so let's plan something."

"Count on it. And good luck getting everyone's taxes filed on time."

Jen groaned. "I'll need it. Thanks."

Marin ended the call feeling cautiously hopeful. Whether or not Jen could get through to Nancy, her support meant a lot. Marin hurried to the front door. She saw Charlotte almost every day, and yet the anticipation and the chemistry she felt in Charlotte's presence never seemed to diminish. Charlotte was the highlight of her day, every day.

Marin opened the front door. Charlotte had on a green knit dress and black boots. The pink-and-green scarf she'd been wearing when they met on the bus was at her throat. It went perfectly with the dress while evoking an avalanche of memories. "You look amazing."

"Thanks. You look great too." Charlotte pulled her in for a quick kiss as Ember darted out the front door and began to run in circles around her. "And hi to you, too, Ember."

"At this point, it's hard to say who's more excited to see you," Marin joked. She felt pleasantly warm just from having Charlotte's hand on her hip.

"You, I hope." Charlotte kissed her again, and Marin's pulse got even faster.

"Keep that up, and I won't even want to go to dinner."

"Liar." Charlotte's eyes sparkled. "You've talked about nothing but our double date with Audrey and Michelle all week."

"That's true," Marin admitted. "But afterward . . . stay here tonight?"

Charlotte nodded. "I brought an overnight bag with me."

Marin pulled her in for another kiss. "Perfect."

Charlotte had been a little bit intimidated about going on a double date with another sapphic couple, but she needn't have been, because Michelle and Audrey were great. Charlotte was really enjoying herself. Although she was the only person at the table without a background in academia, her parents were both professors, so she could hold her own when the conversation inevitably turned to Northshire University.

"I don't miss it a bit," Michelle said as she lifted her wineglass. "That place was sucking me dry."

That drew a surprised chuckle from Charlotte. "Really? I thought everyone loved teaching there."

Michelle shook her head. "Not me."

"You loved it once upon a time . . ." Audrey gave her fiancée a bump with her shoulder.

Their dessert arrived before Michelle could respond. She and Audrey had ordered an enormous slice of carrot cake to share, while Charlotte and Marin had chosen separate desserts, a chocolate torte for Marin and crème brûlée for Charlotte. Marin had asked if she wanted to share something, but that felt too much like a date activity. Charlotte was still wary of people she knew seeing her and realizing this was a date instead of an outing with friends.

She hated feeling like she had one foot in the closet and the other one out, double-dating with Marin while not being ready to acknowledge Marin as her girlfriend to anyone else she knew. She had to make up her mind about coming out, and soon.

While they ate dessert, Audrey entertained them with tales of mishaps at the pottery wheel, and then they split the check and walked outside. It had begun to rain, and the temperature had dropped. Charlotte shivered as they lingered under the awning to say good night.

"We should do this again sometime," Audrey said. "It's so fun having another sapphic couple to hang out with."

"Definitely," Marin agreed, then darted a hesitant glance at Charlotte. "If you think so too?"

"I do." Charlotte grabbed Marin's hand and gave it a squeeze. "That sounds really nice."

As they got into their respective cars and pulled out of the parking lot, Charlotte was reminded that Audrey and Michelle lived just down the road from Marin, because she and Marin ended up following them out of downtown Middleton and onto the winding series of rural roads that led toward their houses.

The rain had really picked up now, making the already muddy roads even worse. Charlotte truly hated mud season in Vermont. What a mess. Luckily Marin's Outback had all-wheel drive and enough ground clearance to make it through unscathed.

"Dinner was fantastic, but I hope you're not *too* full." Marin glanced at her with a coy smile.

"Why's that?" Charlotte asked, although the warmth in her stomach said she already knew.

"Because I'd really like to take that dress off you when we get home."

"I'm fully on board with that plan," Charlotte confirmed.

The sun was setting to their right, although it wasn't much to see this evening through the heavy rain, just a hazy golden blob over the mountains. Ahead of them, the red taillights of Michelle's BMW were just visible in the gloom.

A pickup truck came over the hill in front of them, careening down the muddy road. Charlotte opened her mouth to make a comment about careless drivers, but before she could speak, the truck swerved directly into the BMW's path. For a moment, it looked like the two vehicles would hit head-on, but then the BMW turned sharply. It lost traction in the mud and veered off the side of the road onto the steep embankment.

"Oh shit!" Charlotte exclaimed as adrenaline punched her in the stomach. The black BMW plunged through a gap between trees and disappeared from view.

"Oh my god." Marin's voice sounded high and tight as she slammed on the brakes, bringing the Outback to a stop at the side of the road.

"Fuck. *Fuck.*" Charlotte looked around wildly, trying to see where the car had gone. Through the trees, she glimpsed a lake below. A big lake. As she watched, the BMW careened down the bank and splashed into its dark depths.

This was bad. So bad. Charlotte fumbled for her seat belt, yanking at it with frantic hands. Vaguely, she was aware of Marin punching the button for the hazard lights before they both scrambled out onto the muddy roadside.

Marin had her cell phone in hand. "No service," she said grimly.

"Fuck," Charlotte cried again. It was hardly surprising on this rural road. The mountains around here often blocked cell service, but it was extremely unfortunate during an actual emergency. Charlotte spun in the road, blinking cold rain from her eyes. The pickup truck had stopped at the bottom of the hill. Its driver, a middle-aged man, was just stepping out of the cab.

"Go find cell service and call 911," Charlotte shouted.

He nodded and climbed back in his truck.

Mud sucked at Charlotte's boots as she grabbed Marin's hand and started half climbing, half sliding down the rain-slick embankment toward the lake, following the trail of destruction left by the car. The BMW's red taillights were still illuminated. The rear of the car stuck up almost vertically out of the water now, but it was sinking fast. Were Audrey and Michelle okay?

Charlotte's knees shook, and tears pricked her eyes. She and Marin skidded down the muddy slope, tripping over rocks and tree roots to the water's edge, just as the BMW's taillights disappeared from view, slipping below the surface of the water.

CHAPTER TWENTY-FOUR

Marin pressed a hand to her chest. Her heart was pounding so hard, she feared she might go into cardiac arrest for the second time in her life. Her legs had turned to granite because the car . . . the car . . .

Only bubbles remained on the surface.

"I'm going in." Charlotte stepped toward the edge of the lake, her boots sinking into deep mud with a horrible squelching sound. Cold rain beat down on them. Charlotte's blond hair was plastered to her face as she waded into the lake. In seconds, she was up to her knees in the water, skirt clutched in one hand.

Marin couldn't breathe. She couldn't move. The lake must be ice cold. She was freezing just standing on the bank. Frigid rain ran down her face and soaked through her clothes. Now that the sun had set, the temperature had dropped sharply. Charlotte was up to her waist now, arms out in front of her.

With a splash, Charlotte dove under the water, leaving Marin alone on the bank. She tried to force herself to move, but her legs might as well have turned to ice. They were frozen, like the rest of her. Everything about this moment was cold and unforgiving.

She blinked, and she was back on that snowy Manhattan street, feeling the impact of the car as it slammed into her, the agony of broken bones as she lay prone on the pavement. The cold. The crushing pain. Charlotte holding her hand as her life slipped away.

Help.

Marin screamed internally. She blinked again, trying desperately to free herself from this mental prison. Raindrops blurred her vision, and she still couldn't move. Then . . . a head broke the surface of the lake, right where the car had gone under. And a second head!

There were two women clinging to each other in the water now. Marin choked on her own breath. *Oh thank god.* Audrey and Michelle were alive! They'd made it out of the car. Charlotte was swimming toward them, all three of them bobbing in the lake.

Someone was crying. It might be Marin. She wasn't entirely present in her body right now, still vacillating between the muddy lakeshore and that slushy Manhattan street. Terror swamped her senses, paralyzing her.

The three women were together now, swimming toward shore. Charlotte's pink-and-green scarf floated around her head like a mirage, a tangible bridge between this moment and the day Marin had almost died.

Marin should be doing something. She needed to help! She flexed her hands and blinked water from her eyes, rain or tears, she wasn't sure. Maybe both. Then she forced her foot forward. One step, then another. Her shoe sank into the muddy water. The cold was instant and shocking, probably only a few degrees above freezing. So cold it *hurt.* She could only imagine what the other women were experiencing, being fully submerged in it.

But they're alive!

As they approached the shore, she saw that Audrey was crying, her face contorted with misery. Beside her, Michelle was stoic but pale. Charlotte brought up the rear, guiding them in. Soon, they reached water shallow enough for them to stand, and they struggled toward the bank through deep mud. Marin took another step into the lake and reached for Audrey's hand, tugging her gently toward the shore. Audrey's fingers were ice cold in hers, and her skin had a bluish tinge.

As soon as Audrey was out of the water, Marin reached for Michelle, who had fallen to her knees in the mud. Charlotte joined her, and together they lifted Michelle to her feet and helped her out of the water. Marin saw a red bump on Michelle's forehead where she must have hit it in the crash.

"Can everyone make it up the bank to the road?" Charlotte asked, sounding remarkably calm despite the way her teeth chattered and her body shook. "Hopefully the pickup truck driver has already called for help, but I think we need to get into our car and get the heat going to try to warm up while we wait for the ambulance."

Indeed, hypothermia was a real concern. They were all shivering, lips purple from the cold. Audrey wrapped an arm around Michelle, who seemed to be struggling a bit.

"Let's hurry," Audrey said, her voice tight and shaky. "She hit her head pretty hard. I think she blacked out for a second when we went into the water."

Marin wrapped her arms around Charlotte as her paralyzing terror began to fade into a more manageable level of fear. Yes, they all needed to get to the car, and fast. Both couples held on to each other as they began their climb up the embankment to the road.

It was much harder to climb than it had been to descend. Each step was a struggle, brambles and vegetation clawing at their clothes as mud mired their feet. Rain still fell heavily, and it was cold, *so* cold. Marin was soaked and shivering uncontrollably, her hands and feet numb, and she hadn't even gone into the lake.

They were all a muddy, soggy mess by the time they made it to the road, but Marin didn't spare a thought for the interior of the car as they piled in. Heat was the priority. Heat, and then help. She started the car and cranked the heat to full blast, adjusting the vents to reach Audrey and Michelle where they clung to each other in the back seat.

"Jackets," Marin managed to say, gesturing somewhat wildly to the garments she and Charlotte had discarded on the back seat after dinner. Audrey and Michelle reached for them to wrap up in something dry.

A sharp rap at the window nearly made Marin jump out of her skin. Adrenaline flooded her system all over again. She looked out to see the pickup truck driver standing there. Marin's hand shook as she lowered the window to speak to him.

"I called 911." He glanced anxiously into the back seat. "Everyone okay? I'm real sorry about this."

"Everyone is alive," Marin told him curtly. "As for okay, I'm not sure yet. The two who were in the car that you ran off the road need to be seen by EMTs as soon as possible."

"Help should be here any minute," he said, expression contrite. "Again, I'm so sorry."

Marin nodded. "We appreciate that. Could you please wait in your truck until the authorities get here?" Because the lowered window was letting cold air into the car, and while she wanted to raise hell about his dangerous driving, this wasn't the time or the place.

He walked away, and Marin raised the window. Beside her, Charlotte was quiet, arms wrapped around herself and shivering. In the back seat, Audrey was still crying while Michelle leaned against her, resting her head on Audrey's chest.

They were still sitting like that when sirens approached a few minutes later. A fire truck arrived first, followed by a sheriff's deputy. Charlotte and Marin got out of the car to explain what had happened, and Marin was relieved to see the ambulance pull up soon after.

She watched as Michelle was loaded into its interior with Audrey at her side. They were on their way to the hospital. Thank *god*. The ambulance lurched down the muddy road, and Marin's body seized again. The flashing lights. The siren. She'd thought she had no memory of her time in the ambulance. She'd been mostly dead at the time. But now . . .

Marin heard Charlotte's voice against her ear, telling her it was going to be okay. She was vaguely aware that she was clutching Charlotte against her. Then a sheriff's deputy was approaching them, and Charlotte pushed hastily out of Marin's arms.

What an awful night.

Charlotte and Marin had gone to the hospital, where they sat for hours in the emergency room while Audrey and Michelle were examined. Someone brought Charlotte a clean set of scrubs so she could change out of her wet dress, but she still couldn't seem to get warm.

As witnesses to the accident, they spoke to the sheriff's department, and Charlotte tried not to mind the way Marin kept clinging to her without paying attention to who was watching. Charlotte hated that she minded, but she *did* mind, because this was a small town where everyone knew everyone, and her dad had lived here his whole life.

Marin was an out lesbian on campus, so if Charlotte was seen holding hands with her, it might get back to him. And much like Marin had wanted the chance to tell Nancy herself, Charlotte wanted to tell her dad . . . when she was ready.

They left the hospital just before midnight. Michelle had a mild concussion, but she and Audrey were otherwise unharmed, which felt so goddamn lucky. Marin drove them home before she and Charlotte *finally* made it back to Marin's house, where poor Ember was practically bursting to get out of her crate.

Marin took her out, and then they got into a hot shower together. Charlotte still couldn't stop shivering, even as hot water rained down on her. She'd been so scared when the car went into the water. She hadn't been that terrified since . . .

The fateful day on the bus.

Marin had been weirdly quiet all evening, and Charlotte might have just realized why. She tipped Marin's face toward hers, then tucked wet strands of hair behind her ears. "Did tonight's accident bring back memories of your own?"

Marin nodded, her bottom lip trembling. "I froze . . . there at the lake. I didn't do a thing to help."

"That's perfectly understandable. It was a trauma response."

"That doesn't excuse it," Marin whispered. "What if they'd needed my help?"

"But they didn't, and you're only human. I'm so sorry that tonight brought up bad memories for you."

Marin buried her face against Charlotte's shoulder and sobbed. The sound shook something loose in her, and Charlotte cried, too, as she held on to Marin beneath the hot spray. Gradually, the steamy shower chased away the last of the lake's icy grip, and Charlotte felt warm for the first time all evening. Once they'd cried themselves out, they went to bed.

The next morning, Marin called to check on Audrey and Michelle, then relayed that Michelle was taking it easy because of her concussion. They weren't up for visitors, but they were okay. It was a relief. Sitting here in the light of day, Charlotte could hardly believe that had really happened, that it hadn't been a bad dream.

Watching that car disappear into the lake . . .

Marin was quiet and subdued, still upset with herself for not doing more to help, but Charlotte knew they would get through it. They'd already survived worse, and this time they had each other. They both called out from work and spent the day snuggled on the couch, watching silly television shows in the hope that it would cheer them up, and it worked . . . mostly.

Last night's trauma wouldn't heal in a day, but as Marin was always reminding her, they had time. That night, Charlotte decided to stay over again, sensing Marin still needed company. Truthfully, Charlotte did too. Already, it felt so natural to stay at Marin's house, probably because they'd been such close friends before making the transition to lovers.

On Friday morning, Charlotte reluctantly admitted that it was time to return to the real world. She had showings today she couldn't miss. As she was getting her things together, her next-door neighbor texted to say that a sheriff's deputy was at Charlotte's house.

Charlotte sighed. Right. She was supposed to go in and sign her official statement about the accident. She and Marin both needed to do that, although she hadn't actually expected them to send someone to her door about it. Sure enough, her phone began to ring, and the caller ID read "Northshire County Sheriff's Department."

She answered the call. "Hello?"

"Good morning," a male voice said. "I'm Deputy Ainsbury with the Northshire County Sheriff's Department. Is this Charlotte Danton?"

"Yes, it is."

"Ms. Danton, are you available to come down to the sheriff's department this morning?"

"Could it wait until this afternoon? I was just on my way to work. You need me to sign my statement about the crash at Shady Lake, right?"

"Actually, this morning would be better. Some new information has come up that we'd like to talk to you about."

"Um, okay." Unease prickled between her shoulder blades, although she wasn't quite sure why.

"Do you need the address?" he asked.

"I can google it."

"Yes, ma'am, you can. Just ask for me—Deputy Ainsbury—at the desk when you arrive."

She ended the call and filled Marin in, wondering belatedly why the deputy hadn't called her, too, if this was about the accident. Something felt vaguely off, or maybe she was still out of sorts from her dip in the lake. They took Charlotte's SUV. The Outback would need a thorough detailing to get all the mud out before they used it again.

At the sheriff's department, Charlotte asked for Deputy Ainsbury. A young white man in a neatly pressed uniform came out to greet her and Marin. He invited them to follow him to a small conference room.

"What's this about?" Charlotte asked again once they were seated, because she was definitely getting a weird vibe now.

"When we retrieved Ms. Thompson's BMW from the lake yesterday, we found another vehicle in the water, a Saab 90 that appears to have been submerged for some time. It's registered to Terri Danton."

Charlotte's vision flashed black, and she might have fallen out of her chair if not for Marin's hand on her shoulder, steadying her. The Saab. Her mom's Saab. It was in the lake. What . . . ?

"I'm very sorry to tell you this, ma'am, but there were human remains found inside the vehicle."

Charlotte felt as if she'd gone underwater, as if she were submerged in that ice-cold lake. She was so cold, and she couldn't breathe . . .

Human remains.

"We understand that your mom went missing about thirty years ago. We'll need to run a DNA test or compare dental records to be sure, but there was a purse found in the vehicle as well. The driver's license and credit cards inside all belong to Terri Danton, so it does appear to be your mother's remains. Again, I'm very sorry to be the bearer of such bad news."

"Oh, Charlotte . . ." Marin murmured, sounding anguished.

"I don't understand." Charlotte's face felt numb, and she was so cold.

"It appears that your mom's car went off the road, probably the day she disappeared. The car wasn't visible from the road, submerged as it was, and there was never a reason to search that lake since it wasn't on the route she was supposed to have taken the night she disappeared."

"My dad . . ." Charlotte whispered as a strange buzzing sensation built in her head. She looked down at her hands and saw them shaking violently in her lap.

"A deputy is with him now," Deputy Ainsbury said. "I do have some photos of her effects I can show you, in case you recognize anything. We can't release them to you until the official investigation has been completed, but there's no sign of foul play. We believe this was just a tragic accident."

Charlotte watched numbly as Deputy Ainsbury placed several large color photographs on the table in front of her. She saw her mom's purse, along with a series of photos showing its contents. The missing overnight bag was there, too, the one her dad had mentioned. In the photos of its contents, she saw two partially degraded bikinis and a bottle of sunblock.

Her mom had been on her way to that tropical island after all.

"It's only a weekend bag," Marin said. "She was coming back."

Vaguely, Charlotte heard the deputy telling her that her dad was on his way, but she couldn't focus on anything but the photos in front of her. Charlotte's chest ached, and her eyes were overflowing with tears.

Her mom was dead. All this time, she'd been in a lake on the outskirts of town. What had she been doing on that road? Was she on her way to the airport?

Tragic accident, the deputy said.

She was coming back, Marin said.

Charlotte saw herself swimming through that lake yesterday, passing above the submerged car where her mom lay dead and forgotten. Her stomach clenched painfully, and she almost threw up right there in the conference room.

"Would you and your girlfriend like something to drink while you wait for your dad to arrive? Coffee? Water? Soda?" Deputy Ainsbury asked.

Girlfriend.

"I need some air." Charlotte lurched to her feet, swaying slightly before Marin caught her.

"Of course," Marin said. "Let's wait outside."

Charlotte let Marin lead her into the bright sunshine outside the sheriff's building. Her dad was on his way. He couldn't meet Marin like this. He couldn't hear that Charlotte had a girlfriend today of all days. How obvious had she and Marin been since they entered the station? How obvious had they been for the past month? Did her dad already know?

Did *everyone* in town know?

Charlotte was spiraling, and she just . . . couldn't do this. "You should go home," she whispered. "Before my dad gets here."

"What? Why?"

"That deputy called you my girlfriend."

Marin blinked at her. "*That's* why you rushed out of the station so fast?"

Even in Charlotte's slightly hysterical state, she heard the hurt in Marin's voice. Charlotte had just found out her mother was dead. It was a big fucking deal. Momentous. Charlotte should be leaning on Marin in her time of crisis.

Instead, Charlotte was fixating on the way the deputy had called Marin her girlfriend. This was all wrong, and she knew it. She also knew this was *her* problem, not Marin's. Charlotte needed to get her shit together so she could be the girlfriend Marin deserved, but . . . she needed to do this next part alone. Tears coursed over her cheeks. "I . . ."

"Charlotte, talk to me."

"My dad's going to be here soon," she sobbed, "and I can't have him see us looking like . . . like girlfriends. I just lost my mom. What if I lose him, too, when he finds out I'm not straight? I don't know if I can take it."

"Okay."

"I know I promised you that I'd eventually be ready, but I just . . . I'm so scared . . ."

"This isn't the right time to have this conversation," Marin said, sounding as calm as Charlotte was hysterical. "You've just had a shock, and I totally understand why you don't want your dad to find out about us this way, so yes, I'll go. Text me when you get home, and I'll come over?"

"Yes. Please, just take my car. I'll get a ride with my dad." Desperation twisted in Charlotte's stomach. She needed Marin to leave *now*. Before her dad got here.

Her mom was dead, and Charlotte just couldn't . . . she just couldn't . . .

"You'll text me?" Marin pressed.

"Later. I can't think right now. Please just go."

"Charlotte . . ." The slightest pleading note entered Marin's voice now, as if she'd realized Charlotte's panic was about more than her dad finding out she had a girlfriend on the same day he found out his wife was dead.

As if she'd realized Charlotte was spinning out, questioning *everything*. The urge to run was so strong, but she couldn't . . . not yet, not until she'd seen her dad.

"Please go." Charlotte's voice broke.

"I'm going." Marin's voice was heartbreakingly soft, gentle. "But it feels like you're pushing me away, like you *always* push me away when you're upset about something. This isn't how two people in love handle a crisis. We should be leaning on each other right now."

That made sense. It did. In the tiny part of Charlotte's brain still processing rational thought, she could see Marin's point. But Charlotte had always handled difficult things alone. It was the only way she knew how. Right now, talking was just *too hard*.

She turned away. "And I'm telling you I need space."

A few seconds later, she heard the car start, and she watched through her tears as Marin drove away.

CHAPTER TWENTY-FIVE

"In some ways, it's a relief."

It had been two days. Two days since Charlotte had learned her mom was dead. The sheriff's department had been able to track down her dental records, confirming that the remains in the car were Terri Danton. Charlotte and her dad had spent a lot of time together, grieving.

She'd spent even more time falling apart on her own. Charlotte had come to Vermont to find her mom, and she'd done that, but in the process, she seemed to have lost herself. What was she supposed to do now? What came next? She felt as if she'd come untethered.

Marin had sent so many texts, checking on her, and Charlotte had ignored them all. She wasn't handling this well. She knew she wasn't, and yet she couldn't seem to do better. She just wanted to be alone. Instead, she was propped at her kitchen table, sitting across from her dad.

"A relief?" she repeated, staring vacantly into her coffee.

He sipped from his own coffee. "In the sense that we finally know what happened. Now we can lay her to rest. For me, that's a relief."

"I guess." She knew what he meant, even if she didn't like to admit it. It *was* a relief to have answers. To know her mom hadn't abandoned her. But she couldn't say it was a relief to learn that her mother was dead.

Truthfully, though, deep down she'd always believed her mom was gone. It wasn't until her conversation with Bev that she'd seriously started to consider that her mom was still alive, living her life somewhere without Charlotte. And now, Charlotte had to consider that maybe she didn't know who she was without the search that had defined so much of her life.

The urge to flee was overwhelming, but at the same time, she felt rooted here in Middleton in a way she'd never felt in the other places she'd lived as an adult. All her life, Charlotte had been looking ahead toward the next move, the next step in her journey. Now she had no idea what to do with herself.

"I can't help wondering . . ."

Charlotte looked up, her heart clenching as she saw the tears in her dad's eyes. "Wondering what?"

"If your mom and I had been more open with each other, would she have felt she could tell me where she was going that weekend? Might I have been with her in the car? If I'd been there, maybe I could have saved her. I could have saved us all this anguish, all the years of not knowing. You'd still have your mom."

"The not knowing ruined my childhood." Charlotte pressed a fist against the tabletop as tears ran down her cheeks. "The rumors at school, the things the other kids said about her, about you, about *me*. It was hell, Dad."

"I know." He rubbed his brow, his expression full of the same anguish she felt. "I heard the whispers from students in my classes. I saw the accusations in their eyes. People looked at me like I was a murderer."

Charlotte didn't know what to say. "I'm sorry."

"I'm sorry too." He stood and pulled her into his arms. "I feel like such a failure when I think about what you went through as a child and how I wasn't there for you when you needed me. I was hurting, too, but that's no excuse."

"I was angry at you for so long." She clenched her fingers in his shirt, furious and heartbroken and desperately needing the comfort of her father. "She disappeared, but you left me, too, even though you still lived in the same house."

"I did a terrible job of managing my grief, and I'm so sorry. Now that you're back in my life, I want to be a father to you, the way I should have been back then. I want to try . . . if it's not too late?"

"I want that too," she whispered. "I just . . . I don't know how." All her happy family memories felt like they were from another lifetime. She'd been on her own for so long . . .

"I'd like to keep doing what we've been doing the last few months," he said. "We've done a pretty good job of getting to know each other again, but maybe now it's time to get more involved in each other's lives than just meeting for lunch once a week."

"Like what?"

"Come over for dinner one evening. You haven't seen my new house. I'd like to introduce you to my friends and meet yours too. I want to know what's going on in your life."

She looked away. "I want to tell you . . . but I'm scared."

"Please don't be. I'm not the man I used to be." His expression was earnest, maybe even hopeful. "Whatever it is you want to tell me, it'll be okay."

"I've fallen in love, and I want to tell you about her, but I—" She froze, her body flushing hot and then cold as she realized she'd inadvertently already blurted out her truth.

Her dad cocked his head slightly to the side. "Yes?"

She gulped. There was no going back now. "I'm in love with a woman. Her name's Marin. Marin Easterly."

"The name's familiar. Does she teach at the university?"

"Yes, she does, but did you . . . did you hear what I said?" Charlotte's heart was about to beat out of her chest. "I'm in love with a woman."

"I heard you, and that part's a bit shocking, I admit. I had no idea you weren't straight. I'm sorry if you felt like you couldn't be honest with me about that." His face fell. "Is that part of the reason you stayed away all these years? Because you're gay and you were afraid I'd be upset with you?"

She shook her head. "I'm not gay. I'm . . . well, I'm new to labels, but I'm going with pansexual for now. I'm attracted to all genders, but I only realized it very recently . . . because of Marin, actually."

"Then I think that's wonderful. I confess that I can't keep up with all the labels you kids are using these days. The things I hear from my students . . ." He shook his head, smiling. "But I embrace it, even if I don't quite understand it."

She just stared at him, too surprised to respond. Apparently, her dad was a lot more open minded than she'd given him credit for. "I'm sorry for underestimating you. I don't really remember us talking about gay rights when I was a kid."

"We probably didn't, and I might not have given the best answers back then if we had. I used to be a lot more rigid in my thinking about, well . . . most things. But I learned the hard way that people are complicated, *life* is complicated. I made a lot of mistakes, but I like to think I've learned from them."

She'd made mistakes, too, so many mistakes, but could she really say she'd learned from them? It felt like she just kept repeating the same pattern, avoiding difficult situations and running away when things got hard.

"I'm so happy that you've fallen in love," he said. "Wait . . . is this what you were trying to tell me at lunch a few weeks ago?"

She nodded. "I let you assume I was dating a man, and I felt terrible about it."

"I'm glad I know now, and I hope I can meet her soon."

"I hope so too." But Charlotte had spent the last two days ignoring Marin. Charlotte had pushed her away because she was scared, because she was afraid to face the future. She'd been a coward, but maybe she could learn from her mistake the way her dad had done.

She could. She *would*.

And she needed to do it right now. "Dad, I hate to cut this short, but you just helped me realize something. I've messed up with Marin, and I need to apologize to her . . . before it's too late."

He patted her on the shoulder. "Sounds important. Go talk to her, and I meant what I said. I want to meet her."

"Assuming I'm able to patch things up with her, you will."

She hurried him to the front door, grabbing her purse on the way because she couldn't waste another minute. She was gripped with an almost frantic sense of urgency, desperate to get to Marin and make things right.

Her dad opened the door, then paused, looking at something . . . or someone.

Charlotte peeked over his shoulder, and a startled cry escaped her lips. Her stomach tingled as adrenaline flooded her system.

Marin stood on her front porch.

Marin's heart skipped a beat when the door opened before she'd had a chance to knock. For a moment, she stared in confusion at the man standing there, but just as quickly, she saw the family resemblance. This must be Charlotte's father.

And Marin was intruding. Probably.

Charlotte appeared in the doorway beside her dad, eyes red and damp from recent tears.

Heat flooded Marin's system because she was *so freaking glad* to see Charlotte, despite how upset she was that Charlotte had shut her out . . . again. These last two days had been awful. Charlotte's silence hurt, so much more than Marin had even known was possible.

She'd fought with Andrew, and that hadn't been enjoyable, but it hadn't hurt like this, probably because she hadn't loved him like she loved Charlotte.

"Hi," Marin said after the three of them had stood in silence that lasted a few beats too long. "I'm Charlotte's friend Marin, and . . . I should probably come back at a better time?"

"James Danton, Charlotte's father." He extended a hand, his expression friendly. "Please stay, Marin. I was just leaving."

She shook his hand. "I understand we're colleagues at NU. It's a pleasure to meet you, Dr. Danton, although I wish it was under better circumstances. I'm very sorry for your loss."

"Thank you. I appreciate that, and I hope we can talk again soon." He stepped past Marin, but Charlotte stopped him with a hand on his shoulder.

"Wait. I want to do this right." Her bottom lip shook as she looked at her dad. "Dad, this is my girlfriend, Marin."

Marin gaped. *Holy shit.* This was an unexpected development. She'd come here with a speech planned, ready to fight for a future with Charlotte, but maybe . . . maybe Charlotte had already beaten her to the punch.

Her dad was smiling widely now, looking at Marin with approval in his eyes. "It's a pleasure to officially meet my daughter's girlfriend. Please call me James, and I definitely hope to get to know you better, but first, I understand you two need to have an important conversation, so I'll leave you to it." With a wave, he headed down the walkway toward a silver Mercedes parked on the street.

Marin stepped forward. "Charlotte, wow . . ."

Charlotte flung her arms around her and held her tight. "I'm sorry, so fucking sorry. Please come in so I can apologize properly."

Marin nodded, inhaling Charlotte's familiar scent. They were going to be okay. They had a lot to talk about, but . . . this was fixable.

As she followed Charlotte into the house, the knot of tension that had been lodged in the pit of her stomach since Charlotte sent her home from the sheriff's department two days ago finally loosened.

"I was just on my way to see you," Charlotte said. "I was talking to my dad—a really good talk, as you might have noticed—and I realized how desperately I needed to apologize to you. We opened the front door, and there you were."

"Here I am." Marin stood facing her in the living room. "And I want to hear all about your conversation with your dad. I'll take the rest of that apology, too, but first . . . I have a few things to say."

Charlotte's brow furrowed. "Okay."

"I had a lot of time to think these last few days, while I waited for you to get in touch, and I realized something. You told me once that you've spent your life searching, but I think you're a runner, Charlotte. When things get hard, you run and hide, but . . . I don't think anyone's ever chased after you before. When you left Middleton after high school, no one tried to stop you, not your dad or your friends. You ran from your feelings for Elena, and she just let you go. Darren didn't fight for you after college or when you left DC last fall."

The wrinkle in Charlotte's brow had deepened now, and tears shone in her eyes.

"So here I am." Marin's voice had grown rough with her own tears. "To tell you I love you, and I'm here to fight for you, Charlotte, because I think you're worth fighting for."

Tears streaked Charlotte's cheeks. "Oh, Marin . . ."

"Unless you tell me to leave you alone, of course, because I'm not a stalker." Marin laughed, her throat tight.

"Never," Charlotte whispered.

"I get that you aren't used to talking things through. I think maybe you've always handled difficult things alone, but you don't have to do that anymore, because you have me. And it sounds like maybe you have your dad now, too, which is fucking fantastic." She smiled, tasting salt from her tears. "I couldn't talk about my feelings for a long time, either, when I was closeted, but the difference is, I was fighting for the freedom to speak my mind, and I think you've been running from these conversations your whole life. So I'm here to ask you to stay this time. To fight for what we have. To love me and let me love you. Will you?"

"Yes." Then Charlotte was in her arms again. "God, yes. That was maybe the most romantic speech I've ever heard, and I'm so fucking sorry for how I acted at the sheriff's department. I panicked, which is no excuse."

"I know you panicked, and your apology is accepted, but . . . you can't shut me out like that again, okay? That's not the kind of relationship I want. We're adults, and adults talk things through."

"You're right. They do, and I want us to have that kind of relationship." Charlotte's voice shook. Hell, her whole body was shaking. "I guess . . . I spent thirty years searching for answers about my mom, and when I got them, I didn't know how to process it. I don't know who I am without that search looming over my head, you know?"

"I can only imagine how overwhelming that was for you."

"And on top of that . . ." Charlotte gulped. "I watched you lose your relationship with your sister, which was so scary for me as I was coming to terms with my sexuality. After finding out my mom was dead, I was terrified I'd lose my dad, too, if he found out about us, and I handled it in the very worst way."

"You did, but you're here now." How overwhelming that must have been for Charlotte . . . Sometimes Marin forgot just how fast Charlotte's journey from sapphic awakening to committed relationship had progressed. She'd had so little time to process any of it.

"You're right that I've been running . . . hiding." Charlotte swiped at her tears, but more kept falling. "I'm a total mess, but I want to be better."

Marin folded Charlotte back into her arms and held her while she cried. She held Charlotte until she stopped shaking and the tension left her body. "You can stop running now," she murmured into the blond depths of Charlotte's hair.

Charlotte nodded against her shoulder, her breath hitching before she exhaled in what sounded like relief.

"What happened at the lake made me realize I still have some trauma from the accident. PTSD, maybe," Marin said. "I'm going to start seeing a therapist, and . . . maybe you should think about it too."

"Me?" Charlotte peeked up at her through her hair, then sighed. "Maybe I do need help, so I can process what happened to my mom and truly stop running, because I want to be able to keep my promises to you, Mare. I really do. Okay, let's both look for therapists."

"Our healthiest couple decision yet, I think."

"Yes." Charlotte pulled back far enough to meet Marin's eyes, her own still brimming with tears. "Most of my life, I've felt adrift, like I was just . . . looking for something. I needed to find my mom, but it turns out she was here all along, and I . . . I think my journey was meant to lead me to you. It all comes back to you, doesn't it? We met on that bus, and somehow that horrible day led us to the same small town in Vermont, where I happened to be your Realtor, and you're it, Marin. You're what I've spent my life searching for. It's you."

Tears spilled over Marin's cheeks. "Oh, Charlotte . . ."

"I feel like I say this a lot with you, but what are the chances? Of us meeting on that bus? Of reconnecting like we did? What are the chances of *any* of this?"

"Not very high, that's for sure."

"One in a million, I think," Charlotte declared.

"If you want to be particular, based on the current world population, it's one in eight billion."

Charlotte's eyes crinkled with a wide smile. "Then you and I are meant to be. There's no other explanation."

"I can't argue with that." Marin leaned in for a kiss, as everything inside her seemed to settle. "I love you so much."

"Same." Charlotte smiled against her lips. "I'm so glad fate brought us together."

"Me too . . . and that you convinced me fate is real."

"It all started with a horoscope . . ."

"And it ends with you . . . naked . . . in bed with me."

Charlotte's eyes heated. "Yes, please. Take me. Right now."

EPILOGUE

Nine Months Later

The water was a shade of turquoise Charlotte had only seen in photos before she and Marin arrived at their waterfront bungalow on St. John in the US Virgin Islands. It was the first week of January, winter break from the university for Marin and a slow period at work for Charlotte, so they'd flown out for a week in the Caribbean. This was their first real vacation together, but also the first time in years that either of them had taken a vacation at all.

Too many years, for both of them.

"I can't get over how beautiful this is . . . or how relaxed I am."

Charlotte turned her head to stare at her. Marin sat reclined in a lounge chair, wearing a blue-patterned two-piece swimsuit that revealed a thin strip of skin at her waist. She had a tropical drink in one hand, while palm fronds overhead shielded her from the sun. She looked so sexy, and indeed, so relaxed.

They had been going up to the main resort for meals, but other-wise they were enjoying the seclusion of their private villa. Powdery white sand stretched out before them, and there were no people in sight, only a couple of seagulls pecking along the waterline.

Yesterday, they'd chartered a boat to take them out so they could scatter her mom's ashes at sea. Charlotte had given it a lot of thought in those first months after receiving her mom's remains. She'd discussed it with her dad and with Marin, and in the end, they'd all agreed that Charlotte should set her free in the place she'd died trying to reach.

Charlotte had said a few words and tossed some flowers into the waves, and it had been overwhelmingly peaceful. It had also brought her a sense of closure. Now she could look ahead to the future, which shone as bright as the Caribbean sun.

"I understand why people enjoy tropical vacations so much." Charlotte slipped off her lounger and climbed onto Marin's. She lay on her side, cuddled against the woman she loved, and it was bliss. The air was warm but not unpleasantly so here in the shade.

"Distracting, having you pressed against me in that adorable little bikini," Marin said, her voice lower, slightly throaty the way it got when she was aroused.

"Oh yeah?" Charlotte reached down to tug at the bust of her purple bikini. She was displaying a lot more cleavage than Marin, a lot more skin in general, but Marin's modest two-piece was sexy as fuck.

Marin might give off the appearance of being reserved, but Charlotte knew the truth. Marin had a spine of steel, the heart of an adventurer, and she was brimming with passion. After waiting so long for a fulfilling relationship, Marin was ready for anything and everything when it came to love.

Case in point? She was looking at Charlotte like she had ideas for less relaxing things they could do right here in this lounge chair. That made two of them, because Charlotte had been low-key aroused since she joined Marin on this chair. She slid over so she was straddling one of Marin's bare thighs, arching her hips until she felt pressure against her clit. Oh. *Yes.*

Marin's breath hitched, even though Charlotte hadn't touched her yet, but then again, Marin had always gotten off on Charlotte's pleasure. Charlotte sat up, rocking her hips against Marin's thigh, and

Marin watched with the most deliciously erotic glint in her brown eyes.

Then she slid her hand inside Charlotte's bikini bottom. Fuck. Just *fuck*. Charlotte would never get over how good this felt. Marin's fingers toyed with her, and Charlotte shamelessly ground herself against them. She threw her head back, nearly blinded by a brilliant beam of sunshine that filtered between the palm fronds overhead.

Somewhere, a bird squawked, and this must be the definition of paradise. There was just enough alcohol in her system to give her a slight buzz. The ocean was nearby, providing a melodic backdrop to her and Marin's rendezvous. Charlotte was already halfway to an orgasm as she stared up at the swaying canopy of palm trees.

She moved her hips faster, chasing her release. It rushed through her in a cleansing wave, leaving her gasping, sweaty, and so freaking happy. She dropped her gaze to Marin, lying beneath her on the lounger, looking awfully damn pleased with herself. Charlotte sucked in several deep breaths, enjoying the tingling aftereffects of her orgasm.

Then she leaned forward to capture Marin's lips, simultaneously cupping her over her swimsuit. She felt the sharp intake of breath that betrayed just how aroused Marin was from getting Charlotte off. Charlotte kissed her deeply while she teased her over her swimsuit, stroking with just enough pressure to drive Marin crazy.

Marin was patient with her at first, returning her kisses with enthusiasm as she attempted to adjust the angle of her hips to get more friction, but after several long minutes of this, Marin whimpered. "Charlotte, *please*."

"Oh, I do love it when you beg." Charlotte smiled against her lips. "I really want you to come against my tongue. Can I do that for you? Right here?"

Marin blinked at her, then darted a quick look around. They were secluded behind their bungalow, but there was always some risk inherent to having sex outdoors. Charlotte thought that, in this situation, the reward greatly outweighed the risk, and Marin must have agreed because she nodded, her hips pushing more insistently against Charlotte's hand. She *loved* it when Marin was this turned on. God, she was beautiful.

Already, Charlotte was working her hand below the band of Marin's swimsuit bottom, pushing it down before dropping it into the sand. Marin let out the sexiest little gasp when Charlotte bared her to the tropical breeze, and Charlotte wasted no time scooting down to nestle herself between Marin's parted thighs. She looked up, and the view of Marin, naked from the waist down with a background of sand and palm trees? It was the most beautiful thing she'd ever seen. And the sexiest.

Charlotte throbbed between her thighs as she pressed her tongue against Marin. She'd done too good of a job with her teasing, though, because Marin's breathless cry when Charlotte licked her clit indicated she was already close. Still, Charlotte prolonged her pleasure as long as possible, licking and sucking, driving Marin closer to the edge.

Marin writhed against the lounge chair, hips rocking up against Charlotte's mouth, hands clenched around the cushion beneath her. "I'm so . . . *so* close," she panted with another whimper, arching her back.

"Come for me," Charlotte murmured against Marin's soaked flesh.

Marin's body went taut against the chair, and she let out a long, low moan as she found her release. Charlotte swirled her tongue around and around her clit, helping her wring every bit of pleasure from her orgasm, until Marin pushed gently at her shoulders.

She looked down at Charlotte, her eyes glazed with pleasure, a pink flush staining her cheeks. "That was perfect. *You're* perfect."

Charlotte scrunched her nose. "Hardly."

"You're perfect for me," Marin clarified.

Charlotte gazed up at her, happy and content. "And you're perfect for *me*."

"You know, I checked my horoscope this morning," Marin said, her expression suddenly serious. "And it said that today, I should tell the person dearest to me what I really want."

Charlotte sucked in a breath. "What do you want?"

"You, Charlotte. Always. I want to make it official. Once we're back in Vermont, let's get married. What do you say?"

Charlotte's heart lurched. "Oh my god. Are you . . . are you proposing?"

Marin nodded, eyes glistening with tears. "I have a ring back at the bungalow, but this moment . . . I just couldn't wait. You're the love of my life, my one in eight billion. Will you marry me?"

Charlotte swiped at happy tears, already nodding. "Yes. God, yes. After everything we've been through together to make it to this point, I think we must be written in the stars."

Marin exhaled. "I'm so happy."

"Me too." Charlotte slid up beside her, nestled against Marin so she could kiss her lips. "Remember what I told you about vacation being more about the person than the place for me?"

Marin nodded, rubbing Charlotte's ring finger with her thumb, as if picturing her ring there.

"I spent so long searching for my mom," Charlotte said. "At some point, I don't think I even knew what I was looking for anymore. I was just wandering from place to place, city to city, job to job. Nowhere ever felt like home."

Marin wrapped an arm around her shoulders, holding her close.

"Then I met you on that bus, and something shifted. I didn't know what it was at first, but now I do." She blinked back tears. "I realized that for me, home isn't a place. It's a person. Marin, it's you. You're my home. Wherever you are, that's where I'm meant to be."

ACKNOWLEDGMENTS

This book has a big piece of my heart. I wrote it at a very difficult time, both personally and in the world around me, and there were many days when Marin and Charlotte gave me a much-needed reason to smile. Helping them overcome trauma to find happiness was very therapeutic for me, and their story is one I'll hold near and dear for a long time.

It's also one of those rare books that I wrote in the same place and season as the story itself. Yes, I drafted this book during a Vermont winter, which helped me really immerse myself in their world and capture those extra sensory details about their surroundings. This has only happened to me a couple of times, and it's so magical when it does.

That's not the only way life imitated art in this book, though. While I was writing *Margin of Error*, we brought home our own black lab puppy. Fun fact: My sassy girl is Willow, but Ember was an early name we considered for her. I love the name, but it just didn't suit our puppy, so I gave it to Marin's puppy instead (and totally fell in love with the fictional Ember in the process—what a sweetheart!).

The biggest thank-you to Lauren Plude and Lindsey Faber for all your encouragement with this book, for the planning calls that have become one of my favorite parts of the writing process, and of course for your editorial insight. I appreciate you more than I can say! Thanks also to the rest of the amazing team at Montlake for always making my books shine.

Thank you to my awesome agent, Sarah Younger, and to my wonderful critique partner, Annie Rains. I wouldn't want to do this without either of you.

Quinn Riley, I am unbelievably thrilled to have you bring *Margin of Error* to life with your amazing narration. This is our fifth book together, and I'm so grateful to work with you again and even more grateful to call you a friend.

I owe a wealth of gratitude to the people who helped make this book more authentic. Thank you so much to Mia Bonello-Day, Jen Lyon, MJ Monica, Lisa Boyer, and Brenda Bentley for your expertise and advice.

Last but certainly not least, a huge thank-you to everyone who's read, reviewed, recommended, or otherwise supported my books. Your support means the world to me!

xoxo
Rachel

ABOUT THE AUTHOR

Photo © 2013 Kristi Kruse Photography

Rachel Lacey is an award-winning contemporary romance author and semireformed travel junkie. She's climbed a mountain in Japan with a monkey, gone scuba diving on the Great Barrier Reef, and camped out overnight in New York City for a chance to be a movie extra. These days, the majority of her adventures take place on the pages of the books she writes. She lives in the mountains of Vermont with her family and a variety of rescue pets.

Rachel loves to keep in touch with her readers! Check out her website at http://RachelLacey.com for information about the author, her books, and more. For exclusive news and giveaways, subscribe to her e-newsletter at www.subscribepage.com/rachellaceyauthor. You can also connect with the author on Instagram @rachelslacey and on Facebook.com/RachelLaceyAuthor.